A GUARDIAN
ANGELINOS
NOVEL

NEW YORK TIMES BESTSELLING AUTHOR

ROXANNE
ST. CLAIRE

SHIVER
OF FEAR

DON'T MISS THE SEXY NOVELS IN THE GUARDIAN ANGELINOS SERIES!

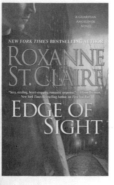

Available now

Available in May 2011

Please turn to the back of this book
for a preview of each novel.

Just

Marc lifted his head.

"I thought about this the lobby of the F

"You did, him.

"I did, looked in

"Sweet

"No, I'

"That's me. At le wanted."

"Shh. No more talking." He lowered his head.

She reached under his chin and tipped his face upward toward her. "But if it counts for anything," she said. "I did pretty much want to jump your bones the minute I saw you."

That made him smile.

"Then stop talking, Dev. And jump."

**Praise for Roxanne St. Claire and her first
Guardian Angelinos novel, *Edge of Sight***

"With Roxanne St. Claire, you are guaranteed a powerful, sexy, and provocative read."

—CARLY PHILLIPS, *New York Times*
bestselling author

EDGE OF SIGHT

"Deliciously intriguing...mystery, deep emotion, a tortured hero, and a woman with purpose, *Edge of Sight* delivers romantic suspense...If the rest of the series is as good as this, I'll have to have a bookcase made just for her to hold all of her keepers. Keep 'em coming!"
   —NightOwlRomance.com

———————————

"Great passion and suspense makes this a good read for all."
   —Romance Reviews Magazine

———————————

"A heart-racing story...a true suspense novel that will enthrall you all the way through...Roxanne St. Claire has a deft hand with suspense novels that are full of passion."
   —RomRevToday.com

———————————

"Hot romance and sizzling suspense...Steamy love scenes, a scarred hero, and a passion that won't go away add up to a thrilling read."
   —BookPage.com

ALSO BY ROXANNE ST. CLAIRE

Edge of Sight

ROXANNE ST. CLAIRE

SHIVER OF FEAR

FOREVER

NEW YORK   BOSTON

Forever
Hachette Book Group
237 Park Avenue
New York, NY 10017
Visit our website at www.HachetteBookGroup.com.

Forever is an imprint of Grand Central Publishing. The Forever name and logo is a trademark of Hachette Book Group, Inc.

The publisher is not responsible for websites (or their content) that are not owned by the publisher.

Printed in the United States of America

First Printing: April 2011

10 9 8 7 6 5 4 3 2 1

*For Kresley Cole, Louisa Edwards and Kristen Painter,
who shower me with support, laughter, perspective,
advice, and motivation (okay, and a little wine) from
chapter one to the end. I love you and treasure our
extraordinary friendship.*

ACKNOWLEDGMENTS

Huge debts of gratitude are owed to some patient, generous, and really smart people who were behind me on this book:

Jessica Odell, my eyes and ears in Belfast. Fact checker, map maker, and exceedingly kind recipient of way too many e-mails that all started with "I have one more question." Thanks, Jess. I owe you a Guinness or two.

Beta reader and Brazilian buddy Barbie Furtado who read, reviewed, then reread and rereviewed, then *reread* until we were well beyond beta and zooming toward zeta. She is a superstar, cheerleader, and keen-eyed first reader.

Former FBI agent Jim Vatter, my go-to guy on anything that has to do with federal law enforcement; microbiologist Dr. Peter F. Bonaventre, who offered layman's language for a complicated subject; the numerous individuals at the Ulster Historical Foundation Research Center and the "parish people" of St. Macartin's Cathedral in Enniskillen. All of these folks (including the really nice guy with the sexy accent who answered the phone at the Europa Hotel but did not give me his name) did everything to keep me from stumbling on a fact. If I erred, don't blame them.

The entire team at Grand Central Publishing's Forever Romance imprint. Starting with editor extraordinaire Amy Pierpont, who knows exactly how to take good and make it better; to the crew of production, publicity, art, and sales professionals who work tirelessly to put my stories into the hands of as many readers as possible. A round of chocolate for everyone!

My patient, brilliant, supportive, and delightful literary agent, Robin Rue, who lets me gallop but skillfully takes the reins when she needs to keep me on track.

And, as always, my enduring love to my husband, Rich, and our amazing kids, Dante and Mia who don't complain (much) when they hear the words "as soon as I finish this scene." Even though they know the scene is never really finished, they love me anyway.

SHIVER
OF FEAR

PROLOGUE

Cambridge, Massachusetts, 1978

The moment Sharon Mulvaney slipped the cushioned case containing three sealed vials of purified botulinum toxins into her handbag and left the microbiology lab, she became a criminal.

Before that, she'd never done anything worse than protest the administration on the lawn in front of MIT's Dome. Drinking whiskey while talking trash with fervent Irish Catholic supporters in the basement of a bar in Harvard Square certainly hadn't gotten her arrested. Even loving a man with deep ties to and deeper sentiments for IRA dissidents didn't qualify as illegal, although the fact that he was married and almost thirty years her senior pushed the boundaries of what was kosher.

But stealing the most toxic substance known to mankind—after isolating, purifying, and crystallizing the spores herself and knowingly handing over the whole concoction for secret delivery to Belfast—was most definitely punishable with some prison time.

She wished her brush with crime thrilled her. Since it didn't, she chose to believe she didn't have an evil soul, just a weak heart.

The bitter wind buffeted her across a winter-break-deserted campus. She pulled her scarf over her mouth and dragged her cap down to her brows while navigating the ice and traffic-blackened snow. Fueled equally by the fear of getting caught and the desire to get out of the freezing cold, she shouldered the handbag deep into her down coat, kept her head low, and marched toward her apartment.

Even on a warm spring day when the only thing on her mind was grading papers as a graduate student TA, this was a long walk. But in a frigid New England winter, carrying enough poison to paralyze a regiment of British soldiers, knowing she was breaking the law and taking chances with every single thing she held dear, the trek became a brutal hike that pained every muscle in her body.

By the time she crossed Binney and the student pedestrian walkway widened into Sixth, her toes tingled with the bite of cold, her fingers were stiffened with numbness, and every brain cell was too deadened to even scare up some rationalization for what she was doing.

Anyway, she was way past rationalizing; she was in love.

She turned onto her street, carefully switching the bag to her other shoulder. It wasn't heavy physically, but metaphorically, the weight of her crime pressed on her heart.

Sometimes a few have to suffer for the good of many.

Had Finn said that? Knowing him, it was probably

more like, *Do this for me, my darling girl, and I'll...*
Leave my wife for you.

Right. Did she really believe that? She must, or she
wouldn't be taking a chance like this.

She stepped gingerly around a snowdrift and headed
down the stone steps to the front door of her garden-level
apartment, already imagining what she'd wear tonight. The
black dress he liked, with the big gold buckle, and some high
heels. Her lover brought out the girl in her. And the criminal,
evidently, she thought as she turned the key and pushed.

"Did you get it?"

She gasped at the voice, squinting into the living room
to see Finn, a drink in one hand and his three-hundred-
dollar loafers propped on her coffee table, jacket open,
tie loose, hair tousled like he'd been running his hands
through it while waiting for her.

All the ice inside her just...melted.

"I got it," she said, easing the bag down to her elbow and
holding it out to him. With the other hand, she yanked off the
knit cap, fluffing hair that was probably a flat, flyaway mess.
Not to mention that the down jacket made her look like the
Michelin Man, and she didn't have a speck of makeup on.

He didn't move to take the bag or, as she foolishly fantasized, rise to give her a kiss. Instead, he sat stone still,
exuding power, control, authority, maturity, and knee-
weakening sex appeal. How a fifty-three-year-old man with
tiny creases at the corners of his eyes and a few threads of
silver glinting in golden hair could make a twenty-five-year
old microbiologist go so damn rubbery was a mystery.

One she had no desire to solve.

"And no one saw you." It wasn't a question. With Finn,
everything was an order.

She shook her head.

He raised the amber liquid of Jameson she'd splurged on just so she'd have it in the apartment for him, cocking his head as eyes the color of summer skies raked over her appreciatively. "We should celebrate."

Despite the automatic response of her body, her brain screamed out a protest. *Should they celebrate a crime?*

"Darling girl, you aren't having second thoughts, are you?"

Naturally, he could read whatever subtle cues her non-verbals were shouting. "It's a little late," she said with a soft laugh. "The deed, as they say, is done."

"I told you, no one's going to use that stuff." He jutted his chin toward the bag as if its contents were harmless, meaningless. "It's a bargaining chip, and in Belfast these days, you just can't get enough of those. I'm only sending that stuff over there to give them some power."

Power? She suspected there was more *cash* than *cache* involved.

"That's the name of the game these days," he continued. "And they are, after all, family, however distant."

Very distant. She'd done a little digging through a friend who studied the various clans of Ireland and couldn't really find a connection between the names Finn had mentioned and the MacCauley clan. In fact, that spelling of his last name didn't even show up, but she knew better than to question this man. He hated to be questioned. When she did, he punished her by disappearing for a few days. Sometimes more.

"I realize that," she said, feeling as weak and ineffective as she sounded. "I thought we'd celebrate over dinner."

Then he stood, his gaze locked on her as he clunked

the drink on the table. "That's not what I had in mind. I don't have time for dinner tonight."

"Plans with Anne?" The question was too sharp; she knew it instantly. Instead of facing his fierce look, she turned to take off her coat.

"I have business tonight," he replied. "So no dinner."

She tossed the coat over a chair, her back still to him.

Business. *That* she wasn't stupid enough to question. They pretended she didn't know exactly what his business was, and in return, she got...

His hands slid around her waist, possessive and strong. She got *this*.

"You're one of us now, sweet girl of mine."

One of whom? A bunch of criminals? "Truly Irish?"

"Truly fearless." He pressed his body, already hard, against her backside, nuzzling her neck with kisses, the tangy smell of Irish whiskey like a familiar trigger that warned her body to brace for an onslaught of Finn.

"I'm not..." She lost the ability to speak as he reached up under her sweater and took ownership of her breasts. "Fearless."

Not for one minute was she naïve enough to think a man as powerful and important as Finn MacCauley saw *fearlessness* in her. But he must have seen something in her, other than her ability to get inside the microbiology lab to make and steal weapons of mass destruction. She had to believe that.

He turned her to face him, instantly feasting on her mouth, sliding his hands down to her buttocks, pressing her against his erection.

"Look what you do to me, darling girl." He guided her back toward the bedroom, kissing her, pausing at the table to lift the strap of her bag. "Let's not let these get too far out of our sight."

She refused to look at the purse and think that it represented her utter willingness to give him whatever he wanted. Her body. Her heart. Her very reputation.

And yet, he wouldn't give her the legitimacy she needed more than anything. Even though she could give him what Anne could not: a child.

He nudged her forward, already taking off her sweater, her bra, his jacket and shirt. By the time he lowered her to the bed, they wore nothing but pants, and those came off quickly.

He angled his head toward the bathroom, pushing his boxer shorts over a throbbing red hard-on. "Get your protection."

She fought the urge to shake her head. He was always so adamant about not taking chances and making her wear her diaphragm. Why? Because he didn't want to be tied to her, and a baby would bind them to each other forever.

He could never disappear if she had his baby.

She swallowed and made an impulsive decision to lie, looking him right in the eye without wavering.

"I already have it in." At his slightly surprised look, she gave him a sly smile and eased her legs apart. "I knew you'd be waiting here when I got home, Finn."

He was inside her before she had a chance to change her mind, pumping and sweating and swearing until he came ferociously. He fell on her, spent and satisfied, while she waited for an endearment that didn't come.

"Listen, Sharon, if anyone, and I mean *anyone,* asks you about—"

"I don't plan to tell a soul what I did today," she interjected.

"Just when, or if, anyone asks you, you have to deny knowing me. Anyone at all, even—"

"I do deny you, Finn." But she wouldn't have to if he was the father of her child. Had they just made a—

A heavy pounding on the door silenced that thought, and the conversation. He rolled over and grabbed his clothes wordlessly.

"Miss Mulvaney, we need to speak with you. FBI."

Finn mouthed the word "fuck" and seized his jacket, his eyes on fire as he pointed to the door. "Get out there and stall," he ordered in a harsh whisper. "Don't give me away, Sharon, or you won't live to talk about it."

For a moment, she couldn't speak. He'd kill her?

"FBI! We're coming in."

He grabbed her arm, fingers digging into her flesh, and flung her onto her feet with a shockingly strong jerk. "Go!"

She stood there, naked and stunned, as he lunged for her purse. Another hard rap forced a reply from a throat thick with fear.

"Just . . . a second," she called, her heart thundering so loudly she could barely hear her own voice.

Finn pushed her again, rougher this time, and she stumbled out of the bedroom and into the hall. "You have to cover for me, Sharon." He closed the door and left her naked in the hall.

"I'm coming," she called at the next insistent knock, spying her down coat on the chair. She slid the cool nylon over her bare skin, shaking fingers working the zipper.

"Miss Mulvaney, this is the FBI. Please open the door."

She'd been a criminal exactly one hour, and the FBI was already at her front door.

You have to cover for me, Sharon.

Taking a deep breath, she opened the door to find two clean-cut men who looked like they'd been sent from Hollywood to play FBI agents.

"How can I help you?" she asked, blocking the entrance with her body.

Two ID badges were flipped open in front of her eyes, but her head was spinning and the words and pictures just blurred, her ears not even registering their names.

"We'd like to ask you some questions."

She blinked, nodded. " 'Kay."

The taller, darker of the two men looked pointedly at her coat. "Are you on your way out, miss?"

"Just got in." From the lab. Where she'd stolen weapons of biological warfare that would be shipped to the distant cousin of the married man who led one of Boston's largest organized crime syndicates—a man who just happened to be naked in her bedroom.

"May we come in?"

"No, you may not come in."

That got her double takes of surprise. Well, one of surprise. The other guy, the stocky blond, looked suspicious. He must be the smart one.

"I'm sorry I can't let you in," she said, steadfast and stalling. "I see you have badges and all, but a woman alone can't be too careful."

"Do you know a man named Finley MacCauley?"

Blood drained from her head and landed low in a nauseous stomach. "I don't know." Stupid, stupid answer.

Suspicious Blond Agent lifted both eyebrows. "You've never met a man named Finn MacCauley?"

"I might have," she said, certain they could hear the drumbeat of her heart rattling her rib cage. "Who is he?"

"He's a criminal, Ms. Mulvaney, and if you aid and abet his activities, you'll be a criminal, too."

Too late for the future tense. "Do you have a picture of him?" she asked, desperate for a stall. "Maybe I'd recognize him."

"You don't recognize the name?" the other man asked.

"I . . . I . . . don't know."

"Let us in, Miss Mulvaney." He was definitely the bad cop, that blond one.

"Why?" She directed the question to the nicer cop, but the other one answered.

"Because we've received a tip that Finn MacCauley would be here today, and if you don't let us in, we're going to arrest you." He took a step forward, his body enough of a weapon to force her back.

Before she could stop them, they were inside. Balling her fists in her pockets, she watched the nasty one walk right over to the coffee table and pick up the drink, sniffing.

"Jameson," she offered before he asked. "Is that illegal?"

The other agent was already striding down the hall, weapon drawn and held with two hands as he shouldered his way into her bedroom.

She didn't breathe, waiting for a shout or a shot. Seconds later, the agent emerged. He shook his head and muttered, "Nothin'."

Nothing? Where was Finn?

She waited for the next question, but it didn't come as they searched the tiny apartment, stuffed their guns away, and returned to the front door.

"You better watch your back, miss," the dark-haired agent said. "You're hanging around with some pretty dangerous people."

She just nodded, remarkably cool considering the somersaults her stomach was doing, the blood coursing through her veins, and the question screaming in her brain.

Where was Finn?

They left and she remained still for a long moment, vaguely aware of the dribble of sticky moisture down her thigh, a reminder that minutes ago she had been making love to a man wanted by the FBI.

"Finn?" she whispered, dragging her feet toward the bedroom, stepping in to see what the FBI agent had seen. A rumpled bed. Her clothes strewn on the floor. The window wide open.

Finally, she exhaled, dropping on the bed from the weight of what had just happened. Her gaze shifted to the bureau. No surprise, Finn had taken her bag.

Tears burned. Her throat closed. And a painful punch of regret hit her in the chest. God, she was a *fool*! A stupid, childish, trusting fool.

And he was the worst kind of man—a user.

For a long moment, she just sat there in her down coat, tears brimming but unshed. She listened to the silence of the apartment, inhaled the bitter fragrance of sex that hung in the room.

And she waited.

Not for Finn; he'd never be back. Not until he needed something only she could give him again. Then he'd charm her and coerce her and weaken her defenses and . . . get exactly what he wanted from her. That was Finn.

But she could say no.

So she waited for the agony in her heart to transform into something else. Visualized the change taking place deep in the molecular level of her soul. Harmless, healthy proteins of love gradually degrading into deadly toxins of hate.

After all, wasn't this her expertise? Creating poison from something as common as dirt? Love. What could be more common? Or dirtier?

Minutes passed, maybe hours. Finally, she made a decision. She wasn't sure how or when, but someday she'd find a way to use Finn MacCauley the way he used her, and then she'd watch him suffer.

Until then, she damn well hoped some other molecular transformation wasn't taking place inside her. Remembering her impetuous decision, she pushed off the bed, slid out of the coat, and headed into the shower to wash away the remnants of Finn. *Please, God, let the hot shower water be enough to eliminate every drop of him from inside me.*

Because the last thing she wanted now was a baby. She had something different to live for—revenge on Finn MacCauley.

CHAPTER 1

Present Day

The halogen headlights sliced through the downpour like laser beams, turning the rain eerily white and illuminating each sudden turn in the nick of time. With every near miss on the twisty roads of the North Carolina woods, Devyn Sterling cursed the rental car company for not offering GPS, damned the weather for delaying her flight until this late at night, and wished to God that she had a clue which street was Oak Ridge Drive.

And threw in one more vile curse for the impulsive nature that landed her in this situation.

Arriving on the doorstep of her birth mother to shatter the woman's life should really be done under sunny skies. But Devyn couldn't wait another day. Or night. No matter the weather.

Squinting into the downpour, she tapped the brakes

at a cross street, slowing to a crawl to seize the millisecond of clarity between windshield wipes to read the street sign, aided by a sudden bolt of lightning.

Yes. Oak Ridge. Thank God.

Thunder rolled just a second or two later, but Devyn powered on, inching down the residential street, peering at the houses, set far apart on acre-sized lots, most of them dark for the night. As she reached the end of a cul-de-sac and neared the address she'd memorized, Devyn drew in a nervous breath, practicing what she would say when Dr. Sharon Greenberg opened the door.

No matter how many times she rehearsed, the words came out wrong. Especially because Devyn doubted she could get through the whole story before she got the door slammed in her face.

Still, she needed a game plan for this encounter.

Her icy New England upbringing told her to be brutally blunt. Just knock on the door, open her mouth, and say, *I'm the daughter you gave up in a secret adoption thirty years ago.*

But deep inside, because her blood wasn't truly the chilly WASP of her Hewitt upbringing but some cocktail of hot Irish, she wanted to tell Dr. Greenberg the story with all the drama that had unfolded a few months earlier on the streets of Boston so the woman could fully appreciate the reason for Devyn's visit.

I hired an investigator, found out your identity—and that of my fugitive mobster father—and told my husband, who decided to betray me, only to get murdered by his mistress and a dirty cop who tried to frame Finn MacCauley for the crime. Uh, can I have some shelter from this storm?

Without knowing much about Sharon Greenberg, it was hard to be sure if that tact would work any better than cool bluntness.

She slowed at the last home, the brick ranch house bathed in the headlights of her rental car. Snapping the lights off, Devyn turned into the empty driveway and stared at the house. Maybe she should go for the heartfelt approach.

I'm sorry, Dr. Greenberg. I know you don't want to meet me, and I really planned to respect that wish, but I told my husband your name and I don't know if he told anyone else before he was murdered. Just in case he did, I thought it only proper that I be the one to screw up your life....And while I'm here, can we talk about why you gave me up?

Don't go there, Devyn. Not at first. The woman had every right to give up a child fathered by a legendary street thug like Finn MacCauley. She didn't even have to *have* a baby.

Still, Devyn thought as she looked at the darkened house, maybe...maybe they would talk about it. But first, Sharon had a right to know that her secret was no longer buried. And Devyn had a right to know who gave birth to her.

Another flash of lightning illuminated the night, followed almost immediately by a quick explosion of thunder. Chills feathered Devyn's skin despite the warm blasts from the dashboard. The storm was close.

As her eyes adjusted and the rain washed the windshield, she studied the large picture window in the front, nine panes of glass, the blinds behind them closed tight. Water sluiced out the gutters, noisily splattering mud below.

Proper New England upbringing pinched at her conscience. A lady would call before arriving.

Okay, she could do that. Devyn picked up her cell phone and pressed the speed dial she'd foolishly programmed in while delayed at Logan. Back when she was still waging an internal debate, considering abandoning the plan and driving home. But rationale won over reason, and she'd stayed at the airport, gotten on the late plane, and...here she was.

If she hit Send, maybe she'd wake Sharon, and then when Devyn knocked on the door, it wouldn't be such a shock. The older woman would have a minute or two to prepare. That seemed fair.

Devyn watched the words appear on the tiny screen: *Calling Dr. Sharon Greenberg.*

Oh, God.

The fourth ring cut off halfway and clicked into voice mail. Devyn pressed the phone to her ear, blocking out the rain beating on the car so she could listen and absorb the sound of her birth mother's voice for the first time.

"Hey, it's Shar. I'm not able to take your call, but do what needs to be done and I'll get back to you. Leave a message, try my office, text me, send a smoke signal. Peace out."

Devyn stabbed End and slipped the phone back into her purse, staring ahead at the shadows around the house, her heart matching the rhythm of the rain. Fast. Hard. Loud.

Was she going to turn back now? Away from a woman who invited callers to send a smoke signal? Obviously Sharon had a sense of humor. But did that mean she had a heart?

What she had, Devyn thought, was a right to know that somewhere, someone might know her darkest secret. That information could be damning to her career...or worse.

So, really Devyn was doing her a favor.

Holding tight to the justification that had gotten her this far, she scooped up her bag and opened the car door, soaked before she could jog up the three stone steps to the covered front porch. There, she intrepidly opened the screen door and rapped hard on the front door.

Fifteen endless seconds passed; then she knocked again. Emboldened, disappointed, and frustrated, she pounded with the side of her fist, an unwanted lump forming in her throat.

"You have to be home," she murmured, her hand sliding down to the large brass handle. A blinding burst of lightning tore a gasp from her throat, making her squeeze the latch in fear and hold tight as the thunder cracked the night air.

And the door opened.

Devyn jerked her hand away the moment she realized *she'd* unlatched the unlocked door. The next blindingly close bolt of lightning pushed her inside, survival instinct trumping everything else.

"Dr. Greenberg?" she called, still knocking on the open door. "Are you here, Dr. Greenberg?"

This was so not how she wanted this meeting to unfold.

Pitch-black inside, the cloying scent of candle wax and potpourri fought with the muskiness of a closed-up house.

"Dr. Greenberg, are you home?"

Obviously not. And Devyn, with the blood of a man who once topped the FBI's Most Wanted list cascading through her veins, took another step into a house where she hadn't been invited. Her adopted mother would keel over in disgrace. But right now, her adopted mother didn't matter. Her *real* mother did.

Two months had passed since Devyn's husband had been murdered. Two months she'd waited for the investigation to close and the police to clear her to leave the Boston area. Two months she'd struggled with a question no one had ever asked and only Joshua Sterling could answer: Had he taken the name of Devyn's birth mother to the grave? Two months was too much time not to have this conversation and deliver the potentially bad news to Dr. Greenberg.

And have the perfect excuse to meet.

All she had to say was, *Your secret is no longer safe.*

In fact, under the circumstances, a simple note could do the job. Not as satisfying as face-to-face, but maybe this was what was meant to be.

She called out again, blinking to get night vision, able to make out an entry table in the shadows where brown sticks surrounded by curled, dried leaves poked out of a vase.

Either Sharon had been gone a while, or she really didn't care about living things.

And, really, wasn't that what Devyn had traveled to North Carolina to discover?

Somewhere to the left, an antique clock ticked. The soft hum of the refrigerator buzzed from a kitchen around the corner. Rain thumped on the shingles, but there were no other sounds.

On her right, through French doors, Devyn could see the green light of a printer and the shape of a large desk stacked with papers and files. The office was the place to write and leave a note . . . or find a clue as to what made Dr. Sharon Greenberg tick.

With a shiver of apprehension and a stab of guilt, she pushed open the door and walked to the desk, flipping on a tiny halogen lamp to scan the mess. There were little hills of papers, files, articles, medical journals, a leaning tower of DVDs, and a half dozen candles melted into various sizes and shapes.

For a moment, she just drank in the first impression. Mom was a slob, she thought with a slight twist of a smile. An untidy, disorganized, hardworking scientist who... had sex with mobsters?

Curiosity burned, along with something else Devyn couldn't identify. Something that felt like hunger. A burn to...bond.

Let it go, Devyn.

She lifted some papers, eyeing the magazines, the arcane terminology, seeking clues to who this woman was. The investigator she'd paid dearly for bits of information said Dr. Greenberg was divorced, childless, and working as a researcher at the University of North Carolina teaching hospital.

The tabs on a stack of file folders confirmed her life as a scientist. Retrovirology. Immunology. Serology. Pathology. Belfast.

Belfast?

The word was scratched in pencil, light enough that it looked like it had already been erased. Devyn tugged the file, something pulling at her as the manila folder slid out from under the others.

Belfast. The city conjured up twenty-year-old newscasts of bombings, violence, deaths, Irish mobs, and...

Irish mobs.

Slowly, she opened the folder, her pulse kicking up

after it had finally slowed. Inside, there were several pages of notes, some drawings, an e-mail. And on a "Recycle for Life" notepad were the words *US Air Arrives 2:45 pm Belfast w/layover Heathrow 8/29. Rtn open.*

August twenty-ninth was almost two weeks ago. She glanced at the papers in the file, obscure scientific drawings, several printouts of e-mails, a magazine article with the name *Liam Baird* underlined. She lifted it to read the story, but her gaze was pulled to a grainy photograph in the file behind the article. Taken from a distance, the image was of a girl on a bike, a backpack on her shoulders, her hair in a pony—

"Oh my God." The words stuck in her throat as she stared at the photo. She knew that bike, that street, that girl.

It was her.

Which meant Sharon knew her identity. She knew enough about Devyn to have a picture of her!

Trembling, she flipped the picture over and stared at the small handwriting.

Finn 617-555-6253

Finn? Finn MacCauley with a Boston phone number?

Lightning flashed blindingly bright with a simultaneous, deafening crack of thunder. The desk light went black, and thunder rolled with such intensity that the hardwood floor vibrated under Devyn's feet.

Had the house been hit? She stood there, the file still in one hand, as the thunder stopped, followed by the soft digital sound of her cell phone. Grabbing her phone, she read the caller ID.

Dr. Sharon Greenberg.

"Oh my God." Sharon was calling her?

She took a moment to breathe and think, too paralyzed to answer. Sharon must have just redialed, curious as to who had called her a few minutes ago.

But she has my picture in a file on her desk.

With unsteady fingers, she tapped the green button and put the phone to her ear. "Hello?"

Nothing. Silence. But someone was there; she could tell.

"Dr. Greenberg?" She pulled the phone away, checked the name again to be sure she hadn't imagined it. "Hello?"

No response. The house was silent around her, all electrical buzzing dead from the power outage. Devyn stood in the pitch blackness, holding the lifeline to her birth mother... which was just as silent. She'd lost the call.

With a soft cry of frustration, she hit Redial. From down the hall, a digital ring cut through the silence.

Sharon was in the house? The call that just came in was made... from this house?

Slowly, like someone was guiding her with puppet strings, she walked around the desk, through the darkness, her arm automatically slipping through the shoulder bag she'd set on top of one of the piles.

The phone stopped midring, and there was a soft click in her ear.

Someone had picked up the phone. Someone in this house.

"Dr. Greenberg?" she said it loudly, not to the phone but toward the hall. "Are you there?"

Silence.

Icy panic prickled over her skin, sending the hairs on the back of her neck straight up. She wasn't alone.

Fumbling through the dark, she found her way back to

the entry hall. There, she stood still, listening, then turned back to call out to Sharon one last time, just as a hand clamped over her mouth and yanked her back into a solid man's chest.

"What are you doing here?" The man growled the words, adding so much pressure that her neck cracked.

White terror flashed behind her eyes, a scream trapped in her throat.

"What?" he demanded, lifting his hand enough for her to breathe and speak.

"Looking...for...Shar—"

"Why?"

"I...I wanted to..." She tried to think of a reasonable answer. "Leave her something."

"What?"

Whoever this guy was—a husband, a boyfriend, or a guard dog—he probably knew where Sharon was. She had to be calm and come up with a plausible story.

"I'm her student," she said in a controlled voice. "She needed me to give her some papers. In person."

He tightened his grip, pressing so hard across her chest she could feel her heart beat into his forearm.

"Who sent you?" he ground out.

"Nobody sent me. I'm a student—"

"A student who broke in?" He lifted his left hand, palming the side of her head while a beefy arm pinned her. Slowly, he pushed her head to the side until her neck muscles strained and tendons snapped. Pain ricocheted down her arm and terror shot up her spine.

"Who sent you?"

"I came on my own. It's personal." Miraculously, her voice didn't crack like her neck. "I have to talk to her."

He pushed her toward the door, which she just realized was open. Had she left it that way? Had he followed her in? Or had he been waiting?

She dug her feet into the mat, refusing to be pushed into the screen and out into the rain. "I have to talk to her," she said again, trying to squirm around to see his face, but he wouldn't allow it.

Had he hurt Sharon? Was her body lying bloody in the back of the house?

"When you find her, give her a message." A shove sent her flying against the screen door, popping it open. She twisted just enough to see a glimpse of his face, older than she expected, light eyes, grim mouth.

He whipped her around and braced her again. "If she comes back here without getting her job done, she's dead."

Devyn squirmed, finally getting her brain to work enough to try fruitlessly to jerk out of his grip. "What job?"

"She knows what job. She steps into this house a failure, she'll leave in a box. We're watching and we're waiting."

He shoved her outside, still holding her so tight she couldn't turn to see him. One more push and she was out from under the overhang, drenched, as the screen door was slammed shut behind her.

She spun around to get a look at him, just as an ear-splitting sound sent her jumping backward, staring in disbelief at the hole in the screen.

He'd backed into the shadows of the house and shot at her! Instantly, she pivoted toward the driveway, slipping on the concrete. Using the banister to right herself, she sailed down the stairs, taking another look over her shoulder.

Fear vibrated through her, her heart hammering as if it

would explode out of her chest. The rush of blood and rain drowned out the little cries that escaped her lips as she stabbed in her bag for the car keys.

Had she left them in the house?

Panic almost knocked her over, just as the keys scraped her knuckles. She whipped them out and promptly dropped them in a puddle.

"Shit!" Falling to her knees, photos and papers she'd taken from Sharon's file fluttered to the ground. The picture? Everything was soaked before it hit the pavement.

One more shot exploded out into the night.

Abandoning the papers except what she could scoop in one shaky grab, she snatched the keys and dragged open the car door, scrambling inside and tossing the remains of the file and her purse across the console. She found the ignition, turned on the car, and jerked it into reverse. With her full weight on the accelerator, she launched backward out of the driveway.

She stole one last glance at the picture window, the reflection of her headlights illuminating the blinds. They parted briefly as her attacker watched her leave. A man who would kill Sharon Greenberg if she returned... *without getting her job done*. What kind of job was that? Research for UNC? In Belfast?

She managed a quick look at the papers she'd thrown on the passenger seat; the picture was still there.

A picture of Devyn taken seventeen years ago. *Why would Sharon have that?*

A hundred answers clobbered her brain, all dizzying in their possibilities. But only one electrified her. Her birth mother had been keeping track of her.

Her birth mother *cared*.

Was that possible?

She had to know. The burn intensified until she could taste the metallic, bitter flavor of need in her mouth. She had to know why Sharon had that picture. And she had to warn Sharon that her home was under surveillance and that she was in danger.

But how?

Trembling, she followed the darkened street back to the curvy Carolina roads. Finding Dr. Sharon Greenberg had just gone from an impulse to a mission. *Belfast.*

Fortunately, she'd brought her passport.

CHAPTER 2

The offices of the fledgling security and investigation firm sat directly above a lingerie store on Newbury Street, giving Marc Rossi one more reason to like his new job.

He loitered at the window of Silk, drinking in the display of autumn gold thongs and russet front-clasp brassieres. While he briefly imagined the pleasure of putting them on—and taking them off—the right woman, he answered his vibrating cell phone without looking at caller ID.

He knew who it was anyway.

"I see you staring at the unmentionables, Marc."

Inching back, he grinned up at the bay window that protruded from the second floor and saw his cousin looking down at him with an amused expression on her devilish features.

"You can mention them, Vivi. I just don't remember my father's offices having such excellent downstairs neighbors."

"That's because Silk was a Chinese laundry when Uncle Jim used this suite. But I'm thinking we can add a tagline to the Guardian Angelinos Web site: 'We're just above the underwear'."

Marc laughed. "I like it." He pulled open the glass door that led to a small entryway, throwing one more wistful smile at the lace-covered entrance to Silk before heading upstairs. Like so many buildings in Boston's Back Bay, offices and apartments were stacked above high-end retailers, accessible by steep, narrow staircases or rickety elevators. "And it'll make Christmas shopping so much easier for me," he added.

"I wear a small. Bottom and top, sadly."

He took the stairs two at a time. "I wasn't thinking about you, little cousin."

"I've no doubt your shopping list is long and heavily weighted to the Silk customer," she countered. "But no lingering in lingerie. We have ten minutes until your FBI buddy shows up, and I want to have our act together to meet a potential new client."

"Will do, boss." He ended the call as he reached the top landing and continued down a familiar hallway to the suite of offices where his father had practiced law for almost twenty years before becoming a judge. But Jim Rossi had kept the lease on this prime Back Bay real estate and had generously offered the unoccupied offices to house the company Marc's cousins had just started.

The faint scent of cleaning solution and paint wafted into the hall, because the official move had taken place just this past weekend. Marc had been unable to leave his weapons shop to help, but he'd successfully trained a few managers, which left him free to make the leap from small-business owner back to the life he missed and loved—not the life of FBI agent that he'd once enjoyed, but that of consultant.

The brother and sister team of Vivi and Zach Angelino had planned a venture that was very appealing to him. When they asked him to consult for the Guardian Angelinos, he went all in, and proved his enthusiasm by bringing the company its first official new business lead.

He opened the door, and the smell of fresh paint grew stronger, along with the colors. The walls were deep purple and gold, showcasing the ultrahip reception chairs and the glass desk.

"Good-bye, Rossi Law and hello, Guardian Angelinos," he said with a soft laugh.

"You like?" Vivi spun around from the bay window, her smile as cheery as the September sun that backlit her, her dark eyes glittering like the diamond stud in her nose. "Because Zach hates it."

Marc shook his head, chuckling. "Your brother is a killjoy."

"I am not." Zach Angelino's distinctive baritone rolled out from the back offices. "I let her go with the ridiculous name, didn't I? Do I have to like the . . . the . . ."

"Jewel tones?" Vivi supplied as she waved Marc toward the rest of the suite. "He's full of it. He loves the Guardian Angelinos. Makes him feel so important to have the name on the door."

"I love the *concept*," Zach corrected as they entered his office. "I still think the name is . . . regrettable."

"How'd you get the office with the better view?" Marc glanced around at his father's former law office, the wall of windows overlooking the bustle of chic Back Bay.

"I'm one minute older," Zach said, grinning at Vivi from behind a cheap fiberboard desk placed in the very spot where James Rossi's antique oak monster lived before it became a permanent resident of the family's Sudbury basement.

"And he got the high-end guest chairs," Vivi said, indicating two folding director's chairs with the Ford logo on the back. "They came free with the company Expedition, and I blew the furniture budget on the reception. First impressions and all."

Mark dropped into one of the wobbly chairs. "Don't make excuses. You two have done an amazing job already."

Zach snorted. "We need more clients, but we're getting there." For the first time since he got back from Iraq, Zach seemed completely comfortable in his own skin—as scarred as that skin might be. It wasn't just his role as CEO of a new company, either. Marc knew exactly what—or rather who—made his cousin look so content.

"How's Samantha?" Marc asked.

Although his missing left eye was covered with a simple leather patch, Zach's happiness was still easy to read. "One week into law school, and she's killin' it already. We're looking for a bigger place than her apartment in Somerville."

"What's that I hear?" Vivi asked, curling her lithe little frame into the other chair and cupping a hand at her ear. "Why, it's the sound of bells. Wedding bells."

"Seriously?" Marc turned to Zach and knew instantly that this wasn't Vivi's usual hyperbole.

Zach lifted a casual shoulder, but his smile was anything but nonchalant. Something twisted in Marc's gut. Envy? Impossible. He couldn't love his cousin more or want to head back into marriage less. "When?" he asked.

"June, assuming this business takes off the way my sister believes it will."

"And that's where you come in," Vivi said, her hand on Marc's arm.

"Best man?"

"Best consultant," she said. "Please tell me this FBI gig is really going to happen. We need cash so badly."

"Assuming Assistant Special Agent in Charge Colton Lang shows up here in the next few minutes, I think it is. And, trust me, if this goes well, the bureau is always on the lookout for outside help on special projects. Colt could be your biggest client."

"*Our* biggest client," Zach corrected, pointing at Marc. "Vivi and I need you as a regular on the payroll, Marc, not just brought in here and there. As long as you understand that payroll is slim for now."

Marc shrugged. "I know what it is, and you know how much I would rather do work in security and investigations than own a gun shop."

"You should be solving crimes and taking down bad guys, Marc," Vivi said. "Not selling Glocks and Walthers so someone else can do the job."

Vivi and Zach, raised with the Rossi family since the two of them were orphaned at age ten in Italy and sent to the States to live with relatives, knew Marc as well as any of his siblings. They'd all been there for Marc when his seemingly perfect marriage to a seemingly perfect woman turned out to be anything but perfect, and trust had cost him the job he loved almost as much as he loved her. They knew how much he missed that job. But not that woman.

"I'm here for the long haul," he assured them. "Not for the slender paycheck."

The squeak of the front office door ended the conversation. Vivi popped up so fast she almost toppled the flimsy chair. "To the conference room, gentlemen. Let's try to look official. This is a client."

The two men shared a look, and Zach pointed to his sister's trademark cargo pants and tank top, a sweatshirt tied around her narrow waist. "We'll follow your lead, Vice President in Charge of Investigations Angelino."

She flipped him the bird and disappeared to greet the guest.

Zach stood but Marc didn't, still eyeing his cousin. "You sure?" he asked simply.

"There are no words for how sure I am," he said, obviously knowing what Marc was referring to. "Just 'cause you're jaded doesn't mean the rest of the world is."

Marc stifled a soft hoot. "Says the guy who invented jaded."

"I'm unjaded now, thanks to Sam."

"The love of a good woman and all?" Marc rose to follow him.

"You don't need to be so bitter."

"Who's bitter? I'm a realist."

Zach laughed. "You've never been a realist, Marc. You're a perfectionist, and that's fine in business, but as long as you're looking for perfection, you'll only be disappointed."

He didn't agree, but just followed Zach into the hall.

"Your marriage didn't work out. Mine will," Zach said confidently. "And, anyway, you picked the wrong person first time around."

"First?" Marc snorted at the optimism. "As if there'd be a second."

"A second what?" From behind them came the calm and authoritative voice of ASAC Colton Lang, which was familiar to Marc since they'd worked together a few times when he was still with the bureau.

Marc ignored the question and exchanged greetings while they all moved into the conference room, where Vivi's decorating hadn't yet started. The bookshelves were still stocked with legal tomes, and the long mahogany table that seated a dozen or so still seemed stodgy and old school compared to the colorful ambience of the reception area.

Short-haired, conservative, suit-and-tie man Colton Lang fit right in.

"I'm here because you all did a masterful job of finding Joshua Sterling's killers," he said without preamble, standing at the head of the table, his gaze moving from one to the other. "I know you took a bullet in the process, Ms. Angelino," he added to Vivi. "How are you feeling?"

Vivi smiled proudly, her hand moving to her stomach. "I'm back on my skateboard," she said with a laugh. "So looks like everything's normal."

Colt covered a rare smile with a single nod. "Glad to hear it. As you know, the bureau wasn't really involved with that case, but we are appreciative of your success."

"Maybe you should have been involved," Zach said dryly. "Since the Boston police had a vested interest in not solving it."

Colt acknowledged the understatement with another tip of his chin. "If you hadn't led us to the dirty cop who was working with Joshua Sterling's mistress, we might have fallen for their scheme to pin the murder on Finn MacCauley. It would have been an easy mistake for us to make, since, as you know, he's a fugitive who remains on the FBI's Most Wanted list."

"I really hope you're here to give us the job of finding him," Vivi added, leaning forward with a sparkle in her eyes. "Because we could do that."

Colt held her gaze for a minute, assessing her with a fraction of surprise that made Marc suppress a smile. Vivi was constantly being misjudged, thanks to her funky style and choice of skateboard as a means of transportation. But being underestimated and sometimes dismissed as too young or too frivolous had helped Vivi crack some of the toughest stories when she was a journalist. As an investigator, he suspected that vibe would be her most powerful secret weapon.

"I'm not here to ask you to find Finn MacCauley," Colt said.

"Still, we could."

He gave in to a smile. "While I admire your spirit, Ms. Angelino, I have to let you know that unearthing an ancient fugitive isn't really a high priority for the bureau."

Marc choked. "Any man on the Most Wanted list is a high priority, Colt. Who are you kidding?"

"I don't kid. For one thing, he's been missing for almost three decades, there's doubts he's still alive, and he hasn't been linked to a new crime since 1983."

"He's linked to enough old ones," Marc said.

"You were still in the FBI post-nine-eleven," Colt replied. "You know what happened to our priorities. Terrorism is job number one, two, three, and four now. Finding a man who was involved with mobs that don't even exist anymore, especially since more than a few people believe his body was buried under the Central Artery when they started the Big Dig, is not on my to-do list. Finding him is as low on the crime totem pole as stopping the sales of knockoff designer handbags."

"Then why are you here?" Marc asked.

"To find his daughter." Colt pulled out a color photo and placed it on the table, and Marc instantly recognized Devyn Hewitt Sterling, the widow of Joshua Sterling and, for a very brief time, a person of interest in that murder.

"I thought she was cleared of any suspicion in her husband's death," Marc said.

"She's not guilty of anything," Colt assured him.

"Except being stupid." Marc eyed the picture of the widowed socialite with striking cheekbones and sky-blue eyes. "If she hadn't told her ambitious husband that her biological father was a wanted criminal, Joshua Sterling might still be alive." Although she was probably better off without him.

"I don't think she's stupid," Colt said thoughtfully. "And that's why we need somebody very smart for the job of finding her."

"What did she do?" Vivi asked.

"Nothing," Colt replied, settling into his seat. "Right now she's traveling, in Belfast as far as we can tell, and I'd like you to track her down and bring that trip to an end."

"Why?" All three of them asked the question at the same time.

Colt reacted with raised eyebrows, hesitating. "You don't need to know that."

This time, he got three silent stares.

"You really don't," he said firmly. "The job is simple. Find her and convince her to leave the country, preferably to come back to the States, but frankly that's not important. Just get her out of Belfast *without* raising her suspicions about who you are or who you are working for. Just somehow get her out of there."

"Why don't you just apprehend her?" Vivi asked, but Marc already knew the question was moot. It didn't take all of his twelve years as an FBI agent to know they weren't getting the whole story. And since Colton Lang had a reputation as a hardass rule follower, he suspected they might never get it.

"She hasn't committed a crime," Colt said.

Vivi looked at her brother, then Marc, clearly not ready to accept this level of information. She opened her mouth to object, but Colt cut off her question before it was asked.

"Do you want the assignment or not?"

She closed her mouth.

Zach put a hand over hers. "Sometimes it's going to work this way," he said quietly. After his years in the army, Zach understood that missions could be carried out without everyone knowing the full reasoning behind the strategy.

"What kind of support will we have from the bureau?" Marc asked.

"None." Colt leveled his gaze with the single-word response. "And you'll have no contact with the bureau except for me. No negotiating on that."

Vivi blew out a breath, but Zach waved away her frustration again. "Let's talk fees."

"When Devyn Sterling is out of Belfast, preferably out of Northern Ireland completely."

"What?" Vivi almost jumped out of her seat. "You want us to take this on contingency? An assignment that's practically a black hole of information?"

"Yes, I do," he said. "If you are official FBI consultants, then I have to show casework, and I'm afraid we don't have time for that. You need to leave immediately, tomorrow if not sooner."

Marc turned the photo of Devyn around to look at it, studying the coolness in her gaze, the distance in her expression. Like she was dead cold on the inside. Why did the FBI want this widow out of Belfast?

He had a very strong suspicion that he was too smart to voice.

"Give us an hour to discuss it," Marc said. "And during that hour, arrange a retainer check for expenses. I'm certain you can do that without getting tied up in red tape."

Colt nodded to the concession, sliding the pertinent files toward him. "I'll be back before noon. Please have a decision for me by then." He glanced at Vivi and Zach. "I can show myself out."

He left and none of them said a word until the door to the reception area closed behind him.

And then they all talked at the same time, Rossi-Angelino style.

"Contingency!"

"He's holding back."

"We need this job." Zach took the lead, holding up his hand. "We *need* this job," he repeated to be sure he was heard over the others. "Even if it's contingency," he said to Vivi. "And even if he's not telling us everything. We know enough to at least attempt to do what he wants. That's the assignment and that's what we'll do."

"Spoken like a true Army Ranger," Vivi said, pushing back from the table. "But not the CEO of a company."

"Hang on, Vivi," Marc said. "Zach's right—we don't

have to know everything, and we do need this assignment. If my gut is right, this has to do with finding Finn MacCauley, and there's no way he's going to trust an unproven operation like ours with that information."

She tilted her head in acknowledgment. "Then let's get proven. Let's find him."

Zach snorted softly. "We're good, Vivi, but we aren't quite equipped to go after a fugitive who's eluded the FBI for thirty years. We prove ourselves by working with him, not against him, and by taking it one step at a time. Marc goes to Ireland, finds this woman, convinces her to leave Belfast with him."

"How are you going to do that?" Vivi asked.

Marc grinned. "Have you met me?"

She laughed but shook her head. "You are charming, but without knowing why she's there, or what she's doing, you'll have to do some fancy footwork."

"I will. And Colt didn't say I couldn't ask her what's going on. He just wanted me to get her out of there. Let me get some intelligence on her situation, create a personal relationship with her, and get her out of there. Then we'll figure out if there's more we can do. All of that is within the parameters of what he wants from this firm."

"I hate parameters." Vivi stood and paced the room, her hands deep in the pockets of her cargo pants. "What if we did bring in Finn MacCauley?" she said.

Zach and Marc shared a look but didn't say anything.

"You know damn well that would put the Guardian Angelinos on the map," she said. "The national press coverage on that would take us right to the next level."

"Vivi, we haven't even reached the first level yet," Zach said. "Let's just do this right and see if we can get more business from the FBI. Marc says they use outside security and investigation firms all the time."

"They do," Marc agreed. "And they don't always tell them everything about a case, so I believe this is legit and has potential."

"Boatloads of potential," Vivi said. "You go find her and we'll give you whatever backup support you need here, and..." She hesitated, locking gazes with her brother.

"Don't turn this into a hunt for Finn MacCauley," Zach said. "If that's what the client wanted, he'd have asked for it."

"So let's overachieve," she shot back.

While the twins stared each other down, Marc grabbed the files, taking one more look at Devyn Sterling. Perfect women made his skin crawl...even though they were the only kind he ever wanted. "I wonder what she's doing traveling around Belfast two months after her cheating husband was killed?"

"I did some research on her when we were working on the Josh Sterling murder," Vivi said. "You know she's a Hewitt, right? The bluest blood in Boston and richer than God's little brother."

"I know." Marc studied the fine features and soft waves of warm blond hair. "Except," he mused, "her blood isn't really blue. She's Finn MacCauley's illegitimate daughter. Her blood is...bloody."

"And no one even knows who her mother is," Zach added. "It was the big hole in the story Joshua was going to take public."

Marc nodded, closing the file. "Can you make some calls and get me the flight information?" he asked Vivi. "I'm going home to pack."

"So we are definitely taking this job?" Vivi asked.

"Final decision is up to the CEO," Marc replied. "Zach?"

"We'll take it exactly as the client has asked us to," Zach said. "He's a straight-up guy and we're not going investigating behind his back. We do the job, we get paid, we get another job. We do this the conventional way, Vivi."

Vivi rolled her eyes. "You know what a fan of convention I am. What do you need from us, Marc?"

"Information on the Belfast hotels. And I don't mean room availability. I need guest lists."

"Chessie," Vivi said, referring to Marc's youngest sibling, the hacker of the family. "She can, um, *research* the hotels in Belfast and see if we can find where Devyn Sterling is staying." She put a hand on her hip and looked at her brother. "That is, if Chessie's creative database searches are still within the *parameters* of what the client wants us to do."

Zach pushed up from the table. "Of course. We still use our secret weapons as long as we do what the client asks and do it well."

"I plan on using every one I've got," Marc said, tucking the file under his arm as he headed to the lobby.

Vivi was beside him in three strides, bounding on her purple and white zebra-striped skate shoes. "You'll stay in touch with me, won't you?" she said, soft enough that Zach couldn't hear. "And tell me everything you find out."

"You know I will. You just move carefully, Vivi. Finn MacCauley may be buried under the Central Artery, or he may be hiding out on an island in the South Pacific. Wherever he is, there are people who don't want him found."

"Got it." She opened the door for him and put a hand

on his shoulder. "So what's your plan? Seduction? Heartbreak? A fellow traveler in need?"

"I'm just going to find her weakness and exploit it."

"Whoa." Vivi inched back, a smile threatening. "I didn't think you were such a bastard, Marc."

"I didn't used to be."

CHAPTER 3

"Did I hear you say you were looking for a Dr. Greenberg, miss?"

For the first time since she'd started her search, Devyn felt a surge of hope. She blinked at the smooth-faced concierge and hesitated a second, making sure she understood the thick Belfast accent. "Yes."

He angled his head to the side and sent his thumb in the same direction, silently telling her to separate from the other guests lined up for help in the lobby of the Europa Hotel.

"She's here, but she's not here," he said, his youthful eyes wide, a sweet flush of color on his pale cheeks, as though getting that close to a woman didn't happen every day. "What I mean is she's checked out but left bags."

Hope soared for a moment. After all the B and Bs, hotels, and hostels she'd tried throughout Belfast and the surrounding area, this was the first time someone had given her any concrete information. She resisted the urge to grab his arm and demand more, asking calmly, "Are you certain it's Dr. Sharon Greenberg, an American?"

He flicked his fingers around his cheeks. "Lots of silver hair, kinda curly?"

She'd seen Sharon's pictures on the university Web site, and the description of Sharon's distinctive white waves fit enough that optimism took a stronghold in Devyn's chest. "So she's coming back here, to this hotel?"

"Thursday," he said. "She told me herself."

Two days. She almost kissed him. "Did she say where she was going?"

He shrugged, but something about the gesture indicated he knew more than he was telling. "A side sightseeing trip, I assume. That's why most guests leave their luggage here. Are you a guest at the Europa as well, miss?"

She should be. "Yes, I'm checking in today," she announced without giving it a moment's thought. She'd chosen a much smaller inn, rather than one of the few glitzier hotels in Belfast, but with the possibility that she'd found Sharon, she would definitely move into the Europa to wait for her. "Can you call me when she shows up for her bags?"

"Of course. I'm Patrick." He smiled self-consciously.

"Thank you, Patrick." She automatically reached for her bag to tip him, but he waved her off.

"No, not necessary, miss. I'm happy to help you find your friend, as she was a lovely lady, right down to the bone."

That was reassuring. "And you're sure she's coming back Thursday? Could it be sooner?"

"She was quite specific, but you know, there's plenty to do in Belfast while you wait."

"I'll just wait here," she said.

"You can, of course, but most people who are sightseeing in this part of Northern Ireland go up the coast for the day. Maybe your doctor's up there. I can arrange a car for you, if you like, and you can see our sights. The Giant's Causeway is quite famous, as is the Carrick-a-Rede Rope Bridge. It's a lovely day for a ride, and I can have you taken care of by the best driver we have."

She'd love to get out of Belfast and see the coast, but since she'd arrived in Northern Ireland, her entire focus had been on trying to find Sharon—without even knowing if she was here—not sightseeing. So the suggestion was tempting.

"I may do that, but I'll get my own car, thank you."

"Be careful if you get a private driver, ma'am. They'll rip your pocket book 'round here. Are you sure you won't let me arrange one?"

"I'll rent a car," she said. The freedom of driving up the coast, holding on to that hope that she'd found Dr. Greenberg, suddenly appealed to her immensely. "I'll be back this afternoon. Will you be here?"

"Until six tonight," he said. "After that I'm on the graveyard, so you'll only see me if you're an insomniac."

"Patrick!" Another concierge called from the desk with a dark look and a gesture to the line. "We need you, man."

"Go." Devyn gave him a friendly nudge. "And thank you."

Feeling lighter than she had for days, Devyn turned to survey the hotel she'd just decided to check into, heading to the front desk to hold a reservation for a few days. There, a sweet-faced young girl helped her and then iced the cake by nodding and clicking a keyboard when Devyn asked if she could check on the status of another reservation.

"Yes," she said, eyeing her screen. "Dr. Greenberg is due back on September fourteenth, holding a reservation until the sixteenth."

Life was suddenly all sunshine and roses after days of doubt and dead ends. "Thank you so much," Devyn said, hoisting her handbag over her shoulder.

As she passed the rack of brochures, she snagged one with the words "Antrim Coast" in large yellow letters, flipped it open, and walked right smack into a six-foot-tall man.

"Oh, I'm sorry." She backed away, feeling a heated flush rise along with a bump where her ankle had slammed the corner of his luggage.

"Excuse me," he apologized, hurriedly rolling the bag away.

"Not at all," she assured him, holding the brochure as evidence of her clumsiness. "I wasn't...looking." And she should have been. Because he made the Irish coast-line pale in comparison.

"Not very smart of me." His voice was melodic, warm. And American.

"Nor me," she replied.

He melted her with a smile that lit eyes the color of ripe black olives, revealing straight white teeth that stood out from a sexy shadow of whiskers. "You're from the States. Where?" he asked.

"Boston." The truth was out before she could think,

but then her brain had flatlined the minute he'd turned around. "You?"

"New York." He winked at her. "We're practically neighbors. Are you staying here?" he asked with just enough hope to give her an unexpected tingle of pleasure.

"I just checked in." She wanted to step away, but something magnetic kept her there for a beat too long.

"You're off to the Antrim Coast?" he asked.

She drew back. "How do you know that?"

"Lucky guess." He tapped the brochure. "Heard it's pretty up there."

"Looks like it's"—she fingered the brochure—"pretty."

He smiled again, a tease in his eyes that made her stomach flutter. Then he reached out his hand. "I'm Marc Rossi."

His palm was warm and dry, his grip strong, his fingers long. "Devyn...Smith." A New Yorker could easily have heard of Joshua Sterling's murder last summer, and she just wasn't prepared to deal with that. This stranger in the lobby didn't need to know her real name. "It's nice to meet you, Marc."

In return, she got one more flash of a smile, a hint of dimples embedded in hollow cheeks, and warmth in his remarkable eyes. "You're not going to invite me along on your day trip, are you?"

She withdrew her hand slowly. "No. But I'll take a picture for you."

"I'll look for you this evening, then. In the bar, right over there?"

"I have no idea what time I'll be back. Maybe. We'll see." She gave him a wistful smile and stole a glance at his expensive cotton shirt, but she really only noticed how nicely his shoulders filled it out. "Sorry for walking right into you like that."

"I'm not."

She laughed softly. "You're good at that," she volleyed back, still not moving from the magic of his eyes. "But you're not getting the invitation."

"Then I'll work harder next time."

Like he was so sure there'd be a next time. "Bye." She turned away and headed to the door, the reason she'd come to the hotel and the successful outcome of her discussion with the concierge momentarily washed from her mind.

It had been a long, long time since a man had made her feel...alive.

Outside, the sun met her mood, threatening to break through a gray sky, underscoring a sense that she'd just breathed clean, sweet air and wanted more. More warmth. More flirting. More...of a man like that.

After the last few years of ice and misery and daily disappointments from the man she'd married, that little shot of flirting with a stranger was like downing a tumbler of Irish whiskey.

And it left her just as warm.

Hesitating at the curb, she looked for one of the London-type cabs she'd been using to get around Belfast. She was already used to the hum of the city and the open-air feel of the low-rise buildings, although the Europa and the few modern buildings in the little square were taller than most. In the past few days, she'd become familiar enough with the main streets and some of the neighbor-hoods that renting a car and taking a trip seemed like a brilliant and beautiful plan.

Speaking of brilliant and beautiful...She glanced behind her through the glass doors, somehow not surprised to see the man she'd just met doing the same thing from the front desk. Their gazes met and he zapped her with a smile again.

"Cabbie, miss?"

She was about to say yes, but then shook her head. The B and B wasn't that far, and for the first time in a while, she didn't feel like hiding in the back of a cab, cornered and considering her options. She'd found Sharon, sort of; she had time and a place to go; and she maybe had a semi-sort-of rendezvous that night.

Was it too soon to talk to a man, too close to Josh's death to think about being with someone else? No. After four years of marriage to one of the coldest cheaters in the world, it wasn't too soon to at least think about having a drink with Marc Rossi. Great name, too.

He was probably in town on business, she decided as she headed around the building toward Great Victoria Street. Lonely, looking for company...married? Undoubtedly a charmer like that had a wife and three kids back in New York. He didn't look too young, mid-to-late thirties, with a sexy kind of fierceness under that charm, like he could slam you up against a wall and pin you there—right before he kissed the living hell out of you.

She almost stumbled on the uneven sidewalk. Was that why she'd turned him down so quickly? Because what was wrong with a little distraction? Assuming he *wasn't* married and really was just a friendly guy from New York looking for company.

Maybe she'd have that drink with him. It couldn't hurt, and it might feel...really good.

She paused at an intersection, orienting herself to the left-side drivers, when a dark sedan slowed down, inching over to where she stood. She stepped back, and the window rolled down and the driver smiled at her.

Delivering the same little bolt of lightning through her blood.

"It's a long walk up the coast, Ms. Smith."

A cool breeze lifted her hair but did nothing to reduce the heat level of his gaze. "I'm on my way to rent a car."

"Now, that's just a waste of time, money, and gas. I've already got one, and I'm going sightseeing. My offer still stands."

She hesitated, but not for long. Why shouldn't she have just one afternoon of enjoyment on this mission?

Still…she wasn't sure. She took a step closer. His right hand rested on the window, but that wasn't the one that mattered. The left was on the wheel, and she took a surreptitious dip to see it.

"Looking for a ring?"

So much for surreptitious. "Actually, yes, I am. I'm suspicious that way."

He held up his bare hand. "Truth in advertising. Divorced and traveling alone, wildly attracted to honey hair and blue eyes, and on my way to spend the day sightseeing and have no desire to do that alone. Would you care to come along?"

This wasn't the reason she'd traveled across the ocean and traipsed all over Belfast. This wasn't in keeping with her plan to find Sharon, to have that personal meeting with her and warn her about the man watching her house. This wasn't—

"If it's that tough a decision for you, Ms. Smith, I'll

back off." There was nothing but sincerity in his tone, no more flirting, no more seduction. Just consideration and kindness.

And, God knows, she could use some of that, too.

"That's not necessary," she said, tucking her hair behind her ear and making yet another spontaneous decision. "I'd love to go sightseeing with you. And, please, call me Devyn."

He grinned like she'd given him a gift, hopping out to walk her around to the opposite side of the car, moving with grace despite his six-foot height and nicely built muscles. As he stepped in front of her to open the door, she stole a look at his back, lingering on the jeans that hugged his backside and narrow waist.

She was going sightseeing, all right. And the view was spectacular.

"So what brings you to Belfast?" he asked when he climbed into the driver's seat on her right and tugged on his seat belt. "Business or pleasure?"

"Both," she said. "You?"

"Same, but mostly pleasure." He threw her another toe-curling look. "Pleasure today, definitely."

"What do you do?"

"Invest," he said. "How about you?"

Of course there'd be questions. Many personal questions. She should have thought of that before she hopped into the car with a sexy stranger. "What do you invest in?" she asked instead of answering.

He maneuvered through a roundabout, surprisingly comfortable with the left-side driving. A competent man, confident and easygoing. Joshua had been that way...an easygoing liar.

"I invest in companies."

"Like a venture capitalist?"

"Something like that, but a little more in the background. Angel investments. You didn't answer my question," he reminded her. "What's your business here in Belfast?"

"It's personal," she said, hoping her tone would not invite another question, but his look was expectant. So she added, "I'm waiting for a friend from the States who gets back in a few days."

"Back from where?"

Instead of responding, she made a show of opening the brochure she'd been holding in the hotel. "There's a map on the back of this. We've got quite a scenic route up the coast."

He kept his gaze on her and not the road for a few seconds. "So you're secretive as well as beautiful."

Looking down at the brochure, she let a lock of hair fall and cover her expression. Would she have to ask him outright not to probe with personal questions?

Stopping at a light, he reached over and lifted her hair, brushing her cheek with his knuckles, the contact surprisingly warm. Damn near electric.

"Am I right?" he asked. "You're secretive?"

"I'm private," she replied, turning her head enough to escape the heat. "There's a difference."

"Still beautiful."

"Thank you." She felt a flush rise to her face as the voice of the woman who'd raised her echoed in her head.

Beauty is skin-deep.

It wasn't until Devyn used her considerable resources to find out her real bloodline that she learned exactly why her adopted mother loved that phrase. Because under the skin is the blood...and the blood in her veins was not Hewitt. It was MacCauley, and there was nothing beautiful about it.

The thought reminded her of why she was here—not to sightsee with charming strangers. Still, she'd made the rash decision—that bloodline acting again—and now she had to live with the consequences.

She pointed to a main highway. "That's the M2, I believe, that circles Belfast. Take it a little west, then go east up to Ballyclare." She gave him a forced smile. "Sounds lovely, doesn't it? Have you been to Ireland before?"

"I have, but I spend most of my time in Dublin. Never been up this far."

"Me neither."

His smile wasn't forced or unnatural. It was just... inviting.

"I know you don't want a barrage of personal questions, but I have to ask one, since I don't see a ring. Single as well?"

"I am now," she said, looking away, out the window.

"Ah, divorced, too, then?"

She waited a beat. "No, actually, I'm a widow."

"I'm sorry. How long has it been?"

"About two..." *Months.* "Years."

"Kids?"

"No," she said quickly. "What about you?"

Maneuvering onto the highway stole his attention momentarily. "Not yet," he replied, a hint of something like wistfulness in his voice.

"But you want them?"

He glanced at her. "What was the clue?"

"The word 'yet' and the sound of longing in your tone."

"Wow." He laughed, shooting her an admiring look. "Private, beautiful, intuitive. Look how much I learned about you in just this little bit of time."

Reminding her that she'd better keep the conversation about him or she'd be telling him far too much. "We're even, then. I've learned you're open, charming, and, oh, let me guess, the oldest in your family."

"You got all that out of 'not yet'? Amazing. But I hate to ruin your perfect record. I'm the second out of seven, not quite the oldest."

"*Seven?* That's a huge family."

"Now we're even," he said.

"Excuse me?"

"I hear longing in your voice."

Was it that obvious? "I was a lonely only," she admitted. "Seven kids sounds like pure heaven."

"With moments of hell. To be fair, there were only five kids and two cousins raised with us. Plus a grandfather, Uncle Nino."

"You call your grandfather Uncle Nino?"

"Mostly we just called him Nino, which became his de facto grandfather title, like, you know Boompa or Gramps. My cousins came to live with us and he's their great-uncle, so they call him Uncle Nino."

"Sounds like a great way to grow up. Rossi, right? So this must be an Italian family. Where in New York?"

But he just shook his head. "You know, Devyn, I have only a day with you, and an overview of my huge family—and yes, we are Italian—could take up most of our time. Unless, of course, you promise me I can have more time until your friend gets here. What day does he arrive?"

"Thursday and . . . it's a she."

He lifted a brow, his dark eyes glittering with a tease. "Well, that's encouraging. Not a romantic rendezvous, then."

Damn, he was good at the conversation volley. She purposely shifted in her seat and avoided eye contact. "It's two more miles to the turn to Ballyclare. You know, I just like saying that, such an Irish word. Have you noticed how different the accent is up here? More British than brogue, don't you think?"

"You know, Devyn," he said, gently placing his hand over hers on the console. "This will be a very long, very frustrating, and very uncomfortable day if you refuse to tell me anything about yourself. Unless, of course, you're on the run from the law, in hiding from an ex-lover, or on a secret mission for the government and can't tell me anything. In that case, I'll let you get away with being chatty and vague."

She slid her hand out from under his, taking the brief moment to try and swallow. "What if I were guilty of all of the above? Would you still want to go sightseeing with me?"

His expression shifted and softened. "More than ever."

The last time a man believed her, he took her story and tried to sell it to the highest bidder—and it cost him his life.

"Then you better be careful, Marc Rossi," she said quietly. "Because nothing about me is as it seems."

He smiled, an expression so sexy and endearing it made her stomach plummet to her toes. "There's nothing I like more in a woman than mystery. I take solving it as a personal challenge."

A challenge, she swore to herself, he would fail.

CHAPTER 4

"Make a wish, Marc."

I wish she weren't so damn perfect. "I wish I didn't feel like such a tourist." He settled into the cool, mottled rocks, the particular arrangement of stones shaped like a chair.

"Too bad, you are. And at this moment, the tourist is in the Wishing Chair." Devyn waved the guidebook they'd picked up at the visitor's center, the wind whipping off the Atlantic coast and howling over the wide stretch of bizarre geology called the Giant's Causeway. "Whatever you wish will come true, according to legend. And if I've learned anything in the last few hours, it's that legends rule the day around here."

"Right. I better make a good wish." He leaned back, squinting up at the silhouette of a woman against a misty sky and gunmetal seas, still amazed at how different she was in person than in two dimensions.

And not just her features. Yes, she was even prettier

than he'd anticipated, but he'd braced for an ice queen and got a surprising blast of heat. He'd expected a bland and bored rich widow, maybe uptight and withdrawn, but discovered a woman with a smile that came from her heart, a laugh that sounded like chimes, and windblown hair that was ten different shades of butterscotch and caramel.

Not to mention a lithe, lean body that moved with a magical mix of grace and sexiness.

Too perfect.

"Come on," she urged. "What do you want most in the whole world?"

Nothing he could wish for here and now. Nothing the legends and lore would grant him. Nothing he could ever expect to have again in this lifetime.

"Now you're the one who's thinking too hard," she said, those wind chimes ringing again as she laughed, a sound as intoxicating as the view from the sharp, limestone cliff jutting out to the ocean behind her.

"I'm not thinking. I'm enjoying the view," he said, looking right into eyes the color of his first Corvette. Arctic Blue, the Chevy guys called it, a mix of glinting glaciers against azure sea.

"You have about ten seconds before the next busload of tourists forms a line. Wish."

He closed his eyes, the outline of her curves against the milky sky still burned behind his lids. "I wish you'd have dinner with me tonight."

She just laughed and reached for his hand, offering help he didn't need but certainly wanted. "You're greedy. You've got my whole day already."

"Not greedy. I just like to plan for the future." Still holding her hand, he brushed her lower lip with his thumb, because it was the next best thing to pressing his mouth there. "And dinner isn't exactly a lifetime commitment. You've got to eat. Why do it alone?"

She gave him that don't-ask-me look she'd laid on him mercilessly in the car, until he backed off and kept the conversation impersonal and light.

Once he'd done that, she'd relaxed and the day had unfolded from his well-orchestrated "accidental" meeting to something that felt very much like a first date. He couldn't think of a better way to get her off course than good old-fashioned seduction, but nothing about this effort felt forced.

"Let's go to the edge," he said, keeping their hands locked as he closed his arm around her back.

She hesitated, a little off balance on the slabs of slippery rock. "I don't think so."

"You afraid of heights?" he asked.

She nodded, her color deepening with the admission. "They make me dizzy."

He tightened his grip and lowered his face to her ear. "I'll hold you," he said softly, his words caught in the wind. "Then *I'll* make you dizzy."

"Wow." Easing away but still holding his hand, she shook her head, stepping gingerly over one of the thousands of flat-topped rocks that formed the unique shoreline. "You're scary good at flirting, you know that?"

"Come on, how can you not be a little romantic? It's Ireland, for God's sake, and this whole thing"—he gestured to nature's spectacle around them—"was created by a lovesick giant."

"Or an erupting volcano, depending on whether you believe lore or fact."

He laughed, slowing her steps with a gentle tug. "I guess I'll add pragmatic to the list of things I'm discovering about you."

"And I'll add world-class *play-er*." She dragged out the word.

With a grunt, he pounded a fist to his chest, feigning a stab wound. "Ouch." But the truth hurt a little. She had no idea how much he was playing her right then.

"Not denying it, I see."

"I'm not a player," he assured her. "Just a hopeless romantic. Like you're private and not secretive. Obviously, between us, semantics are important." He guided her closer to the cliff's edge. "C'mon, Devyn. Face your fears."

Another gust whooshed over them, so he had to place his arm around her waist or stumble in the stiff breeze. She looked out at the water, giving him a chance to study her profile.

"It's hard to be scared in the face of such beauty," she mused, unaware of his scrutiny.

"It sure is."

She turned then and caught him. "You're flirting again."

"I'm admiring the view again." The stunning, perfect view that really should be a red flag to Marc.

She looked back at the sea, letting the compliment drop.

His former wife had been a flawless specimen of womankind, too, and he'd been foolish enough to believe that meant her heart and intentions were perfect as well. At least he had the advantage of already knowing this woman was hiding something.

Something he needed to know in order to accomplish the simple assignment of derailing her and getting her to leave Belfast. At least he'd gotten her out of the city for the day, but the job was bigger in scope than one day, and if he was going to accomplish it quickly, he'd better work harder.

"So," he said with a light squeeze, "you've stood at the edge of the Giant's Causeway. Surely you're ready for the rope bridge at Carrick-a-Rede? It's next on every tourist's agenda."

"I don't know..." She suddenly looked around, her attention moving to the crowds instead of the scenery. "Every tourist?"

"Yep, even the ones afraid of heights." He guided her back to the car, across the thousands of hexagonal rock columns, arm in arm over the uneven terrain like a couple who'd been together for years instead of three hours.

What exactly would it take to get her to leave before the person she was waiting for arrived? It depended on who that person was, he decided. Time to find out.

As they passed the Wishing Chair, he wended them toward it. "I know what my wish is now."

She let him take her there, and when he sat, she didn't fight the pull to sit on his lap. He put his finger under her chin and turned her face toward his.

"I know what you're going to wish for," she said with a laugh. "And you're wasting your time. I'm not going to kiss you."

"That's not what I was going to wish for at all."

A flash of surprise and maybe disappointment darkened her eyes. "Then what?"

"I wish you'd tell me who you're meeting in Belfast this week."

Color drained from her face. "Why?"

"I'm curious."

"Not important. Just a friend." She got up from his lap, the move fast and forceful. "Let's go, Marc."

He stayed in the chair and watched her make her way across the stones without him. He'd have to be more creative.

Less than thirty minutes later, they were at the base of another seaside cliff, the entire promontory swathed in classic Irish green grass, a winding stone path leading up to the top.

Way up to the top.

A few hundred butterflies woke up in her stomach, making Devyn wonder if they took flight because of her fear of heights or her attraction to Marc.

He was right about one thing—he made her as dizzy as the extreme elevations.

Their fingers brushed as they started toward the path, passing dozens of tourists along the narrow walkway, groups coming down from the rope bridge that joined two towering land masses, the water crashing beside and below.

Devyn wanted to join the laughter and chatter in the air, but she'd been purposefully quiet on the ride over here, a debate raging internally.

She wanted to tell him why she was here. It would be such a relief to share the burden but, oh, the explanations and questions. So, she curbed the impulse and said nothing, and being a gentleman, he let that silence feel comfortable instead of awkward. Which was just another thing she liked about him.

Without taking the time to consider why, she slipped

her hand into his much larger one and they started up the hill.

A group of tourists hustled by, noisy and happy, joking about the terrifying trip across the bridge. As Devyn and Marc came around the next corner, they could see why.

"Whoa." She almost didn't breathe as her gaze traveled up to the narrow, handmade walkway that joined the highest peak on the mainland to the cliffs of tiny Carrick Island. About sixty feet from end to end, the bridge hung a good eighty feet or more above a watery chasm. Devyn felt the breath rush out of her at the thought of crossing that bridge.

"C'mon." He tugged her gently, obviously sensing her reluctance to move. "Can you imagine the view off the other side? You can see Scotland."

"Not today you can't." A fenced-in path rimmed the top of the huge rock, offering glorious views back at Ireland, but straight across the ocean was nothing but clouds and mist.

"There's nothing to be afraid of, Dev."

Her heart flipped. "Oh, yes, there is." Starting with a man who called her "Dev."

"I'll be with you the whole way."

"So we go down together."

He grinned. "What a way to go." He took her hand and placed a strong, protective arm around her waist, the gesture so close and comforting it made her eyes tear. Or maybe that was the wind. And raw fear of what she was about to do.

No, she decided, the emotional tug was because of him. No one had ever protected her before. On the contrary, anyone she'd ever trusted had betrayed her. And yet, this man, this total stranger, just made her feel . . . safe.

"Don't think so hard about it—just do it," he said.

"I'm not thinking about the bridge," she said quietly. "I was actually thinking about you."

He slowed his step, searching her face with a hint of a smile. "And what were you thinking?"

"That no one calls me Dev."

He lifted a brow. "No one? Not your mom or dad?"

"Especially not them." Both of whom would jump off that bridge if she referred to them as "mom" and "dad" instead of "mother" and "father."

"Not your"—he angled his head gently—"husband?"

"Not him, either."

For a heartbreakingly long minute, he held her gaze. "Then it's a day for firsts, Dev." He pulled her a little closer. "First nicknames. First trips across scary bridges. And, if we make it...first kisses."

Something inside her slipped, falling into an exciting cocktail of feminine response low in her stomach. She *wanted* that kiss. "Then I'm motivated to cross that bridge when we come to it."

He laughed at the pun and hugged her, warmth flowing from him into her whole body. With the cold breeze off the North Atlantic and the cloudy sky, Devyn almost ached with the desire to hold tight to the warmth and security he was offering her.

Without exchanging another word, they continued arm in arm, drinking in the breathtaking scenery, occasionally glancing at each other with appreciative smiles. By the time they reached the top of the hill, her skin felt flushed and her heart was beating double-time again.

A small crowd gathered in groups at the precipice, forming a single line to cross the bridge.

"Ugh," she said softly. "It's a long way down."

"You're not going down, Dev. You're going across. With me." He led her over to read a placard explaining that the bridge was built—and rebuilt every year, he pointed out—by fishermen who wanted to reach the island to catch the salmon that circled it during spawning season. After a few minutes, they joined the crowds moving toward the stairs that led to the rope bridge, and Devyn's throat grew drier.

By unspoken rule, people crossed with their groups, with no more than two or three on the bridge at the same time, pausing to take pictures or share giddy, terrified laughter. Some held hands. Every once in a while, someone froze in fear and had to be coaxed one way or the other.

"I'll hold your hand," Marc promised as their turn approached.

He went first, his fingers threaded through hers. The first step was pure hell, a jolt of terror going through her as the planks of wood wobbled under her sneakers. Instinctively, she let go of his hand to grab the braided ropes on both sides for balance.

"You okay?" he asked.

"Define 'okay.'" She managed a rough laugh, proud that she could find any humor at all in this. "Just...don't stop. Let's get over there."

"Offer a woman a kiss and look at the heights she'll scale."

She laughed again, nerves making this one come out like a giggle. "Go, Marc."

He turned and went a few feet ahead. With her gaze planted on his back and not the narrow body of water almost a hundred feet below, she took a step. The ropes creaked, the wind whined over her ears, and somehow they managed to make it to the middle.

Where Devyn froze. Her feet refused to move, no matter how much she willed them to take the next step. Mind won over matter; fear beat out the promise of a kiss she wanted more than she was willing to admit.

A few feet ahead, Marc turned and reached out a hand. "Come on, Dev."

"I want to." She really did, but she couldn't let go of the ropes, couldn't take another step. In fact, she couldn't breathe as fright clutched every cell and paralyzed her. "I can't."

"Yes, you can."

With a few fearless steps, he returned to her, and she heard a soft "aww" from the bystanders waiting their turn. Still she didn't move.

Her gaze slid exactly where it shouldn't have, over the side and down. So. Far. Down. The fall would be terrifying, her body in free fall, gravity taking ownership, the crash deadly.

"I can't," she repeated, even when he placed his hand over hers.

He looked right into her eyes. "You can do this," he said softly. "I've got you, I promise." He squeezed her hand and eased it off the rope. "I've got you, Dev. Show me what you're made of."

The words had their intended effect, kicking her forward, spurring her on. What *was* she made of? Wasn't finding that out the whole reason she'd come to Northern Ireland?

Not that she expected to find out on a flimsy rope bridge almost a hundred feet above certain death.

"Come on," he coaxed. "We'll take every step together."

She squeezed his hand in a death grip, her gaze pinned on him. One foot. In front of. The other.

After about thirty endless steps, they reached Carrick Island, terra firma glorious under her feet.

"I knew you could do it," he said, pulling her into him for a congratulatory hug.

"Thank you," she managed to say. "I couldn't have done that without you."

He grinned at her. "Yes, you could have, but I'll take the credit. And also be the bearer of bad news."

"What?"

"There's only one way back." He wrapped an arm around her and guided her toward the dirt path that encircled the top of the rock. "Let's explore for a little while before we tackle the return trip."

So he was either forgetting the kiss or delaying the gratification. Either way, she didn't let the disappointment show. They strolled along the path that circled the rock, leaning against the fence to look way down the limestone cliffs, which was only a little less terrifying than the rope bridge. But the salt air was cleansing, the squawk of birds and crash of waves like nature's symphony, and the man she was with made her feel so *steady*.

As they approached the end of the path that led back to the bridge, they stopped one last time to enjoy the view.

"That is just one of the prettiest things I've ever seen," she said, trying to memorize the beauty of the endless rolling green hills.

"So are you."

She looked up, only a little surprised to find him gazing down at her, his expression a mix of interest and desire. "You're flirting again," she teased.

"I never stopped." He lowered his head, his intentions clear as he turned his back to the view and reached out for her.

Her heart did a little soar and drop, and she moved closer, their bodies easing into each other in the most natural way. An unfamiliar and exciting ache started very low, very deep inside her, tingling up her stomach and spine, up to her mouth, which suddenly ached to touch his.

"You know, Marc," she whispered, "I haven't been paid for my act of bravery yet."

He cocked his head and gave her a sexy look. "Is this you begging for a kiss?"

She laughed, giddy with an overload to every sense, including the sixth one that said she could and should trust this man.

"I'm not begging," she said. "In fact, I'm not even asking." She stood on her toes and closed the space between them. "I'm just going to take my reward."

She lightly placed her lips on his, barely brushing them as he drew her into his body. Their bodies molded to each other, aligned, instantly like one.

He intensified the kiss, his hands sliding up her back until they settled on the nape of her neck. He wove his fingers into her hair, tilting her head possessively with both hands, opening his mouth, inviting her tongue to touch his.

Fiery sparks exploded in every nerve ending, burning her skin and sending lightning bolts of pleasure from her mouth to her toes.

From across the water, a bird shrieked, and someone on the bridge let out a little hoot of panic and pleasure. She knew exactly how they felt, poised at a death-defying height, facing a free fall.

She couldn't stop the kiss any more than she could avoid that bridge back to the mainland. His lips were soft, his whiskers rough, his tongue hot and sweet. It took all the power she had to finally stop.

When she did, she opened her eyes and got a little lost in his.

"I wasn't expecting you to do that," he said.

"I'm impulsive. My mother says it's one of my worst traits."

"Your mother's wrong. It's a wonderful trait. Be impulsive any time you want."

Smiling, she hugged him, still full of hope and happiness, putting her head on his shoulder just for the sheer joy of having someone strong to lean on. Her gaze traveled over the crowds, across the bridge, up to the lookout platform on the other side of the chasm.

And landed on the most distinctive white hair she'd ever seen.

Sharon.

She blinked at the woman in a dark green jacket, far enough away that she couldn't be certain it was Sharon, but the woman bore a striking resemblance to the pictures she'd seen when she'd researched Dr. Sharon Greenberg on the faculty of UNC.

"What is it?" Marc turned to follow her stunned gaze.

"Sharon!" The man's voice was far in the distance, carried by the wind and the water, the sound coming from the opposite side of the bridge. The woman with the white hair spun around to follow the call. "Come here, Sharon!"

The woman waved at whoever had called her and started walking toward the parking lot.

"Oh my God, it's her! She *is* here. The concierge said she might be."

"Who?"

Devyn shoved Marc to the side, trying to get a better look. "Come on!"

Without explanation, she grabbed his hand and started jogging toward the bridge, navigating around people, trying to keep her eye on those white waves of hair.

"Devyn," Marc said sharply, giving her hand a jerk as she muscled through the crowd. "What are you doing?"

"I have to get to her. Excuse me," she said urgently to a small group of tourists. "Can we get through?"

She was rewarded with a vile look from one and a loud "tsk" from another.

"I'm sorry," she said, her heart hammering with the need to reach Sharon Greenberg. "I have to get over there."

"And ya kin wait yer turn, lass," a man said roughly, blocking her way.

Devyn let out a soft grunt of frustration.

"What the hell is going on?" Marc demanded, pulling her to a real stop. "You can't just barge through all these people."

She ignored him, standing on her tiptoes to see over the group of about a dozen people in front of her. The woman she'd seen was gone, probably headed down the hill back to the visitor's center and the parking lot. Maybe she could catch her there.

"I see someone I . . . have to talk to," she said, throwing the words over her shoulder as she practically jumped up and down to see over a tall man in front of her. "Excuse me, could I get by?"

"Slow down," Marc said. "We'll get there."

She just shook her head, staring at the spot where she'd seen the woman who looked—from a distance—so much like Sharon Greenberg. A woman *named* Sharon. That *couldn't* be a coincidence.

"Oh, come on," she whispered under her breath at a couple pausing to take pictures on the bridge, earning another dirty look from a tourist in front of her.

She could feel Marc behind her, silent, not happy with her behavior, probably boring a hole in the back of her head trying to get an answer to her bizarre behavior. But she didn't owe him an answer. She didn't owe him anything just because she had given in to a little atmosphere and kissed him.

So she used every ounce of energy to focus on the lookout platform across the chasm, willing the woman to show up again, to walk toward the railway, to head back toward the rope bridge.

But there was no sign of her. They must have both been on this little island across the bridge at the very same time. What were the chances of that?

Finally, it was their turn. Without even looking back at Marc, without dawdling for one heart-stopping second on the rubbery, bouncing bridge, she bounded across, as close to a run as one could make on a rope bridge. Marc kept up with her, one second behind her as her feet hit the other side.

"Dinna like it, huh?" An older man on the other side teased, but she ignored him and muscled through the crowd, determined to reach the lookout point where she could see all the way down the hill along the pathway.

There were a lot of people, even some with gray hair, but no white curls, no green jacket. No Sharon.

Disappointment coiled through her, and she let out a half sigh, half cry of frustration. "She's gone."

A few cars pulled out of the lot back onto the highway, but they'd be long gone even if Devyn ran down the hill at full speed.

"You want to tell me who could make you try to mow down perfectly nice strangers like that? When half an hour ago you needed to be begged to get across? Who is that important?"

She turned, focused on him again. Why would she tell anyone why she was here, let alone a complete and utter stranger?

Because she wanted to trust him, and she just didn't want to do this alone anymore. "My mother."

He drew back. "Well, she was right when she called you impulsive."

No, she thought. *The* other *mother. The one who never called me at all.*

CHAPTER 5

Sharon dug deep for composure. She couldn't lose it now. She couldn't possibly let him know the thoughts exploding in her head. Maybe if she didn't *think,* she wouldn't give herself away or show any sign of weakness.

That's what they'd trained her to do—never show weakness—so she certainly couldn't risk an emotional response. She was a scientist. She *had* no emotions.

But the word rushed through her head, like the wind over that cliff, and with it came *feeling.* Ancient, buried, long-dead *feeling.*

Rose.

No, not Rose, she chided herself. Devyn Sterling. That was her name now. The last picture she'd seen was recent enough for her to know exactly who that young woman was. Her daughter.

How in God's name had Devyn found her?

"Well?" Next to her, Liam Baird shifted in the backseat

of the sedan, his hazel, Irish eyes narrowed in question. "Did you see her?"

"Yes," she said, brushing back a wave of wind-whipped gray hair, a reminder that she was too old for this cloak-and-dagger stuff.

"And?" the man prodded, his impatience palpable as always, making him seem younger than his forty-some years.

"I just told you, I have no idea who she is. I've never seen her before in my life." Not since handing her over, signing some papers, and moving on.

Liam dropped back against the leather seat with a dramatic sigh, running a hand through thick, sandy locks. "Then you better have an explanation for why this woman is gallivantin' around Belfast askin' for you at every corner."

"No idea." But she sure as hell better come up with one, and fast. She went with the story she'd been concocting ever since Baird hit her with this news. "My guess is she's a former student who heard through the university that I'd taken leave over here, and she's trying to find me. I just don't recognize her from this far away."

"Then perhaps we should bring her closer."

Oh, God, no. She turned to him, skewering him with a look she knew from experience could buckle anyone. She'd perfected the power of her gray-eyed stare. "Are you as stupid as that?" she asked. "An American girl? Whoever she is, you don't want that kind of publicity. Get her out of here, put her off my track rather than send her right into it like you did today."

"It worked," he said with a shrug. "One suggestion where you might be, planted by one of my people, and—*wham*—she shows up. She should be quite easy to manipulate."

Would she be? What kind of woman had Rose grown up to be? Sharon only had an inkling. A fine family, a rich lifestyle, oblivious to her dirty roots. Except there was the nasty incident of her husband's murder. Sharon had tried not to follow the news, but it had been impossible.

"Then use your considerable powers to convince the young woman to leave," she said. "Scare her off. Threaten her. Send a man to woo her away, whatever it takes, Mr. Baird. We have work to do and can't afford a distraction like this."

Baird just eyed her. "You better not be lying. About anything."

She never even blinked. "Don't suggest that again, Baird. You don't want to offend me. If I take my toys and go home, you are in a lot of trouble."

He shifted his long, lean frame and bent forward to talk to the driver. "Did you get a good look?" he asked Danny, who glanced into the rearview mirror to make eye contact.

He nodded. "I got a good look. I can find her." Danny's hands curled around the steering wheel. Deadly, strong hands. Hands of a man who would kill without compunction.

Even a woman.

No weakness, Sharon. No weakness. They'd use weakness against her. They'd kill anyone in this operation who showed weakness.

"Then find her," she said coolly, throwing the order at Danny as if he worked for her and not Baird. "And get her the hell out of Belfast. She's a young woman, for crying out loud. How hard can she be to handle?"

"She's got a man with her," Baird said. "Did you see that? Do you know him?"

"No, I do not. But you said she's been alone up until this point. She probably picked him up in a bar last night."

"She's been alone, my contacts tell me," he said. "Alone, all over the city, knocking on every door in Belfast, seeking a Dr. Greenberg."

"Maybe she's looking for someone else."

"She's described you."

Sharon's stomach tightened. How? How did she know who Sharon was, what she looked like?

Of course, she'd followed the death of the girl's husband a few months ago, a murder committed by some dirty cop and Joshua Sterling's mistress. Could there be a connection somehow? The only person they had in common was . . .

He *wouldn't* have sent her, would he?

"As I told you, Mr. Baird, I'm sure there's a perfectly legitimate explanation. Without causing a stir of any kind, I suggest you use your considerable resources and network of contacts to get that girl to give up and go home."

He sniffed, but Sharon just stared out the window. *Go home, Rose. Get out of here.*

"Unless we can use her somehow," Baird said. "She might be useful to us."

She didn't react, letting her head rest against the glass as the questions slammed her brain. *Why is she here? How did she find out? Is this a trick, a way to trip me up, or test my loyalty?*

Because if Devyn Sterling was sent here by who Sharon thought had sent her here, then . . .

She swallowed, an ancient phrase replacing all the questions.

Sometimes a few people die for the good of many. But which people? And who made those decisions?

"Can we get back to the business at hand, Mr. Baird?" she asked briskly. "This has been quite a delay tactic, and as far as I'm concerned, completely unnecessary."

"Not unnecessary, Doctor." Liam stretched his legs. "This young woman has raised a red flag in my organization. I wanted you to identify her so we can stop her. No matter who sent her here."

"No one sent her here," she shot back with a glare. "And I know you're testing me. Don't lie about what you're doing, Mr. Baird. You think she's some kind of plant or decoy or *spy*."

"You're right," he acknowledged. "I was testing you. I didn't get where I am by trusting anyone."

She barely shrugged, indifference rolling off her. "Let's just get back to the job I came here to do," she said coolly. "These delay tactics aren't helping your cause."

"*Our* cause," he corrected.

She reached over and put a hand on his arm, noticing her veins popping up to reveal her true age of fifty-five, reminding her it had taken Finn MacCauley thirty damn long years to give her this opportunity to ruin him. She wasn't about to let age stop her now, and she wasn't about to let his daughter stop her, either.

"Let's just get one thing straight, Mr. Baird."

He met her gaze. "I know, it's not your cause."

"It's not *your* cause, either," she said. "You're in it for the same reason I am. Cash. And as long as we're straight on that, we can do business. That's how I work. That's how I've always worked."

"Obviously, I—*we*—need cash in order to reinvigorate

the political forces and win the Republican cause we never should have...lost." He stumbled over the words, backpedaling under her gaze.

"Shut up," she said simply. "You're pushing drugs, girls, and guns to make money. And now you want to dig into some deep and dark pockets to get more." She added a little pressure on his hand. "Don't bullshit me, Mr. Baird, and I won't bullshit you. I'm not interested in the Republican cause or your mafioso schemes."

"What are you interested in, Dr. Greenberg?"

She'd wanted it for so long, there wasn't even a word in her head to describe the feeling. Revenge. Payback. Destruction. "What I want should be obvious by now. And since I've passed your stupid little test today, the second payment should be made to my account."

He withdrew his hand. "It'll be made when you do what we hired you to do."

"If there isn't two hundred and fifty thousand dollars in my account by noon tomorrow, then I will not take one more step to help you."

He deliberately moved to show the Walther on his hip. "I think I'm the one calling the shots in this organization, Doctor. You are here as my guest."

She laughed softly. "Brains trump guns, my friend. And you know that or I wouldn't be here. What will your client say if the delivery is late? Or worse, if it's ineffective?" She arched a brow. "You'll be dead long before I will."

He smiled at her, barely hiding his fear at how very right she was. "You're shrewd and heartless. If you were twenty-five years younger, I'd be in love with you."

"If I were twenty-five years younger, you'd be useless

to me." She turned her body, shifting her attention to the coastline outside. "As it is, you're beginning to annoy me."

"Danny," Baird said softly. "Take care of the girl."

"Will do, sir."

Sharon didn't want to *think* about what that meant. But she knew.

Emotion clutched her again, and she tamped it down.

She needed someone on the outside to help. Someone she could trust. Someone Devyn Sterling would trust—and then Sharon would have to do the unthinkable. She'd have to contact Devyn and convince her to leave.

But she'd have to be very, very creative.

It wouldn't do any good to grill Devyn on the way home. She was visibly shaken by what had happened at Carrick-a-Rede. So Marc mentally reviewed what he already knew.

Her mother—the one who had raised her, at least—was definitely in Newton, Massachusetts. While Devyn stopped in the bathroom after they reached the bottom of the hill, he'd texted Vivi with a request to confirm that, and while they were driving back to Belfast, the answer came in.

So this "mother" in Northern Ireland was her biological mother? Devyn must have more information than what was in the FBI files, then.

Next to him, she quietly watched the scenery pass along the coastal road, obviously not ready or willing to reveal more than she already had: She thought the woman she saw on the hillside was her mother, and she'd been looking for her. She didn't say if that was who she expected to meet later that week, but he was going to assume it was. He didn't press for more.

The best thing to do with a woman wound this tightly was to just let her uncoil on her own. He could think of a dozen quite pleasurable ways to help that process along, but pushing too hard would lose him all the ground he'd made today.

But he did have to know one thing—would seeing her mother make Devyn more determined to stay in Belfast or more amenable to his secret agenda to get her out of there?

No, he had to know something else as well. Did her mother have anything to do with why ASAC Lang wanted her out of there?

"I guess I kind of killed the mood," she finally said as they made their way into the beginnings of Belfast traffic, the skyline marked by a few distinctive buildings and the silhouettes of two cranes poking up from the waterfront shipyard.

"No worries," he said, glancing over at her. "Are you okay?"

She nodded, her smile tight. "Just a little blown away by seeing her, and missing her."

"Are you sure the person you saw was your mother?"

"I think so. I don't..." She turned her head and mumbled the rest of the sentence. "I don't really know her."

"Excuse me?"

She hesitated a long beat, then looked at him, misery in her eyes. "I've never met her."

He didn't react at all, except to slowly nod, hoping that would coax a little more out of her. She just swallowed and then whispered, "I'm adopted."

"Ah, I see. She's your birth mother and you are trying to track her down?"

"Yes."

He maneuvered through the traffic, purposely quiet until he stopped at the last light before the Europa. "Does she know that?"

"No." One syllable with a world of emotion.

He couldn't help reaching to hold her hand and wasn't surprised when she clasped his back. "But I have to speak to her whether or not she wants to meet me."

"Why?"

She just shook her head, and he didn't push it any further. "Back to the hotel, then?" he asked.

She checked her watch with a sigh. "You know, I haven't checked out of the Windermere, where I'm staying, so I guess I'll spend the night there and figure out what to do tomorrow."

"I can take you to the Windermere and wait while you pack and check out, then drive you back to the Europa. You can get settled and wait for her."

She looked at him, a question in her eyes. "I didn't tell you she was the person I'm waiting for."

"I'm making an assumption. Am I right?"

She nodded without elaborating.

Something just didn't ring true of a typical "birth mother search." Why would she fly all the way to Belfast instead of waiting in the States until her mother returned? "How long is she going to be here?" he asked.

"I don't know," she said. "I wasn't even sure she *was* here. I just came on a whim because I have to tell her something."

"That's a pretty big whim."

"I'm impulsive, remember?"

There had to be more than that. "What do you have to tell—" Her look stopped him. "Never mind, Devyn. It really is none of my business."

She gave him a quick smile. "Thanks. The Windermere is right down Lisburn near the university. I'd really appreciate if you just dropped me off there."

"Of course. Unless I can talk you into having dinner with me."

"I'm sorry, Marc. I need to be alone to sort things out."

He nodded as he turned at the intersection and headed south through Belfast's colorful university district. The streets were jammed with tourists and students, the traffic slow enough for him to take plenty of looks at his passenger, but she stayed closed up tight.

"I'm not trying to pry," he finally said, "but if she doesn't know you're here, don't you think it's an incredible coincidence that in all of Northern Ireland, you'd see her at a remote bridge on the coast?"

"I thought of that," she admitted. "But that's such a common tourist attraction, and the concierge did think she'd left to take a brief sightseeing trip, leaving some of her bags behind. He even suggested I go up there, so... not that much of a stretch. Just serendipity."

"*And* a coincidence. Which I'm no fan of, by the way."

She shrugged. "Maybe. Maybe I was just meant to see her. You know, like the universe lined it up or something."

"You believe in that?" He couldn't keep the incredulity out of his voice.

"Not for a minute," she said with a soft laugh. "But there's not a lot of other explanations."

"I'd still like to spend an hour over a nice meal discussing all those possibilities, but I understand you're no longer in the mood. Maybe I can get a rain check before you head back home."

She dropped her head back, and her smile relaxed into one he'd seen dozens of times during the day—pretty, natural, comfortable. "You're a damn nice guy, you know that?"

"Then my evil plan to fool you worked," he said with a laugh, hoping it hid how close his statement was to the truth. Because he didn't particularly like conning a woman who was wrapped up in a personal cause, no doubt seeking closure or answers on the heels of her husband's murder. It didn't feel completely right to be taking her away from Belfast when that cause was an emotional connection with the person who gave her life.

Except, *why* did ASAC Lang want her out of Belfast? Did it have something to do with this woman she was searching for?

"Well, Marc," she said as they neared the B and B, "this afternoon's events probably weren't at all what you had in mind when you asked me to go sightseeing."

"Depends on what events you mean," he said smoothly. "I had every intention of kissing you. I just didn't expect you'd shove me aside and go running over a bridge that ten minutes earlier left you paralyzed with fear. Doesn't say much for my kissing, does it?" But it said plenty about what she was willing to risk to talk to the woman.

"You're an excellent kisser," she assured him. "Next time I promise not to get distracted."

"So there will be a next time?" He didn't have to fake the hope in his voice as he slid into a parking spot across from the Windermere.

She eyed him again, her walls threatening to crumble. She really didn't want to be alone tonight, he suspected, but she didn't trust herself with him, either.

So he better get damn creative if he was going to succeed in his mission.

"I don't know about a next time," she finally said. "I have to find Sharon, and then..."

He lifted her hand to his mouth and placed a gentle kiss on her knuckles. "You know where I am," he said, holding her gaze. "Room four-twelve at the Europa."

"Thank you," she said, her eyes filling a little.

He lowered their joined hands and leaned closer, the magnetism between them completely genuine. "I had a wonderful day with you, Dev."

She smiled. "I like when you call me that."

"I like you," he said simply. "And if you need anything at all, just ask."

Sighing, she met him halfway for a kiss. He slid one hand under her hair and brushed over her mouth, able to feel her internal battle waging, the victory almost his. He opened his mouth just enough to heat up the kiss and invite her tongue to touch his, not forceful or fierce, but warm and sweet.

The muscles in her neck relaxed under his hand as she inhaled softly and shuddered a breath into his mouth. On his leg, her fingers splayed and tensed. He deepened the kiss, not too much, not too fast.

Her eyes were still closed when he broke the contact, opening slowly to reveal she'd been a little lost in the kiss.

But she focused quickly, then unlatched the door, stepping out without smiling.

"Bye, Marc." She didn't look back as she darted into the inn.

So now it was time for Plan B.

CHAPTER 6

The air chilled Devyn's heated skin as she dashed out of the car, stealing the warmth Marc had just created. She clutched her jacket, shivered, and shouldered open the door of the B and B, torn over her decision to leave him.

And as much as she wanted food, libation, and about two hours more of nonstop mouth-to-mouth with the guy, she didn't want to have him pulling secrets out of her.

She'd shared enough secrets, broken enough confidences, taken enough reckless risks.

Anyway, that man was attracted to Devyn Hewitt, the socialite debutante blue-blooded Bostonian who could make small talk and witty repartee. He was obviously a classy guy, despite the undercurrent of sex that oozed from his every pore. A few more questions and he'd know exactly who and what she really was.

The bastard child of a wanted fugitive.

Not to mention that this quest wasn't for some joyful, heartstring-tugging reunion with a mother forced to give up her child because she was only a child herself when she gave birth. Sharon Greenberg had made no effort to find Devyn.

And, frankly, this potential meeting could be dark and ugly. Not only did she have to tell Sharon that Joshua might have shared her secret before he was murdered, but she also had to tell her someone else was waiting to pounce on her when she got home.

Once she delivered those messages, then maybe Devyn could think about dating and flirting and kissing a man like Marc Rossi.

Not that it would change who she was. But maybe...

Nodding to the young woman at the front desk as she passed, Devyn glanced at the cozy lobby, happy she hadn't yet checked out of this precious, undersized inn. The Europa was big and impersonal and cold.

And Marc Rossi was there.

Here, a fire crackled and the thrum of conversation and laughter floated out from a pleasant little restaurant and pub where she would have dinner tonight.

Alone.

She turned the corner and walked up the wooden staircase to the second floor, heading down the narrow corridor to her room, determined to stop all rationalization and second thoughts and focus on what mattered.

Tonight she'd sit down with the few pieces of paper she'd retrieved from Sharon's home office and try again to put the puzzle pieces together. If only she had a computer and Internet, she probably could have figured out exactly what the drawing was, and maybe who'd sent Sharon the e-mail about her airport pickup.

Marc Rossi probably had a laptop with him.

If you need anything, just ask.

She needed...everything. Everything a man like that had to offer, except as soon as he found out the truth, she doubted they'd be offered so easily. And even if they were, what made him any different from Joshua or her parents? People she loved and counted on, only to find out her second-class-citizen status made her unworthy of their love and trust.

And what about Sharon Greenberg? Who knew Devyn's name and saved pictures of her. With Devyn's biological father's phone number jotted on the back.

Once again, the realization squeezed her heart so hard it hurt. Why had Sharon kept track of Devyn? Worry? Regret? Curiosity? *Love?*

She stabbed the key into her door and smashed an imaginary boot heel on that last one. A childish, baseless fantasy. If Sharon loved the daughter she gave up for adoption, surely she would have tried to make contact by now.

Inside, she took off her jacket and began unbuttoning her blouse, the familiar battle so loud in her head she didn't pay attention to the footsteps outside her room. But she froze mid-button at the soft rap on her door.

Another knock. "Devyn?"

Oh. He'd come back for her. She couldn't help smiling because, deep down inside, she wanted to share all of this with someone. With Marc.

"I'll give you this," she said, walking toward the door, "you're persistent."

Hand on the knob, she glanced down at her unbuttoned blouse. But something stopped her from rebuttoning and hiding the peek of lace and cleavage. Something? How about *attraction*?

There was no peephole or she'd have checked to see if he was smiling like she was. Instead she unlocked the door and safety bar, only to have the wood whiz right at her face, knocking her back.

A soft gasp strangled her as a man stepped inside, a mask covering his face.

"Oh my God," she cried softly, stumbling and blinking in disbelief.

He was tall, big, and coming right at her. She opened her mouth to scream, but he smashed his hand over her face, whipping her around and snapping her arm up behind her so hard she heard it crack.

She felt hot breath on her ear and the strength of him, the faint smell of something sour on his breath.

"Get out of here. Do you understand? Out!"

How had she thought he was Marc? This man had an accent. Irish. Or English. Thick and as gruff as his handling.

She tried to cry out again, but his hand silenced her scream.

"Get out or it'll get much worse than this." He pushed her hard, releasing her, but the force was enough to buckle her knees and take her to the floor. She froze there, crouched and unwilling to turn and face him, waiting for something else—a blow, a kick, another threat.

But the door slammed behind her and he was gone.

She stayed on her knees, shaking, the words reverberating in her ears.

Get out or it'll get much worse than this.

What was he talking about? And who was he? Finally, she turned, terrified that he'd still be there. But she was alone.

Not really. She didn't have to do this alone. Not anymore.

Very slowly, with the dead bolt in place, she packed her bags.

It would cost him a little, no doubt, but Marc was ready to part with some cash, and the ruddy-faced concierge who looked nearly seventy and far too tired for this job seemed willing to take some payment for his labor.

"I might be able to help you," the old man said as he made Marc's twenty-pound note disappear with the ease of a magician. "But if I get caught, I'll deny I've ever laid eyes on you."

As he would expect. "Deal. All I need is ten minutes, max, in your baggage hold room." Long enough to get a last name to go with Sharon, the name Devyn had let slip in the car.

The concierge frowned. "A dozen or so years ago, you'd be arrested just for asking that, you know."

No doubt this man remembered the Troubles all too well. "Times have changed."

"Some." He shrugged. "But ya better not be planting a bomb in my closet, lad."

"I'm not. I'm looking for some bags that a woman left here. A friend of mine was told by the concierge on duty this morning that the bags are there, and if you can take me right to that luggage, we'll be done in no time."

He shook his head. "You can't have them without a ticket. Sorry."

"I figured that, but could I look at them? Just to make sure they're here? You can watch me."

He glanced toward the lobby, which was quiet for

the moment, then back at Marc. "I don't know, lad. It's unusual."

Marc lifted his hand, this time sliding a fifty-pound note across the counter. "It's important. And I don't have to be in there alone if that'll make you feel any better."

As he palmed the bill, two more guests approached the desk. "One minute," he said to Marc. "Let me handle this first."

Marc stepped away and waited while the man helped the other guests with a question about local restaurants. When they'd left, the concierge signaled Marc closer.

"Let's go now," he said, nodding toward the door behind him. "And be fast about it."

The storage area was less than twenty square feet, crowded with bags and a few packages waiting for pickup.

"What's the name?" the concierge asked.

"Sharon."

He got a quizzical look in response. "Surname, please?"

Marc shook his head. "I'll just look at the names on the tags." How many Sharons could there be?

"No, sir, I can't—"

The bell rang from the desk outside. "Excuse me, is anyone here?"

Thanking his good luck and some woman's impatience, Marc gave the man a nudge. "Go, I'll be out of here in less than three minutes. I just need to check to see if she's picked them up yet. I'll be sure to stop by the desk and thank you properly." His gaze dropped to the name tag. "Thomas."

"Hello? Is there a concierge?" The voice grew louder, and Thomas blew out a frustrated breath.

"Just hurry it up," he said, stepping out the door.

As soon as Thomas was gone, Marc started in one corner, grabbing each bag to look for a luggage tag or ID, moving like the wind because Thomas would be back to order him out at any second. He scanned names. Michael, David, Mortimer, Eileen, J. Macmahon, Tim Ballough—there were five bags with that name. Damn, that was half the room.

On the other side, he started at the top. R. Fink. Thomas MacAvoy. Dr. S. Greenberg.

Sharon Greenberg? Doctor? The luggage tag was handwritten in black scratchy letters, UNC Microbiology Dept, Chapel Hill, NC.

He checked the rest—no Sharons among them, no S first initials on these. He went back to S. Greenberg from North Carolina and tried the zipper, but the bags were locked tight. Still, Marc had enough to start.

He almost collided with Thomas as he left, slipping him another twenty pounds with his thanks.

In his room, Marc fired up his laptop and shot an e-mail to Vivi, hoping she'd look for any detailed background on Dr. Sharon Greenberg. Then he started his own search by Googling the UNC site. He found a faculty member at the teaching hospital with the same name who had a specialty in immunology, pathological diagnostics, and retrovirology.

Could this be the woman who had had an affair with an Irish mob boss and gave birth to an illegitimate baby? He might be on the wrong track. He dug some more, into the microbiology department, into the faculty files, finding some papers she'd published. He was able to log into one, and found her bio.

He skimmed it, zeroing in on one line.

After participating in the Master's Program at the Massachusetts Institute of Technology in 1978, Dr. Greenberg transferred to the University of North Carolina at Chapel Hill . . .

MIT in Boston. That would put her in the right city in the right year.

Still thinking about the incongruity of Finn MacCauley sleeping with a microbiologist at MIT—and creating the beautiful, lively woman he'd just kissed in the car—he stripped and took a shower, considering where to have a drink and dinner. And how much better it would have been with Devyn Sterling.

Scratch that—Devyn *Smith.*

Not a real surprise that she'd choose a fake name. Her husband's death made some notoriety, since he had been a well-known columnist for the *Boston Globe* who had made frequent appearances on cable TV as a talking head.

Slathered in shaving cream, he took one swipe with a razor when someone knocked on his door.

"Marc? Are you here?"

He recognized Devyn's voice immediately—and a note of desperation. Grabbing a towel, he wrapped it around his waist, tipped the laptop screen down as he passed, and unlocked the door.

Her eyes were red, her cheeks as white as the shaving cream he'd just applied. "I need you."

He reached for her, pulling her in, cold fear palpable from her body language and the look in her eyes.

"What's the matter?" He instinctively put his arms on her shoulders, realizing she had her bags with her.

"Can I come in?"

"Of course." He eased her into the room, glanced at the empty hall, and closed the door behind her. "What's wrong?"

She swallowed, a little breathless and flushed. "I just don't want to be alone."

"Okay." He didn't hide the doubt in his voice. "You're welcome to stay here."

"I just want to"—she looked up at him, a helpless, anxious expression tearing his heart right out of his chest—"have dinner with you."

"I see you brought your suitcases," he said with a half smile. "Should I be really optimistic about that, or are you planning on checking into another room?"

"I don't want to check into another room."

What was going on with her? She was oozing fear, not pheromones. "All right. Let me finish shaving and change, and we'll go out for—"

"Room service."

He laughed softly. "Stay in, then. Hang on." He grabbed his clothes from over the chair and headed back into the bathroom, moving quickly, fearing she might up and change her mind.

Picking up the razor, he considered not shaving at all, just to get out there with her faster. Then he'd have one stripe down his whiskery face. He took a second swipe.

"Did you take a cab here?" he called, hoping small talk would relax her.

She was quiet for a moment, then, "Yeah, I did."

He couldn't think of another question except to ask why she'd changed her mind, but he wanted to do that face-to-face. He nicked himself going too fast, then splashed water on his face, shook his hair, and dressed in jeans and a shirt. Without taking the time to button his shirt, he stepped out into the bedroom.

The laptop was open in front of her. Instantly he knew why she'd been quiet and what was on the screen in front of her. And why her expression was stricken.

"Why were you looking up my birth mother's biography?"

"Why are you looking at my laptop?"

"I need one," she said. "I thought I'd check to see if you had Wi-Fi here." Her expression shifted from shock to flat-out anger, dismay, and distrust, all powerful enough to make him momentarily consider the benefits of telling her the truth.

But then he'd be completely compromising his assignment.

"I thought I was helping you," he said. "I asked the concierge about the luggage and figured if I could find out—"

On the dresser, his cell phone beeped with an incoming call, and she shot to her feet.

"All right, I overstepped my bounds," he acknowledged, ignoring the phone. "But it was only because I thought it would buy me some more time with you."

"I should have known better than to trust you." She spat the words. "To trust anyone."

"I meant to help, maybe help you find out for sure if she was coming back. I found one set of luggage that was a possible match—it said S. Greenberg—so I did a search. Is that the right person?"

"Yes." Her eyes narrowed in anger. "Which means that of all the Sharon Greenbergs in the entire world, you somehow zeroed in on exactly the right one. That is beyond amazing. That is an absolute unbelievable coincidence." Her shoulders squared a little as she slowly inched back. "From the man who is no *fan* of coincidences."

The phone stopped ringing, and Devyn grabbed the door knob.

"Please, let me explain," he said, striding to stop her, but the landline hotel phone chirped loudly with a distinct European double ring. Someone wanted him badly.

"Wait," he said, torn. "Don't go yet. You can trust me." She just eyed him as he picked up the receiver. "What?"

"It didn't take long to get some very interesting information on Sharon Greenberg, that's what," Vivi said in his ear.

But Devyn bolted, leaving her bags and letting the door slam behind her.

Damn. "Vivi, I'll call you back."

"No, you have to know this." Something in her voice stopped him from dropping the phone. "It's mission critical."

"E-mail it to me. I gotta go." With that, he threw the receiver down on the desk, scooped up his shoes, phone, and room key, and tore outside to an empty hall. Swearing, he jogged to the elevator bank, smashing the button as he spun around looking for stairs.

He ran down the hall, whipped open the door under an exit sign, and jogged down to the lobby, but she was gone.

He headed for the street, searching left, right, and into the square across the way. Dusk was turning to dark, and a light drizzle made it even more impossible to find her among the pedestrians.

The smell of fried chips wafted from a street vendor

whose cart and customers blocked Marc's view. He ducked to the left, stepped off the curb, then powered through, walking fast through the crowds, pausing at the sight of a woman with similar-colored hair and a dark jacket, then moving on as time ticked away, along with any chance of finding her.

Just as he was ready to give up and go back, he caught a flash of caramel hair over a navy jacket, dashing into a doorway a few blocks from him.

Got her.

CHAPTER 7

Devyn powered through the group of smokers outside the pub door, the stench of their cigarettes strangling her. Inside, the place was as dark and crowded as she hoped it would be, the patrons in tight groups around the bar, a soccer game on TV, all drowned out by the sound of unfamiliar and screechy rock music. Perfect.

As she hustled toward the back, her sneakers stuck to beer residue on the floor, and a few curious gazes bored boozy holes through her. She slipped into a back booth, tucked away but still able to see the door, breathless from the impetuous decision that sent her running through the streets of Belfast.

Maybe her gut had been right when she answered her hotel door? Maybe it *had* been Marc behind that mask, and he'd done that to scare her and send her to him? No, that made no sense. But why did she feel so violated?

He couldn't have honed in on Sharon that quickly... could he?

She wanted so much to believe him, to trust him, to lean on him. But that had never worked out for her, not since... well, not since the day she was born and the first person who was supposed to love Devyn decided she wasn't worth it.

And if that hadn't been Marc in her room, then who *had* broken into her room to threaten her, scaring the life out of her? And why?

God, the irony was she needed him now more than ever. But how could that be? She'd only met him today, by accident. Or *was* it an accident?

She dropped her head back and closed her eyes for a moment, remembering the way she'd bumped into him, entirely unexpected and unplanned.

A hand landed on her shoulder from behind, making her jump and whip around. She expected Marc, but a different man loomed over her. Fairer, older, definitely a local.

"Whadya havin', lass?"

She shook out of his touch, her mind blank.

"A pint?" he prodded.

"Yes, fine, thank you." The door opened and she looked beyond the waiter, her eyes widening as Marc Rossi pushed his way in, already scanning the place.

The server glanced over his shoulder, then automatically stepped to the side to block her from sight. "You runnin' from him?"

She looked up and nodded. "I am."

He pointed behind her. "There's a back door. I'll cover for you."

She almost took a second to think about that, but pushed up instead, murmuring her thanks as she rounded the back of the booth and darted to a dimly lit corridor. She still needed space and time, and Marc was barreling down on her with questions and an agenda.

What was it?

The back hall was little more than two closed doors and an overpowering smell of beer and bathroom. At the far end, an exit to outside. She pushed a latch and stepped into a narrow alley, a brick wall right in front of her, nothing but filth and shadows in either direction. She'd have to pick one way and run, though.

Unless she wanted to face him. Which she had to do eventually. She'd left her bags in his room, after all.

She hesitated, leaning back against the door as it closed, the image of Dr. Greenberg's bio on his screen replaying in her mind. What had that man in her room said?

Get out or things will get worse for you. Her heart ratcheted higher than she thought possible as fear and confusion racked her body. What had she stepped into over here? And what part did Marc Rossi play in this?

She cursed herself for trusting him in the first place, for kissing him like a teenager in heat.

Idiot!

Taking a breath, she took another glance left, then right. Escaping would literally mean plucking through trash and God knew what else. Marc couldn't hurt her inside that pub, and he'd have to answer some questions. She should go back in and face him.

She turned to open the door, yanking hard and jolting her shoulder. Locked.

She tried again, fiddling with the latch, but she was most definitely locked out. No choice now. Stepping back, she chose the route with the least amount of trash and started walking toward the busier of the two streets. Her head throbbed from the foul smell and the vicious frustrations that had piled on her one after another the past few hours.

Behind her, the hinges on the pub door squeaked. Looking over her shoulder, she saw a man step into the alley. Not Marc, and not the waiter who'd helped her escape—someone beefier than both.

Hesitating and dropping back into the shadows, she waited to see which way he was going, tensing when he started toward her. She squinted at him, about to continue, when she caught his direct gaze and froze.

"Not another step." Broad shoulders flexed as he took direct and purposeful strides toward her. She retreated, her feet hitting a broken bottle and crunching on glass.

He kept coming.

Damn it, she hadn't even taken her handbag when she ran out of Marc's room. She could have thrown money at this guy and...

He was five feet away, his nostrils flaring with each breath. Shaved bald, thick-necked, fat lips. Scarily silent.

A shiver of fear vibrated through her. This man didn't want *money.*

She stumbled, reaching for the brick wall to keep from falling. He got two feet closer, and she whipped around to run, but he snagged her elbow in a viselike grip, wrenching her right back to him.

"Let me go!"

He shoved her against the wall, hard enough that the brick slammed her skull. Bile rose in her throat as he smacked his hands on either side of her head and rammed his knees around her thighs. She pushed his chest, but she might as well have been pushing the wall behind her.

"Get away from me," she ground out, ready to bite, spit, kick, or kill to protect herself.

He did just the opposite, closing in on her face, his dark eyes cutting her. "Listen to me." His voice was low and thick with a Belfast accent, but the words were spoken eerily slow.

"You..." He growled the word, dragging it out. "Are coming with me."

"No, no," she said as he breathed hot air on her face. "I won't. Please, don't hurt me. Let me go."

"You're coming now. Is that clear?"

She shook her head. Nothing was clear, except his breath smelled like pretzels, and droplets of spit stung her cheeks with his every word.

"Then let me make it clearer." He increased the pressure of his legs, locking her in place, then slid both hands to grasp her shoulders. Something in his right hand glinted.

Oh, Lord, he had a knife.

"Please..."

"I'm gonna make it real easy for you, miss." The tip grazed under her jaw. "You're gonna get the fuck out of Belfast. Right now. Wi' me."

She opened her mouth to scream, and the blade pressed right against her side.

"You'll be dead before anyone hears you." He slammed her against the wall. "There's a car coming down that street." He jerked his head in the opposite direction. "We're gonna get into it. Or I'm gonna cut you to ribbons. Is that clear?"

So, so clear.

She fought for inner strength, but there wasn't much

but watery terror and rushing blood inside her. Oh, God, where was Marc now?

"Let's go."

"No," she said, spinning through every self-defense class and article she'd ever come across in her life, her brain a useless blank.

Don't fight him. Let him take down his guard, then... She had no idea what then, but it was all she could come up with. She forced her body to relax, and sure enough, the pressure from the blade eased up. Still, he kept a firm grip on her shoulder.

"Go," he said simply, shoving her forward.

She staggered on the uneven bricks but found her footing and went with him, light-headed.

"Where are we going?" she managed to ask.

"Just move it." He pushed her hard, passing the door to the bar, which she glanced at longingly. Where was the waiter who'd said he'd cover for her? Where was Marc? Suddenly he seemed like the much lesser of two evils. "You shoulda never come here," he mumbled.

She slowed her step, processing that. "What?"

"You're not wanted around here." He punctuated that with a spit to the side.

That was basically the same thing the man at the hotel had told her. Was it the same man? Is this what he meant by things would get worse?

"Diggin' around for trouble is what you're doin'. We know you had someone look at her bags."

Oh, God. This wasn't random. It wasn't a mugging or a kidnapping. This was about Sharon.

"Who are you?" she demanded.

"None of your fucking business." He grabbed for her

again, but she dodged him, scooting to the side and breaking away.

"Who are you and how do you know me?" she demanded. She'd fight the damn knife if she had to, but she wanted answers.

He lunged for her, but she managed to throw herself out of his way, rolling to the ground and scrambling to her feet, glancing over her shoulder to catch the glint of the knife as he launched toward her.

"Bitch!" He jumped on her, pushing her back down with a crack of her back on the brick pavement, his weight like a truck on her. "No trouble, huh?" Spittle flew as he growled the words. "The doctor was fucking wrong about that."

The knife came down right next to her face, and Devyn turned her head and shrieked, the blade just missing. He slammed his knee onto her stomach, making her grunt in pain.

He raised his hand to stab again. Time froze as she stared at the knife, her elbows locked, her hands fisted on his shirt, trying desperately to hold off the inevitable. She could feel the bones in her arms almost snap with his weight as she choked on another scream lodged in her throat.

She shook her head, her only hope to be a moving target. The knife came straight for her throat, the air moving as it fell. The world exploded with noise and light and the punch of pain as his whole body fell on hers, and everything went black.

Marc vaulted over a crate, his Glock still aimed at the dark figure he'd just shot in the alley. The body slumped over Devyn, and Marc didn't dare take another shot for fear of hitting her.

The guy rolled off her or she pushed him off; he couldn't tell. But all that mattered was that her attacker still had enough strength to haul himself to his feet. Marc aimed again, but Devyn was getting up, too.

"Stay down!" he ordered.

"Don't kill him!" she yelled.

He ran closer, not sure he'd heard her right, giving the guy just enough time to take off. Marc whipped the pistol directly at him, cupping his right hand to get a dead aim.

"He knows..." She couldn't finish the sentence, too breathless from the fight.

Holding his shoulder, the guy stumbled to the end of the alley. Marc reached Devyn, dividing his attention between the assailant and her, making sure she was okay.

As he did, a BMW roared up to the alley entrance, slowing down as someone in the backseat threw open a door. Devyn's attacker leaped in, and the engine and tires screamed as they peeled away.

Marc dropped to his knees. "Jesus, Devyn, what the hell happened?"

"Hey!" From the pub, several men poured out of the door, drawn by the gunshots, no doubt.

"Are you okay?" he asked her.

"What's going on?" one of the men yelled as they hustled closer. "Who's firing out here?"

"I'm fine," she said, pushing hair off her face and looking anything but fine.

The men reached them, one of them holding a pistol of his own. "Let 'er go, you bastard."

Marc ignored the order and asked them, "You know who came out here after her?"

The two men looked at each other, then at him. One of

them said, "Don't lie, lad. I know she was runnin' from you." He bent down on his knee in front of Devyn. "Come with me, miss."

For a second, Marc thought she would. But she just shook her head and held up a hand. "Thank you, but I'm okay."

"You don't wanna stay with him, do ya?" The man pointed at Marc. "No need to, lass. Come inside."

But she bit her lip and shook her head, glancing at the street for a second. "No, really. This man didn't attack me—someone else did." She turned to Marc, her eyes bright from the trauma. "He saved me," she said softly.

The thin-haired Irishman stood slowly, contempt on his face. "You don't have to lie. I know you're scared of him."

"I'm not," she said. "Honestly. You can go back."

They did, grumbling and throwing looks over their shoulders as Marc helped her stand, squeezing her hands to stop the trembling. When they were alone, she took a deep breath, and as she let it out, she said, "I think my mother just tried to have me kidnapped."

"What?"

"At least"—she glanced at the street again—"whoever that was knows Sharon Greenberg."

He searched her face, all the options on how to respond flipping through his brain.

"Do *you* know who that was?" she demanded.

He shook his head. "No." And that was no lie. "Why would I know?"

"You tell me. Was our meeting an accident? Or was it because of Sharon?"

"I didn't even know the woman existed until an hour ago," he said, purposely not answering what he'd been asked.

"You're a liar. A good one," she conceded as she brushed her hands on her jeans. "But you're lying."

"I am not."

She practically spit when she puffed out a breath of disbelief. "Look, pal, I just knocked on death's door twice in one night, and I want *goddamn* answers."

"Twice?"

"Somebody broke into my room, a guy in a face mask. Made the same threat—told me to leave Belfast."

"Then maybe"—he reached for her, but she swiped his hand away—"you should listen to them. Maybe it's time you leave Belfast, Dev."

She narrowed her eyes at him, anger and frustration rolling off her. "Maybe it's time you tell me the truth, Marc. What are you doing here, and what does it have to do with my mother? The *truth*."

"The truth is you are being told by all kinds of not real nice people that you should leave this city. You have no idea why your mother is over here, but if your instincts are right and she just tried to have you kidnapped, then you're not safe and you should abandon this search. Let me take you out of this city—"

"Go to hell." She started walking away, but not fast enough. He grabbed her arm and she shook him off. "Touch me again and I'll scream so loud you will spend the night in the nearest Belfast jail. I already have friends in that bar who're ready to kill you. And if you don't give me a straight answer, I might do it myself."

"I'm not here to hurt you, Devyn. I swear."

She studied him, her body stiff, her beautiful face in a cold, unrelenting expression. "Then why *are* you here, *Mr. Rossi*? What do you want from me?"

"Drinks, dinner, and—"

She slapped his face, the smack echoing through the alley, the sting fiery on his freshly shaven skin.

"I've had enough people lie to me," she said through clenched teeth. "My whole life I've been lied to. My mother didn't want me. My adopted parents bought me, then never let me forget I didn't share their precious blood. And my husband? My husband—"

"Tried to betray you and got himself shot in the head for it."

She stumbled backward a little, no words coming from her open mouth.

"I know who you are, *Mrs. Sterling*. But I swear I don't know anything about your missing birth mother."

Slowly, she raised her hand to her mouth. "You knew all day?" The hitch in her voice broke his heart.

"I did."

"Oh." It came out as a sigh, almost like she expected the answer and it hurt. "So what do you want from me?" she asked in a whisper, the plea on her lips as heart-wrenching as the pain in her eyes.

He stayed silent. She'd been threatened and the rules of the game had changed. All bets were off. She had to know why he was there, even if that was all he could tell her.

"I want what everyone else seems to want from you. I want you to leave Belfast."

"Why?"

"I don't know."

She blinked at him. "Then who sent you?"

"The FBI."

"Are you an FBI agent?"

"Not anymore. But I am working for them."

She swallowed, nodding, thinking, scrutinizing him. "This is about...Finn MacCauley, isn't it?"

"I honestly don't know. I've been sent here with a simple job—to get you to leave Belfast."

"You think I have information about him. That's the only reason the FBI would want me."

"I didn't say they wanted you. They want you to leave."

"Well, you can tell the FBI that you failed on your mission, Mr. Rossi. I'm not going anywhere." She turned and headed out of the alley. He stayed close behind, eyeing the road for the BMW.

At the curb, under the harsh red light of another pub, a gaggle of smokers outside the door watched them.

"Why not?" he asked.

"Because I'm going to find my mother."

"But you think your mother just sent a thug to kidnap you."

"I don't know that for sure. I just know there's a connection. I want to know what it is." Determination drenched every word and step.

He steered her away from the crowd to an empty section of the sidewalk. "Why?"

She eased out of his grasp but was smart enough to avoid the crowds. "I guess a person happily ensconced in a family of seven would ask that. But put yourself in my shoes, Marc. I want to face my birth mother and find out her deal. I want to tell her that her secret might not be a secret anymore, because she has a right to know that."

"A right? After you think she tried to kidnap you?"

She shrugged off the question. "All I know is I have nothing—and I mean *nothing*—to lose by finding out."

"Your life," he said quietly. "You could lose your life."

"I have no life." The words were flat and bitter, and he didn't believe them for a minute.

"You have a death wish?" he countered, pulling her deeper into the shadows, rocked by the urge to protect her from everyone around, every potential threat—real and imagined.

"I have a wish not to spend another day torn by not knowing which side of the gene pool I belong on, and frankly I don't care if you understand that or not."

He didn't, but he could tell it mattered to her, a lot.

"I know I'm not a crusty purebred Hewitt, and I don't think I'm a vile, murderous MacCauley...that leaves Greenberg. Or Mulvaney, as I believe her maiden name was. But you know what? I came across the ocean to find the woman and meet her, and that's exactly what I'm going to do. If she's made of the same evil as my biological father, then I just have to know that. If she's not, then maybe..." She swallowed, unable or unwilling to finish.

"Maybe what?" he prodded.

"Nothing."

Probably not *nothing* at all. "You think you'll have some sort of mother-daughter epiphany and you'll feel all whole again?"

She gave him a look of disgust, and he felt bad for the sarcasm, but not if it got her off this quest.

"You never know, do you?" She turned and tried to walk away, but Marc stayed with her, let her walk and think.

At the next block, she slowed her step and looked at him. "I don't really want to do this alone and unprotected."

"Then don't."

"I don't suppose I could...pay you?"

Talk about double-dipping and pissing off the biggest, and only, client of the new firm. "I'm already working for the FBI," he said. "And if you don't leave, as they've asked me to coerce you to do, then...I failed." And nobody got paid. But right now, money wasn't the issue. Her safety was.

"They want Finn MacCauley," she said quietly.

"I don't know what they want," he admitted. "Other than you out of Belfast."

"What if you delivered Finn?"

"You know where he is?"

She didn't answer for a good ten seconds. "I might."

"And you're offering this information in exchange for protection while you hunt down your mother, or at least wait for her to show up."

Her expression grim, she nodded. "I can even sweeten the deal," she said. "I'll leave the minute I've talked to her. So you accomplish your goal *and* you get Finn."

It was a sweet deal. If he got her to leave and turned over a lead to one of the FBI's most wanted, everybody would win.

"Are you in touch with him? You're certain he's still alive?"

"You're just going to have to trust me on this."

"I don't like the sound of that."

"Why not?"

He slowed his step, placing his arm on her back, inching her closer to make his point. "The last time I trusted a woman—another beautiful, perfect woman who happened to be my wife—I lost."

She stopped and stared at him. "You lost what?"

"Everything." They stood face-to-face, the challenge

hanging in the night air. "So you're going to have to give me more than your word. I need proof."

They both took slow, even breaths, their gazes locked. "My word is all I've got," she finally said. "Will you help me or not? Because if the answer is no, I want my bags and I want you to disappear."

"And if the answer is yes?"

"Is it?"

How could it be anything but? He wasn't about to leave her to fend for herself against kidnappers and street thugs. He wasn't about to get on a plane as a failure and face Colton Lang or his cousins. He had no choice but to help her, to trust her.

"Yes."

She rose up on her toes and put her hands on his cheeks, her palms cool against the skin he'd just shaved. "Thank you." Without a word, she kissed him, her lips parted, her breath warm, her mouth sweet and soft and full of promises.

Promises he couldn't make or keep.

But, apparently, he just had.

CHAPTER 8

The Guinness tasted bitter, but Devyn managed to swallow it, needing the Irish salve on her soul as Marc told her his role in bringing in the people responsible for having her husband killed. He chose his words carefully, but even his diplomacy couldn't soften the blow of reliving the day Joshua was shot in cold blood in the wine cellar of a Boston restaurant.

"I'm sure this is tough on you," he said, sipping his own ale across the small table in his room, watching her reactions to his words.

"I've accepted his death, and the fact that he planned to betray me in the most public way," she said. "But honestly? Your version isn't anything like what I've been told by the police or read in the papers."

"The Guardian Angelinos weren't in it for credit or publicity. Our only goal was to protect the witness, Samantha Fairchild."

But they had closed the case, helping to bring in a dirty

cop and one of Boston's most highly paid madames, who was Joshua's lover. That woman had wanted Joshua dead, and when she'd learned he was about to do a revealing story on the fugitive Finn MacCauley, the elusive Irish mobster became the perfect person to take the rap for the murder.

And they might have succeeded, if not for Marc and his brothers and cousins, who'd unearthed the truth.

"Frankly, I'm happy to know the real story of what happened so I can tell you how much I appreciate what you did."

"Zach did the most," he said. "But I always wondered if you knew about the story your husband was going to write."

She pushed her half-eaten food away. "I found out that day, and I decided to leave him."

"Yet you went out to dinner with him that night?"

"I didn't want him to know I knew. I had to get a lawyer, figure out a plan. Then"—she closed her eyes, remembering the melee in the restaurant—"he was murdered that night."

He wiped his mouth with a napkin, tossing it on the plate before getting up from the table, kicking off his shoes, and dropping his long body on the bed, arms locked behind his head as he regarded her.

His bare feet were just inches from where she'd propped hers on the end of the bed, the almost touch of skin sending an unwanted tremble through her. She carefully lowered her feet.

"Sorry your marriage had to end in such an ugly way," he said.

"Sounds like yours wasn't much better."

He waved his hand, fending off the subject, so she took the cue and let it drop.

"I'd read Joshua Sterling's columns in the *Globe* for years," he said. "He was a very insightful guy and had a real handle on local politics."

"He was," she agreed. "And I'm very, very sorry he had to die so young. But I won't be a hypocrite and act like a grieving widow. My husband was a liar, a cheater, a user, and a pig."

He grinned. "Tell me how you really feel."

"Well, notice that I didn't say he was stupid." She shifted in the chair. "Sadly, he was smarter than I am, and counted on me being exactly what I'd always been."

"Which is?"

"Raised to protect the hallowed family name and willing to smooth things over to avoid a scandal."

"Is that what he expected you to do when he broke the story?"

She'd often wondered that, but he had died before she ever got the answer. "Maybe, or perhaps he thought it would make me agree to a quick divorce so he'd be free to marry his mistress. He wasn't thinking about me; he was thinking about himself. He was either going to land a cable news job with the notoriety or get my father—my adopted father—to pay him millions of dollars before he went with the story."

Marc considered that. "Is it possible he knew Sharon Greenberg is your biological mother?"

"Anything is possible," she said. "I didn't tell him that. I only told him about Finn, but I really don't know how much he knew or shared."

She pushed up from the chair with a long sigh, pacing

away from him, away from the interrogation. "It's really complicated and doesn't have anything to do with why we're here."

"I want to know."

At the demand, she turned to him. "I don't want to tell you. I told him about Finn, that's all. Sharon's name wasn't on any of that paperwork because it had been expunged. But I found someone who . . . unexpunged it for me."

"Could that person have told anyone your mother's identity?"

"I don't think so, but I don't know. I suppose anyone who knows about Finn and really, really wants to figure out who had his child might eventually come up with her name. I know that's possible, and that's why I'm here, to tell her." Not the only reason, but it was the initial prompt.

"Why'd you look up your biological parents in the first place?" he asked. "The usual reasons?"

There was nothing *usual* about it. "Yes, the usual reasons." If wanting a baby was usual.

She crossed the room and returned to the chair, feeling trapped. "I wanted to know my medical history." That much was true. She wanted to know her medical history because that was the only way Joshua would agree to father a baby—and that was all she really wanted. Ever. *Still.*

But some people really shouldn't reproduce. And until she met Dr. Greenberg and found out what the woman was made of, then she wouldn't indulge in that dream.

"My adoption was completely closed, handled by a lawyer, and no medical records existed. My adopted parents insisted they had no idea who my biological parents were. They really wanted me to drop the whole thing, as the fact that I was adopted was a bit of a black eye to my mother."

"Why?"

"Not being able to have a baby made her less than perfect. And if there is one thing Bitsy Hewitt values, it's perfection."

"Then she should value you."

Devyn snorted softly. "I'm not a Hewitt, therefore I am not perfect. Not by a long stretch in my mother's—my adoptive mother's—eyes."

"So how did you unearth your birth mother's identity?"

It had taken two years and many thousands of dollars, but every minute and dime had been worth it. "The private investigator was eventually able to find the women who'd given birth at Brigham and Women's Hospital on my birthday, then he tracked each one down, interviewed them, and finally narrowed it to this scientist at University of North Carolina, who was Sharon Mulvaney back when I was born. Apparently, she married briefly in the eighties, then divorced."

"You didn't tell anyone about her? No one at all?"

She had no one to tell. "I don't have a lot of friends." Boy, she must sound like a poor little rich girl. Could he possibly understand what it meant to carry around the weight of being a Hewitt? "My social circle is made up of people who are enamored of my maiden name or my connections."

"That must suck."

She smiled, appreciating the fact that he didn't judge her. "It does."

"But you trusted your husband enough to give him the name of your biological father, a wanted fugitive, but not your mother's identity?"

"You really are an FBI agent," she said, feeling the sting of embarrassment.

"Was," he corrected. "But I believe that getting all the facts out can help you solve a problem."

Marc didn't need to know about her desire for a child. He knew enough. "I told him because he was my husband and I wanted to be honest," she said, hoping it was enough of an explanation. "I had to explain to him how we could never really find out about my father's medical files because he's a fugitive. That was a year ago. Things between us were still on track. Kind of."

She shook her head, dropping the act and the rationalization. "I was grabbing at straws to avoid the shame of a divorce," she admitted.

"Divorce is more shameful than murder?"

"Marc, first of all, I had no idea the information about my biological father would get him killed. And secondly, as far as the shame part, I assume you've done your homework and know exactly who and what my family is. A Hewitt protects the family name."

"And the big-ass money."

She choked on a dry laugh. "Yep, Boston Brahmin A-List." She picked up the glass of Guinness and took a sip. "And you can believe that's why Joshua Sterling—whose real last name was Silverman and who hailed not from Manhattan but from a two-room walk-up in the Bronx—married me."

"I'm sure he was attracted to far more than your last name."

An unexpected wisp of heat curled through her at the statement, at his deep voice and intense gaze. She didn't reply.

"So why'd you marry him?"

"I was never really close to anyone until I met him. And he was handsome, kind, and adoring." Until...he wasn't. She stroked the beads of condensation on the smooth, thick glass. "And he offered something I'd never had before."

"Which was?"

The potential for a family, the one she'd dreamed of. He'd promised they'd have children. He'd sworn her unknown biological history didn't matter. And he'd lied. The day after they married, he started talking about his concerns about what he called "her unknown DNA map."

She finally looked up from the glass, fully aware her eyes were misted. "Stop. Now."

He just looked long and hard at her, then rolled over and pushed off the bed. "You're right. Time to get to work." He grabbed the laptop and opened it. "I'm expecting an e-mail from my company with some information that might help us."

His company, the Guardian Angelinos. On the way back to the hotel, he'd told her about the loosely formed organization run by his cousins, which was when she realized just how much she owed him.

Would a scribbled phone number that she found on the back of a picture be enough to thank him? A pang of guilt hit again, but she squashed it. She needed his protection and his help. A phone number with the name "Finn" on it had to be enough.

While he clicked a few keys, her gaze drifted from his head to his feet, lingering on the faded jeans over rock-solid thighs, narrow hips, and a muscled, masculine torso.

His face was tilted down as he worked on the computer, reading intently, his dark hair a little tousled, his shave done so quickly he'd missed a few spots.

Hours ago, she'd been kissing him on a hillside over the water. Then she'd gone from ready to kill him to trusting her life to him. Her whole being ached from swinging on an emotional pendulum.

"What is it?" he asked, catching her scrutiny.

"I just realized you know an awful lot about me, having just squeezed out some of my deepest and darkest secrets, and I know nothing about you except what you told me today. Obviously, you're not an investment professional traveling on business and having some fun."

"I'm on business, and some people might consider this fun. But I'm not from New York," he admitted. "I live in Marblehead, where I have a weapons store, and just recently made the decision to work for my cousins' firm. I have no kids, I grew up in Sudbury, and I like to fish, cook a little, and am going to be thirty-nine next month. Feel better?"

"It's a start."

"Now, c'mere. You need to read something." He gestured for her to join him and read the screen. "An e-mail from my cousin Vivi. She's a former reporter for the *Boston Bullet* and a damn good investigator." He angled the laptop so she could read the e-mail, skimming the words until she landed on her birth mother's name.

Dr. Sharon Greenberg happens to be one of the few microbiologists in the world who has the skill set necessary to grow and reformat botulism spores into a substance that can be used in a bioterrorism attack.

"I know she's quite highly regarded in the area of

immunology and neurotoxins. Possibly one of the best scientists in the world," Devyn said.

"Look at the e-mail Vivi forwarded." He clicked to another message. The sender's name was unfamiliar, but the address ended in fbi.gov.

Current investigation open: Reported theft from University of North Carolina Chapel Hill Department of Pathology and Laboratory Medicine's faculty lab… 19 grams of Clostridium botulinum bacterium, purified for growth of toxin…multiple lab employees have been interrogated. Notes from interviews available through investigation team…CIA has been alerted…currently monitoring Internet chatter among known terrorist cells…

"Oh my God," she whispered. "You think she's involved with this?"

"I don't know. The spores have been stolen. This woman, with a confirmed expertise in this science, disappears in Northern Ireland, at one time a hotbed of terrorism, and she has connections to a man who, among his many crimes, is believed to have openly supported Irish terrorists in the 1970s. It might explain why the FBI wants you away from the potential problems."

Her heart, what was left of it after every word he said crushed it into bits, fell deep into her stomach with a thud.

Was the other side of her "unknown DNA map" just as evil and criminal as her father?

Oh, God, what did that make *her*?

"We can't ignore this," he said.

But how she wanted to. "I know. What do we do with that information?"

"We're looking for clues, trying to connect one dot

with another." He clicked through a few more pages as the sickening thoughts took hold.

Both her parents were criminals?

"Look at this."

The screen changed to a blotchy image of a partially handwritten form, a report scanned in at an angle, the seal of the FBI top and center.

Her gaze landed on the date, December 22, 1978, and the city, Cambridge, Massachusetts.

Acting on a tip to find person of interest Finley MacCauley, investigators visited the apartment residence of Miss Sharon Mulvaney, MIT grad student, who cooperated with agents and allowed them into her residence w/o search warrant. No evidence of MacCauley.

Her heart stuttered as she glanced back at the date, about nine months before her birthday.

"Nothing shocking there." Except absolute proof of what she wished weren't true. "I'm living proof they knew each other. I have no doubt the authorities watched her if they suspected a relationship."

"Then this one." He clicked to another page, a similar document. The handwriting was different, but the seal was the same. And the date was about three weeks later.

Investigators interviewed seventeen students and faculty members related to the MIT laboratory reporting a theft of Clostridium botulinum bacterium, detaining six for further questioning.

She didn't have to read every one of the six names. They were meaningless to her, except for the fourth one on the list. Sharon Mulvaney.

All were released without charges; investigation remains open.

With an achy weight on her chest, she stood and walked to the suitcase she'd left by the door.

"I have something to show you," she said softly.

"What is it?" he asked.

"More dots to connect."

CHAPTER 9

Liam Baird braced himself against the ancient window frame of the third-floor parlor, his gaze drifting where it always did when he looked out over the Milltown Cemetery. The vast acreage of graves was lit only by the moon and ambient light from the Falls Road streetlamps.

His mother's grave, adorned with only a torn Irish tricolor flag and a modest Catholic cross with Celtic carvings, sat on a crest at the far western slopes of the famed burial ground. Milltown was closed for the night to the tourists who came to stroll past the heroes' monuments and whisper famous names as though they'd been sainted. Every night, the cemetery was locked to stop the black-hearted Unionists who snuck over from Shankill to dribble paint and spit on the graves of men who were killed by their fathers. But there were many ways in and out of those ten thousand plots, even at night.

Still, no one would bother to deface Colleen Baird's burial site, tonight or any other night. No one braved the bramble bush and broken stones or wandered into the area of "lessers." Visitors came to Milltown to stand in reverence at the graves of men who'd managed to become "political prisoners" instead of ordinary dissidents.

Liam would never be ordinary. Not with the money he planned to make. Money could buy anything. Even...

His gaze was drawn back to his mother's grave. The first thing he'd do was build a monument to her.

And if the shrewd and manipulative scientist from the States was as greedy as he hoped she was, she held the ticket to the vast sums of money he wanted.

Not that he hadn't done well, creating a business by riling up the young boys who burned to be like their fathers and uncles before them, dying for a Republican cause. He just hadn't done well enough.

His boys were willing to twist arms, take cash, move drugs, and sell women. They liked the dirtiness of it, these bricklayers and ironworkers, these plumbers and butchers and working-class Catholics who had no more excitement in their dreary lives since peace replaced passion in Northern Ireland. They needed an outlet, and Liam provided it, putting the work into a political framework to justify the deeds and pocketing the cash.

But there was always a lot more cash to be pocketed.

He looked down at his cell phone, which was still silent even though the appointed time for the conversation had come and gone. A satellite signal could be hard to obtain in Pakistan. Especially in a cave.

As he looked at it, the phone vibrated, but the name on the caller ID wasn't the one he expected.

"Did you get her, Danny?" he asked without greeting.

"It's Magee. Danny's been shot."

"Jesus Christ."

"He'll live. But he's got to see Doc Russell."

"Did he get the woman?"

The brief hesitation was enough of an answer, and Liam bit back a dark curse.

"He did get a warning in before some bloke fired on Danny," Magee said. "And I've no doubt she'll blow out after that."

Blowing out wasn't enough. He wanted to know who had sent that goddamn woman who was asking too many questions. And he wanted to stop her before she alerted the wrong person that Dr. Greenberg was here.

"Where's the doc?" Liam asked. "You can't take him to the hospital—they'll file a police report."

"He's meeting me upstairs at Four Points. You want to come?"

"I might. I'm waiting for a call." Disgust rolled through him. "The girl is a problem. If she's been sent by the British fucks, we'll give them a nice, clean message."

"Well, she *was* almost a nice clean message tonight. Danny had a knife on her."

"Did he cut her?"

Behind him, he heard the pine board of the top step creak under the pressure of a foot. He turned to meet Dr. Greenberg's slicing silver gaze.

"No," Magee answered. "But he scared the living shite out of her."

"Good. We want her scared."

"We want her *gone*," the doctor corrected, crossing her arms. "What happened?"

"Keep me posted, Magee." He ended the call and pocketed the phone. "Danny didn't get her into the car, but he scared her and managed to get himself shot."

"She shot him?"

"No, she had backup, conveniently enough." He peered hard at her. "Who *is* this young lady, Dr. Greenberg?"

She just stared him down. "Did you arrange for the cash transfer?" she asked.

Christ, she was one tough bitch. Except this bitch had a skill no man, woman, or scientist—at least not one who could be bought—had to offer. So he had to put up with her. "Everything is taken care of. Have you been in the laboratory?"

She nodded. "Everything's growing as it should. There are no problems. For the time being, a few days at least, we have nothing to do but observe the process."

"I have plenty to do," he countered. "Marie'll have dinner ready in an hour. I'll be out for the evening."

"Where are you going?"

He felt his nostrils flare. "To a fucking pub, ma'am, and you would not be welcome there."

"Why?"

"Sectarian place. Not real open to outsiders, so I'd rather not explain you to anyone. You stay here and eat whatever my housekeeper makes you."

"You won't have to explain anything to anyone," she said, a tight smile in place. "Tell Marie to save the trouble. I assume they serve food at the pub."

"If you wanna call it that. Four Points is better known for the stout."

"I like beer," she said, canting her head toward the door.

The vibrating from his pocket saved him. "I have to take this call."

She didn't move.

"I have to take this call *privately*," he said. "That is, if you want that cash transfer to happen."

"I'll wait for you downstairs."

When he heard her footsteps on the landing, he checked the ID and blew out a breath of relief.

"*Salam*," he said, knowing it was the only way to greet the Muslim on the other end.

"How much longer, Baird?" Obviously, his client didn't worry about etiquette. The accent was thick, the subtext clear. *Time's running out.*

"Not much longer," he said. "But I will need more in the advance."

"I don't think that's possible."

"Look, this is a very expensive process, and some of it is out of our hands. I need a little more time and a little more money. At least a week."

"And then it will be done?"

"If Allah has his way," Liam said, despising that he had to use the wrong God's name but knowing it would give him points.

"Allah always has his way," the man said simply. "And we have a timetable to follow for this project. Unfortunately for you, I have found another supplier."

Fuck. "This tactic doesn't scare me." Although it did. Because Malik Mahmud Khel held every card in this game. And every dollar. Liam had no doubt there could be other suppliers, probably right there in the Middle East, too.

Still, he dug for the confident leader's tone that he used on his men. "My process is much further ahead than anyone's, and I have the quantity that no one else has. You know that and I know that. Please put two hundred and fifty thousand U.S. dollars into the account you have for me."

"Every good leader has a backup plan," Malik said. "I have one, and so should you. I will give you your additional funds, Baird, but then you have three days to deliver. At that point, you will receive one million U.S. dollars."

"One?"

"When the substance is proven effective, you will receive the rest, and after our strike, the name of Tehrik-e-Jafria will be on the lips of every man, woman, and child in the world. They will forget Osama bin Laden. And they will remember the heroes of Tehrik. You can be one of those heroes."

Fuck that. He wanted the two million dollars they'd agreed on, but the line had gone silent. He'd been dismissed.

Behind him, a step creaked. Furious, he stomped to the doorway to catch her spying, ready to strangle the doctor. But instead Marie stood there, a question in her sad blue eyes. Always sad, all these years since her husband lay bloody and dead on Botanic Avenue, the victim of a British bullet.

"No dinner, Mr. Baird? The doctor said you're going out."

Baird closed the phone. Maybe he *should* take the doctor to Four Points. Maybe she needed a little lesson in what happens when you delay and demand more than you're supposed to.

But he couldn't hurt her. At least, not yet. He needed her. Once again, he looked out to the rolling fields of Milltown and sent a silent salute to his dead mother, Malik Mahmud Khel's heavy foreign accent still ringing in his ears.

Malik wasn't the ultimate leader of Tehrik-e-Jafria, but he was close to the top, and he managed the money of that Islamic sect. Which must keep him busy, because those Pakistanis had a bundle and they were going to spend it to get what they needed.

And Liam Baird could provide what they needed. Assuming he could manage the demanding doctor and the troublesome young woman asking too many questions around Belfast.

Sharon was waiting with a coat on at the front door.

"I'm ready," she said cheerily, as though they were longtime mates going out for a pint and darts.

"Then we should go." He gave her a tight smile, ready and willing to placate this woman who held the key to what he wanted most.

And if getting what he wanted most meant doing away with that nuisance of a girl, then so be it. Too bad Danny couldn't get the job done. He didn't have many men who'd take out a female.

Well, too fucking bad. He'd do it himself if he had to.

Marc leafed through the scant pages tucked into the manila file folder Devyn had pilfered from Dr. Sharon Greenberg's home office. On the bed, Devyn crouched over his laptop, her eyes burning as she clicked her way through academic sites and online scientific journals.

"I have to admit," she said, "this is such a relief."

"To have a computer with Internet access?"

She gave him a sincere look. "And a second brain. Between us and the search engines, surely we can find something that explains what that drawing is, other than the obvious—a synaptic vesicle." She pointed to the screen. "Which I now know is a small membrane-bound structure in the axon-bound terminals of nerve cells."

"You understand that?"

"Not a word. And none of this was what got me on a plane to Northern Ireland when I found these papers."

"So what was?"

It was a fair question, and one she'd been dreading. "I found a picture of myself as a little girl, so..." *I hoped she cared about me.* "I knew she must know who I am. And I felt compelled to tell her how and why Joshua was killed."

"I wonder how she got that picture?" he mused.

And the phone number written on the back. "I did, too. But..." She bit her lip, still hesitant to trust him with more. "Someone was in Sharon's house the night I got this file."

His head shot up. "What?"

"He attacked me."

Marc just stared at her, not even blinking. "When were you going to tell me this?"

"I'm telling you now," she said. "I don't know who he was or if he was waiting for Sharon or working with her. There was a powerful lightning strike and the lights went out, and as I made my way to the front door, he grabbed me from behind and made me leave."

"Another person who wanted you out."

She nodded with a sigh. "There does seem to be a pattern."

"And a message you refuse to get."

"Don't," she said sharply. "My decision is made. I'm not going anywhere until I know who she—I mean, where she is. And why."

He looked positively disgusted with that decision. "What else did this guy in her house say to you?"

She closed her eyes, remembering the darkness, the strength of him, the fear that blocked out parts of her memory. "He wanted to know who sent me and told me if Sharon came back there without getting her job done, he'd kill her."

"You shouldn't have come over here alone," he said quietly.

"I didn't have a choice. My husband is dead. I don't have brothers or sisters or cousins, like you. I'm a loner, always have been. And impulsive, just ask Bitsy Hewitt, the woman who raised me and never let me forget that all my flaws were a result of the wrong blood."

He looked at her as though he didn't believe her again, then his dark eyes softened into something like pity. "Mom sounds lovely. No wonder you're looking for the real thing."

The words hit hard. "I'm not..." Yes, she *was*. "Fooling myself into thinking I'm going to have some special relationship with this stranger who gave birth to me, Marc. But wanting to know what I'm made of doesn't make me a freak. It's pretty common, I think."

He smiled, putting a warm hand on her leg, making her instantly aware that they were side by side on a bed and all they had to do was fall backward and into each other's arms.

Like that wouldn't complicate things any worse than they already were.

"First of all, Devyn, there's nothing common about you." He added some pressure. "Second, finding her isn't going to answer all your questions. It's just going to raise a lot more."

She put her hand over his and removed it. "Lots of questions, like"—she jutted her chin at the computer screen—"what does all that arcane scientific stuff mean?"

"I don't know, but while I look through it, try Googling this e-mail address, from the person who sent her instructions on where to go when she got here. It's puggaree17@connectone.com."

She typed it into the search engine while he turned back to the file. The screen flashed. *Address invalid.* "That's not an active e-mail account."

"No surprise. I'll send it to my office in Boston," he said. "They can probably find out who owns it or at least the location of the server it was on when this e-mail was sent. From that, we can probably get a more exact location."

She glanced up. "Really?"

"My sister's a hacker," he said with a sly smile. "And my older brother's a cop. And my other sister's a shrink with an expertise in criminal profiling. Oh, my other brother's a spook, my cousin's a former Ranger, and, well, I already mentioned Vivi, who can suck information from sources like a tornado."

She laughed softly. "They sound amazing."

"They are," he agreed, still studying the diagram that was in the file. "But not without their downsides, trust me. Hey, pull up that screen you had a minute ago. The biochemical mechanism of toxicity."

She did, and they compared the two images. "We've got a match," she said.

The string of scientific terminology ran together under her exhausted eyes—*neurons...endocytosis...SNAP-25 proteins...*

"But this is Greek to me."

"Not entirely," he said. "This has to do with the spores that create toxic chemicals. Very toxic. Botulism toxic."

She pushed the computer screen toward him and backed away, sliding down the bed to drop on the pile of pillows, closing her stinging eyes and her stinging heart.

What the hell was Sharon Greenberg *doing* over here?

"You know, it could be something entirely innocent," he said, as if reading her mind. "She could be participating in some kind of international conference on chemical substances."

She opened one eye. "And that would be why some nitwit in the alley tried to kidnap me. Why some goon came into my room wearing a mask and threatened me. Oh, and don't forget the nice man at her house."

He reached out, closing his hands over her ankles, gliding them up her legs to add pressure to her calves. He meant it to be comforting, she had no doubt, but the contact was intimate and sexy, even through her jeans.

"You could just go home now, and be safe and smart."

"And never know? I can't go through my life wondering anymore. I just...can't." She cursed her voice for breaking, and him for looking like he could possibly understand. "Stop it," she ordered.

He instantly lifted his hands, and she regretted the loss of warmth.

"I mean the way you're looking. Sympathetic."

"I am sympathetic."

She shook her head. "Sorry, but you have no idea how it feels to know your blood is tainted."

"Better tainted than spilled," he replied.

He didn't argue her point, though. Didn't tell her that blood wasn't important. Because it was. It would be extremely important to a man who came from such an impressive bloodline, cops and soldiers and spies.

No doubt he'd hate to water down that gene pool. "I need a shower and some sleep," she said suddenly, rolling off the bed to stand up.

"Make yourself at home. And I'll sleep on the chair." When she didn't answer, he looked up. "Unless you'd rather I slept in the bed with you."

She managed not to let any response show on her face as she connected one more dot—one that led to her and that bed.

"So was that your plan?" she asked. "Were you going to seduce me into leaving Belfast with you?"

"The thought never crossed my mind...until I saw you."

"And then it crossed your mind?"

He smiled. "And hasn't left since. But don't worry. I have no intention of taking advantage of you."

For a moment, she just looked at him, not sure if she was disappointed or relieved. A little of both, she imagined.

"While you shower, I'm going to call Boston," he said. "I want to send someone down to Sharon's house in Raleigh to check it out."

"Good idea. I suppose any of the people in your organization can handle whoever they meet."

"My family can handle anything."

Must be nice, she thought as she grabbed the smaller of her two bags, which held toiletries, and slipped into the bathroom. There, she locked the door and flipped on the water, stripping down and climbing into the shower before it reached the usual feverish temperature she liked.

His family could handle anything. And hers? Daddy is a fugitive and Mommy is a...God knows what.

She dropped her head back and let the warm water roll over her, closing her eyes to block out those thoughts and think about the good ones. About Marc Rossi.

He'd lied to her, yes. He had an agenda, yes. He wanted her to leave before she found out what she needed to know—all true.

So could she trust him? She had to.

Would she sleep with him? The thought heated her a lot more effectively than the water. He admitted the possibility had crossed his mind. And stayed there. The thought had crossed her mind, too. Crossed her whole body, in fact, every time he was six inches away.

No, Devyn. There was impulsive...and then there was stupid.

Climbing out, she dried herself and her hair, and realized she hadn't brought in any clean clothes. Curling her lip at the clothes that had been in the filth of the alleyway, she wrapped the towel tighter under her arms, but it wasn't long enough to tuck and knot. Holding it with one hand, she turned the doorknob, inching it open silently... to find him digging through her suitcase.

"What the hell are you doing?"

"Finding you some clothes."

His fingertips were inches from the zipper compartment where she'd tucked the picture with the phone number. Is that what he was looking for?

If he had it, he didn't have to help her. Hell, he could just force her out of Belfast at gunpoint if he really wanted to. That phone number was her only bargaining chip.

"I'll get them," she said.

His gaze dropped over the towel. "I was trying to help."

Clutching the towel to her chest, she walked to the bag and grabbed a T-shirt and sweatpants, dipping at the knees to keep from exposing her body under the towel.

She had to tuck the clothes under her arm so she didn't drop them as she slipped her hand to the back of the bag, searching for a bra. None was in reach.

With a bemused expression, he stood and watched.

Abandoning the search for a bra, her fingers slowed. Should she take the picture? Would he see her do that? She could memorize the number and destroy the photo in the bathroom.

But there was something about that picture. Like it had been taken... with love. She *couldn't* destroy it. She could drag the whole bag into the bathroom, which would be awkward and obvious that she was hiding something in it.

There was only one solution.

Straightening, she opened her fingers and the towel fell to the ground with a soft thump. He barely reacted, except for his eyes, which traveled over her naked body. Hot and slow and up, then down. And again.

"I wouldn't have looked for whatever it is you're hiding," he said.

"I don't trust you."

"Obviously you do." One more time he scanned her, appreciation and desire in his eyes.

She stepped into her panties, holding his gaze when it returned to her face. Then she pulled on the pants and T-shirt. When she zipped up the suitcase, he shifted his attention back to the laptop.

"If you're done tormenting me, I think I finally made sense of that drawing."

She stopped just short of locking the suitcase. "Really?"

He turned the laptop toward her. "That drawing is a diagram for how to make a toxin, in this case botulinum, more deadly than a nerve agent and probably delivered through an aerosol, most likely to affect hundreds, if not thousands, of people."

"Do you think that's why she's here? Because she knows how to do that?"

"I don't know. But if she is planning on making this, then we better find her and stop her."

"And if she isn't?"

He just nodded. "It'd be good to know that, too."

Yes, it would. If only to save Devyn's heart from breaking all over again.

CHAPTER 10

Vivi stood over her younger cousin's shoulder and read the computer screen. "How much are we paying you, Chessie?"

"Nothing."

"God, you're worth so much more than that."

Chessie let her head fall back, looking straight up at Vivi, as stunning upside down as she was right side up. "At least minimum wage."

"Keep hacking like a beast and you're gonna get health benefits, too." Vivi pointed at the screen. "Where exactly is Bangor, Northern Ireland, and why are you sending Marc there?"

Vivi had finally had a conversation with her cousin last night, and he'd brought her up to speed on the assignment. Which was a lot more complicated than Mr. Secretive FBI Agent Lang led them to believe.

But when Marc told her what was at stake—a direct connection to Finn MacCauley—Vivi agreed he should proceed with caution. As she would, when she flew down to North Carolina today to dig around and find out what she could about the questionable Dr. Greenberg.

Chessie clicked a few keys to open up another page. "See that e-mail sent to Sharon Greenberg? The address is no longer valid, and the IP address is untraceable, which is kind of interesting and odd. Given enough time, I may be able to crack it. But I found this." More keystrokes and a new page, rich with code and virtually unreadable to Vivi.

"And that is?"

"The server location," she said as if a moron should be able to decipher that. "At least, I'm ninety-nine percent sure that's the location. That server handles Internet messages sent from small towns just east of Belfast, most of them from Bangor." More clicks, then a map, and some pretty pictures of a harbor tucked into rolling green hills dotted with sweet little cottages. "Which is that precious seaside resort right off Belfast Lough." She gave the Irish word a thick brogue. "*Lough.* I love saying that."

Vivi rested her hip on the side of the desk, studying the pictures. "What exactly are they going to look for there? I mean, having the server location doesn't exactly tell them who sent it."

"I have ideas. The e-mail address is 'puggaree17', so I did a search for every single person in that area with the letters 'p-u-g' in their name."

"Very creative," Vivi said, tapping Chessie's shoulder in admiration. "What did you find?"

She returned to the keyboard and called up yet another page. "The Puggetts, the Pugmires, and, listen to this, the Puggley family! Cute, huh?"

"Very."

"And, wait, how about this?" One more click. "Three pug breeders in Bangor and the surrounding area. Hey, call me crazy, but it's something to go on."

"He better not call you crazy," Vivi said, her heart swelling with love and respect for Chessie, who, as the baby of the family, took a hard rap from her older brothers, and from Zach. "You're saving his ass. What did he say?"

"I just sent him all this and he hasn't answered. To be fair, it's only five-thirty in the morning there, so he's probably still asleep." She arched her dark brows. "Or *they* are."

"You think?" Vivi asked.

"Wouldn't hurt him to get laid."

"Chessie, if your mother heard you talk like that, she'd cry."

Chessie snorted. "Ma cries if I say 'shit'."

"You're her last great hope, that's why. And, listen, Marc's a flirt but not a player." Still, she had heard a little something in his voice when they'd talked last night. A level of tenderness she hadn't heard in a long time. Not since Laura. "When he called me about going to Raleigh today, he told me he came clean with her on why he's there. I'm telling you because you have to know this, but if Lang calls and asks you anything, play it dumb."

"He's the client."

Yes, he was, which was why his caginess irritated her. "He's also not shooting entirely straight. It makes me wonder."

Chessie looked up at her. "You investigated too many bad cops when you were a reporter."

"Hell, yeah, and that's why my nose is so adept at smelling a rat."

"You think Mr. Lang's a rat? He's so...straightlaced. And kind of cute, don't you think?"

Vivi would rather die before she admitted she agreed. Mr. Lang was hot in a way that made her want to...mess up his hair. With her teeth.

"Cute if you like the Dudley Do-Right type. Which"—she pointed a finger in Chessie's face—"I know from experience can be an act to hide the insidious evil underneath."

Chessie laughed but pushed back from the desk to pop her feet up, purple-tipped toes peeking out of black strappy sandals. "I know this is totally not part of my job, but don't you think we should be straight with the client even if he's a little evasive with us?"

"I do and I don't," she admitted. "But Marc's pretty damn sure they're in a hornet's nest of some kind, and Super Special Assistant Whatever Agent Lang never even *mentioned* Dr. Sharon Greenberg to us. I don't know if he knows she exists or if she's the reason he wants Devyn out of there. But Marc said Devyn's not going anywhere and happens to have a little something that could earn the Guardian Angelinos a big, fat bonus and national acclaim."

Vivi walked to the picture window to look down at the lunch crowds milling about the brick sidewalks of Newberry Street. She wanted to bring in Finn MacCauley so bad she could taste it.

"We just have to be very careful not to blow it," she said. "There's a fine line between not playing by the rules and taking a risk that costs us everything."

"I have a feeling we're going to walk that line every day," Chessie said.

Vivi turned and smiled at her cousin, who was so much like a sister to her. "And that's what's going to make the Guardian Angelinos the best in the business. There are a zillion security firms that offer bodyguards and investigations. We have to be different, better, sharper—riskier. And that Lang character? Shoot, he probably never took a risk in his life."

"He took one by hiring us," Chessie said.

Vivi grinned. "Touché on that one. So, we have to make it pay off for him."

"What if your gut's right and he's not, you know, a good agent?"

"Then he's a bad agent," Vivi countered. "In which case, I'll nail his ass to the FBI headquarters' front door, and his boss will be my new best client. We can't miss."

Chessie swiped a lock of dark hair over her shoulder and rounded the reception desk she'd poached as her home base on her first day. "What you can't miss is your flight, which leaves in less than two hours." She grabbed a black tote Vivi had dropped on her way in. "Are you staying overnight? Is that why you have this?"

"No, but I have to check a bag so I can bring my pistol." She looked at her watch. "Damn, I really wanted to talk to Zach before I left."

"Call his cell. I told you, he's just house hunting with Samantha. You can call him."

"I was hoping to kind of read his mood in person."

"His mood's good," Chessie said. "He's ridiculously in love. We should all be so lucky."

"All the more reason for me to not bore him with the details of this assignment."

Chessie tilted her head and gave Vivi her best get-real look. "You don't want him to know what Marc's doing over there, do you?"

The girl was smart, and intuitive. She'd make a great Guardian Angelino. "Look, Zach might be my twin, but he's more conservative than I am about these things. That's why managing the business is his area and pushing the envelopes is mine. Just tell him I'm doing some intel in North Carolina and I'll bring him up to speed when and if I have to."

"When will that be?" Chessie asked.

"When I'm able to say 'Hey, Zach, the Guardian Angelinos brought in one of the FBI's most wanted.'"

Chessie laughed. "I want to be you when I grow up."

Vivi tipped her chin. "You're twenty-five, baby. You are grown up. Be you. I'm a mess."

"A beautiful mess."

But Chessie had no idea what she was talking about, and Vivi loved her for it.

"Oh, don't forget this," Chessie said, grabbing a file from her desk. "All the information Marc sent me about Dr. Greenberg. And I printed out some stuff about microbiology and the UNC campus and her lab as plane reading."

"Good, because I'm going to start at her office before I go to her house."

"Oh, and I hacked the airline site again and got you out of that window into an aisle."

"Damn, you're becoming downright indispensable in this business."

"That's my evil plan." She waggled her brows. "I might get paid."

"You will get paid," she promised. "Before anyone else."

Chessie screwed up her face. "Dude, there *isn't* anyone else but Uncle Nino. Who, by the way, wants to put a stove in the employee kitchen so he can cook for us."

"God love that man." She gave Chessie a quick kiss and added a hug of gratitude. "I'll call you when I get there."

Still smiling, Vivi darted into the hall, holding on to the scarred banister as she rounded the corner and looked down to the Newbury Street entrance. And stopped as the front door opened and a tall, imposing man walked in and looked up at her.

"Special Assistant Agent in Charge Lang."

He nearly smiled at the title she knew she'd botched again. "Just 'Mr. Lang' is fine."

Not, she noted, *Colton.* He'd never suggest she call him that.

He stayed at the bottom of the stairs, right outside the door to Silk, watching her as she descended.

Damn, she didn't want to miss her flight. "We weren't expecting you," she said.

"That's the best time to pop in, I find." He was kind of a great-looking guy, handsome in a clean-cut way—if there was such a thing—with hazel eyes that could go green or light brown, depending on the light, and thick, short chestnut hair.

"I'm afraid I'm late to catch a flight, and Zach is at an appointment. Can we reschedule a meeting tomorrow?"

"I'll drive you to the airport."

"Not necessary, but thank you. I'm planning to take a cab."

"I'm parked right out front."

The only person to get a parking spot on Newbury, naturally. "The traffic will suck at this time."

"Traffic sucks all the time." His smile widened, as if it amused him to use the word "suck." He probably didn't drop F-bombs, either. "I'd like a chance to talk to you."

Well, hell. She'd lost this battle. "All right." She'd just be careful. The text of Marc's e-mail remained top of mind, including his clear instructions that she tell Lang nothing about what he'd discovered—specifically the clouds surrounding Dr. Sharon Greenberg and the fact that he'd broken cover with his target.

Just for good measure, she imagined the headlines: *Newly Formed Security Firm Zeroes in on Fugitive Missing for Three Decades.*

Oh, yeah. She could do this.

"What did you want to talk about?" she asked brightly.

"Marc's progress."

Of course. "He's found Devyn in Belfast, has made her acquaintance, and is spending time with her. I really don't know any more specifics than that." That would be her mantra.

"When is she leaving Belfast?" he asked, his hand just hovering over her back as they navigated some foot traffic outside.

"Well, she isn't in such a big hurry to do that, so he's working on it. I'll keep you posted the minute he succeeds."

"Has he been able to figure out why she's there?"

A tiny alarm bell dinged in her head. Not because of the question, but the wee bit of concern hidden deep inside his tone. Most people would have missed it, but investigative journalism had honed Vivi's skills. "She's on vacation."

"A vacation? Who vacations in Northern Ireland?"

"Plenty of people." They reached a black sedan so nondescript it might as well have had a placard that said "undercover law enforcement" on the side. "It's not a bomb fest over there anymore, you know. Bangor, for instance, is a darling little seaside town."

He shot her a sharp look. "That's where she is?"

Way to vomit information, Vivi. "I think they're taking a day trip there. But from what he says, Belfast isn't the center of a civil war anymore."

"It's not completely over," he said, as if he had inside knowledge. "Hot spots bubble up, believe me, Ms. Angelino."

She shot him a smile and caught him looking at the diamond stud in her nose. "Call me Vivi," she said. "Since I seem to butcher your title on a regular basis."

Opening the door, he fought a smile. "I think it's cute."

You think that, FBI guy. Her youthful appearance had fooled plenty of sources into giving her more information than they wanted to. No one took a skateboarder with a nose stud seriously. Big mistake.

As he climbed into the driver's seat, she took in his long, lean body, his slim but predatory hands over the wheel. Without looking at her, he said, "I'd like you to tell me everything that he's discovered about the target."

Oh, boy. This was going to be a very long trip to the airport. "I really don't know much. He's still, you know, working his magic, trying to get her comfortable enough with him to consider leaving." *Lie, lie, lie.*

"Has she mentioned anyone?"

Anyone like Finn MacCauley? "I have no idea."

"Let's call him."

"He's with her right now," she said quickly. "I don't think that would be a very good idea."

"So, Vivi." He glanced at her, down to her bag, then back to her face. "Where are you going?"

She never questioned her gut, and right now it was screaming not to tell him anything about this trip. "New York," she said, grabbing at the first thing that popped into her head. "To see...my cousin."

"The one who works for the Bullet Catchers?"

Very little got by Colton Lang. "Yes," she lied. "The very same."

Yep. A very long trip to the airport.

Devyn hadn't slept much, and she doubted Marc had, either, as he'd spent the night in one chair with his feet propped on the other. Even though she'd made a half-hearted invitation for him to sleep on the bed, he'd turned down the offer.

Either he was a perfect gentleman or he wasn't the least bit attracted to her.

The truth, she suspected, lay somewhere in the middle.

They'd risen early, had breakfast, and headed out, armed with the information his company had sent. He drove them past a sprawling shipyard, which boasted the dubious distinction of being the birthplace of the *Titanic* and looked pretty dismal and deserted, even in the early morning sunshine.

Still, it was one of the more hyped tourist spots in Belfast, marked by huge shipbuilding cranes that towered over the water and dry docks. She leaned forward to check out the monstrosities.

"I've heard you can arrange to climb Samson and Goliath," he said, referring to the colloquial names for the two yellow cranes with arms and flatbeds swinging hundreds of feet in the air.

"Are you forgetting how I froze on the rope bridge? You couldn't get me up there with a gun to my head." She shifted her attention to the papers he'd handed her when they got in his rental. "Your assistant is thorough. The pug surnames is a stroke of genius. As far-fetched as anything I've ever heard, but clever."

"Chessie? She's all that, and more. But she's not my assistant. She's my baby sister."

"What's Chessie short for?"

"Francesca, like my mom. I guess she's going to be everyone's assistant in the company. I haven't had one since I left the FBI, though a couple of good managers run my gun shop for me."

"Why'd you leave the FBI?" she asked.

"Eh, long story."

"Is that code for 'don't ask'?"

"Pretty much, yeah."

Ignoring the clusters of redbrick and gray stone homes, warrens of winding streets, and the occasional village sprouting up from the hills as they left Belfast behind, she looked at his profile instead. Roman and strong, handsome and square. The man came from gorgeous stock, she'd bet.

And she suddenly really wanted to know why he'd left his job with the FBI.

"You're awfully young to retire. You don't look like you got injured, and—correct me if I'm wrong—you like this kind of thing."

He laughed softly. "Ignore code much?"

"I'm curious," she admitted.

"Why does it matter?"

"Because I noticed that you came alive around the time the trouble started."

He considered that, narrowing dark eyes in a quick glance her way. "I wasn't dead during our trip up the coast yesterday."

"Not at all," she agreed. "You were nice and entertaining and . . . fine."

"Nice and *fine*?" He took his hand off the gear shift to stab his heart. "Ouch."

"And pleasant," she added teasingly.

"And after all that pleasant niceness, what, my killer instinct reared up?"

"Not exactly," she corrected. "But once you got your gun out, I saw something in your eyes."

"The willingness to kill the guy trying to kidnap you?"

"What I saw was . . . your passion," she told him. "Like you came alive."

"That's interesting," he said slowly, a look of appreciation in his eyes. "I've had people who were . . . close to me never figure that out."

Like his ex-wife? The one who cost him *everything*?

"But, yeah," he agreed. "I do like the work, generally."

"Then why'd you quit the FBI?"

"Look." He pointed to a green street sign. "The Ulster Folk and Transport Museum is right up ahead. We could stop there."

"Nice try." She lowered his arm, making sure it didn't land on her thigh. "Why'd you quit the job?"

"And 'relentless' can go on that attribute list, too," he said, laughing.

"Answer the question."

"It's personal," he said simply. Whatever the reason, he wasn't going to share. She of all people should respect that. "But you're right—work is my passion. What's yours?"

"My passion?" She glanced out the window, wishing she had one. Other than the one she didn't have: children. "Oh, you know, stuff."

"Stuff?" He coughed a laugh. "What kind of stuff? And remember, I've read your file. I know more about you than you realize."

"I'd like to forget I *have* a file. But, since you've read it, then maybe you know my passion and you can tell me."

He tore his gaze from the road, intrigued. "I admit, when I read your file, I thought your life looked pretty... vacant."

A chillingly accurate assessment. "And now that you've met me?"

"Hey, it's just a file."

Vacant. "I guess it looked kind of empty because I don't have a job, lived vicariously through my husband, and haven't ever accomplished anything of note." God, that sounded bad.

"I did notice that despite a Wellesley education, you're not working," he said diplomatically.

"I didn't figure out what might interest me until I met Joshua. I was twenty-five then, about the same age as your 'baby' sister."

"And what interested you?"

"Joshua," she admitted, a little sadly. But why lie? She had thought she was in love with him, and he promised her that family she wanted so desperately. "Before that, I certainly didn't need to work. My parents have more money than they could spend in three lifetimes, and my husband had enough ambition for both of us."

"Ambition isn't passion. What do you love?"

She tried to look at the scenery, but it blurred. What did she love? All she'd ever wanted was to have a child—or four—and create a home she never had. A simple, old-fashioned, kind of embarrassing goal in this day and age, but it was hers nonetheless.

"I do volunteer work," she said. "That's where I met my husband."

"What kind of volunteer work?"

"For kids, mostly. Troubled or disadvantaged."

"And Joshua Sterling did that kind of volunteer work, too?" He sounded surprised. "Doesn't fit with the sarcastic political columnist image."

"There was media coverage," she said dryly, "so he was there. I'd helped manage the fund-raising for a new facility for autistic children, and, anyway, that's how we met."

"Was it love at first sight?"

"Not even close," she said, remembering how she'd bristled at his ego at first. She should have paid attention to that first impression. "How about you? How long were you married? How did you meet?" *How did she make you lose everything?*

She knew better than to ask that, though.

"We were married for six years and met at a mall on Christmas Eve."

She laughed. "*Who* goes to the mall on Christmas Eve?"

"Guys." He grinned at her. "I was with my brother Gabe and my cousin Zach."

"The Army Ranger and the spy?"

"I like a woman who listens," he said with a wink. "They are, but not in that order. Gabe's the spy; Zach's the soldier."

"And...at the mall...you met...," she coaxed.

"Laura," he said quickly. "Was there with a friend."

Laura. His ex-wife. She filed that, but her brain had already gone back to his impressive family. "You must have had great family Christmases."

He frowned at her non sequitur, probably expecting questions about his wife. She was interested, but more riveted by the big family. "Christmases in my family are great, once we get back from the mall and have the feast."

"What's the feast?" she asked.

"The Feast of the Seven Fishes is a big Italian tradition on Christmas Eve. My grandfather goes nuts and cooks for days, and we eat for hours until it's time to go outside and..." He laughed self-consciously. "I know it sounds preposterous to an outsider, but we go out and play in the snow until, you know, Santa comes."

For a minute, she couldn't speak, choked by emotion.

"I know, ridiculous," he said, still chuckling. "But it's a holdover from when we were kids and my parents needed to get us out and get the stuff under the tree so we could open presents all night long and sleep late."

She had to work hard not to cry. "That sounds wonderful."

He glanced at her, his mirth fading a little as he realized he'd struck a chord. "It's tradition now. We still go out and have a snowball..." His voice faded. "Are you okay?"

No. She wasn't okay. She was envious and empty and emotional. "You have no idea how lucky you are," she said softly. "I've always wondered what the big, happy families were like."

"They're great," he said, splitting his attention between her and the road. "I know I'm lucky."

"And..." She had to ask. Had to. "You want a family of your own, don't you?"

He swallowed, his expression shifting. "I take it your childhood wasn't so happy. Tell me."

Of course he wouldn't share his dreams about creating a family of his own. Not with a woman who obviously could never qualify for that job. Her bloodline would have no place in a family like his. That's what Joshua had said, over and over again.

"My childhood was...cold." She gave her arms a rub, the chill of the subject all too familiar. "We should be there soon. Where to first? The Pug families?"

He tapped the brakes and slowed at an intersection. "You should talk about it," he said. "My sister, Nicki, is a shrink. She'd tell you to talk about that childhood to make it go away."

"My childhood was fine," she said coolly, turning from him. "Now let's just focus on finding Dr. Greenberg, okay? The sooner I can close this chapter of my life, the better chance I have for starting a new one."

And she couldn't forget that, not for one minute.

CHAPTER 11

When I'm on a job like this," Marc told her as they reached the outskirts of a small but thriving coastal city centered around a horseshoe-shaped marina, "I like to sniff around. We'll keep a low profile, just a couple of quiet American tourists."

"Looking for a bioterrorist."

He shot her a look. "You believe that now?"

"I don't know what I believe." She dropped back on the seat rest, letting out a heavy sigh.

"There's plenty of time to turn back, get on a plane, and go home. Or Paris, if that sounds like a better plan."

A smile lifted her lips. "You could do me a favor and not be so damn sweet."

"Sorry."

"I don't want to like you," she chided.

That made him laugh. "That makes two of us."

"I know," she said softly. "I don't blame you."

He didn't understand the comment, so he gestured toward the town.

"Looks a lot like Marblehead and Gloucester," he said, taking in the waterfront atmosphere as they meandered closer to the heart of the city.

"Or Bangor, Maine," she added, indicating the pastel walk-up Victorian houses with bowed windows that lined each road, the first levels all shops and restaurants catering to tourists and, more likely, day-trippers from Belfast or even up from Dublin.

"Don't think we're going to run into any pharmaceutical companies up here or international conferences on botulism," he said. "So don't get your hopes up that there's a simple explanation."

"My hopes aren't up."

He pulled into a parking lot near the heart of the harbor, squinting into the sun to look around and memorize their location. "Let's see what we can find out."

They got out and started down a narrow main street, the salt air much more intense here than it was in Belfast, and warmer, thanks to the sun. The weather brought out lots of locals and tourists, and the shops had opened their doors and put items for sale in the street.

They passed a few cafés and food vendors, the smell of coffee and pastries mixing with the brine in the air.

"Have you heard of the needle and the haystack?" she asked.

"Have some faith and patience, Dev," he said, sliding an arm around her and tucking her neatly into his side. "She isn't going to walk out the door of one of these stores and magically appear."

Sea breeze and sunshine made a picture-perfect day for touring a seaside resort, but not, it seemed, for finding missing persons. After a few hours of walking every cobblestone and brick, they'd stopped in multiple eateries to quietly chat up the locals and tracked down every lead Chessie could send their way. They even visited a small kennel where they saw some cute dogs, but they met no one who might have contacted a microbiologist in North Carolina and arranged for her to fly to Belfast.

They finally ate a late lunch in a pub, where they ordered a pint they both deserved and asked the waitress for a local phone book so Marc could peruse it while they ate.

"We've been to the three Pug name families," Devyn said, shaking her head at the phone book like it was a lost cause. "And the breeders. What are you looking for?"

"Boxing."

She lowered her sandwich to her plate, frowning. "Boxing as in…" She made a fist and punched the air.

"Yep. We're thinking 'pug' not 'puge.'" He pronounced it with a long vowel and soft g. "Like pugilist."

"A boxer," she said, her eyes bright. "See what you can find."

He did, skimming through the business section looking for anything related to boxing. "Here's a trainer, Padraig Fallon. Not too far from here, on the outskirts of Bangor. Other than that, there are some boxing rings in gyms but nothing specific."

"We can try," she agreed. "Nothing to lose."

"Look." Marc turned the book and pointed to the address. "He's in building number seventeen."

"And the e-mail address was puggaree17." She lifted her mug in a mock toast. "Well done, Sherlock."

When they each sipped, he held her gaze, something tightening in his gut. Lower.

Of course lower. Devyn Sterling was a gorgeous woman, as perfect as he liked his women to be, but perfection usually went hand in hand with misery and heartache, and he'd had enough of that in this lifetime.

He looked away, paid the bill, and hustled her out, ignoring the little flash of disappointment in her eyes.

A few minutes later, they met Padraig Fallon, a fireplug of an Irishman with clear eyes and spare words. Marc pretended to be an amateur boxer on holiday, looking for a possible place to work out, and while he talked to Padraig and tried to understand an incomprehensibly thick brogue, Devyn looked at his trophies and pictures, then spent a few minutes in the back office talking to Mrs. Fallon.

When she came out, she gave Marc a little head shake, a silent "nothing here."

He was already feeling the same way after a conversation with the former professional boxer, and the frustration at the futile investigation of the day made him skip further questions. Instead he joined Devyn as she studied some yellowed photographs of a much younger Padraig in shorts and boxing gloves.

"I think we're wasting our time here," she said. "We should get back to the Europa to see if Sharon's checked in. Maybe she came back a day early." But he could tell from her voice that she doubted it as much as he did.

"Don't be frustrated. This has been a purposely lowkey search. If she doesn't show up, we can come back and start asking more specific questions."

They left and headed back to the car, taking a different

route through the more residential area, turning a corner, and smelling curry. This street held all businesses, doors open to retailers selling glittery jewelry, brass art, and porcelain pieces with a heavy Indian influence.

The strings of a sitar and bells played from speakers placed over the door of one storefront, and at another, a woman in full Indian garb set small tables for lunch, smiling up at them as they passed.

In his pocket, his phone vibrated. "Maybe another lead from Chessie," he said, taking it out and trying to decipher the caller ID in the sunshine.

"Who is it?"

"Not sure. Hello?" They slowed down in front of an empty table at a café.

"Mr. Rossi? Thomas from the Europa here." The concierge who'd let him check out the bags.

He gave Devyn's arm a squeeze and nodded. Maybe Sharon *had* come back a day earlier. They needed something to break in their favor. "What've you got?"

"The bags you had under watch? They're gone."

"Really." Marc held up a finger to her and stepped away, not wanting to relay anything to Devyn until he had the full story, but she was already drawn to a rack of colorful scarves at a shop door.

When he was out of her hearing range, he asked, "Did Dr. Greenberg check in, then?"

"On the contrary. We had a bit of a fluffle here trying to figure out what to do with the note."

"The note?"

"The doctor left a note for a guest, but there is no guest by that name."

"What's the name?"

"Devyn Sterling. The front desk brought it to me, or I suspect it would've just been tossed as so much rubbish. Since you'd asked about Dr. Greenberg, I kept the note for you, figuring you could tell the doctor that the note wasn't delivered."

Marc was quiet for a second, processing this.

"You are interested, aren't you? 'Cause it might get *lost*."

Extortionist. "I'm very interested," Marc assured him. "Please don't let it get lost."

"Will do, sir."

"As far as Dr. Greenberg, you're absolutely sure she hasn't checked in?"

"She?" The concierge gave a dry laugh. "Dr. Greenberg was as much a man as you and me."

A man? "Did you see his ID? You're certain it was the right person you gave the bags to?"

"He had the ticket—I had to give him the bags."

He glanced over at Devyn, who was already in a conversation with the shop owner, animatedly discussing a long piece of black and yellow material. "Okay, thank you, Thomas."

"Cheers."

He signed off and turned to Devyn. The shopkeeper stepped inside, so he came up behind her, possessive hands on her waist, but before he could tell her his news, she held a small sign up to his face.

"I found another needle."

Puggaree—any color—£5.

He held on to his bad news while they chatted with the shop owner, and all they came away with was a pretty black and gold silk scarf that Marc bought for Devyn after the owner informed her it was a classic Indian design symbolic of good fortune.

Well, they'd need a little of that.

Devyn fingered the creamy silk around her neck and shoulders as they left, her shoulders slumping as though weighed down by defeat.

"At least tomorrow's Thursday," she said as they walked to the car. "And I know she's coming back to the hotel."

"Maybe not." He hated to break this news, even more when she looked up with concern in her eyes.

"What do you mean?"

"The call I got before you started sleuthing around the shop? It was from the concierge." As he told her what he'd learned, the sun slipped behind a cloud, and Devyn's eyes grew as gray as the sky.

"A man took her bags and left a note for me?"

He nodded. "It could be a trap just to get you again."

But she stood rooted to the spot, her eyes searching his face, her expression stricken. "What if both my biological parents are criminals?" she asked, her voice barely a whisper.

"Isn't that what you're so determined to find out?"

"What does that make me?"

"Come on," he said, attempting to guide her across the street to the lot where he'd parked, a strong arm over her shoulders, but her legs moved like they were leaden.

"They're my biological parents," she said. "They *are* who I am. They have *everything* to do with me."

"It's just genes and DNA, not your character, not your soul," he told her, the words sounding hollow as he said them.

Family is who you are; he knew it, and she did, too.

He unlocked her door, his gaze hard on her as she folded into the passenger seat. He jogged around to the right side, opened the door and slid in, key poised to start the ignition.

"Really, Dev—"

"Neither one of you should move."

Devyn let out a shriek at the man's voice, while the only muscles Marc moved were his eyes as he gazed into the rearview mirror.

The boxer had followed them here.

"Hello, Padraig," he said calmly, lifting both hands to show he wasn't armed.

The older man didn't have a weapon, at least not aimed at them, but his hands were deadly enough, and they rested like huge slabs on the backs of their seats, ready to attack.

"I have information you want."

Marc stole a glance at Devyn, who sat stone still, eyes wide.

"No need to break into a car to give it to us," Marc said.

"I didn't want to be seen talking to you," he said, his words running together like brisk Irish breezes.

"Why not?" Marc asked.

"Because it would be very dangerous for . . . someone," he said, drawing out the word "dangerous" with a guttural inflection.

"Who?" Marc inched around, burning the man with a look.

But Padraig's attention was on Devyn. "She wants your phone number."

Devyn visibly paled but didn't respond.

"Dr. Greenberg," he said in response to a question she didn't have to ask. "She wants to get in touch with you."

"Okay," Devyn said quietly, reaching for her bag. "I'll write it—"

"No, just tell me. I'll remember."

Devyn glanced at Marc, uncertainty in her eyes. He gave a nod, sensing she needed a little coaxing.

She said the phone number once, slowly, and Padraig nodded. "Now I have a message for you from her," he said.

Devyn leaned forward. "You do?"

Marc put his hand on the seat, looking hard at Padraig. "It better be an explanation about where she is and what she's doing, and why someone attacked Devyn in an alley last night and mentioned her name."

"I can tell you where she is," the man replied. "Finding out the rest will require you to go there."

Marc blew out a breath, but Devyn quieted him with a wave. "Please tell us."

"Enniskillen," he said.

"Who are you?" Marc demanded. "How do you know her?"

"Where is Enniskillen?" Devyn asked, as though Marc hadn't spoken.

"Devyn, we're not going anywhere until we find out who sent us and why."

Padraig lifted a shoulder as if he expected this, then reached into his pocket. Marc braced to get his own gun. But all Padraig pulled out was a photograph, an older picture, taken before color printers and digital cameras.

Devyn turned and took the picture, the little bit of color left in her cheeks draining away. "Oh, God."

"Your graduation day?" Padraig asked.

She nodded.

"I guess she was there, then."

Devyn brought a shaky hand to her mouth, looking at him, her eyes filling. "How did you get this?"

"She gave it to me as a way to convince you to go."

Devyn studied the picture, then the man who'd given it to her. "What is this all about? Marc's right—we need to know something before we go."

The collar of a beat-up peacoat brushed against the few hairs he had left as he leaned forward, the thick fingers tightening on the seat. "You'll find your mother in Enniskillen," he repeated. "I've a sense she'd like to meet you before she dies."

Devyn responded with a gasp.

There was no way he'd convince her to ignore this lead, that much Marc knew. "Where do we go when we get there?"

"Someone will meet you when you find the notes."

Jesus, this was getting ridiculous. "What notes?" Marc demanded, leaning forward and itching to get his weapon. "Just spell it out and quit the cloak-and-dagger business. Devyn's traveled across the ocean to find Dr. Greenberg, so just tell us where, when, and why."

Padraig ignored the order. "Just go there. It'll be clear to ya." He inched to the side door and started to climb out. Halfway, he paused, dipped his head back down, and stared at Devyn.

"You know, miss, you favor your mother much more'n your dad. At least, on the outside."

That was it, Marc knew. She'd go anywhere he said now, no questions asked. And Padraig Fallon was gone before Marc could ask anything at all.

CHAPTER 12

Devyn damn near vibrated all the way back to Belfast. Padraig's parting shot had hit her hard, and it took all of Marc's willpower not to pull over and take her in his arms until she did what he suspected she wanted to do—sob. To her credit, she didn't cry.

She didn't talk, either. Or look at him. What she did was stare at that picture and occasionally give in to a shiver despite the fact that the windows were closed and no air-conditioning chilled the car.

Near the hotel, she finally took a deep breath and looked at him. "I'm going. You know that, don't you?"

"I figured that."

"She..." Her fingers grazed the picture of a teenage girl in full high school graduation garb crossing a stage to receive a diploma. It had been taken from quite a distance. "I have to go and find her."

And he had to be very careful with how he proceeded. She was emotionally raw, obviously clinging to a hope she'd tried to talk herself out of, and they had nothing but questions.

"Before we—you—make any decisions, we should think this through. We don't know who Fallon is, what his agenda is."

"She's in trouble."

"Possibly. Or it could be a trap to get you where they want you."

She closed her eyes, not about to be talked out of a decision she'd already made. "She's...followed me. She knows me. She wanted my phone number."

"And she appears to have been at your high school graduation." He waited a beat. "The operative word being *appears*."

When she didn't reply, he reached over to her and said, "You know we can figure this out."

She turned, blinking as though trying to bring herself back to the moment, then nodded. "I'm going to Enniskillen."

Not until they had more information, she wasn't. "Devyn, listen to me. Several unsavory characters have suggested you leave, to no avail. Now this guy produces a picture that, frankly, anyone could have taken—"

"This is me, Marc." She waved the picture.

"Anyone could have taken *of you*," he finished.

"But anyone didn't. Sharon Greenberg did. On the back, in handwriting, it says 'Rose on her Grad Day.' "

He frowned. "Rose?"

"On my birth records, it says Rose Devyn. She named me before giving me up. My parents have never called me anything but Devyn. No one has. No one...until now."

"Still—"

"It isn't the first picture," she said, cutting him off. "I think"—her voice finally cracked—"she needs me."

"Or someone does. And they know just how to get you."

She just closed her eyes, unwilling to discuss it.

"This is really the first concrete lead I've had," she said when they reached the hotel.

"No, you had word that her bags were here. Now they're gone."

"And going to Enniskillen is exactly what you've been trying to do—get me to leave Belfast." She wasn't listening to him. "I don't know why you wouldn't just agree to go."

"Let's go read this note left by the man who took the bags."

"Maybe it's one of the notes that Fallon guy says we need to have to find her."

He nodded, considering that. "Maybe it is."

Parking the car, he turned off the ignition and sat still for a moment, listening to his gut. "After we read the note, we can reassess." He turned to her, reaching for her hand to make his point. "But I have to ask you, for your own safety, please let's not go running to Enniskillen. At least wait until morning, until I have more information on Padraig Fallon. Until we know more."

"Where *is* Enniskillen?" she asked.

Nope, she wasn't hearing a word he was saying.

"I'm pretty sure it's in the middle of Northern Ireland, maybe a little closer to the western border. We'll have to get some intel on the place before we make any decisions."

Her eyes sparked bright blue. "So it's only a few hours' drive?"

"Devyn." Her name came out harshly, and she blinked at him. "You're not listening."

"I just can't believe it," she said, lifting the picture to her chest, tears threatening again. "After all these years. If she needs me, if she's in trouble, I have to go, Marc. I have to."

"I can understand how you feel, Dev—"

"No, no, you don't." She pushed his hand away. "You can't possibly understand how I feel. Not with your big, perfect, happy family that works together and plays together and still has Christmas dinner together. No. You don't understand."

"But I—"

"Either go with me to Enniskillen or get the hell out of my way."

As he turned the engine off, she flung open her door, almost getting out before he grabbed her arm.

"I'm serious, Marc," she ground out, trying to wrest free of his grasp. "Help me or leave me—those are your only two options. Our deal still stands. I'm willing to pay you with information on Finn."

He tightened his fingertips and inched her closer. "If I wanted, I could have it by now. I know your information is in your suitcase."

She remained very still, barely breathing. "Then why don't you take it?"

"I want to help you." He waited a beat, their gazes locked and steady. "My way. The smart way. Maybe take an hour, a night, but figure out what we're doing and why."

She shuttered her eyes, a silent consent. He released her arm and she instantly climbed out of the car. He did the same, meeting her at the back.

This time he didn't fight the urge, pulling her into an embrace that let him feel those vibrations humming through her. "Don't, don't be impulsive. It could get you killed."

"That's like asking me not to breathe." Against his chest, he felt her shiver.

"Are you cold?" he asked.

"I'm always cold," she admitted. "I've been cold since I was born."

He draped an arm around her, snuggling her against his chest. "Let's get inside and get warm and safe, and pick up that note."

She didn't argue, and they walked to the back entrance, toward a long corridor of meeting rooms that led to the lobby. As they reached the glass doors, a man came out, holding the door to let them in, watching Devyn as he did.

Marc wanted to catch the man's eye and nod a thank-you, but his gaze never left Devyn.

"Come on," he whispered as he guided her into the hotel and down a wide corridor, hesitating near an elevator, considering a change in plans. They could take this back elevator instead of the one in the middle of the lobby, lock her in the room, and he could get the note.

And she might be gone when he got back.

"How do you think Padraig knew?" she asked, her gaze wandering toward a ballroom draped with white netting and stars, obviously the site of a wedding later that evening.

"Million-dollar question, sweetheart. You've asked a lot of people about Dr. Greenberg in the past few days. I suspect the wrong people." He tucked her closer, scanning the people in the lobby, on guard for anyone or anything that seemed out of place. But tourists and guests gathered in groups, many in formal wear for the wedding, a festive buzz in the air.

At the front desk, they waited a few seconds for the next clerk, then separated as Marc stepped forward to speak to the woman who waved him over.

"Marc Rossi, I'm a guest."

"I recognize you, Mr. Rossi. Is everything in order with your room?"

"Thomas, the concierge, left a note for me."

Out of his peripheral vision, he saw a man texting into a cell phone approach Devyn. Marc turned to look, just as the man bumped into her, his gaze glued to the screen.

"Oh, excuse me," they said simultaneously, and instantly Marc moved to her, his hands on her shoulders to get her away.

"So sorry, lad," the man said in thick Irish, lifting the phone in apology. "My fault entirely."

Marc bumped the man's hand as it came back down, knocking his phone to the ground. A flurry of apologies from her, from him, as Marc and the man both bent to retrieve the phone. Marc reached the device first, and as he lifted it, he read the screen.

They're at the desk now.

Marc's head shot up as the other man snatched the phone immediately darkening the screen as they both came up. He muttered a few more apologies, backing away quickly.

"Mr. Rossi?" the woman at the desk called. "I have that package you were looking for."

His arm firmly around Devyn, one eye on the man with the phone as he returned to the desk to take a plain white envelope the woman held.

"Uh, one more thing," Marc said quietly, leaning in for complete privacy. "I'd like another room." Because anyone could know their room number by now, and that was the last place they were going to go. Next to him, Devyn gave him a surprised look but didn't question him in front of the clerk.

"Use the credit card you have on file, put the room under the name M. Burns, and give me a room key right now, just slide it across the desk, please."

The young woman did as she was told, completely discreet.

He thanked her and stepped away, holding the envelope, hiding the key, and nudging Devyn toward the bank of elevators.

"Can I see it?"

"Not here. We're being watched."

He felt her small intake of breath, but she didn't look around, just kept step with him. "How do you know?" she whispered.

"I just do." He smiled, acting as though nothing were wrong. "We'll be in the elevator in one minute. You can read it then. I know you're dying to."

Just as they reached the bank of elevators, another man approached, pressing the call button as Marc checked him out. Medium height, early twenties, classic Irish face and carrot-colored hair, seemingly not interested in them as he shoved his hands into the pockets of his khakis and pursed his lips, blowing a silent whistle.

The bell rang and the doors opened, the entire car

filled with white lace and the sound of giddy, nervous laughter, reminding Marc of the ballroom set for a wedding downstairs.

The bride had arrived.

Behind her, a photographer held up a camera, his shot of the bride aimed right at them. Marc nudged Devyn quickly to the left, trying to get both of them out of the picture, the flash momentarily blinding.

Someone called out, and a camera flashed again. Devyn and Marc stepped far to the side to let the bride out of the elevator, and she was instantly surrounded by a crowd, excitement rising up from the group.

He managed to get Devyn around them and into the elevator as the doors wobbled to a close, the bride and her spontaneous entourage blocking the other man who'd waited.

Marc leaned on the Close Door button, willing the rubber strips to roll toward each other. Just as the doors were about to seal shut, a hand shoved in between and forced them back open with a clunk.

Damn it. Tension coiled through him as the redheaded young man stepped inside. Marc purposely waited until the guy chose a floor. Four. Where their first room was.

Without hesitation, Marc stepped in front of Devyn, blocking her in the corner to press floor three. The young man took note of the floor but didn't react. Then he turned, pinning his gaze on Marc, the challenge in his eyes sending Marc's hand closer to the Glock hidden on his hip. The elevator was small, wood and glass—the worst possible place to fire a gun.

The car thudded to a stop at the third floor. Marc led Devyn out and away from the car, relieved when the door closed. He had to act, fast.

"Go to three-fifteen, and don't move," he said, slapping the card key into her palm. "Chain the door, and don't stand in front of the door or window. Don't let anyone in but me."

Her eyes were saucers now. "Why?"

"Just do it, fast." He gave her a little shove, nodding toward the sign that indicated where 315 was, just a few doors away.

The minute she was in the room, he jogged toward the stairwell, taking the steps two at a time, reaching the fourth floor in seconds. He eased the door open silently and peeked around, just in time to see Red approaching 412, Marc's room.

With a fucking key.

He inched out, ready to time his attack for the instant the other man had one hand on the card key and the other on the knob, but suddenly the guy stopped, reached into his pocket, and pulled out a phone, reading it.

"Jesus," he mumbled. "They fucking moved."

Marc backed behind the door as the kid started toward him, holding the heavy metal door so it closed without making a sound.

Back in the stairwell, he pressed against the wall, deep into the corner.

If the door didn't open in three seconds, he'd run downstairs and meet the elevator when it stopped at the third floor.

The door popped open loudly.

The man took a few steps down, completely unaware that Marc hid behind him. Then he stopped and took out a cigarette, obviously not in any hurry.

A match flared, bathing the shadows in an orange rush,

the sulfur smell taking over, then a thick waft of cigarette smoke. Marc waited until the nicotine hit his brain, then moved silently behind the guy until his weapon touched the red hair.

"Jesus!" The man jumped and spun around, the cigarette flying as he grabbed for the railing to keep from falling. "Fuckin' A, man."

"Who you working for?"

His eyes narrowed at Marc. "The hotel."

"Doing what?"

"Security."

"Does that include breaking into rooms?"

"If there's a problem." He lifted his hands and backed up toward the stairs he'd just descended. "Back off, man."

"Who sent you to four-twelve?" Marc demanded.

"Front desk. Guests moved—we need to be sure everything's gone from the room."

"So if we call the front desk right now, they'll confirm that?"

"Of course they will."

Marc held out his left hand, his right holding the pistol over the man's heart. "Give me your phone. Take out a gun and I pull this trigger."

The young man reached into his pocket and produced the phone.

"Put it on speaker and call the front desk."

The man glanced at the phone but did nothing.

"Now!" Marc ordered.

He pressed one button; then his hands started shaking, obviously an act. He fumbled the phone and dropped it, looking at Marc.

"Sorry," he said. "Let me get it."

"Get this." Marc slammed his knee up, nailing the guy in the groin and sending him straight backward down the stairs. He landed at the bottom, curled in half, moaning.

"Who do you work for?" Marc demanded, hustling down the steps to get in his face.

The phone lay next to his head, buzzing with a text. With the gun at the guy's head, Marc picked it up and read it.

Did you deliver message to 412?

"What message?" Marc demanded.

He had seconds. Seconds to get what he could out of him, then he had to get Devyn. Someone else could know what room she was in.

Lifting his right hand, Marc smashed the gun into the man's face, earning a low growl of misery and causing some pain but not nearly enough to knock him out. Under him, the other man writhed, one hand out to the right but smart enough not to take a swing at someone who pinned him with a gun.

"Who sent you?" Marc demanded, raising his hand again.

"I...I...don't know. I swear to fucking God, I don't know."

The gun came down again, no easier this time, smacking flesh. "Next time I shoot it."

"I swear...I don't know the guy's name."

"He just texted you."

"I took his money." A bruise darkened over his eye, angry and red.

"To do what?" Marc demanded.

"Tell her..." Blood oozed from a cut on his lip. "To leave."

"Why?"

He looked terrified, tears building. "I swear to God, man, I don't have a clue."

"Give me a name." As Marc readied for one more hit, the man's arm came up, smashing the burning cigarette onto the back of Marc's hand.

"I don't fucking know!" he insisted over Marc's hiss of pain.

He had no more time for this clown. "Tell him she got the message, and if anyone comes near her again, they're dead."

Marc gave him one more vile look, bending over to take the phone from the floor and the room key that had fallen next to it, then backed down the stairs, catapulting through the door when he reached it.

The hall was empty.

At 315, he rapped twice. "It's Marc."

No answer.

Son of a bitch, did they beat him here? "Devyn?" he called, knocking again.

Still no answer.

He glanced at the key he'd taken and stuck it in the reader, getting an instant green light and access. A master. Whoever wanted to warn Devyn had definitely infiltrated the hotel staff.

He pushed the door open, snapping the security latch. "Devyn!"

She peeked through the two-inch opening, her face bone white.

"What's the matter?" he asked.

She closed the door partially, then opened it for him, stepping back to let him in. She held the envelope in one hand, a piece of paper in the other.

"What does it say?" Whatever it was, it couldn't be good.

"Absolutely nothing. It was blank."

CHAPTER 13

Sharon touched the switch and waited for the familiar flicker of milky yellow fluorescent lights to illuminate the two lab tables and glass-enclosed shelves that ran alongside the row of airtight coolers against the back wall of the room. The basement, not ten by twenty feet, had become her workplace for the past several weeks.

Stuffing her fingers into sticky latex gloves and pulling them tightly over the cuffs of her lab coat, she checked her mask, grateful that it not only blocked a deadly spore from finding its way into her system but also covered the distinct smell of wet earth that permeated the basement walls. From the cemetery, no doubt. So close to this house, so full of tens of thousands of dead Irish men and women.

The little people who thought they were dying for a cause.

She slid clear goggles over her eyes and crossed to the coolers, her sneakers making no sound. Using a key to open the first cooler, she tugged the handle until the air-tight rubber strip made a suctioning noise, assuring her that the contents inside were sealed.

The bacteria was growing nicely. She peered at the blackened dishes, needing no microscope to tell her that she was looking at raw botulinum toxin, grown from spores harvested from Irish soil.

"Got anything yet?"

She jumped at the voice, nearly dropping the dish.

"Jesus Christ, Baird," she mumbled behind her mask. "You want to kill me?" She turned to see him, bare face, bare hands, no lab coat. "Or yourself?"

"I thought they weren't toxic yet."

She lifted the petri dish. "This one is. Get suited up and I'll show you."

He left and she breathed into her mask, her body tensing as usual around this deadly young man. She forced herself to relax, setting the dish back in its proper slot.

She slid the microscope out and switched it on, finding a glass plate and swab. Baird would want to see for himself, of course. He was, after all, the paying client.

"I don't have good news for you," Baird said as he returned, a mask hanging around his neck as he tugged on some gloves.

Don't react, Sharon. Don't take the bait. "Does that mean there hasn't been another deposit in my account?"

"The money is there," he said coolly. "You know damn well it is because you logged into your account today."

No secrets here. She couldn't forget that. "Then what's the bad news?"

"It's about the young woman on your tail."

She looked up, surprised at how much his next words mattered. "Yes?"

"She's a wily one, it seems."

It's in the blood. "How so?" She lifted the petri dish full of deadly toxins.

"She's working with someone."

Her fingers tightened on the glass, but her voice was utterly unconcerned. "What do you mean, working?"

"Working to find you."

A lifetime of freezing out emotion took over by instinct, icing down the tendril that threatened to wrap around her heart. *No feelings.* They were dead, like the people buried in the cemetery next door. "Who is it?" she asked.

"We don't know, but he pistol-whipped one of our men."

Oh, sweet Jesus. This was not good. "Did your runner get the message to her anyway?"

"We shall see, won't we? What do you have here?" He pulled the stool out, taking it for himself without even offering it to her, his hands greedy for the microscope.

"Be careful," she chided. "What we have is phase two of the project. As you know, the spores were easy to harvest. But now we've grown bacteria, and this is when they start to become dangerous."

"If I touched one?"

"Nothing would happen, unless you had an open sore. This has to be ingested, but in this form it is not easily ingested."

He looked up, excited. "So it's nearly ready to go?"

"The chain is thickening nicely."

He had no idea what she was talking about, which was exactly how she liked it. Fighting a smile behind her mask, she continued. "The light chain of the type A toxin degrades the SNAP-25 protein, and the SNAP-25 protein is required for the release of neurotransmitters from the axon endings."

He blew out a disgusted breath. "I don't care. How soon will we be ready?"

"You want toxin purified and stabilized to work, not one that will be like what the Shinrikyo tried in Tokyo back in the early nineties, correct?"

"Did you do that, too?" He sounded impressed.

"I can't take credit for that." But they'd asked her, that was for sure. "And I assume your client wants to transport this material into an aerosol that will impact a large segment of the population."

"Impact…"

"Paralyze and kill, Baird," she said, impatience in every word. "Aerosol or not?"

He pushed off the chair and left the room, returning a few seconds later with a large crate that he dumped on the table. Opening the lid, he pulled out a long silver canister with a black top. "Aerosol."

That would do the job. "I'll have quite a bit of work to do to get this into a gas that fits in there."

"And you say that'll take a week still?"

A day, maybe two. But no need for him to know that. Everything had to be lined up just so. "That's what I said."

"Speed it up."

"I fill orders, Mr. Baird, not work miracles."

He dragged off his gloves carelessly and threw them on the lab table. She worked with the dishes for a moment, and right before he left, he said, "I'm going to take care of the girl. Permanently."

The vial in her hand didn't even wobble. "An American woman killed in Ireland would attract a lot of attention. I strongly suggest you use a less high-profile means of getting rid of her and simply get her out of town."

"She's stubborn."

Like her father. "Be creative."

"Trust me, we are."

"Trust you." She gave a scoffing laugh. "That's rich."

He glared at her. "She pissed off one of my men, and I really can't say what he'll do for retribution."

"Don't you have control over your men?"

"We'll take care of her."

She set the petri dish down hard, damn near cracking it. "You do that."

He responded with a slightly surprised look, and she turned to hide any reaction she might have, modulating her breathing as his footsteps landed on the concrete stairs heading up.

She had to *do* something. If they got to her...No, that was just bad on every imaginable level.

Deep in the lining of her lab coat, a soft vibration alerted her. Certain Baird was gone, she took out the phone and read the text, a tight smile pulling. Their network was remarkable, really.

Returning the dishes to their proper places, she locked the cooler and stepped out of the lab, stripping off her coat, goggles, mask, and gloves to properly dispose of them in the bin, unlike Baird.

She locked the door and shuffled through her options again, finding only one, despite the risk of it.

In her second-floor bedroom, she slipped on a Parka, the feeling of silky down always reminding her of another dark day in her past. The day all of this was set in motion. The day she became a criminal.

And a mother.

Quietly descending the stairs, she jumped when Baird stepped out of the first-floor parlor, where several other men were meeting with him.

"Where are you going?" he demanded.

She gave him a haughty look. "I'm not your prisoner, Mr. Baird. And as I'm not in your meeting"—she nodded pointedly to the room behind him—"I'm going for a walk."

"The cemetery's closed."

"I'm aware of that."

"It's not smart to just walk around the Falls Road neighborhood at night. Some of those bastards from Shankill love to cross the Peace Line and harass our girls over here."

"No one will mistake me for one of your *girls*," she assured him. "And I know the safer areas to walk."

He eyed her suspiciously. "Did you finish in the lab?"

"I did what I could," she said, lowering her voice, tucking her hands into the deep pockets of her coat, the outline of her phone pressing against her palm. "Can't rush the process," she reminded him. "Good night, Mr. Baird."

"How long will you be gone?"

She just closed her eyes and shook her head, like he was nothing more than a nuisance to her.

Without another word, she continued to the door, aware that he watched her. She walked out, the crisp night air a welcome sensation on her face. She splashed through a puddle as she marched down the hill to Milltown Road, away from Liam Baird's house.

With each step, she played out what she would say when she made this call.

No words sounded quite right in her head.

She followed the road to a busier area, where more traffic made her feel less vulnerable, the grounds of Milltown off to her left, some shops, more houses, and pubs to the right. A young couple passed her, nodding, and then two men, both on cell phones, one rambling in an accent so thick it was unintelligible to her. She glanced behind her and saw no one, picking up her pace to really get some distance between her and the house.

The smell of fresh paint on a pub wall mixed with the night air and scents of fried food and beer, the mural an homage to the lost hope for a united Ireland.

The image and smells overwhelmed her with a memory of Finn. Amazing how, after thirty years, every once in a while, a sense will awaken a memory. A selective, unrealistic, stupid-as-hell memory of a day with Finn, or a night.

Footsteps behind her pulled her from her reverie. She slowed her pace, and so did the steps behind her. She turned the corner and rounded the building where the fresh mural had been painted. The sound of footsteps followed. She picked up speed and walked back on a different street, and whoever was back there did...not.

After a few blocks, she looked over her shoulder into the dark shadows, seeing nothing move. She kept her pace up, her eye on the walls of the cemetery so she didn't lose track of where she was. She crossed two streets, then Falls Road, and reached what she assumed was the southwest corner of Milltown.

She finally stopped in the shadows, listening. Her follower had given up, and none of the pedestrians who'd been shopping or drinking made it to this remote end of the street, which was lined with parked cars.

After one more furtive glance up and down, behind and around, she dug the phone out, holding it close as she reread the message she'd just received. She inched closer to the high, wrought-iron fence that enclosed this section of the cemetery. The "lesser" were buried here, in mass graves. All those babies, all those victims of plague and poverty. These folks didn't merit a brick wall, just a fence with thick, thorny bushes.

After a moment, she dialed the number, squinting at the words when given the option to call or text.

Text would be the easier way, of course. But would it be as effective?

A nudge was all she needed, and Sharon was just the person to give it.

But something paralyzed her. Once contact was made, life would never be the same. Maybe she should text it. But Devyn would never know who was texting her. What could Sharon say to prove who she was? What would she know about Devyn that no one else knew?

Her birth name. If she had been resourceful enough to dig up long-buried paperwork, she would know that. And Finn wouldn't. If she responded to the name, then it answered a lot of questions, too. It meant Devyn was doing this on her own, and Finn wasn't behind it.

Yes, using "Rose" would be a brilliant move.

Text or call?

She typed a few words, just to see how they looked.

Rose, please go. I need you

Light poured over her, making her jump backward with a gasp.

The high beams of a car parked on a side street bathed her in yellow. The engine revved and the car shot forward, heading right for her.

She started to run, the phone still in her hand, the message unfinished. The car swerved, continuing to head toward her. If it hit her—when it hit her—she'd be smashed against the iron fence.

She turned, unable to let out the scream trapped in her throat as the vehicle picked up speed. She stumbled back, into some brush and the fence, squeezing the phone.

Her hands clutched the phone behind her, squeezing every button on the pad.

The car bore down on her, the engine screaming, not twenty feet away. With one fast move, she whipped her arm backward through the iron rails and released the phone, praying that it would be lost in the brush, destroyed by the next rain, the batteries dead before anyone ever found it.

And as she opened her mouth to scream and held up her empty hands in a last-ditch plea for mercy, she threw out one more prayer. That death wouldn't hurt too much.

CHAPTER 14

It's blank?" Marc reached for the note, cringing. A light sheen of sweat dampened his face and temples, his irises nearly black, adrenaline so thick Devyn could taste it in the air.

"What happened?" she asked, the disappointment of the blank note momentarily forgotten as her gaze moved to his hand, where he shook off the pain.

"Cigarette burn. Son of a bitch got me." He glanced at the paper she held. "Of course it says nothing," he spat. "It might as well have said 'you've been duped.' They wanted to find us. And they did. We have to get out of this room."

She took his hand to examine the burn, sucking a breath at the raw, festering skin. "What son of a bitch?"

"I don't know. But I don't think it's safe to leave the hotel right now."

"Then where do you think we should go?"

In his uninjured hand, he held a cell phone and a room key. "Anywhere we want. This is a master." He nudged her to the door. "We'll go to the fourth floor, get our stuff, and find an empty room. We have to move fast."

She followed him into the hall and to the elevator, instinctively knowing by the fact that he drew his gun and kept it at the ready that it wasn't the time for questions, complaints, or demands.

Thankfully, the hall was empty. At room 412, he used the master and they slipped inside, wordlessly gathering their belongings. In under two minutes, they had their bags zipped and were out the door, headed back down the hall.

"Best bet is right by the ice machine and side door," Marc said. "Gives us easy access and it's the last room they generally book on a floor."

"You know this how?"

He barely smiled, hustling in that direction. "I'm guessing."

No one answered their knock at 435, the room next to the ice and exit. Marc unlocked the door and peeked in, closing it silently. "Suitcase and shoes. Move on."

Directly across the hall, he tried 434, then nudged her in. "No one's coming in here tonight."

Inside, the king-size bed was stripped bare and a second dresser blocked the middle of the room. "They're using it for storage," she said.

"And we're using it for tonight."

Tonight?

But she held the argument inside for the moment. "What if they electronically change the locks?" she asked.

"When we leave, we're not coming back."

Because we are going to Enniskillen. She held back

the words, letting go of her suitcase and slicing him with a demanding look. She'd kept her questions in long enough. "You need to tell me what the hell's going on, Marc."

"You say that like I know." He threw his bag on the bare mattress and checked out the rest of the room, shaking his hand again.

"I think I have something for that," she said, turning to her suitcase. "Let me dig it out."

"It's not serious." He was already moving around the room at warp speed, closing the room-darkening drapes to cut out what little light there was, then grabbing a towel to stuff in front of the door. "No lights," he said in a whisper. "We don't want to alert a sharp housekeeper. No sound, no running water, no nothing."

"For how long?"

"For as long as I say."

Irritation made her squeeze the tube of aloe she'd found. She was trapped with him. He had the keys to the car; he called the shots—he had the power.

Finished setting up the room, he sat next to her on the bed. "Whatever you have, I hope it's strong."

"It'll help," she said, taking his hand and giving her eyes a second to get used to the darkness. "How did you get a master key?"

"How did our mystery man get it is a better question. My guess would be the hotel staff is easily bribed."

"What happened?"

He sucked in a hiss when she dabbed white cream on the festering burn. "He got a call informing him we'd moved, so I got him in the stairway."

She rubbed gently over the wound, holding his hand

with both of hers, aware of his eyes on her. "Looks more like he got you."

He puffed a breath. "He's in worse shape. He said he was sent here—wouldn't tell me who, if he even knew— to deliver a message to you."

"Don't tell me. Leave Belfast."

"Bingo." With his other hand, he tipped her chin up, forcing her attention off his burn and on him. "That doesn't mean leave Belfast and go where they sent you."

"We don't know who 'they' are, Marc."

"*They* aren't good. You need résumés?"

"Then why did the FBI send you here with the same mission?" she countered. "Maybe some of them are good." Like her mother. Maybe.

"To be perfectly honest, the FBI, per se, didn't actually send me here."

She inched back, her jaw loose as this fact landed on her heart and in her head. "What? You lied about that, too?"

"You say that like I'm a pathological liar. The FBI allegedly sent me here, but the directive was given by one man, and one man alone. He was clear we weren't supposed to discuss the assignment with anyone else in his office, and frankly, back then, I didn't have much reason to question it."

"Really? I'd question it."

"Considering who's involved, I didn't."

At first she didn't understand the comment, then his meaning became clear. "Finn MacCauley," she said.

"Yep. When we got the job of getting you out of here, I assumed it had something—I honestly don't know what— to do with them bringing him in. I figured the agent was being cautious because getting a fugitive of his caliber has to be a very high priority for the FBI, despite him saying it wasn't."

A fugitive of his caliber. She tamped down the sensation those words sent through her. "And now what do you think?"

He blew out a breath loaded with frustration and, no doubt, pain he was trying to act like he didn't feel. *Join the party, pal.*

"I don't know what to think, Devyn."

"What I know is it doesn't make sense to hole up in here all night when we have a place to go and try to find out," she said. "Enniskillen. When do we leave?"

He released his hand from her grip and cupped her face. "Impulsive and relentless is a very dangerous combination."

She shook out of his touch, standing for some measure of power to make her argument. "I am not being impulsive. I've followed every move you suggested for the last hour. Day. *More.* Now I want to go, which is exactly what your original goal was with me anyway. Why can't we leave?"

"I'm not sure we'd get through the lobby without being shot."

She closed her eyes and let him pull her back to the bed. He was right, and she hated that.

"It's true getting you out of Belfast was my original assignment," he said, putting a hand on her shoulder to make her face him. "But everything's changed. I need to protect you, first and foremost." She opened her mouth to argue, and he placed a single finger on her lips. "And," he added emphatically, "I promised you some answers about your mother. Let me do that. Please."

She saw something then in his eyes, something more

than determination to get the job done. Could he be genuinely concerned for her? Just then her belly grumbled in protest, and hunger. "I don't suppose you grabbed a minibar key when you got that room key."

He smiled. "No, but I'll break the lock for you and we can dine on peanuts and candy."

"And Guinness." They said it at the same time, and she smiled. "I'll share one with you."

While he used muscle and a sharp tool on his keychain to break open the minibar, Devyn moved to the far corner of the window, squinting out a tiny crack to see outside. Night had fallen, but four stories down was the large balcony of the ballroom, where she saw wedding guests gathering.

She turned at the pop of a bottle top, and the prospect of food and drink.

There were no chairs in the room, just the extra dresser and bare bed, so she met him on the mattress and they settled next to each other, eating and drinking in silence.

"So you think she's been following you your whole life?" he asked, the question squeezing her heart because it was unexpected—and all she really wanted to talk about.

"I have to wonder," she admitted. "She had a picture of me on a bike at thirteen, and another almost five years later. Both taken from a distance. I wonder if she's been visiting Boston and watching me." The thought stabbed her with longing.

Was that what she really wanted? For Sharon Greenberg to secretly care about her? To love her, even from afar?

"Or if Finn has and sent her the pictures."

Oh, God. "I never thought of that." Because she never *wanted* to think of that.

"They could still be in touch, Devyn. For all we know, they could be close. Together, still."

No, it wasn't possible. "I always imagined she had nothing to do with him. You know, like he was a one-night stand. A big mistake in an otherwise well-lived life. I mean, she has a legitimate job, and she was married, but only briefly."

"This is just making you want to find her more, isn't it?"

She handed him the rest of the beer, disinterested in the bitter ale. "Yes. So stop eating and do whatever it is you have to do to get the information you want."

He didn't argue but moved away, silently taking out his laptop, firing it up, and clicking away.

"I've sent a request to the Guardian Angelinos for assistance. Now let's find out where Enniskillen is."

She watched him work, letting her thoughts roam to places she had been effectively refusing to go.

She wanted to kiss him again.

Or did she just want comfort and connection? Warmth. He made her warm, and not just in the obvious way. He made her feel so—

"It's a few hours' drive, a straight shot on a few main highways."

"What kind of town is it?"

"Small. An island in a lake, it appears. Historic. Nothing that screams 'terrorism.' "

She swallowed hard. "Is that what you think this is about?"

He hesitated, considering his response. "I don't think she's making Botox to treat the wrinkled women of Northern Ireland."

His tone said it all. *You can't ignore the obvious anymore.*

"Let's stay here until I get some word from Boston on the town, and on Padraig Fallon. I've asked my sister, Chessie, to do some digging, and she's a freak on the computer. There isn't a database in the world she can't hack, so let's just wait for a while until we know more, okay?"

"Then we'll go?"

He came back around to join her against the backboard. "I have to figure out a way to get us out of here safely."

She nodded as his weight shifted the mattress, making her roll a few inches closer.

"In the meantime, you should rest." He eased her head down to his chest. "I can be the pillow."

She let him comfort her and nestled under his arm. It felt good and right and warm.

"Just rest, Dev."

"What are you going to do?"

"Watch you rest."

She smiled against the cotton of his shirt, the hardness of his muscle pressing her cheek. "You're doing it again," she whispered.

"Calling you Dev?"

"Being sweet."

"Sorry."

"No, you're not."

He chuckled, stroking her hair lightly. "We'll figure it all out," he said, his voice low and reassuring, his touch absolutely magical.

"That's what I'm afraid of," she said. "I'm not sure I want to know all about my mother."

"You're going to pretty extreme lengths to find out something you don't want to know, then."

She sighed. "I have to know, don't I? And I can't help

if I harbor hopes of something…better than what I suspect she is."

"What she is doesn't affect who you are," he said.

So easy for someone like him to say that. "Then you are discounting the power of DNA."

"If she's a criminal, that doesn't make you one." His hand stroked her cheek and rested under her chin, lifting her face toward his. "You are obviously nothing like her."

But he didn't know that. More important, she didn't know that. But she didn't want to argue or plant the seeds for him to think the things that had plagued her for so long. What was she? *Who* was she? Who could possibly want her with that bloodline?

Joshua hadn't.

But Joshua was dead. And she was alive and in the arms of someone…someone kind of amazing.

"What are you thinking, looking at me like that?" he asked, the hint of a smile pulling his lips.

"I'm thinking…" *That I never met anyone quite like you.* "That you are very good at curbing my impulses."

"That's a shame." He glided his thumb along her lower lip. "Because I was kind of hoping you'd have the impulse to kiss me right now."

"I do," she admitted. "And I think I should fight it."

He nodded slowly. "It's a bad idea," he said. "Complicated."

"Stupid."

"Rash."

"Impulsive."

She waited for his comeback, but he kissed her hair, pressing his lips to her forehead with restrained pressure, like it was all he could do, so it would have to be enough.

But it wasn't. Unable to stop herself, she lifted her face so that his mouth met her cheek. He kissed again, this time on her lips.

Or she kissed him. It didn't matter, because her eyes stayed closed and she just gave in to the bone-deep pleasure of connecting mouth to mouth, of sliding her hand over his chest to pull him into her, of blocking out everything except the sweet, sweet sensation of...

His tongue. He curled it against hers, eliciting a soft moan from her throat, easing her against him at the same time, scooting down so they were lined up on the mattress.

"Marc," she moaned into his mouth, knowing she had to stop.

She would stop. In a minute.

He answered by deepening the kiss, opening his mouth, and wrapping her in his arms so securely she felt like she could never fall.

And that feeling gave way to something else, something sharper and needier. Like fire licking at her skin, burning, making her take her leg over his. He stroked her back, dragging his hand over her hip, over her backside, urging her onto him.

Her thigh pressed against his erection, and she heard him suck in a breath, then release a soft moan and her name as he suckled her throat and collarbone, pulling her body over his, taking them to the most natural position.

Natural. Thrilling. And wrong.

But nothing felt wrong about this, Devyn rationalized, arching just enough for her hips to rock against him, for his hard-on to roll against her crotch, for everything in her to invite him to go further.

With his hand behind her head, he pulled her into him

for another kiss, rolling her over, changing their position in one fast move, taking the top, taking control.

Because hers was gone. Above her, he intensified everything. The pressure, the kisses, the touching.

Each breath was more shallow, more impossible as he cupped her breast, then caressed, slow and sure, her nipple instantly hardening to the insane pleasure of his touch.

She had to end this. And she would...as soon as she took one more kiss, let one more wave of sheer dizziness roll over her as their tongues played and his fingers traveled and their bodies moved with an ancient rhythm.

He slipped his hand under her sweater to get closer to flesh. Her stomach muscles tensed as he seared her skin with his palm, breaking the kiss long enough to absolutely slay her with a look of hunger and longing.

"Devyn," he whispered. "I'm not going to stop until you tell me to."

She tried to breathe, but it came out as a ragged sigh. "I want you..." She couldn't finish the sentence.

What did she want? Sex. Him. Comfort. Closeness. *Sex*.

She just moaned, and he took it exactly how she meant it, a plea for more. His hand delved under her bra as he kissed her again, keeping his eyes open, adding pressure between her legs.

Sweet, sweet pressure that made her wet with need and physically incapable of not moving to meet every roll of his hips.

"Your hands are so warm," she whispered.

"It's your body." He pushed her top up, out of the way, unsnapping her bra in front and admiring her as he did.

"I'm never warm."

"This is way past warm, honey." He thumbed her nipple, teasing, torturing, taking his time to make her crazy.

Possessed, she pressed just enough on his shoulder to tell him what she wanted.

He closed his mouth over her breast, sending sparks over her skin, squeezing between her legs, bringing her to the shocking edge of an orgasm.

It controlled her. He controlled her, his hands everywhere, on her stomach, on her jeans, on her zipper. With one more kiss, slow and sexy, rich with meaning and intent, he pushed her jeans over her hips and dipped down to trail kisses on her exposed body.

He kissed over the silk of her panties, slipping his tongue along the lace, sliding his fingers into the tiny strips of satin that held them on her hips.

"Oh my God." Her voice quivered with the feeling, the raw pleasure when his finger touched her.

She threaded her fingers through his hair, added some pressure on his head, and spread her legs enough to draw him closer. With one finger, he pushed the silk aside and drew his tongue along the exposed center, like a hot, wet stroke of fire that made her want to scream.

Blood pulsed and throbbed everywhere. Under his tongue, through every vein, in her head like a drumbeat, keeping the rhythm of his licks. Harder, faster, deeper as he curled inside her and—

Froze, lifting his head.

"What?"

"That's your phone." He gave her a questioning look, ready to ignore the text, but then she remembered Padraig.

"It could be her," she said, easing him off her.

He assisted by reaching over and grabbing her bag and

her phone. Hope surged when the screen said *Unknown Caller.*

Please, please be Sharon.

She sat up, her nakedness forgotten as she pressed the button and read.

Rose, please go. I need you

"It's from Sharon." The words whooshed out in one breath.

Over her shoulder, he read the screen. "How do you know?"

"No one else would call me Rose. That was the name on my birth papers, and no one knows it but her." She started to get off the bed, but he grabbed her arm.

"How would she know you would know it?"

She considered that for a moment, shaking her head. "Marc, I don't know, but I do know what I'm doing next and you cannot stop me. I'm going to Enniskillen."

He blinked as if his head were exploding in frustration. "It could be a trap, Devyn. You don't know what it means by 'go.' Go anywhere. It doesn't say go to Enniskillen. There are a lot of ways to interpret that."

"Well, this is how I'm interpreting it. She sent me a private message and she says she needs me. Add to that the fact that a man who knows a lot more about me than anyone else took great pains to find me today and tell me to go to Enniskillen. If I go there and she's not there, I haven't lost anything."

"If you go there and get killed, you've lost *everything.*"

She met his gaze in a long, silent, visual showdown that she would not lose.

"How do you propose to get out of this hotel without being shot at or followed?" he demanded.

During the silence of her inability to respond, the strains of the wedding music played outside the window. And gave her the answer.

"Did you bring any nice clothes?"

He just frowned, then his expression changed from confusion to a mix of admiration and resignation. "Yeah."

CHAPTER 15

Nothing about Oak Ridge Drive was remarkable. Middle America tucked into the hills and woods. A touch of Southern comfort here and there in the form of red brick and white columns. Expansive manicured lawns, cookie-cutter houses, a bicycle in one driveway, a gardener finishing up a day's work at another.

So, was some lug nut waiting around the corner to attack?

It sure seemed unlikely to Vivi.

This place was Raleigh's version of the Boston suburbs, where she'd landed at the age of ten, after the dark days of being orphaned in Italy. Sudbury had seemed a little like a fairy tale at the time, not as wrenchingly beautiful as her homeland, but it was...home.

Still, the suburbs had their dark side, and that's what had made Vivi itch to run like a city rat. She'd never live in a place like Oak Ridge Drive in Raleigh, North Carolina.

She drove the rental to the end of the cul-de-sac, following the detailed directions Marc had e-mailed her. They included everything, except how to get in, and a warning that the last time Devyn Sterling had visited, the house hadn't been empty.

But the brick ranch house looked deserted today. According to the one person she could find at the university, Dr. Greenberg was on an extended sabbatical, traveling through Europe on a speaking circuit. She had no classes this semester, and her lab was closed.

Vivi parked on the street and headed straight to the front door, not at all sure what she was looking for—just the *unusual*. After her years as a reporter, she had a pretty good nose for finding unusual when it didn't want to be found.

Around the yard, dead autumn leaves formed a brown blanket under the ubiquitous oak trees that gave the street its name. There was no sign of any life at all. No mail, no papers, all the windows closed, blinds drawn in the front, no sign of life.

She rang the doorbell, waited, and after a few minutes and another ring, she rounded the house to the back, inspecting what she could on the way. The last time she broke into an empty house, she nearly ended up dead.

But this time she'd been warned and was armed, so she powered on. The back door was locked, but not dead bolted. It didn't take five minutes to pick the simple latch, making as little noise as possible. Before she went inside, she took out her Glock, racked the slide, then stepped into the kitchen.

After standing perfectly still for five minutes, she felt relatively sure she was alone and dead bolted the door to make sure no one followed her in, then she waited again for any response to the echo of the latch. Nothing.

Setting her tote bag on the floor, she started a slow and quiet search. With each room, she grew more confident she was alone. As she combed every inch of Sharon Greenberg's life, she found nothing too extraordinary. The woman might have had a green thumb, but all the plants were now dead, and she had no obvious family ties, since there wasn't a personal photo in the whole house. A workaholic, Vivi surmised, as most of the household activity seemed to take place in her office.

The room looked the way Marc told her it had when Devyn was last there: laden with files, magazines, and paperwork.

She finished in a spacious master bedroom, clearly added on after the house was built, with a more modern, crisp feel, an oversized fireplace, a luxurious bathroom. And a jewelry safe hidden behind an innocuous door in that luxurious bathroom.

She touched the knob and the safe popped right open. So it was probably a freebie from the builder, or someone had beaten Vivi to the punch, because the velvet posts and hooks for jewelry were all empty.

Maybe Devyn was wrong and the intruder had been a garden-variety thief who'd taken what jewelry he could find and left everything else.

She slid her hands down the sides of the unit, poking into the velvet for a false opening that she knew these things sometimes had. And found one.

With a little "Oh!" of delight at the discovery, she pushed the ledge that ran across the bottom, and it flipped up on an invisible hinge, revealing another compartment.

And, holy shit, there was stuff in there.

Not jewelry, but tiny scraps of paper, handwritten notes

or a letter that had been torn to teensy bits and stored there. A fine chill fluttered down her spine as she touched a few pieces of paper, reading random words like *decision* and *promise* and *never* and *please*....

Shreds of something far more personal and valuable than hidden jewelry. This pile of paper bore the fingerprints of emotion. Someone had torn it in anger, then saved it in remorse. No single piece of paper contained more than two words. Was this *one* ripped document, or many?

She picked up one more piece, blank on one side, and turned it. Her heart stopped and her eyes widened. She'd found the signature of the person who had sent this letter, and everything changed.

Best, Finn.

The paper almost burned her hands. Finn MacCauley had written this diatribe. How old was this? Could this be criminal evidence that could be key to finding a most-wanted fugitive, or was it just a lover's torn missive?

That wasn't her question to answer. This should be turned over to the FBI, stat.

Her hands trembled a little as she carefully fingered the shreds, rationalizations screaming in her head.

She had a possible key to finding Finn MacCauley, right in her hot little hands. These shreds were more valuable than the freaking Constitution to her. To her *business*, which could explode if they brought in a high-profile fugitive.

"I have to keep this," she said, silencing any internal argument. "I can't give this to Lang. Not yet anyway."

Decision made, she turned, looking around for something that could hold the torn treasure. Still holding the find, she headed back into the office and returned to the shelves where she'd seen half a box of standard business envelopes. She pulled one out and tapped the bits of paper into it, her gaze moving around the office, stopping on a wall calendar.

The quintessential image of emerald Irish hills rolling down into a vast spread of bizarre rectangular stones, the words in a Gaelic font: *The Giant's Causeway.*

Wasn't Marc just there yesterday? Sealing the envelope, she walked to the calendar and lifted the page, sucking in a little surprised breath at how familiar it was.

"Too freaky," she whispered, staring at the image of the seaside resort of Bangor, exactly where Chessie had just sent Marc. The month, September, was empty of any notes, except for one date, circled in red. The 17th. Three letters written: PUG.

Something clicked in place. *Puggaree17.* The e-mail Marc had them checking.

She looked to the next page. This one had a church spire over a sweet little village called Enniskillen. She had to squint to read the tiny notations on most of the days in October. Single letters—A, B, B, D, F, G. And every so often, a number sign.

This definitely qualified as *unusual*, so she took the calendar and the precious envelope and headed back out the way she came in, trying to figure out who to share this with.

She knew who *not* to share it with—Colton Lang.

Buttoning his shirt in the pitch-black room, listening to the sounds of Devyn dressing in the bathroom, Marc tried telling himself that getting dressed up and sneaking out of the hotel by blending into a crowded wedding was

a smart way to achieve what still was his original goal—
to get Devyn out of Belfast.

So of course he hadn't put up a fight, and it wasn't just
because he was temporarily blinded by lust.

Although he was that, too.

He was going along with her escape plan because of
another male weakness he harbored—the need to help
women with a cause. And not just any kind of woman, oh,
no. That would be too easy.

The worst kind of woman—flawless and perfect on the
outside and scarred and wrecked and ruined on the inside.
Marc Rossi to the rescue.

Except hadn't he learned from Laura that he couldn't
fix those internal scars? Women like that despised themselves and were incapable of love. He couldn't make Laura
love herself after her mess of a childhood, but he didn't
accept that fact until the day she stuck her sweet little Ber-
etta 92—the one he'd given her for her birthday—in his
face and damn near killed him.

Because no matter how he'd tried to show Laura he
loved her, she refused to believe that deep inside she was
worthy of that love. So all that effort was wasted.

And she was an embezzler. He couldn't forget that.

Devyn was no criminal, like his ex-wife. But she was
lost, alone, and longing for something he didn't think her
birth mother was going to give her. He could help her find
that out, but he couldn't, absolutely could *not*, let himself
get involved with her.

Rescuing her was not his job. Getting her out of Belfast was.

"Hey, I'd dance with you."

He looked up from the cuff he was tugging through a

sports coat sleeve, his night vision easily strong enough to see the *vision* in front of him.

The *wrong* woman who looked very, very *right* in a short black dress, a deep V at the neckline, the waist tapered to show the curves of her narrow frame.

The memories of the woman he'd married—last seen by Marc on her way to prison—faded instantly. "We'll dance right out the door and to the balcony if your plan works."

"It'll work. It has to." Her whole face lit with a renewed spark for her not-so-secret fantasy for a mother-daughter connection that would erase the pain he sometimes saw in her eyes.

He wasn't going to be the one easing that pain, not in any permanent way. He had to remember that.

No matter how much he wanted to.

"I have an idea about our bags," he said. "Let's stash what we absolutely need into that small carry-on, and I'll just tote it over my shoulder like a camera bag or something. It's not that noticeable."

"And the laptop?" she asked.

"I downloaded everything we might need onto a jump drive and deleted the rest. We'll just leave everything here in the room safe, not that it's any guarantee of safety. Just pack very light. Like, almost nothing."

He indicated her suitcase and went into the bathroom to let her have privacy. Whatever she was hiding in there—her clue to finding Finn—would be going with them to Enniskillen, he supposed. "Just take what's mission critical, Dev."

When he came back out, she was waiting, the little bag zipped up. He took the rest of their stuff and pushed it deep under the bed, although he wouldn't be surprised if it was all gone when they got back. Nothing of earth-shattering value there anyway.

A few minutes later, they were waiting at the service elevator in an empty hallway, to all appearances a couple on their way out for the evening. When the elevator doors opened, the car was empty. Inside, alone, they shared a look.

"Step two accomplished," she said.

He frowned at her. "What was step one?"

"Getting you to agree to this."

With a whisper of a smile, he leaned closer and put a kiss on her forehead. "Evidently I can't say no to you."

"That makes two of us," she said. "Sorry we got so carried away before."

"I'm not." He slipped his free hand into hers. "Listen, don't leave me, not for one millisecond. Is that clear?"

"I promise I won't."

"Do exactly as we planned. Stay to the outside perimeter of the room and keep talking to me or listening. Just fake like we are in the deepest, most riveting conversation of our lives. We don't want to talk to anyone else, and our goal is to get in and out as fast as possible."

"What if someone questions us? Or chases us?"

"Just follow my lead." He added a squeeze to her hand. "Don't question, don't argue, don't act suddenly with a better idea. One of us is in charge, and it's me."

The elevator doors opened to a crowded hall full of wedding guests who had spilled out of the ballroom, which was already noisy from the effects of an open bar, the music in the main room loud enough to make talking out here difficult.

As she scanned the crowd, her gaze stopped at a man standing at the large double doors outside of the ballroom, looking in as he talked on a cell phone.

"Oh my God, Marc, it's—"

Before she had the name out, Marc whipped her in the opposite direction, blocked her with his body, and pushed her into the crowd. "Move!"

CHAPTER 16

I got 'em," Padraig Fallon whispered into his cell phone. "They just got off the elevator, dressed for the wedding."

"The wedding? What the hell for?"

"Blend in, I guess. And they—shit—spotted me. He's taking her farther away."

"That's not a problem, is it?"

The truth was, he wanted them to see him. "Not if they're going to Enniskillen, it isn't. If they go there, stay there, and get lost there, everyone's going to be fine." He scanned the faces again, none familiar, none threatening. "Anyway, I don't care if they see me. It's the others I'm worried about."

And he hadn't been smart enough to dress to fit in, as they had. He'd already gotten some sideways glances from other guests, but no one had spoken to him.

"Are they going outside yet?"

"It's a long way to the parking lot door," he said.

"They've gone into the ballroom, staying at the edge. Probably working their way toward the back balcony." Smart again. If someone was going to take them out right here and now, they'd most likely not be in this wedding room.

Padraig wasn't in the ballroom, and he couldn't bloody well walk in there, either. A cheer went up from the crowd inside as a groomsman took the mike and the dreadful music finally died down. Toast time. A few guests hurried by him to get back inside for the speech, giving Padraig an opportunity to reposition himself and see his targets.

"Okay," he reported. "They're way in the back of the room, slowly working their way past one of the bars. No one seems to have noticed them."

"Can they get to the parking lot from there?"

"The ballroom leads to an aboveground terrace. There are stairs that go down to the side, then around to the lot. Not the easiest way, but smarter for them."

"So he knows what he's doing."

"He's well trained," Padraig agreed. "Former FBI. I surely hope he knows what he's doing."

In his ear, a soft snort. "Now where are they?"

"Still walking...Oh, fuck."

"What is it?"

"Trouble."

A man had risen from one of the tables and kept his head down as he walked to the back of the room, but Padraig recognized the profile.

"What kind of trouble?"

"The kind we don't want."

But the wrong person had his young couple on the

radar, and although they were getting close to the wall of doors that led to the terrace, they might not be fast enough. Padraig had two choices—run into the ballroom, in the middle of the best man's droning toast, and swing all of the attention to him and off them, or haul ass out the back, run around the backside of the building, and somehow get them first.

With no more than a split-second deliberation, he bolted down the hall, thrusting the phone into his pocket without bothering to end the call. He had to sidestep a few surprised guests, but he still had that low-to-the-ground speed that had saved his life on many occasions, in the field and in the boxing ring.

They could have taken this route, but the wedding path was so much smarter and safer, moving through innocent guests instead of by a gunman who could be waiting to take them down. Padraig moved as though a bullet could hit him at any second, because it could.

Using his full body weight, he threw the back doors open, whipping around to the right, and running down the hill behind the hotel, reaching the bottom in seconds, surrounded by Dumpsters and the employee parking lot. The steps that led from the ballroom terrace to the hotel guest lot were thirty feet away, an eternity, even with how fast he was running.

As he ran, he looked up at the railing along the balcony, catching a glimpse of couples leaning over, a few smokers strewn about, no sign of the two he wanted or the man he was relatively certain had them in his sights as well.

He reached the stairs and hesitated in the shadows, hoping he'd see them hustling down, their plan to sneak out executed without a flaw. But no one ran toward him. No one even walked down the stairs.

Enough doors were open to the ballroom that he could hear an outburst of laughter, then applause. Some more talking and another round of applause.

They couldn't have gotten by him, could they? Marc Rossi wasn't *that* good, was he? He couldn't outsmart a guy like Padraig—

The kick from behind hit his kidney at the same moment an arm looped around his neck, cracking it to the right. Fuck.

"What are you doing here?"

Evidently, he *was* that good. "Just making sure you got the message, mate."

"Who are you?"

"Padraig Fallon," he said, the pressure of a pistol at his back replacing the knee.

"Ask him!" The female voice was more distant, even deeper in the shadows, as though Rossi had made her stay back while he did the dirty work.

"How do you know Devyn?" he demanded. "How do you know so much about her?"

Padraig managed to get a look up the stairs and saw movement. Or at least he thought he did. Had Rossi seen it?

"You better get the fuck out of here, lad," he warned.

"Not without answers. You think I'm stupid enough to go exactly where you want us to go without knowing why, who you are, or who you work for?" He yanked Padraig's head farther to the side and jabbed the gun barrel into him. "Let's go. We're gonna talk."

Definitely someone at the top of the stairs. Listening...about to take aim...about to fire.

"You want her to live?" he asked.

Rossi slid his hand around Padraig's throat, curling a finger into the chain around his neck and twisting it like a noose. "You are in no position to bargain, Fallon. I want answers, and I want them now."

The chain snapped and his medal spit off to the side, clunking to the ground. "Someone's about to shoot her."

"And that's why you're sending us to some obscure town across the country?"

"That's why—"

A shot exploded, noise and white light and the whiz of a bullet right next to them. Instantly, Marc thrust him away, so hard Padraig stumbled to the ground, hitting his hip with a bone-jolting smack.

Rossi flipped around, using his body to shield the woman and turning his Glock toward the top of the stairs to take aim. But another bullet whizzed by, the flash showing them the shooter had made it halfway down the stairs.

Rossi was already pushing the woman in the other direction, trying to get her out.

"Padraig, what the hell is going on?" The voice came from the phone in his pocket, still on. He ignored the plea, reaching instead for his weapon, getting it out just as the man on the stairs took another shot at the couple running away.

He could stop this. He could save them, or he could roll into the darkness under the stairs and let them make it on their own. The shooter reached the bottom of the stairs, possibly still unaware of Padraig. He could get one shot, take this bastard down, let the couple get away where they could do no harm.

If he missed, he'd be dead.

He lifted his gun and steadied his arm, waiting for the man to come two feet closer, and pulled the trigger. The bullet went right past the bastard.

Already there were thunderous footsteps as people ran out of the ballroom, some screaming at the gunshots. But right above him, his target, still damn whole, stopped and looked down, recognition darkening his features.

"What the fuck, Padraig Fallon?" He pointed his gun at Padraig's face.

Now he had to kill the guy, no matter what. He shot point-blank, rolling away as he did, catching a glimpse of the former FBI agent looking back from the parking lot to which he'd escaped, just in time to see it all happen.

In front of him, the man slumped to his knees, swearing, as blood gurgled out of his belly.

"You fucker, Fallon," he mumbled, falling facedown. "You fucking bastard."

Padraig ran, knowing that even if he was arrested, it would only mean he'd be detained, not held. He had more clout than all of the police in Belfast.

And he'd done his job—they were off to Enniskillen.

A1 to the M1 to the A4. Marc had memorized the directions and used every brain cell to focus on getting their little rental through traffic, away from any threats, and on to those roads.

Devyn hardly spoke, as if she were in tune with his

bone-deep need to concentrate on the wrong-side driving, the foreign roads, the determination to get the hell out of Belfast.

Sailing along the M1 at top speed and a half hour into the country west of Belfast, they still hadn't discussed what had happened in the shadows of the hotel parking lot. Marc was replaying the scenario in his mind, trying to piece together what didn't fit.

And what didn't fit is that someone tried to kill them, and instead of aiding and abetting that effort, Padraig Fallon shot the assailant and gave them a chance to run. Based on that, and only on that, Marc agreed to follow the man's directions.

"The question is," he mused aloud, finally ready to break the silence, "who's after you, and why?"

"No," she countered. "The question is who's got Sharon, and why does she need my help?"

"We're coming at this from two different angles," he said. "And it makes me wonder if there aren't two different angles."

"What do you mean?"

He didn't answer right away, still mulling it over. "That maybe more than one party is threatening you. Maybe you've walked into the middle of some kind of . . . turf war."

"I don't know," she said, exhaustion coloring her tone. "I'm sorry I convinced you to jump him for answers."

"I'm not." She'd made a compelling argument as they'd worked their way across the ballroom. "Fallon has to know something, and if someone else hadn't tried to shoot at us, I might have gotten the old guy to talk."

"Do you think Fallon was shot?"

"I don't think so, but someone was," he said. "There were, what, two shots?" Then a lot of chaos and Marc had moved on instinct, getting Devyn away from the bullets. "The guy at the top of the stairs was toast at that range."

"Was that the same guy you fought in the stairwell?"

"I didn't get a chance to see. Before we left, I sent a message to Boston asking for a background check on Fallon and a check of the numbers called on the phone I took from the guy who tried to get into our room."

"Maybe we can take a picture of this," she said, holding out her hand and opening her fingers to reveal a small orange and silver medal. "And find out what the symbol means."

"Where did you get that?"

"When you throttled Padraig," she said. "It popped off and I grabbed it."

"Let me see it." Taking it, he glanced at the cross, then back to the road before returning it to her. "He's Protestant—that much is clear."

"From the orange trim?"

"Yeah, and I think the crosses are a little different than the Catholic one. It's something." In his pocket, the phone vibrated. "Maybe that's Chessie."

But it was a male voice that greeted him when he answered, and it surprised him.

"Where are you, Marc?" Colton Lang asked. "Because nobody seems to be able to find you."

"Didn't know anyone was looking, Colt." When the other man didn't respond to that, he continued. "I'm in Northern Ireland, just as we discussed." He glanced at Devyn, hoping she'd understand his vagueness. If Lang knew the secrecy element was gone, he might call Marc back to Boston. Which wasn't happening. He wasn't about to leave Devyn in the middle of this country without protection. "In fact, I'm driving out of Belfast right now."

Meaning, the job he'd been sent to do was complete, more or less.

Still, Colt didn't respond.

"I'm with a lady," Marc said meaningfully. "How can I help you?"

"You can tell me what the hell is going on."

"Can't really do that right now. As I said, I'm not alone." If Colt thought Marc was staying undercover with Devyn, he certainly didn't expect him to discuss the details in front of her, did he? "I'll check in tomorrow."

"So she doesn't know?"

"Not much." He weaved around a slower car and hit the accelerator to chew up the empty road ahead. "Full report tomorrow, Mr. Lang." Then he had an idea. "But while I have you, I ran into someone over here and was wondering if you had any information about him in your files."

"Who is it?"

"A former boxer by the name of Padraig Fallon. Lives in Bangor, east of Belfast. Can you check to see if we've ever done business with him in the past?"

"I can do a cursory check now," Colt said. "Hang on. You can answer questions while you wait."

"Shoot."

Next to him, Devyn fingered the medal, listening to every word he said.

"Has she mentioned her biological father?" Colt asked.

"Not by name." At least, she liked to dance around the subject of Finn MacCauley as much as possible, so maybe that wasn't a lie.

"How about her birth mother?"

Whoa. Where'd that come from? "What about her?"

"Just curious how much information she's sharing with you."

"Nothing too personal," Marc said, the instinct that had kept him alive and on top of his game for so many years urging him to keep this vague. Or just outright lie.

"Has she told you why she's over there, then?"

"On holiday, as we thought," he said. "Anything on Fallon?"

Colt hesitated a long, silent minute. Then, "There's nothing in our records on him, Marc."

"E-mail me if you get anything on him."

"What time tomorrow will you call?"

Marc glanced at her again, catching her eye, his gaze sliding down her face to her mouth. "Late. I'll be busy." Running around Enniskillen, looking for Mom.

"Where will you be?"

He glanced at a road sign, bathed in his headlights, and read it out loud. "Monaghan," he said. "Some sightseeing."

"Just be ready to leave the minute I give you the word," the agent said.

"I may not be able to, uh, extricate myself that easily."

"Well you better be. *You're* not on holiday, Marc."

Don't I know it. "Got it." He ended the call, put the phone down, and reached over to take Devyn's hand. "That was the FBI agent who sent me here."

She threaded her fingers through his. "Nothing on Padraig Fallon?" she asked.

"Nothing at all."

She just closed her eyes and held out the medal, letting

it catch the lights of a passing car. "Twice now this man has tried to help us. He just appears from nowhere, like an apparition, giving us assistance. Like an angel."

"More like a spook." And that, Marc knew, was the piece of the puzzle that didn't fit.

CHAPTER 17

Even Devyn wasn't impulsive enough to suggest they start their search for "notes" the minute they arrived in Enniskillen. It was the middle of the night, and they had to sleep.

They had to sleep *together*.

In the bathroom of the farmhouse-style inn where Marc had managed to get them a room with a fireplace, Devyn slathered a palmful of body butter down her freshly shaved leg. Closing her eyes, she reached for a tiny crystal snifter of Baileys that they'd found in the room and Marc had insisted she take into the bath, with orders to relax.

She was anything but relaxed. Her head swam with so many unanswered questions that she didn't even know how to sort everything out. For one thing, she might meet her birth mother in a matter of hours. And that would put her lifetime of wondering to bed once and for all.

And speaking of bed...there was Marc, right outside the room.

Closing her eyes, the sensations that she'd felt earlier that night rolled over her again, making her melt. The power of his kiss, the certainty of his touch, the delicious, wild ride her body took when he undressed her and... tasted her.

How could she handle this now?

How could she *not*?

She could barely remember the last time she'd made love with Joshua. He'd been perfectly competent, able to elicit an orgasm, yes, but not... heat. And, always, always, the *fight*.

Every single time, they fought over her desire for a baby and his refusal. He lorded the possibility over her head, using her closed adoption as an excuse, then, of course, gloating over the fact that he'd been right.

She had bad blood.

She shook her head, trying to get him out of there. Maybe she didn't have *completely* bad blood. Maybe Sharon...

She stood and grabbed the inn's white bathrobe from the back of the door, easing her arms into the soft terry, tying the belt, and smoothing the V-neck. Her fingers lingered over an embroidered logo on the pocket and then her breasts underneath.

This thing could come off with the flick of a finger.

She towel-dried her wet hair, glancing in the mirror, unable to ignore the pallor of her skin. But there was something else in her face, something unusual. For the first time in a long time, there was a spark in her eyes, like a little gas burner was lit inside her, burning bright. Marc put that there; she was certain of it.

Was it possible she'd come halfway across the world to find her birth mother... and found something entirely unexpected instead?

Opening the door, she froze at the sight. Marc stood in front of the fire, shirtless, his back to her, silhouetted against the fire. Braced on the glossy white mantel, his hands rested inches from a half-glass of whiskey. He still wore the dress pants he'd put on earlier, but the gun and holster were gone.

He pushed off the mantel, stabbed his fingers through his hair with a long exhale, then knocked back the rest of the whiskey.

"Now what makes a man like you sigh with such sadness?"

He turned, a frown drawing his dark brows together, the firelight and sienna-colored walls casting a glow of gold over olive-tanned skin. "I'm not..." He stopped, fighting a smile. "Nothing for you to worry about."

She tightened the robe self-consciously and stepped into the room. "I was thinking about you in the bath."

He just looked hard at her, his eyes like ebony spikes, his jaw tight. "Funny, I was thinking about joining you in the bath."

She laughed, but he didn't even smile, and for some reason, that was just dead sexy. "And?"

"The door was locked."

Her stomach took a ride down to her bare toes.

"Were you thinking the same thing?" he asked.

"More or less." She took a few steps into the darkened room, drawn to the fire. Drawn to him. "I didn't have much...control. Back there in the hotel. I'm..." *Sorry?* No, she wasn't sorry at all. "I'm sure you understand how much I need..."

"Sex," he said.

"I was thinking *comfort*, but call it what you want."

He laughed softly, walking to the bed and grabbing hold of the eiderdown comforter that fluffed over the mattress. "It's called sex. But if it'll make you feel better, I'll just sleep in front of the fire and you can have the bed."

Disappointment fluttered through her when he snapped the cover off the bed.

No, that wouldn't make her feel better. Only smarter and safer. "Of course." At an antique sideboard, she poured another glass of Baileys.

"Not that I wouldn't want to finish what we started, Dev."

The admission turned her insides as liquid as the creamy drink in her glass.

"But I don't want to take advantage of a woman who is seeking *comfort* while all I can offer is *sex*."

Come to think of it, sex would be fine. "I appreciate that." She took her glass to the bed, which he'd covered in a lighter afghan.

"Will that be warm enough for you?"

Not without him under it, with her, next to her, inside her. "Yes, that's fine. You need the down for the hard floor." She set the drink on the nightstand, pulled the covers back, and slid in, robe and all.

He disappeared into the bathroom, the faucet running for a long time. While he was gone, the fire burned down a bit, and she sank deeper into the pillows of the massive antique bed. Longing squeezed her throat, and some remaining tendrils of lust tortured her between her legs.

She hadn't expected him to be *that* much of a gentleman.

Maybe it was...her. He knew too much about her, knew her devils, knew her secrets. What she needed was a man who would never know where she came from. Was that possible? If Finn MacCauley was ever caught, it was only a matter of time before her name was dragged into it; she knew that.

So how could she ever hope to keep the truth from a man?

She couldn't.

Marc came back in, and she feigned sleep, watching him cross the room through her almost closed eyes. She heard the down rustling, another drink poured, another exhale of exhaustion and...frustration.

The fire crackled and eventually smoldered. He turned again. And again. Another sigh.

A slight shiver shook her body and made her clutch the afghan tighter.

"Are you cold?" he asked, the sound of his voice jolting her.

"I'm fine."

She heard him move, the fireplace screen slide open, a log hit with a hiss. The room brightened in shades of fiery orange, and a wave of heat rolled toward her.

But not enough.

"It's warm down here, Dev."

She swallowed hard, her breath catching, her heart a steady thump against the terry robe.

Warm. Safe. Comforting. Sexy.

Impulse won the battle, not that reason put up much of a fight.

Without making a sound, she slipped out of the bed, finishing what was left in her glass with a fortifying slug. The liquid burned, despite its sweetness, fiery on her throat, giving her a push she really didn't need.

She silently walked to the foot of the bed.

He lay on his back, arms locked behind his head, the

comforter under him and spread open, wearing nothing but boxer briefs, which were tented with a full erection.

"I'm still thinking about you in the bath," he said with a sly smile. "As you can see."

She dragged her gaze over his body, over each cut of defined muscle, over each line of male beauty, to the strained shorts. Her mouth actually watered to taste him; her fingers itched to touch.

Very slowly, her knees bent, as though she had no will to stop herself from kneeling next to him.

Holding his gaze, she felt captured. The connection was real, palpable, a physical pull that she couldn't stop. She placed her hands on his chest, and his heartbeat vibrated up her arms, like she was channeling his pulse.

She lowered her head, letting her hair fall near his face, the scent of Baileys mingling with the malty smell of fine Irish whiskey. She wanted to close her eyes but didn't want to stop looking at him.

What would it be like to love a man like this? The possibility, the longing, the pure want of that stole her breath.

"I'm cold," she whispered.

His gaze dropped to her mouth, lower, then back to her eyes. "I'm not." He released one hand from behind his head, and for a moment she thought he was going to flip the cover over her, but his hand went to the robe's belt. Just like she'd imagined, one flick of the finger, one easy tug, and it was open.

He inched up, using both hands to slide it over her shoulders, the flames behind her sending a wall of searing heat over her bare back. For a long moment, she remained still, letting the warmth of the fire penetrate her skin and the warmth of his gaze break through to her heart.

He reached for her, touching her cheek with his palm first. "I want you," he said simply.

"I want you, too." She tilted her head, getting more of his touch like a needy cat, her hands moving toward him with an ache of their own. She wanted to touch him. She had to.

She fingered the top of his boxer briefs, her palm less than an inch from the hard-on that stretched the fabric. Very slowly, she lifted the waistband and dragged them down, revealing his shaft, pulsing, red, already glistening at the tip, daunting in the dancing firelight.

She just stared at him, her hands trembling, her breath trapped, her mouth aching to close over him.

He barely arched in invitation. She lowered her head, but he scooped behind her neck and pulled her upward to his face.

"Kiss me," he demanded. "Kiss *me*."

She did, letting herself fall on his chest to meet his mouth, the contact so much more intimate than what she'd intended, so much more personal.

So not...sex. Comfort.

She took it greedily. He opened his mouth and plunged his tongue deep inside, the flavor of whiskey bitter and sweet, his lips soft and strong, his arms determined as he pulled her onto him and rose up to make their chests touch, their stomachs, their hips.

Ending the kiss, she backed up enough to study his face in the firelight, memorizing the lines, trying to etch the moment into her brain. No matter what happened to them, no matter what the future held, she'd have this night. This sexy, romantic, loving man. The kind of man she'd always wanted but didn't even know existed.

She stroked his strong jaw, drinking in the shadows formed by his cheekbones and whiskers, the power of his Roman nose and full lips. She dragged her hand over his chest, down the symmetry of his abdomen, and finally closed her hand around his erection.

He closed his eyes and let out a moan.

His tip was wet, slippery under her fingertips. She kneeled again, straddling him, kissing the skin of his stomach, then fluttering her tongue over the head of his shaft. It tasted as creamy as the Baileys she'd been sipping, and just as smooth. She closed her mouth over the top, sliding her hand down the length of him slowly, letting every muscle and vein glide through her palm, taking him a little deeper into her mouth as he rocked his hips forward.

Once, twice, a third time and his hands dug into her hair, stealing another stroke before he lifted her head and eased her back on the pillows, sliding down with her.

"I want to be inside you." The demand was husky and irrefutable. "All the way inside you."

Without waiting for her response, he eased her to the side and got to his feet in one move. Instead of feeling bereft of his warmth, she pulled the comforter around her, watching him open the bag he'd dropped on the settee.

"So condoms were mission critical?" she asked.

"Guess that depends on the mission."

"And I was feeling guilty about a tub of body butter."

Returning to her, he dropped the packet next to them and climbed back into the nest, reaching for her, then caressing her breasts, her stomach, her hips, and finally settling on her backside. "If that's what makes you feel like satin and silk, then it was also mission critical."

He kissed her breast, suckling just enough to make her ball the comforter under her fists; then he lifted his head, his eyes hooded and dark. "I didn't plan to seduce you, Devyn," he said. "I want you to know that wasn't my intent."

"I know." She splayed her hand over his chest, reveling in the mightiness of it and the amazement over what all these muscles covered. A good, good heart. "I came to you, remember?"

"But I was only going to give you five more minutes in that bed."

She laughed softly. "But you know I'm impulsive."

"I was counting on it." He silenced any response with a deep kiss, laying her back and delving into her mouth with his tongue.

He stroked every inch of her, branding her skin with his touch, making every spot come alive when he reached it and making her beg for more when he left. Finally, his hand settled between her legs, watching her eyes as his thumb found the sweet spot of her clitoris.

The shock of his touch stole her breath and made her rock against his hand until he replaced it with his erection. She instantly wrapped her legs around him, and their bodies melded.

Between whispers of her name and groans of pleasure, he kissed her again and again, each wet, warm connection tasting like whiskey and chocolate and heaven, dragging her closer to the point where all she wanted was him inside her.

She rolled her hips and reached down to feel him pulse and grow in her fingers. While she stroked him, he bit open the condom package, letting her slide it over him as part of her strokes.

As he nestled between her legs and braced himself over her, they shared a long, silent look.

She tried not to get lost in the darkness of his eyes, told herself not to attach too much meaning to what he'd freely admitted was just sex, but she couldn't help the bits of daydream that flashed like sparklers in her head.

What would it be like to love a man like this...always?

She closed her hands around him one more time, guiding him between her legs, wanting him in her so badly she almost cried out. She lifted her hips and relaxed as he slowly took ownership of her body. Deeper and deeper, he entered, his eyes half-mast, his arms flexed, his neck strained with the fight against thrusting into her.

And then he was all the way inside her, throbbing against her flesh, still and steady. He lowered himself enough to kiss her but still didn't move his hips. She battled the same urge, aching to just rock and roll and ride, but instead took one more slow, wet, smoking hot kiss.

Her sigh escaped into his mouth, and it was all he needed. He thrust harder and faster, and she met each stroke, building with him, grasping the granite of his shoulders, pulling his head to hers, hearing the sounds of their panting whispers in harmony with the crackling fire.

He touched her, sliding his thumb between them, manipulating her like she'd been made for him to do just that. Dizzy and completely lost, she forgot everything and gave in to the heat, the touch, the need as she finally let the knot inside of her unravel under his relentless, magical fingers.

He kept thrusting, adding to the sweetness inside, holding her with his other arm as she shuddered against him with a long, blissful orgasm.

She barely stopped panting as he hissed in a breath of his own. He pushed harder into her, far less tender as he plunged in and out, sweat glistening on his face, his eyes closed, his lips parted. As lost as she was, he dragged out the pleasure, finally letting go with a ragged groan of surrender as he came inside her.

For that one moment, everything, every single thing, felt right.

"That wasn't sex," she whispered, the words out before she even realized it.

He still couldn't breathe but managed to lift his head and look at her with a rueful gleam in his eye. "Can't wait to hear what you call it."

She was still floating, high on the sensations, numb to reality, all the pain deep inside her just...gone.

"It was like that aloe I put on you," she whispered, no control over the words. "Soothing and healing, taking away the wound."

The gleam disappeared as his expression grew serious. He placed one hand on her cheek, cupping her jaw. "See? The condom and body butter was mission critical. My mission is to make you feel better."

"That went way past better." She closed her eyes and pulled him closer.

"Who wounded you, Dev?"

She wasn't even sure how to answer that. Her husband, obviously. Her parents who never let her forget she wasn't part of their blood. The birth mother who didn't want her. And, of course, Finn MacCauley. The man whose legacy she carried in her blood.

The reason she'd never know the answer to what it would be like to love and be loved by a man like Marc Rossi.

"Dev?" he asked.

She shook her head, shoving the demons into a drawer, wanting to be in his head, not her own. "No, Marc, it's my turn," she said. "Tell me about this woman who took everything from you."

He lifted his head, his eyes sharp.

"You told me the last time you trusted a woman it cost you everything. Did she take you to the cleaners in the divorce?"

"She's in prison."

Oh. Wow. Prison? "Really?"

"Yes, really. I put her there."

CHAPTER 18

Marc didn't want to talk about Laura while he was feeling the aftereffects of mind-blowing sex, still hard and nestled inside Devyn's sweet flesh, riding an endorphin high that was meant for kissing and cuddling and, God, sleeping.

"You put her in prison?" She moved just enough to dislodge him, the separation hurting more than he expected it to.

"She's a criminal. That's what I do. Did. I put the bad guys—and girls—behind bars." He knew he sounded cold; he had to. This wasn't a discussion where he'd ever let his guard down. "Dev, you really want to drag ex-spouses into this beautiful night?"

She sat up, reached for the protection of the robe, scrutinized his face. Not many men had the dubious distinction of putting their own wife in jail. The curiosity was natural.

"What happened?" she asked.

"What happened was that I naïvely believed that no one could be that perfect on the outside and that messed up on the inside."

A shadow crossed her expression, or maybe it was the firelight. "What did she do?"

Besides step on his heart and shatter his belief in womankind and top it all off by taking away the one thing he wanted from her? "Twenty-five counts of embezzlement, one of attempted murder. We divorced during the trial, and she's doing seven years in a state prison."

"Who did she attempt to murder?"

"Me."

She let out a little breath of shock.

He closed his eyes, remembering the night he walked into the office building in the financial district, looking for evidence. Well, he sure found it. He could still remember the smell of the offices, the silence in the halls, until he heard...them.

Laura and her fucking partner in crime. Literally.

"How?"

"Does it matter?"

She tied the robe firmly. "It matters to me," she said. Of course it did.

"The details aren't important, Devyn. I was investigating fraud in a group of small angel investment partners in Boston. When some of the evidence pointed to the firm where my wife worked, I wanted to get off the case. But Laura actually talked me out of that. She said she could help me infiltrate the company, find out who was involved."

"To keep you from finding the real culprit?" she guessed, accurately.

"Who happened to be her boss." He blew out a breath. "Who was also her lover."

"Oh," she said, reaching a hand to him. "I know that feeling. That sense of..."

"Betrayal."

"Yes." She squeezed his arm but still didn't slip down to hold him. "How did she...attempt murder?"

"I caught her in the act."

"Of committing fraud?"

"Of committing adultery." He let out a dry, mirthless laugh. "The coward ran and left us to argue it out. She pulled a gun on me." He was doing a great job of being emotionless, at least on the outside, considering just how much he hated this chapter of his life.

"Did she shoot you?"

"I shot her." His smile was tight. "Just to take her down, not to fatally wound her. But the whole incident was a mess, and...I left the FBI. I felt I had to, after staying on a case I had no right to be on. And we divorced, obviously."

After a long, quiet, endless minute, she said, "We have a lot more in common than I realized. Starting with cheating spouses who get what they deserve."

"She was a user," he said, more roughly than he meant to. "I should have listened to my brothers, my cousins. They couldn't stand her, but I always had an excuse for her. She had a really rough childhood, beaten by her father, actually locked in a closet when she was five. Serious trauma that left her with issues. You understand."

She lifted her eyebrows. "To be fair, the worst thing my parents did was give me the cold shoulder over a formal dinner. Not rough, exactly."

"But you have that...issue"

She gave him a funny look. "What issue?"

"That sense that you're not good enough," he said, trying not to let the words rile, but he could see he'd struck a chord. "It's in the subtext of everything you say. You're the child of at least one fugitive parent and another who is lining up for that job. You wear that identity like...like armor."

"Armor?" Her voice rose a little. "I just let you past it."

"Did you?"

She pushed herself up, but he grabbed her arm to keep her down.

"You have nothing to be ashamed of, Dev. *You* haven't done anything wrong."

She froze and gave him a hard look. "That's very easy for you to say."

"I just told you what I carry around. I feel a lot of things about my ex-wife and what happened, but no shame."

"You *married* her, Marc. You weren't born to her. Big difference. And your family is...is...glorious. I'm sure they're great judges of character." She shook off his grasp. "I have to get some sleep."

He studied her for a while, considering the benefits of arguing. None. "Alone?"

She hesitated, then shook her head. "Of course not. Sleep in the bed with me. We both need company."

Company? Comfort. Sex. Why did that leave him wanting more? It was all he should expect to give or get from her. Anything more, and he'd be...rescuing again.

He followed her into the bed, dragging the cover with him as they silently got into bed together. She kept her robe on, and he didn't argue, turning her around to spoon with her, holding her as tightly as he could.

He wasn't being fair. There was so much more to the story he hadn't told her. But some secrets should stay hidden.

Neither of them spoke as the last of the embers cracked and a cowbell dinged softly on a distant farm. After a while, her breathing grew steady and slow, and so did Marc's. He was just about asleep when he felt her shift, slide, and move away.

He let her go, keeping his eyes closed. He felt her weight leave the bed, heard a bare foot hit the floor.

She took a few steps, slowly and surreptitiously. From under his lids, he watched, wondering what she was doing. Getting another drink? Going to the bathroom?

She very quietly opened the bag they'd brought, glancing over her shoulder when the zipper made a soft sound, checking to see if he was asleep.

She reached into the bag, rooted around, checking him periodically. After a moment, she pulled something out. Not *something*. She turned a piece of paper over, read the back, her head shaking slowly.

With one more look at him, she approached the fireplace and dragged the screen back very carefully, trying not to make a sound.

He purposely breathed evenly, the sound of sleep.

When she turned, he lifted his head to see a match flare, the flame dancing, ashes fluttering into the embers.

On some weird level, he understood.

If Finn MacCauley were captured, it would be next to impossible to keep Devyn Sterling out of the story. Her darkest, most shameful secret would become public information. And that, he suspected, mattered very much to this woman.

The last of the flames ebbed, not as warm, but still... combustible. She stood for a long time and watched the ashes.

Finally he spoke. "What are you doing, Dev?"

She sucked in a guilty breath, looking over her shoulder to meet his gaze.

Please don't lie. Please, please just don't lie, he thought.

"I'm... getting warm."

He could take the questionable genes. But he couldn't take lying. Lesson learned—or relearned, as the case may be.

"Come to bed," he said huskily. "I'll keep you warm."

She glanced at the fireplace, which now held merely ashes. "All right."

And as he held her, he forced himself to remember exactly how betrayal felt. Not good, not good at all.

Every muscle in Sharon's body hurt. She'd broken at least one rib when the car pinned her to the fence. Her face stung where Liam Baird had smacked her, her lower lip swollen and dripping blood. Her wrists burned from the ties that bound them behind her.

If this went on much longer, she'd tell him everything he insisted on knowing.

And then she'd be dead.

She hung her head, her eyes opening and closing in exhaustion and pain, her gaze landing on a few wavy strands of silver hair on the floor. So that's why her scalp hurt.

He'd left her in the lab, the lights on, the cabinets open. Such a fool when it came to science. But no fool when it came to pain and misery. That he could inflict like a professional.

The door popped open, so hard it hit the wall behind it with a resounding crack. She managed to lift her head, making out two men in her blurred vision. One was Liam. The other was one of the men she'd seen come and go in the house.

"Who did you call?" Liam asked her for the twentieth time.

"No one." She couldn't waver.

The back of his hand slammed so hard she felt her brain dislodge and heard her neck crack. "Don't fucking lie to me, *Doctor* Greenberg." He said it as though he didn't even believe she was a doctor anymore.

Her face throbbed, white blades of misery shooting through her head.

"A call was made to an American cell phone number—that much we picked up with our monitoring system. You were seen dialing a phone. Who did you call?"

"I didn't."

He raised his hand again, and she braced for the next blow, but the other man grabbed his arm and stopped it.

"Wait a sec, Liam. Let me have at her."

Oh, God. That didn't sound good.

Liam backed down, wiping his mouth with the back of his hand, a disgusted look directed at her. "She's a plant, Ian. We were had. Fucking *had* with this one."

The other man took a step closer, and Sharon could make out his features, classic black Irish with thick dark curls and deep blue eyes. She remembered his name now—Ian O'Rourke.

He didn't strike her as one of Liam's thugs. More brainy and calm. Maybe that meant he wasn't about to pound the holy shit out of her.

"Dr. Greenberg," he said, his voice soft. Too soft. Like the blow would come when she least expected it.

She squinted at him. Not that she had any choice; her left eye was so swollen she could barely see out of it.

"It doesn't seem likely that you're a plant, now, does it?"

"What the fuck?" Liam asked. "She's running off at night, having secret phone calls, lying about it, demanding more money, all the time delaying everything we're trying to do here." He gestured wildly to the lab. "I don't trust her."

"That might be," Ian continued. "But we went after *her*, Liam. You did the research on this deadly spore business and sought out the world's expert."

Liam snorted softly, as if he doubted she was an expert on anything. "*You* told me to get a woman."

"Usually they're more pliable," Ian said, giving her a harsh gaze, as though she should know better than to not be pliable. "But we found her, so how could she be a plant?"

Exactly what she'd wanted them to think back when this whole plan came together.

"Is this your phone, Dr. Greenberg?" Ian asked.

Oh, Lord. They'd found it in the cemetery. "I've never seen it."

"Ian found it not ten feet from where you were," Liam said.

Did the text go through?

"Where'd you hide the battery?" Liam demanded.

"I . . . don't know what you're talking about."

"The battery could have fallen out on impact," Ian said.

Then it was a miracle. But had the message gone

through? Had they traced it? Could they find out who she'd called? She'd been careful to delete everything else, including the message sending her the phone number. But had she been careful enough?

Baird turned to Ian and they shared a look, and a quick comment, too soft and too thick with Irish accents for her to follow.

One more time, Ian dipped to get face-to-face with her. "Dr. Greenberg, you don't want to die, do you?"

She shook her head.

"Then do what Mr. Baird asks you to do."

"I never said I wouldn't."

"Oh, for Chrissake," Liam said, pushing off from the lab table he leaned against. "This is a fucking waste of time, Ian. Get out of here. I'll deal with her."

But Ian didn't move. "Why don't you go cool off, Liam? Freaking out isn't going to help anyone or anything. Let me have a minute alone with her."

Liam narrowed his eyes at the other man, assessing him and then backing off. "I have to piss," he said brusquely. "Then she gets to work and I don't give a flying goddamn hell if the spores are full grown or not. She can finish the job or die."

And die, more likely. She closed her eyes as another wave of pain cascaded through her as he left. How the hell could she get out of this? Who would help her now? She was in a self-made no-man's-land.

Ian stepped even closer. "You had no idea it could hurt so much, did you, Sharon? We tried to tell you."

For a second, she stopped breathing, sure that she'd misunderstood him over the sound of her labored gasps. We? Who did *he* work for?

"Tried to warn you not to contact anyone."

With superhuman strength, she lifted her head to see him, to dig for the subtext she imagined she heard in his voice.

Did he know who sent her here? Who *really* sent her here?

"You're on your own now, Doctor," he whispered. "You know nobody can help without compromising everything."

She drew a ragged breath. "Do you—"

He silenced her with a deadly look. "You might die."

"What can I do?"

"The job you were hired to do," he said simply.

"What about...her?"

"We're doing everything possible to take care of her."

Who was *we*? Take care of as in get rid of? Or take care of as in protect?

But before she could ask any questions, the door popped open, and Liam looked like he'd done more than go to the bathroom. His eyes were bright as he entered, his cell phone in his hand.

"We're out of time." He jerked his head to the door. "Get out of here, Ian. This woman has work to do. The buyer is ready, and we need to be, too."

When Ian left, without so much as a glance at her, she hung her head again, the fight slipping from her body.

"You ready to give up, Doctor?"

"I can't do anything tonight."

"Then let me spell it out for you. I know who you called, Dr. Greenberg."

Her blood chilled, more at his tone than his words.

"One of my men found the battery, and we traced your little text. Sent me right to her."

He was bluffing. He *had* to be.

"So you better get to work, Doctor. And I wouldn't make any mistakes, because if you do, if so much as one spore is lost or not purified correctly, that young woman dies. And trust me, I will kill her. And then I will kill you."

He turned to the refrigerator and flipped it open, so careless and stupid. "Let's get started."

She didn't move.

"Or do you need more time to think?"

Yes, yes, she did. He would kill Devyn, no doubt about it. But Devyn—*Rose*—might help her very own mother. So, she wasn't in a self-imposed no-man's-land after all. Her *daughter* was out there, and as long as she was alive, she could help Sharon. She *would* help Sharon.

Fueled with hope, she slid off the chair. All she needed was a plan. "Let's get to work," she said, sounding much tougher than she felt.

CHAPTER 19

There were no notes lying around the streets of Enniskillen. No secret directions indicating where they could find Sharon or another clue, and after a long day of discovering nothing, frustration nipped at Devyn's heart.

Along with the fact that Marc had raised an invisible wall between them, starting with the moment they'd awakened, legs and arms entwined. She'd expected morning sex, another slam to her senses, and his mighty erection indicated that he expected the same thing.

But with remarkable self-control, he merely left the bed and took a long shower, emerging from the bathroom fully dressed. While she got ready for the day, he spent the time on his phone, using its spotty Internet service to find out what he could about the town, still unable to get anything concrete on Padraig Fallon or the "notes" he told them to find.

They set off to explore and inspect, barely touching

except when they had to, the conversation strictly on the business at hand, not on each other.

Disappointed but not surprised, Devyn followed his lead as morning shifted into afternoon and then into autumn dusk, and still they found nothing. Hungry and exhausted, they stopped at a café on the main drag, taking an outdoor table nestled on a corner. From there, they could look down the narrow street, up to a church spire in one direction and toward the monuments they'd just visited in the other.

"Let's eat," Marc suggested. "We skipped lunch, and it's almost noon in Boston. I want to try and reach Vivi. We still haven't heard a word about what she found in Raleigh."

"Probably the same thing we have," Devyn said, happy to take a seat at the outdoor table he'd gestured to. "Nothing."

While he dialed his cell phone, she glanced up and down the street, noticing an abundance of orange flags and banners, a sure sign Enniskillen was heavily Protestant and in support of England. They'd passed a few churches, including the one that dominated the skyline ahead of her, its dramatic steeple housing the bells that filled the winding streets of the town with monstrous, melodic chimes each hour.

Along the road in the center of town that led to the church, two- and three-story slate and stone buildings were nestled so close you couldn't slide a credit card between them. Most probably had been erected two or three hundred years earlier, then updated every few decades.

"You *are* there, Vivi," Marc said into the phone. "Why haven't you called?"

As he listened to her response, Devyn gave in to the urge to look at him, to study the way his strong, tanned fingers curled around the glass he sipped, the way he leaned back with ease, grace, and confidence, yet his dark gaze swept the landscape, always watching.

And then those gorgeous eyes stopped on her and scorched her with a meaningful look... only she didn't understand.

What had changed between last night and today?

He'd told her about his ex-wife. Laura. He'd put himself out on an emotional limb and she'd responded by...

Burning Finn MacCauley's phone number.

In the light of day, it seemed a little like an overreaction. But last night, she'd been in abject misery, hearing the echo of his admission in her head as she tried to fall asleep.

He put his own wife in jail for her crimes; he didn't have any sympathy for lawbreakers. How could a man like that ever forget what she came from?

And what about another man? What chance did she have of ever finding happiness if her name was irrevocably associated with one of the country's most-wanted fugitives?

So she'd burned the picture and felt guilty as hell about it.

"A calendar? That's all you found?" Marc's smoky looked transformed to a quick shake of his head, and more disappointment wrapped around her chest.

"We're in Enniskillen," he said, taking a sip of water, then repeating the name of the town. "It's in..." His voice drifted, and she forced herself to stare at the church steeple instead of his mesmerizing face. "Really?"

He suddenly sounded interested, leaning forward, switching the phone to his other ear. "Does it say anything else on that month? What is it, October?"

The server came with sandwiches for them, so she ate while she listened and tried to make sense of his side of the conversation, reviewing the day.

They'd combed the island town for clues but hadn't found anyone or anything except shops, restaurants, apartments, and small businesses up there. No one appeared to even notice them, let alone give them some kind of cryptic message the way Padraig had implied.

They'd roamed through the limestone buildings and narrow streets, seeking any kind of connection to Sharon, finding nothing. They'd even visited the monuments erected in memory of the people who'd died when an IRA bomb ripped through the heart of the city and changed its role in history forever. Plenty of anti-IRA sentiment, but no one stepped out from behind a bush in the gardens surrounding the area to announce they knew where Devyn's biological mother was hiding.

"There are actual letters marked on the days?" Marc asked, pulling a pen out from his jacket to write on a paper napkin. "Read them to me." After a pause, he added, "Because you never know, Vivi."

She watched him write a series of letters, sharing a quick glance with her, his eyes looking a little excited about whatever his cousin had found.

She swallowed hard as he set down his pen and rested his hand, and without thinking, she reached for him, closing her hand around his wrist, longing for that physical connection they'd had the night before, wishing so much that she'd met him under different circumstances.

He didn't even respond.

"Anything else?" he asked, his tone impatient. "Are you sure, Vivi? Absolutely nothing?" A few beats, then, "Did Chessie find anything on Padraig Fallon?"

Devyn pushed her plate away, her appetite gone.

"Keep looking and I'll call you later. Text me anything you have."

He clicked off and set the phone on the table, tapping the napkin covered with letters.

"What is that?" she asked.

"She found a calendar in Sharon's office, with pictures of Ireland. Northern Ireland, it seems."

"And?"

"And August was the Giant's Causeway, September was Bangor—"

"It was?"

He leaned forward. "And October was..." He tilted his head toward the street.

"Enniskillen." They said it at the same time, a little quiver waltzing down her back.

"That is very weird, and oddly wonderful," she said, then gestured toward the napkin. "And what is this?"

"On most of the days in October, there was a letter written in pencil, lightly, in the corner of the date box."

"Oh?" Now that had promise. "Does it spell something?"

"Not unless the message is made up of the same seven letters, A through G. Those are the only letters." He took a bite of his sandwich while she read them.

"Yeah, the only thing that—"

"Finished, luv?" A red-haired waitress stepped up, reaching for her plate, just as a loud chime sounded from the church. "Jesus, they'll deafen you, they will," she said loudly, putting her hands over her ears in a dramatic gesture. "You can see—or hear—why we had a big fight about playin' them bells all hours of the day and night."

"It's beautiful to listen to," Devyn said loudly as the next note rang. "Are they real, then? I know that so many church bells are really computerized now."

The young woman hooted and rolled her eyes. "Good Lord, yes, they're real. We've got ten of 'em, all encased in new steel brackets that God only knows how we paid for, and now Enniskillen is one of only a handful of cities in Nor'n Ireland that can make the claim of having ten real bells. An honor, it is, if a noisy one."

Another note echoed over the sandstone buildings, rolling through the streets, a low, sad clang that hung in the ear long after a clapper hit.

"They ring every hour, right?" Devyn asked, retrieving the napkin Marc had written on when the waitress scooped up the plates.

"Oh, yes, indeed. Sometimes more, just for no good reason like someone sneaked up there an' took a pull. If the church is open and Reverend MacIntyre is drunk—" she leaned closer to add a stage whisper—"which is as likely as not, ya know, well, then, ya can go right up there and hang on a rope. He'll take money to letchya do that, too."

"Thanks for the tip," Devyn said politely.

Marc leaned forward. "How many bells did you say there were?"

"Ten. And each weighs over one ton and cost a bloody fortune. But we got one bell for each note in the scale, and three sharps, if you are one of those people who care. One of those...camp..."

"Campanologist," he supplied. "The study of bells."

The waitress laughed. "That's it. I've heard that before, from tourists who're just that. You'd have to go up there if you're that interested." She took the plate and nodded to some new customers. "'Scuze me, sir."

"Devyn." Something in his voice reached into her gut and squeezed.

"What?"

He took the napkin. "Seven letters and look." He pointed to the napkin. "That's not a number sign—it's a sharp."

"Like the notes of a scale." The realization hit her as they both turned to stare at the spire as the last bell rang out and echoed over the city.

"The *notes* of a scale," he whispered, tugging the napkin out of her hand and fluttering it in front of her. "Sharon had these letters on the Enniskillen page of her calendar. Maybe we're thinking of the wrong kind of *notes*."

A frisson of excitement fluttered through her. "You think the notes on her calendar are some sort of message? Like if they get played on the bells, the message is sent?"

He helped her up and nodded to the church. "Let's hope the reverend is drunk enough for us to find out."

The sense that Vivi hadn't quite told him everything nagged at Marc, but the instant the pieces fell into place with the church and the bells, he felt better. The inaction and brick walls they'd hit all day had his blood simmering, along with the close contact with a woman he'd rather not respond to...but couldn't help that he did.

The renewed enthusiasm for their mission gave him a reason to hold her hand, then place a possessive arm around her shoulders.

He blew out a breath of self-disgust but didn't let go. *Just do the job, Rossi. And move on. Quit rescuing, and work.*

As they turned the corner, the elaborate stone and stained glass of St. Macartin's loomed large, a behemoth of a church topped by a lofty bell tower and steeple. He guided her to the path that led to the church's front door and headed directly there.

"I'm thinking you aren't going to look for the rector to ask permission to go up there."

"You're thinking right."

Inside, the air was cooled by the dark stone and stained-glass lighting, the lingering smell of wood polish and candle wax permeating the mustiness of a closed-up church.

"Based on where the steeple is, let's try this way," he said, taking her to the far right side to an unmarked door. Marc turned the oversize knob, which clicked open effortlessly.

"They're pretty trusting," she noted.

"Or someone is expecting us."

She hesitated on her next step. "You think?"

"I don't know yet. Proceed with caution." Inside, the stairwell was nearly pitch-black, dank with moldy air. He pulled her close but stepped in front to protect her from anyone coming down. "Single file, and watch your step."

They started up spiral stairs that were not even two feet wide, pie shaped and steep, stacked straight up a tightly curved stairwell. Close behind him, Devyn's body tightened and he threw a look over her shoulder to make sure they weren't being followed.

"Who do you think we might find, Marc?" she whispered.

"I'm considering all the possibilities," he replied, giving her hand a squeeze. "Let's get to the top."

Wooden stairs creaked underfoot, and the walls were made of centuries-old stone, cold and unforgiving. A bullet shot from above would ricochet like mad. At the top, he put a hand out to hold her back and he inched around to see where they were.

The bell ropes hung in the middle of a small room, not twelve feet in either direction. Frayed, each had an embroidered badge dangling from the bottom bearing a letter, one for each note in the scale. And three sharps.

Around the perimeter of the room, slender openings in the stone let in light and a cool breeze. Devyn walked to one, squinting out to the streets below. "Now what?"

"Fallon said someone would meet us once we found the notes. Maybe that's how Sharon met her contact over here. By playing these notes."

She frowned at him. "That's all so cloak-and-dagger, Marc."

"Exactly. A spy network that communicates through the bells."

Her jaw loosened. "You think she's a spy?"

"Fallon moved like one," he said, fingering the ropes that hung from the ceiling, strung through eighteen-inch holes. "I just have to figure out what order to play them in."

"Why not the order they were on the calendar? Did Vivi tell you what letters were on what days?"

"Yes." He turned and looked around the room again. "But I'd like to be sure before we ring the bells. We'll only have one chance. There should be some kind of songbook here for a bellringer. Up on that shelf?"

A stone shelf circled the room at about eight feet, too high for him to reach.

"Lift me up and let me look," Devyn suggested, walking to him.

He closed his hands around her waist and hoisted her up, turning to give her a chance to examine the whole shelf.

"There it is."

He shifted her to where she pointed and she reached, pulling out a tattered notebook. They started leafing through the handwritten pages.

No scales, no music, just a page for each song and a list of letters to play. But there were at least two dozen songs.

"If we can find one that matches the notes on Sharon's calendar, we'll know we have it." He took out the napkin as Devyn turned the pages and they compared the notes.

"They're all just hymns."

"Maybe not," he said. "Remember what the waitress said? Sometimes someone just plays a random song, in the middle of the hour? Probably not so random." He shuffled through the notebook.

They flipped through the pages and read the titles.

"Rock of Ages." "Be Thou My Vision." "The Pride of the Parish." "I Heard the Voice of Jesus."

"And look at this acronym," he said, pointing to the title "Sinners Into Saints." "SIS. The Secret Intelligence Service."

She looked up at him. "Is that the MI6? Like, James Bond stuff?"

"More likely MI5, but it's a fine distinction. They're both British spies. Let's compare the notes."

A hand to her mouth, she stepped back. "Sharon is a British spy?"

"Or an American one helping them out."

"That would mean...she's on the side of the...good guys."

He didn't answer, comparing the notes on the napkin with the song book. "We have a match to every other day on the calendar," he said, excitement at the find humming through him. "If you play the notes on the odd numbered days of October, you play this song."

"And then what happens?" she asked.

He turned to her. "There's only one way to find out."

"Do you think Sharon will come?"

He shrugged. "My guess is someone from the SIS will show up."

"And lead us to her," she said, reaching for the first rope. "Let's play."

"No, no. You have to hide." He pointed up to the bell tower. "It'll be loud up there, but you'll be out of sight, at least from someone coming up the stairs."

"Eeesh. Really?"

"Go. Or the bells stay silent."

She looked up into the holes and made a face. "It's a long way up."

"You want to meet your mother?" He put his hand on her shoulder, meaning to give her a light push toward the door that led to the belfry, but he held on to her instead.

"You play dirty."

"Go up there and *stay* up there." He added some pressure, inching her closer, fighting the urge to kiss her after his vow not to give in to the attraction. "No matter what happens down here."

"What if—"

"No," he said sternly. "No matter who shows up, do not show your face until I tell you. Is that clear?"

She didn't look happy but nodded. "You're asking a lot of a woman who has a fear of heights and an impulsive nature."

"Promise me, Devyn. You'll stay quiet and hidden. Promise me."

She started to smile; then it wavered, a little pulse jumping in her throat. "I promise."

He gave her a hard look. "A promise is a promise."

Something in her expression got to him, destroying his determination not to kiss her. He kept it brief, but kissed her. The contact with her mouth only made him want more. "Go. Let's turn some sinners into saints."

She slipped into the small opening, and he heard her feet on the stairs, going up to the bell tower.

With his eyes on the page of letters, he closed his hands around the rope and yanked, expecting it to be a tougher tug than it was, the strike of the clapper against brass vibrating the room with powerful sound.

As it lessened and nearly diminished, he pulled the next. Then the next. As the third F-sharp died down, a melody emerged. And in the distance, he heard the slam of a door echoing up the stone chamber.

He reached for his weapon, turning to face the door and whoever was coming up. He yanked the rope again, hoping Devyn's ears could take the beating, because if it was loud in here, it was deadly up there.

And if his guest didn't want him there, it could be deadly in here, too.

Two more notes and then silence. No footstep creaked the wooden stair, no one appeared around the corner, no pistol snapped into firing position.

And then all hell broke loose.

CHAPTER 20

Just when her head stopped ringing from the chimes, gunfire exploded in a wholly different kind of deafening sound. A shot echoed, then another. And another. Devyn scrambled to the icy stone walls of the bell chamber, her heart hitting her rib cage with the same ferocity as the clapper that just hit the bell.

Holy God, Marc was in a gunfight fifteen feet beneath her.

After the gunfire stopped, she remained frozen for a moment, waiting for a sound, a word, or some kind of exchange, but she heard absolutely nothing below. Pressed against the rounded wall, Devyn blinked her eyes to adjust to the darkness of the windowless turret. In the shadows, she could make out the shapes of the bells, not nearly as big as they sounded but made of thick metal. Above her was one more story, accessible by a ladder bolted into the wall.

Dust tickled her nose and she covered her mouth; she

couldn't give herself away. She jumped as another gunshot cracked, then a footstep scuffed, then nothing.

Questions screamed in her head, one louder than all others. Was Marc down there, dead?

A promise is a promise.

Fear for Marc's life mixed with burning guilt. She'd destroyed information she'd promised to give him for helping her. And here he was, risking his life, making her swear to save her own.

She breathed soundlessly, listening, waiting. At the next gunshot, she'd move. If there was another shot.

Two heartbeats, four, then...another deafening bang. Instantly she launched toward the bells, using a second explosion to cover her sound, stopping next to the closest bell.

The bell wasn't quite as tall as she, but it was wide and about two feet off the ground. Under it, an eighteen-inch-wide hole was cut in the floor. She bent over, moving cautiously so as not to make a noise, trying to see through the hole.

But the floor wasn't single-plank wood. There were two floors, about a foot apart with a huge hollow area between them, probably built like that to absorb sound. She'd have to lie on the floor and actually hang her head and half her body down there if she had any chance of seeing what was—

Another gunshot and a grunt. Was Marc hit?

She dropped to her knees, then flattened her body against the floor, scooting forward until her head was at the edge of the hole. She had to know if he was alive.

She could see down the rope but not much of the room below. She'd have to go farther, dangling more than half her body down that opening in order to see. And what would she see? Marc lying on the floor in a pool of blood? Oh, God, no.

She heard a breath. A quick intake of air, directly below her.

Without making a sound, she slid forward, clinging to the rough wood of the floorboards as she forced her head into the hole. Clammy, cold air filled her nose and burned her eyes, but she bit her lip and dropped farther, managing to inch her upper body completely into the hole. Her legs braced on the floor, she balanced her weight precariously in the middle of her torso. Rat droppings and dust balls filled the open area between the two floors.

Six more inches and she could see partially into the room below. She pushed herself and saw Marc, very much alive.

Relief rocked her. He was smashed against the wall, his focus riveted on the opening to the stairs that led back to the church. He couldn't see around that wall, but from her upside-down vantage point, she could. Squinting into the darkness, she could make out a man, also pressed against a wall, waiting for Marc to give away his position.

It was a standoff.

After a moment, the man raised his hand to fire. Devyn let out a soft breath to get Marc's attention. He looked up and saw her motion for him to duck, just as the bullet cracked, missing him.

He caught her eye and nodded in gratitude. She risked her balance by letting go with one hand to point to the door and mouth, "He's right there."

He tilted his head left, right, then shrugged. *Where exactly?* he wanted to know.

She eyed the man again and used her hand to indicate the left, against the wall.

Marc gave her a quick nod and repositioned himself, aiming at the wall. He shot, the explosion splitting her eardrums. The man jerked wildly to the right. He'd used the angle of the wall to bounce a bullet, but the other guy was too fast.

When Marc looked up at her for a report, she shook her head furiously, holding up her fingers to show he'd missed by an inch. Maybe less.

Again, he gestured the same question: *Where is he?*

The man had moved to the other wall now, unaware Marc had the advantage of eyes in the ceiling. She showed Marc, using one hand and clinging to the splintery wood with the other.

One more time, he steadied, aimed at a different place on the wall, and fired.

The man jerked down and grabbed his arm, and Marc gestured up to show he knew he'd hit the target. Moving stealthily, he slipped out of visual range as he rounded the far end of the tower. Devyn's whole body thudded with each heartbeat, her hip bones pressed so hard into the wood to hold her in place she could feel the bruises forming.

The man let go of his jacket sleeve, which was torn, but no blood was visible. Marc must have grazed him. He still couldn't see either of them as he stood.

Marc got closer, then leaped forward, just as the other guy did exactly the same thing. They slammed into each other, a gun skimming across the floor, landing under the bells where Devyn could see it.

Was that Marc's gun? They wrestled each other to the

ground, grunting as a fist hit flesh. Marc got on top and raised his hand to deliver a punch, but his opponent, about his size, maybe bigger, whipped Marc over on his side and got in his own punch. Marc kicked the guy's gut, and Devyn saw a gun in the melee.

In the wrong man's hand.

They rolled out of sight, and she let out a soft choke of frustration, her whole body hanging precariously, her whole being tensed for the gunshot that would kill Marc.

She could see their feet, tangled and kicking, could hear the thud of knuckles against bone and the growls of violence and deadly intent. They rolled closer, within her view now, but Marc was still too far from his gun, which lay a few feet from him.

The two men were almost directly under her. Marc suddenly popped up onto his feet, his arms wide in surrender. He took a slow step back, the other man taking one forward, his gun aimed right at Marc's chest. With one more step, the other man was directly under Devyn.

If she jumped...

Which would be exactly what Marc told her *not* to do.

But they had the advantage of surprise. Marc had no gun and the guy hadn't said a word but moved with deadly intent.

Should she jump?

Hands in the air, Marc's right index finger moved so imperceptibly that the other man wouldn't have noticed. But Devyn saw the miniscule gesture and read it as a signal. He flicked the finger again, a little faster. He *had* to be telling her to jump.

She reached forward, closed her fingers around the rope and swung her legs out. In the split second it took her weight to pull the rope and move the clapper, she slid two feet. As the man looked up in shock, Marc dove for his own gun, kicking the guy out of Devyn's way as she fell to the floor with a thud.

"Drop it!" Marc demanded, loud enough to be heard over the single chime reverberating over the stone walls.

Devyn rolled onto her backside in time to see Marc pushing the guy toward the wall, one hand on this throat, the other holding a gun at his chest.

When the man's gun clunked to the floor, Devyn swiped for it, grabbing it as she pushed herself to her feet.

"Who the fuck are you?" the man asked, his accent thick, maybe more British than Irish, but it was hard to tell on five words.

"You greet every caller with bullets?" Marc asked, getting right in the guy's face. "That the way you guys work now?"

The man said nothing, his pockmarked face red from the struggle, a beady, pale gaze sharply divided between Marc's gun and his eyes. "Nobody's supposed to have them notes, mate. Not that song. No one."

"How about Dr. Greenberg? Did she play it?" He tightened his grip on the guy's throat and punctuated the question by slamming the man's head against the stone. "Did you meet her with a spray of fire, too?"

"I don' know what you're talkin' about."

"I think you do." Marc ground the words out. "Where is she?"

The guy clamped his mouth shut and stared at him, his chest still heaving with each breath. Devyn squeezed the gun in her hand, letting it slide naturally into her palm, the metal warm against her skin.

"Where *is* she?" He shoved a knee into the guy's groin, getting a loud *oomph* in response but no answer.

"Tell me where she is, and you live. Keep your mouth shut, and I fire." Marc was so close to the guy they were practically kissing, hatred and fury rolling off both of them.

"I can't."

"Can't or won't?" He jammed the gun again. "'Cause either one'll kill you."

"Too much at stake, lad."

"Your life's at stake, pal. Where is she?"

The other man sucked in a breath. "I don't know."

Marc thrust another knee into his belly and slammed the guy's head against the stone wall.

"Liam...Baird...is all...I know."

"Who?" Marc demanded. "Where?"

He could barely rasp out the words. "Liam...Baird. Belfast."

Liam Baird? Devyn knew that name. How? The magazine article on Sharon's desk! "Liam Baird" had been underlined. But the article got lost in the rain when she'd tried to escape Sharon's house.

"Where in Belfast?" Marc demanded.

"She's in Mill...town."

Milltown? That was a *cemetery*. "She's dead?" Devyn gasped.

The man shook his head furiously, a purple bruise throbbing under his eye where Marc had landed a punch.

"She's...top secret....Don't fuck it up." He had his breath now and locked his eyes on Devyn. "She knows you're here. That's why we had to get you here."

"To Enniskillen?" she asked, a new hope sparking in

her chest, so powerful she could taste the sweetness of the possibility. Sharon was a spy—on the right side. "Why send me here?"

"To get you away from her. You asked too many people and got attention on her. She's deep undercover."

She let this information settle over her heart.

"They'll kill you," he rasped. "They'll kill you and they'll kill her. But..."

"But what?" Marc demanded, not loosening his grip at all, but not jamming the barrel of the gun into the man quite as hard.

"I'm gonna tell you she's never gonna make it. She's on a suicide mission."

She was? Why?

He looked hard at Marc. "I'm not saying another word, so pull the fucking trigger and get it over with."

Marc eased his stance, still on the guy but not in his face. "Devyn, open the door to the bell tower."

"Where is Sharon?" Devyn said, not moving. "Why isn't someone helping her? Does it have to be a suicide mission?"

"She's on her own," the man said softly. "And that's the way it has to be. Unless you want a whole helluva lot of dead people in the world."

She couldn't respond, couldn't move.

"Get the door," Marc commanded again.

With leaden feet, she stepped sideways, then went to the opening that led upstairs. She pulled the door open and stepped aside as Marc forced the man into the doorway.

"Move it." Marc pushed him up the stairs and followed while Devyn stayed stone still at the bottom, putting it all together.

Sharon had something to do with the British intelligence agency. She was in a cemetery with someone named Liam Baird, on a suicide mission that, if she failed, could kill a lot of people.

"Devyn, c'mere. Fast."

She ducked through the opening and ran up the stairs back to the bell tower.

"Did you go up there?" he asked, indicating the ladder to the top.

"No."

"Go up and see if the door locks from this side. Hurry."

She hoisted herself onto the ladder, pulling herself up and climbing, moving without thinking, without fear. Because her mind was a thousand miles away. Well, a hundred or so. She knew where Milltown Cemetery was; they could find it easily. And she and Marc were so good together that they could find Sharon. She just knew they could.

At the top, the trapdoor was unlocked, but a strong steel bolt locked it from the outside. She knew why Marc had sent her up there.

"You can put him in there," she said. "No one'll ever find him."

"They'll find him. The SIS know when they're missing one of their agents. Keep that gun on him when you get down here."

She did while Marc frisked him and took a cell phone and a wallet.

He flipped the wallet to Devyn. "Get his ID out. And cover me. I'm taking him upstairs."

Without fighting, the man followed Marc's orders

and stayed a few steps ahead of Marc, climbing into his prison.

She kept the gun on him until he was behind the closed door, and Marc bolted the door from the outside, hurrying back down to her.

Back in the bell tower, he paused only long enough to snag the napkin and leave the agent's wallet. He pocketed the man's ID and cell phone, nudging her to the stairs. "Move it," he ordered. "We don't have much time."

"I know, but we can be in Milltown in two hours."

He froze. "Are you out of your mind?"

She turned to him. "Don't even think about stopping me."

"You're not going into an SIS undercover assignment, Dev. Sorry."

"But you heard him. He said—"

"Go!" He gave her a solid push. "We'll fight about it later."

Indeed they would.

CHAPTER 21

Vivi smelled the tomato sauce before she actually saw Uncle Nino in her office doorway, giving her enough time to whip open her desk drawer and slide in her unfinished project, hiding it just as he lumbered into the room.

Would she ever get some time alone in this place?

"You don't look happy to see me, *mia cara*."

She rearranged her face into a smile, then let it fall. Lying—or at least hiding something—from her twin was hard enough. Pulling one over on her great-uncle, a man she loved wholly and completely without wanting to change a single thing about him? Impossible.

But she had to try. She'd been counting the minutes until Zach left, impatient to get back to the letter bits, as she'd come to think of her find from North Carolina.

"I'm just trying to get some work done, Uncle Nino."

"What work? We have, what, one client?" He glanced around the very quiet offices. "I saw Chessie on her way to get her fingernails painted, so we're not that busy."

"She's caught up on her responsibilities," Vivi said. "Plus, it's not like we're paying her yet."

"She told me business was flatter than my crespelles."

She eyed the glass oven dish he carried. "I hope to God that's what you brought."

He held up the dish. "Eggplant parmigiano," he said, slathering a real Neapolitan accent on the word.

"Eggplants with pajamas on." She grinned, always amused by what her American cousins had called the dish as children. "And Zach just got the microwave to work."

"Microwave?" He *pffft*. "Like I'd cook my food with electrolysis."

She smiled. "Just reheat, no cooking involved."

"Thank God I ordered you a stove and a small conventional oven."

She stood slowly, her brain on that drawer, her stomach on the eggplant. "Chessie told me. You know that's not necessary, Uncle Nino."

"I can't just sit around here and do nothing while we wait for business."

"You don't have to be here," she said, measuring each word. From the moment she'd conceived this idea for a business, Nino had counted himself in as one of the team. No matter that his skill sets were limited to cooking and puzzles, both crossword and jigsaw.

"I love that you want to be here, and so does Zach, and you are always our main source of nourishment, but..."

"But what?" He gave a classic Uncle Nino wave of his hand. "Ehhh? I'm too old to be a Guardian Angelino?"

"No, not too old." Guilt warred with irritation as he entered the office without waiting for an invitation, lifting the corner of the dish cover to let a tantalizing and wonderfully familiar aroma of oregano and freshly crushed tomatoes fill the room. "Want some?"

"Am I human? Of course."

He snapped the lid back on and gave her a not-quite-yet look, then jutted his chin toward the desk drawer. "Whatdya hide in there?"

Her jaw slackened. "What makes you think I hid something?"

"Viviana." He drew her name out, all displeased and Italian. "This is Nino you're talking to. I heard you when I walked in. Little gasp, scrapy scrape into the drawer, fake smile. You're hiding something."

She let out a quick laugh. "That's good, Uncle Nino. That's really good. You could be an Angelino yet."

His face said "no shit" but he just asked, "What is it?"

"Nothing."

He lifted the dish and pulled it away like a petulant child. "No parmigiano for you."

She snorted softly, fighting a smile. And the need to share her plans with someone. Zach wouldn't like it. Marc wouldn't like it. But Nino? The jigsaw man? Her pulse kicked up a notch. He might do more than like it. He might *solve* it.

"Uncle Nino," she said conspiratorially. "What would you think if the Guardian Angelinos brought in Finn MacCauley?"

He lifted his big salt-and-pepper brows, wrinkling his forehead all the way back to his balding crown. "I think I'd get a Viking stove in that little break room."

"Exactly!" She snapped and pointed to him. "It would be such a coup that we'd be turning away clients."

He pointed to the desk. "Is he in that drawer?"

"Part of him is." She sat down slowly and inched the drawer open. "Look what I found down in North Carolina."

She'd only reconstructed about three-fourths of the torn paper, stymied by the fact that so many pieces didn't fit, and some were clearly missing.

But she had enough to know Finn MacCauley and Sharon Greenberg were on a first-name basis, and he wanted something from her, bad.

There was a reference to the year 2009, which told her the correspondence was fairly recent.

Nino put the dish on the credenza and sidled around her desk, dragging one of the director's chairs with him so they could sit side by side. Gingerly, she took out a spiral notebook and opened it to the page where she'd been laying out the pieces of the torn letter. She also had the envelope she'd taken from Dr. Greenberg's house and tapped it so that the remaining twenty or so shreds tumbled out. Some were a half inch in diameter, some even smaller.

She explained where she'd found it and brought Nino completely up to date on who Sharon was, how much they knew about her, and what Devyn was doing in Northern Ireland. While she talked, Nino began to finger the pieces.

Like he did with his thousands of jigsaw puzzles, he turned each one round and round, studying it and the possible places for it.

"I have a few complete sentences, see?" She pointed midpage where she'd been able to match all the words.

There's no one else I'd trust this with but you, Sharon. You have that special . . .

"Do you think they're still in love?" Vivi asked.

Nino just shook his head, not speaking. He never did when he went into the puzzle zone.

At the bottom, she still had the *Best, Finn* piece, which struck her as an odd way to sign off a love letter. And she had *money will be astounding, at least four . . .*

That line really intrigued her.

Nino reached for a random slip that had come out of the envelope, then lifted it. Some pieces had to be missing; some were just so small it was impossible to figure out where they fit. But she had enough to know that Finn MacCauley was very much alive, and had, as recently as 2009, communicated with Dr. Sharon Greenberg. About love and money.

After all, what else was there?

"Look at this," Nino said quietly, lining up three pieces.

They'll put you through some tests and make sure you've got

"Oh," Vivi exclaimed, reaching for the one sizeable piece that said *what it takes.*

"Look at that," Nino said softly. "Big sentence. And what's this?" He twirled another piece that had part of a word—*tox.*

"Toxic?" Vivi asked.

"Hello?" The greeting was accompanied by a hard rap on the lobby door as it opened. "Ms. Angelino? Are you here?"

She bit her lip and jumped up. "Jesus K, it's the client. Quick, put this away."

"You're not going to show him?" Nino looked up in surprise.

"Ms. Angelino?" Lang was coming toward the office.

"Hang on, just finishing a call," she hollered. Then, in

a whisper, "No, I don't want him to see this. He'll be all over it, taking away any chance for our moment of glory."

Nino gave her a chastising look.

"Nino!" she cried softly. "Not until we've finished it. That way it'll be so much more impressive."

"I'll finish it," he said quietly. "Go handle the client."

She shot him a grateful smile and popped around his chair and out into the hall. Lang was already on his way back, moving like he owned the place.

Well, he was their only client.

"Hello, Assistant Special Agent." She grinned, closing the door with two hands behind her. "Did I get it right?"

"Hello, Vivi." He added a just-this-side-of-seductive smile. "You forgot the 'in charge' part."

"How could I?" She smiled, pointing at Zach's far more impressive office. "Let's go in here. My brother's out."

"Does he have a new assignment?"

Yeah, buying a house. She didn't answer and slipped around him to snag Zach's chair behind the desk, wanting a little position of power with this man. "How can I help you?"

"I'd like a full status report on Marc's progress."

"I was just putting that together," she said. "It's a real...jigsaw puzzle."

He frowned, his hazel eyes taking on a green hue today, thanks to a dark green polo shirt pulled just tightly enough to show off his broad shoulders. A golf shirt. Of course Lang would be a golfer. Dull, precise, plodding along the fairway of life.

"How is it a puzzle?" he asked.

"Well, it's all just very small bits and pieces of information." Some less than an inch. "You know, communication is shaky sometimes, and with the time difference, we don't hear from him every single day. But he does try to call in every evening."

"Before I forget." He reached into his back pocket and pulled out a folded business-sized envelope. "Some money toward the advance for expenses as promised."

Her heart danced. "Thank you."

"Call him."

"Now?" Her dancing heart tripped. The possibilities for disaster loomed large.

"This minute."

There was no arguing with this guy, was there? "I can try, sure. Let's see, it's about six o'clock there. We could try to reach him."

"He carries a cell phone."

"Of course." She flipped hers off her belt loop and hit speed dial, half hoping for voice mail. "Let me just tell him you want to talk to him."

He leaned forward, reaching for the phone. Instead of taking it, he put strong fingers on her wrist and lowered her arm. "Put it on speaker, and don't tell him I'm here."

Resentment made her recoil. "Sorry, Mr. Lang. We don't work like that around here."

"From the looks of this place, you don't work at all around here. Unless"—he sniffed lightly—"you call making spaghetti work."

She gave him a hard look. "It's parmigiano." Not that a white-bread guy like Lang would appreciate the difference. "And I'd rather be completely open with Marc and tell him you're here."

"Don't." The single syllable command was clear and unequivocal. "Dial and hit speaker."

She did, just as Marc answered with, "I'll call you back." He was breathless, air whooshing over the receiver as though he were running.

"*Now,*" Lang mouthed.

"Now," Vivi repeated. "We need a status report, stat."

Did Marc pick up the *we*? Lang did. He gave her a dark look of warning.

"We are in a fucking hornet's nest, Vivi."

"What's going on?" she asked, wishing he'd sense her odd reaction was a sign that they weren't on the phone alone.

He didn't answer for a minute, mumbling something, then, "No, just hold the gun. Use it if you have to and run faster!"

Vivi and Lang exchanged a long look, his gaze a mix of horror and what-the-fuckery. Marc was supposed to be taking this woman to dinner, convincing her to leave Belfast, if not the country, not running with guns.

"Where are you running off to, Marc?" she asked, keeping her voice calm.

"Jesus, Vivi, I can't talk now. I only answered on the off chance this was Gabe returning a nine-one-one I just put in to him."

Lang stared her down.

"Gabe?" Getting his brother on the phone would be like pinning down a ghost. Why would he want Gabe? "What's going on that you're trying to reach Gabe?"

"The kind of shit that Gabe knows about," he said.

Lang was pretty much annihilating her with narrowed, accusing eyes, a little vein jumping in his muscular neck.

On the phone, a long pause, then, "There, the car, Dev. Get in, now."

"What is going on, Marc?"

The answer was an engine and squealing tires.

"Vivi, listen to me," Marc said.

She braced for anything, holding Lang's gaze. "What is it?"

"Get me anything you have, anything at all, on a guy named Liam Baird."

Lang tried not to react, but she picked up a very subtle widening of his eyes, and the vein in his neck went ballistic.

She grabbed a pencil and a small notepad from Zach's desk. "B-a-i-r-d?" she asked.

"No clue. Just look up every permutation. Find out who the hell he is and why the MI5 would want him."

The MI5? "You mean, like British intelligence?"

Lang whipped the phone up, putting it to his mouth despite the speaker. "Rossi!"

Silence.

"This is Assistant Special Agent in Charge Colton Lang speaking."

More silence.

"Listen to me, and get every word. You had a simple, clear-cut, safe assignment when you left this office. One woman, one name, one easy job to get her the fuck out of there. What in God's name is going on there?"

The background sounds died instantly, and the silence was no longer a dumbstruck Marc but a dead connection.

"Son of a bitch," Lang muttered, throwing the phone down and looking hard at Vivi. "You get him back on that phone, and you tell him that whatever he's doing, wherever he is, whoever he thinks he's found"—he leaned forward, slicing her in half with a look of pure power and command—"he needs to stop. Is that clear?"

She nodded.

He snapped the sheet off the pad with the word "Baird" on it, and balled the paper in his hand. "And if I were you, I'd forget you ever heard that name."

He stuffed the paper in his pocket and left. She didn't move until the front door opened and closed, her heart clumping against her ribs. She picked up the phone to call Marc, heading back to her office to make the call with Uncle Nino at her side.

When she walked in, he looked up from the puzzle of Finn's letter to Sharon, much further completed than when she'd left. He was just putting two pieces together, nodding. "Now that sounds right."

"What sounds right, Nino?"

He looked up. "The name Liam Baird. So Irish. Mean anything to you?"

CHAPTER 22

Marc hung up on Colton Lang only because his caller ID showed a much more important name. The chances of getting Gabriel Rossi on the phone were slim to none, and right that minute, he could get more information out of his deeply connected, black ops, super-spy younger brother than the FBI agent who was screaming in his ear.

"Make it fast," Gabe said as a greeting.

"Got any MI5 connections?"

Gabe just snorted. Yeah, Marc thought so. "How about a guy named Liam Baird?" he asked.

"I'll look into it. Anything else?" No wasted words with Gabe.

Marc tucked the phone against his shoulder and reached out his hand. Reading the silent request, Devyn gave him the ID card they'd taken from the man in the bell tower. "Does the name Nigel Sutton mean anything to you?"

"No more than John Fucking Doe," Gabe said. "That's

standard-issue SIS no-name identification. They're all named Nigel Sutton when they get captured. Where the hell are you anyway?"

"Enniskillen."

"Northern Ireland?" Gabe sounded surprised. "Well, no wonder. Every other guy in that place'll be named Nigel Sutton. It's a hotbed of SIS activity. A clearinghouse for British spooks. What the hell are you doing there?"

"Long story."

"You in trouble?" Gabe asked. He might be younger by two years, but he was a protector, and the tone of concern came through in just a few words. "'Cause I'm not"—he hesitated—"that far away. Same side of the world anyway. I can be there in less than a day."

"I'm good, but stay reachable."

"No promises, dude."

"You on a job?" Marc asked.

"I'm on a chick, and you're interrupting me." He heard the smile in Gabe's voice. "But I could be persuaded to fly to Belfast if you need me."

"Just get me everything you can on Baird, and get it fast." Marc glanced at Devyn, next to him in the passenger seat of the rental. She wrapped her arms around her middle, a slight tremor vibrating her slender form. "I really need something concrete on what he's doing and where he is. I need an address, near Milltown."

"If he's in Milltown, brother, he's dead."

"I know, but where in the area he'd be. What's it called, the Falls Road? West of the city."

"Gimme some time. I'll get back to you."

And just like that, Gabe was gone. Still holding the phone, Marc considered calling Vivi back, but he didn't want to deal with Lang right that minute. From his standpoint, this assignment was a bust. He tossed the device onto the console and checked out the rearview mirror again.

"Anyone following us?" Devyn asked.

"Not at the moment. We can go back to the inn and figure out a plan."

"Can't we go straight to Milltown?"

He shot her a look, bracing for the fight. "No. We're not going to Milltown."

"Then why did you just ask someone for an address where Liam Baird could be? And your cousin for information on him?"

"Because I'm an investigator first and foremost," he shot back. "I move with information. The only information I have now is that we've just walked into a land mine, and I don't want to get blown up."

"Who were you just talking to? I thought it was Vivi, then you took another call."

He hesitated a minute. Gabe lived a top secret existence. Only the family knew what he did, and some of them, like their mother, didn't know all of it. "My brother," he finally said. "He's pretty connected."

"With MI5?"

"With the CIA, which puts him in the same line of work, with access to a lot of information."

She pushed deeper into the seat.

"You cold?" He flipped on the heater and got a blast of warm air.

She didn't answer but looked out the window. "In a million years, I can't imagine why Sharon would be involved in anything like this. She's a science nerd."

"You really know nothing about her, Dev."

"I know . . ." She hesitated, obviously not able to answer that. "I know I don't. But at least, whatever she's doing, maybe she's not Dr. Evil after all."

"But you still want to risk your life to find her? Even though every person we run into over here seems to think that is a very bad idea?" He heard how harsh his voice was, but he didn't care. At some point, she had to back off. "You have no idea what she's doing, other than it involves some pretty dangerous people."

She turned away completely, shutting him out, silent as they arrived at the tiny inn, parked the car, and slipped into their room, which had an outdoor entrance.

The minute he locked the door behind them, she headed to the bathroom. But before she entered, she turned to him.

"Here's the thing, Marc," she said suddenly, as if she'd been holding the thought in for the entire drive and simply couldn't wait another minute to speak her mind. "You have this big amazing family who are all just one phone call away from saving your life. You have parents you know and trust and . . . and a childhood that was probably like a damn Norman Rockwell painting."

"Not exactly Rockwell."

She just waved off the comment. "You have skills and jobs—more than one, if I understand correctly. And you have purpose. You've never known what it's like to belong to no one, to have no real reason for being on this earth, no connection to anyone, anywhere."

No, he certainly didn't. "Surely you have connections to people. Friends, the parents who raised you, someone."

She let out a soft, rueful laugh. "My parents are like

robots. The house was gloomy, the conversations were distant, the love was... Well, Hewitts don't show affection."

"So that's what you're looking for from your mother?" he asked. "A purpose for living? Some maternal affection? You're willing to risk your life and the lives of others for that?"

Her face fell like he'd slapped her. "You know damn well I want more than that," she admitted forcefully. "I want a *relationship* with her. I want to..." She swallowed. "I want to love her. And have her love me. Is that so wrong?"

"Not at all, in the right time and place. But you need to manage your expectations. Be careful of wanting too much."

"What's wrong with wanting love? Wanting a family? A real mother? A child of my own? I'm not some kind of freak, Marc. I'm just a... *woman*. I just want the same things every woman wants, and for some reason, I can't have them. It's like I don't deserve them."

But she did. More than any woman he could think of at that moment. "You're not *just* a woman, and you deserve all of those things," he said softly, taking a few more steps to close the space, ready to comfort her with his hands, his mouth, his body. "You're a strong, beautiful, smart, brave woman. You've got a soul and heart. You are flesh and blood and—"

She halted him with a raised hand. "Bad blood."

"That's crazy. You are more than your bloodline, Devyn. Much, much more."

"Do you believe that?"

"It's not important whether I do or not," he said. "Do *you* believe that?"

She leaned against the doorjamb as if the question defeated her. "I want to."

"Then believe it."

"You make it sound so easy. You have no idea what it's like to live with this over your head. It's like no matter what I do, it wouldn't change what I am. I can't change the people I'm truly connected to. Blood is thicker than water, and, sorry, but you are living proof of that."

He reached her and placed a gentle hand on her cheek, holding her gaze to make his point. "I think you're living proof that a person can overcome whatever genetic imprint they happen to think they are born with."

She just looked at him, searching his face, a question in her eyes. "You know what I wish?"

He shook his head, stroking her jaw, her lips, her cheek. "What do you wish, Dev?"

"I wish you didn't know any of this about me. I wish we met under different circumstances and that I had a clean slate in your head and we could just...have a connection."

"I don't know about you, honey, but I feel a connection." He wanted to lower his head to kiss her, but something in her eyes stopped him. "You saved my life, Devyn. That's pretty much a bona fide blood-and-sweat connection."

"Is it?"

He nodded, getting closer. But she slipped away and stepped into the bathroom, still looking at him.

"I need to...think about this." She closed the door and left him standing there, getting hard and hungry and frustrated.

He backed away and ripped his T-shirt over his head, air cooling his sweaty skin as he stripped. On the bed, he ran his hands through his hair. What would it be like to live without family, without purpose? He couldn't blame her for wanting it so much, but if finding Sharon Greenberg meant risking her life, he couldn't let her do that, either.

Somehow he'd have to convince her to abandon the plan.

On the other side of the bathroom door, the shower started, just as his phone beeped. He grabbed it, recognizing the number.

"What do you have, Gabe?"

"Enough to tell you to get your fucking ass out of there, fast. This is global, this is big, and you are risking your life if you go one inch closer to Liam Baird."

Or *Gabe* would help convince her. "Who is he?"

"A broker, a troublemaker, a bit of a rabblerouser with big connections. It's the connections they want, not him."

"And who are 'they'?"

"Tehrik-e-Jafria." At Marc's hesitation, Gabe added, "Pakistan's answer to Al-Qaeda. Dude, I'm not shittin' you. Out. Of. There."

"What's Baird doing?"

"Bioterrorism is all I was able to get, and I sold what's left of my miserable soul for that much. My guess is he's selling biochemical WMD shit to the Pakis for loads of cash."

Biochemical weapons of mass destruction. The kind made from...botulism spores. Like the very spores that had been stolen from the University of North Carolina lab right before a certain research scientist with world-renowned toxin expertise disappeared, according to the FBI files Vivi had sent.

"What about Dr. Sharon Greenberg?"

That was met with dead silence. "What about her?"

"I need to find her."

"I wouldn't go there if I were you."

"Why not?"

"Look, she's gone to the dark side. Does the dirty science work that Baird's too stupid to do but smart enough to sell," Gabe said. "And forget that she's an American. They'll take her down in the process of closing in on Baird. They're close to getting him, but nobody would tell me how close."

This would kill Devyn. "You're sure? Maybe she's undercover SIS."

"I think I'd know that."

"You don't know everything."

Gabe snorted. "I know this op is huge and it's dark. Very, very dark. The only thing I got for sure was this: you go near that project, you tip the balance of power, you alert Baird to the fact that he's about to get nailed, and you can kiss your little business, and your ass, good-bye."

"Is there any way this could be misinformation?"

Gabe sighed. "I don't get much of that, but you know, anything's possible. Just get the hell out of there, brother. Take care of business on U.S. soil. Leave the rest of the world to us guys."

And he was gone.

Now he had to go tell Devyn the good news. She was right about her bad, bad blood.

The plastic goggles squashed Sharon's bruised cheekbone, and her breath inside the surgical mask was sour from hours without food and very little water. Her legs throbbed with aches and pains, even when she rested her behind on a stool during each painstaking step of harvesting the isolated toxins from the bacteria, then putting them through purification and gasification. Her head hummed with the rush of blood and worry that she'd made a very big mistake this time.

But Sharon's hands remained steady, the cost of a physical error so high, she refused to make one.

Next to her, Baird's phone buzzed. He checked it, and his entire body language perked up as he answered. *"Salam."*

Okay, Pakistan calling.

"Of course we're ready," Liam said coolly, eyeing the vials and test tubes spread before her. He pointed at the row of aerosol cans, all but three full now.

"I can deliver them when you want them, where you want them," he said, turning away and walking to the door. "Let's discuss the details now."

Don't leave, don't leave! She wanted that information. This was the key to getting Devyn to help her out of this mess.

"The shipyard?" Liam asked, opening the door. "You'll have to get through tough waters. Maybe you'll need"—his gaze fell on her—"a bargaining chip."

Of course, her instincts had been right. Liam would throw her out there as a hostage. But how shocked he would be to learn the truth. The only problem was...No, it wasn't a problem. Not if she could figure out a way to have Devyn help her.

She held the test tube over the flame to transform the liquid inside to gas, listening hard for more information.

But the room was virtually soundproofed, and she heard nothing for a few minutes until the hinges squeaked and she knew she was no longer alone. She stole a glance over her shoulder and met the blue eyes of Ian O'Rourke.

Hope flared like the flame on her Bunsen burner. She looked over his street clothes. "Please get proper covering, Mr. O'Rourke. You could die by breathing in one of these spores."

He picked up a mask from the table and slipped it on.

"Are you almost finished?" The mask muffled his voice, but not the tone of concern.

"Three more cans. He wants twenty-four."

He didn't say anything for a few seconds, watching her work. Her hands didn't tremble, but her insides did. Could she trust this man? Was he SIS?

She thought that occasionally about Marie, the housekeeper, too. That woman lurked around every corner and seemed to have enough of a reason to hate the IRA and its descendants. Both of them could be working part of the same assignment she was, or neither of them. It was time to find out. Because when this was all over, she'd either have no allies or she'd be dead.

And that wasn't the reason she'd put herself through this particular hell. One man had to dangle and die. And only one. She had to remember why she'd agreed to do something so vile as create poison to kill people. The real reason she stood in this room turning spores into canisters of death.

He cleared his throat. "Mr. Baird didn't happen to mention a location on his call?" he asked softly.

If she said or did anything to give herself away to the *wrong* person, she'd be dead and everything she'd done the past few weeks would have been for naught. But...

"The shipyard," she said.

Desperation pressed her down, but her fingers remained steady as she tilted the vial.

"Do you need anything, Dr. Greenberg?" Ian asked.

In other words, a reward for the information she'd just given him?

"I don't think you can get me what I need, Mr. O'Rourke."

He looked hard at her. "Try me."

For a long moment, they stared at each other, unspoken questions hanging in the dank air between them. Should she . . . *try* him?

Behind her mask, she wet her parched lips and took the biggest chance of her life. "Do you have a daughter, Mr. O'Rourke?"

He barely blinked. "I have a son."

She nodded. "You love him."

"Very much."

"Would you do anything for him?"

A smile flickered in his eyes. "I believe I am right now."

She let out a quick breath. "I need you to get a message to someone," she whispered.

He didn't move, but she could see that he knew who she meant. And how to find her. This was either the stupidest thing she'd ever done or the smartest.

She finally exhaled. "Give her . . ." She closed her eyes and reached deep into her pocket, pulling out the picture she'd been carrying since she got here. Taking a pen next to her notebook, she wrote the first thing that came to mind underneath the tiny image, then handed it to him. "This." She stole a look at him, trying to read an unreadable expression. "Can you do that?"

"No promises."

"Please?" Her voice cracked. "Please," she repeated.

"I'll try."

"I have to trust you," she said softly. "I have to trust you work for the right side in all of this."

He nodded. "I do."

"Ian!" Liam barked the name as he threw open the door, and both of them startled a little. "I'll be right back. Don't leave her, not for one second. Do you understand? I don't care if she pisses herself—she doesn't leave this room until the last three cans are done."

Ian agreed tersely.

"And for Chrissakes, put on some fucking gloves," Liam added. "You're no good to me paralyzed, man."

Behind her, the door slammed again. Ian made no move to add the protective gear, even when Sharon reached for a canister and placed its open top over the test tube, a silvery cloud moving inside.

"I have two more to do," she told him.

"And then, Dr. Greenberg, your job is done."

Ian moved to the door, behind her and out of sight, while she went through the motions without even thinking. The hard part, the isolation and harvesting, had been done hours ago.

"Do you need anything else?" he asked quietly.

"Only . . . a chance." A chance *not* to be the hostage.

"Then take it."

She popped the top on the canister, handling it carefully. After she'd returned it safely to the shelf, she turned around to face him.

But the room was empty, and her prison door stood wide open.

For a moment, she just stared, expecting him to appear

at any moment, having stepped away into the vestibule. But he was gone. And she ... she could escape.

Slowly, she lowered the goggles and took a few tentative steps toward the door.

She took one deep breath and stepped into the vestibule. Then up the stairs, expecting to be jumped or stopped or worse. The door at the top of the stairs was unlocked, opening to a dimly lit kitchen. She glanced around the empty room, then entered, her eye on the door.

She put her hand on the knob and turned it, her heartbeat so loud and hard and fast that she could barely breathe. Outside it was cold and wet and dark.

"Run." The voice came from behind a hedge, a familiar voice, a woman's voice. "Run before he kills you."

Marie was crouched in the shadows of shrubbery. The housekeeper's usually sad eyes were bright, and her expression was set in a strong, serious line. Sharon almost reached for her, but Marie pointed toward the pathway. "As fast as you can!"

"Marie, please, come with me," she urged, reaching out her hand.

The woman drew back, horror on her freckled Irish face. "I can't!"

"You can. We can escape. Before the gunfire, before ... You know what's going to happen, don't you? The raid?"

Marie waved toward the road. "Go. You can get out of here."

"They won't care about us," Sharon insisted. "Come with me. Come!" She reached for the woman again, but Marie jerked back.

"She's gone!" Someone shouted from inside.

"Go," Marie said again. "I'll cover for you!"

Footsteps made her decision; she'd go alone. She launched into a run, following the bushes, taking her path to the cemetery. It was locked at night, but if she could make it all the way down the one side, there was that gate where she'd been hit. Maybe it was—

Gunfire cracked through the night, a bullet exploding on the pavement near her feet. Another shot deafened and nearly hit her.

Stretching her legs, she dug for speed and strength, rounding the bushes into the street, staying in the shadows, wind whistling through her ears.

She made it to the thickest of the bushes on one side of the massive cemetery grounds. If she could get in there, she could get lost among those ten thousand graves. There were places to hide, to wait this out.

To wait for the young woman who surely would come to help the mother she'd never met. That had to be what sent Devyn across the ocean—that need to connect. If it was strong enough, she'd come.

She threw herself into the bushes, hitting the wall behind, the bricks scraping her hands. Could she climb it? If she could, if she could just get over it, she could hide among the bramble and bushes of the most unkempt areas of the cemetery.

Placing one sneaker on the first brick, she ignored the pain in her legs, the burn spurring her on to pull herself up. With strength she had no idea she had, her fingers found the top of the wall and she hoisted her whole body up with a grunt.

She lifted her right leg, hooking her calf around the top of the wall, the cone-shaped cement tearing at her clothes and stopping her cold. Her left foot slipped, driving the stone deeper into her right thigh, ripping her pants but not her flesh.

A gunshot exploded, the bullet whizzing right over her head. Jesus, they had her. She had one second, maybe less, to live or die.

With a furious cry, she heaved her body up and finally straddled the top, a sitting target for the shooter. Ducking, she pulled her other leg over and balanced on her hands, ready to leap to the other side just as another shot blasted the night, the sound and fury of it thrusting her to the ground.

She thudded onto the earth, her legs buckling, her teeth cracking with the impact. Frozen, she tried to breathe and listen for the next shot or the sound of them scaling the wall behind her.

In the distance, she heard footsteps and men's voices.

She stumbled to her feet just as a new pain fired through her body, a burn so intense she cried out, slamming her hand over her arm, crying into the mask she still wore as she realized what caused the agony in her arm.

A bullet. Blood poured out and fire coursed over her skin.

Now her fingers trembled uncontrollably. She had only one hope. The daughter she'd ignored for thirty years. Would she come?

CHAPTER 23

The shower water had to be damn near a hundred degrees, burning her face, her chest, right through to her heart.

And still Devyn was cold.

Why was her mother on a suicide mission?

There was no immediate answer, but the voice in her head was still loud: *No one on the good side goes on a suicide mission.*

Or did they? She knew nothing of the spy world, of British intelligence, of the "spooks," as Marc called them. Maybe they *did* go on suicide missions. Closing her eyes, face to the stinging water, she clung to the hope that started in the bell tower. The hope that Sharon Greenberg was some kind of high-level government agent working to bring down a terrorist.

"Jesus, Devyn, it's like a sauna in here."

Marc stood right outside the glass doors of the shower; she could tell by the proximity of his voice. But she couldn't see him through the steam that had turned the door milky white or the puffs of clouds her burning shower water had produced.

"You better have invaded my privacy with an estimated time of departure."

"I did not." His voice was flat, and serious.

She smelled a fight coming on. She smeared her hand on the glass, clearing a section in front of her face, getting a watery view of his bare chest. She swiped her hand straight down the glass a foot or so, getting a complete view of the rest of him.

So, maybe it wasn't a fight she smelled. If it was, he fought dirty.

"Then why are you here?" Almost immediately, the glass started clouding again, but it was still transparent enough for her to see his manhood, nested in dark hair, not erect but alive.

Finally, she started to feel warm.

"I have more information about your... about Dr. Greenberg."

Her lust subsided. "What is it?"

He didn't speak, but she could see his silhouette as he shifted from one foot to the other. He didn't want to tell her. This wasn't good.

"I spoke to my brother again."

"The CIA agent." She let just a little cynicism taint her tone. Because, really, who *knew* a CIA agent, let alone grew up with one?

"He actually doesn't work for the CIA."

She snorted softly. Case closed. "Then you misled me."

"He works for a contractor for the CIA, but he is extremely well connected in the world of dark operations and—"

"Dark operations?" She almost pushed open the glass door so she could really nail him with a look, but she still needed the barrier. "What the hell does that *mean*, Marc?"

"It means he knows exactly what your birth mother is doing and who she is doing it for."

She felt her legs weaken just a little, the familiar cold in her gut radiating over her, counteracting the hot water that still sluiced over her body. All because of the way he said that.

She didn't answer, waiting for the verdict. Good or bad? Guilty or not? Pride or shame?

"She's working for a broker, making biochemical weapons of mass destruction that sources believe are being sold to the Pakistanis for future terrorist attacks."

Her stomach turned to ice. "What sources?"

"Really fucking reliable sources. She's a traitor to our country, Devyn, working on a project that needs to be stopped or a lot of people could die." Each word stabbed, more hurtful than the stinging water.

"Fortunately," he continued, softening the blow with a gentler voice. "There's a whole bunch of guys out there closing in and trying to stop her and catch the real terrorists who are buying and selling and using what she's making. We cannot get in the way of that, Devyn. It would be foolish and stupid."

And she could not have a relationship with a woman who would commit such acts. That would be more foolish and more stupid.

Oh, God, where did that leave her? Alone and ashamed and...*alone*.

Just like that, everything that mattered stopped mattering. Everything she wanted dried up. There would never be a connection with that woman, only another shadow of shame.

"Devyn." He said her name as his hand landed on the door, but she was fast and grabbed the handle, holding the glass shut. "You're deluding yourself if you think—"

"Not anymore I'm not." She closed her eyes as the pain rolled over her.

He tugged at the door again, but she clung to the metal bar, refusing to face him, naked and shredded and vulnerable.

At least she hadn't sold Finn MacCauley's phone number for this information.

"Please," he said softly. "I understand this is difficult for you, but it's time to end this search. We're not infiltrating a terrorist cell so you can face these facts in person."

"Yeah, I got that, Marc." She waited for the fury to rock her, but nothing came. No drive to know the truth. No determination to face her real mother.

"Devyn." This time he was truly gentle, coaxing her. "Please, honey. Come out here."

And do what? Let him comfort her with kisses and sex? All meaningless, without a future, without hope because she could never have anyone. Not anyone who wouldn't betray her. Not even...

But she *could*. She could have someone.

She gave the door a push, and it popped open, a puff of steam trapped in the shower fogging over Marc.

Without hesitation, he stepped into the spray, wrapping his arms around her so that they touched full length, nothing but water between them.

"You know I'm right, don't you?" he asked, no smugness in the question at all.

She nodded.

"You're going to give this up, aren't you?"

Another nod.

"We can go back to the States and you can—"

She put her hand over his mouth. If they were going to do this, then it wouldn't be with him under the illusion she was paying with Finn's number. It wouldn't be under illusions or delusions. She'd tell him the truth about everything.

"I burned Finn MacCauley's phone number."

For a moment, he said nothing, no doubt processing what she meant. Would he explode in anger? Steal this chance before she even took it?

"I know. I saw you."

"Oh." The word came out like he'd punched her. "And still . . . you risked your life today."

"So did you," he whispered. "And this was never about getting information about Finn, Dev." He eased her to the wall, bracing her there.

Against her stomach, his erection grew, and deep in her belly, she responded, unable to stop the twist of longing that made her want to rock against him. Nature's way, of course.

"This was never about fooling you," Marc said, already starting to move against her. "Or seducing you or getting you to do anything except leave Belfast."

"And yet," she said, looking up at him, lost in the depths of his eyes as the first shards of ice began to melt inside her and her need took hold. "You somehow did all those things."

He gave her a smoky half smile. "I'm good like that."

"Oh, yes, you are." So, so good.

Why couldn't she have exactly what she wanted? From him, by him, *with* him?

It didn't have to mean...forever. It was just that he was perfect in every way. So perfect that he could give her the one thing she needed so fundamentally it was like breathing.

Her hope for a bond with her birth mother was gone, lost forever. But her hope for another kind of bond, the one she longed for the most, was right here in her arms.

A baby. He could give that to her.

She curled one leg around his calf, somehow managing to get them closer still.

"Marc." She spread her hands on his chest, the flesh and sprinkling of hair soaked under her fingers, the muscles hard under her palms. "I need something from you."

He stroked her hair, his hand gliding down to caress her breast, filling his palm and thumbing her hardened nipple. "I noticed."

"I need you to give me something."

A slow smile pulled as he rocked his hips against her, the length of his erection branding her. "Right here. In the shower?" He kissed her forehead, already heading for her mouth, already caressing her waist and back possessively.

"Yes, here. Now. Please." Her heart hammered, the mix of hope and lust making her tremble from the inside out.

He found her lips and they kissed under the spray, the water making their mouths slide against each other as he inched her back against the wall. With the hot, wet marble against her back and the hot, wet man pressed against her front, she felt a full-scale ache of need blossom between her legs.

"Devyn." He kissed her, touching her everywhere, his

voice raspy with desire, his breathing already tight. "You sure you're doing this for the right reason?"

There was no other reason. "Yes."

She matched him move for move, caressing his body, adoring every inch of his physique, devouring every wet, hard, sexy piece of him. Their tongues collided, their hands meshed, their legs curled around each other as the blistering hot water pounded on his back and shoulders, exploding droplets on his tanned skin that she licked off.

He sunk deeper against her, kissing her harder, sucking her tongue into his mouth and guiding her hands around his shaft. Stroking him, listening to him moan with pleasure, she spread her legs and let him slide her up the wall enough to get under her.

With ease, he positioned his erection between her legs, and she rolled against the length of it, rubbing, riding, clinging to him with her arms and legs.

"Inside," she murmured, desperate. "Get inside."

He pushed her up higher, bringing them face-to-face, jabbing his tip at her opening. His eyes narrowed and his lips curled back. "Wait."

"No," she insisted, letting herself down so he went in farther.

"Wait." He visibly dug for control, pulling out even though she tried to draw him in.

Didn't he get it? Didn't he know what she wanted? One powerful thrust, a few strokes, and she could have—

"I need to get something," he said, slowly letting her return to shaky tiptoes.

"No, Marc, please don't."

He backed up, frowning at her. "A condom."

"No."

"No?"

"I've been to the doctor so many times," she said. "You don't have to worry about me."

He just looked at her like she was crazy. "Sorry, it's SOP."

She shook her head, biting her lip, knowing the tears were right there and praying he'd think they were shower spray. Didn't he want her enough to ignore standard operating procedures just this once?

"Can't you...please..." Was he going to make her beg? To ask for what she wanted? She would. Right now, she'd get down on both knees and plead. "I need this, Marc. To be whole." Her voice cracked and her throat closed. But she didn't care. "Can't you give this to me?"

Very slowly, realization dawned. "You want to get pregnant."

Shame rolled over her, but she squashed it. So what if she was desperate? What did her pride matter? This was all that mattered. "Marc, I want a baby. That's all I want."

His eyes widened. "So I'm, what, a *donor*?"

"No, no. You're...perfect." She opened her legs more, let him in deeper, moved just enough to see the response he was fighting darken his eyes. "You don't have to have any responsibilities, nothing. I just...want a chance."

For what seemed like an eternity, he just stared at her, no readable expression on his face, except the possibility of a raging internal debate.

"This isn't what you want," he said.

"Yes, it is." Tears rolled now and her whole body trembled. "A child of my own, a chance for that bond, with no one to wonder and worry about what my half of the gene mix would bring."

"Devyn, you're wrong about that. The right man would—"

"You *are* the right man," she insisted. "You are. Everything about you is so good and solid and right." She moved again, barely aware she was grasping his shoulders, clinging to the last shred of hope. "Please give this to me. Please."

"I...can't." He stepped away and she almost cried out.

"Yes, you can. I'll disappear. You'll never have to know what happened. I'll leave you alone—"

"That's not what I want."

"But, Marc, it's all I want. In the whole world, it's all I want." Tears continued streaming, salt rolling into her mouth, the sob choking her. "My mother...my father... my whole life is just empty. This is all I want."

He stared at her for a long, long time, and she waited again for a verdict.

Finally, he put his hands on her shoulders, and she braced for him to say no, but he added pressure, pushing harder, taking her down to the shower floor. All the way he held her gaze, his eyes sharp, his mouth drawn.

"This is what you want?"

She nodded.

Without warning, he was on top of her. Automatically, she wrapped her legs around his hips and lifted her mouth for a kiss, but he refused, holding his head up, bracing his arms on the slick tile, kneeing her thighs farther apart.

He thrust inside her, a hard, vicious jam of flesh into flesh, bowing his back and lifting his head high enough to deny her the ability to see his face. Her eyes widened in shock as he went deeper, his breath growing ragged, his moans unstoppable as he pumped into her.

Each stroke wound her tighter, made her want more, brought her to the breaking point. He was engorged, slamming into her with fury and purpose and sweaty need that matched hers. She reached up to his shoulders, but he remained impassive, a huge space between their chests, connected only at the hips, only by their sex.

She bit her lip hard enough to draw blood. She rode with him, doing everything she knew to pull an orgasm from him, feeling him stiffen, his balls as hard as stones against her.

He was almost there. Almost.

He swore softly, his face reddening, his mouth pulled as he got lost at the brink of an orgasm.

"Marc, please, honey, *please*."

At her words, he looked down at her, and for one flash of a second, their gazes clashed. He closed his eyes and thrust again and again, all the way in, over and over and over right to the very edge.

He gritted his teeth and tendons pulled in his neck, his control nearly obliterated. This was it. He was...

He yanked himself out with a guttural cry. "I can't," he moaned, crushing his erection against her. With a low, long growl of release, he spurted his seed all over her stomach.

All she could hear was the hiss of the shower and the pain of his breathing. She felt the pounding of his heart as a sob lodged in her chest.

"Devyn." He forced her to look at him. "I can't make a baby like...this."

Like *this*...with *her*. Of course. The crush was so hard on her heart that she couldn't breathe. She couldn't move.

But he did. Barely recovered, he kneeled over her

and turned his face up to the water and let the spray pour over him. She touched her stomach, the few drops of his semen sticky, then washed away by the shower water. He remained facing the water, his hands hung at his sides, his chest heaving.

After a moment, he stood and reached out his hand to help her up. She shook her head.

"Leave me alone," she whispered, her voice cracking with shame so deep she could taste it. "Just, please. Leave me alone."

And he did, closing the glass door with a final click. She lay in the shower spray until it turned ice cold, matching the temperature of her heart.

When Zach Angelino got mad, it wasn't a pretty thing.

"What the fuck are you trying to do, Vivi, put us out of business? Not to mention this information is critical to Marc's case. Finn MacCauley recruited Sharon Greenberg to work for this Baird guy?"

The facts were there, in the fugitive's handwriting.

"I'm not trying to put us out of business, Zach," she said. "I'm trying to do just the opposite. Look, there's a phone number right next to his name. A 617 area code, here in Boston."

"Have you called it?" Zach demanded.

"No," she said. "It could be tapped or traced and then get disconnected. That's why I don't know what to do. I've tried to call Marc about ten times, but he's not answering. I thought you and I could brainstorm another direction."

Zach considered the letter again, then looked up at Vivi. "The only direction is downtown to One Center Plaza."

The FBI's Boston office. "I knew you'd say that."

"Then why didn't you do it?" Zach asked harshly. "Quit trying to be a bounty hunter. That's not what we do."

"I'm not," she denied. "I'm investigating this letter. If it leads to one of America's most wanted, can you imagine what that'll do for the Guardian Angelinos?"

He clearly didn't agree. "This could be crucial evidence, and by holding it, we are putting our company in jeopardy." He stood, sliding the letter back to her. "Get your ass over to Lang's office and give it to him. That'll get us more business, and frankly, I want paying clients, not glory."

"I want high-profile clients because they pay more," she countered. "How else can we grow?"

"One case at a time," he said. "But, Vivi, I'm not going to argue with you. Do what's right."

"That's just the problem—I don't know what's right." Before he could argue, she leaned forward, pinning him with a look. "For some reason, I don't trust Colton Lang. He makes me feel funny."

Zach puffed out a breath. "He has the hots for you is all."

"Hah, very funny. He wouldn't look twice at a woman like me, and honestly, I wish it were that simple."

"How so?"

"I can't explain it, Zach, but my gut's on fire."

"It's on fire with ambition, Vivi, and while that's an admirable thing, you can't let your dreams of big business make stupid decisions for you. Lang is one of the top guys in that office, probably in line for an SAC position. Plus, he's a straight shooter. What's not to trust? The fact that he has a crew cut and wears golf shirts? That makes him 'the man' to you?"

She smiled. "I'm not indicting the guy because he's

J.Crew on the putting green. I just get the sense that he's not telling us everything."

"He's not," Zach agreed. "He openly admitted he wasn't."

"And he's told us finding Finn MacCauley isn't a priority. Why should we hand this to him?" She shook her head. "He doesn't even know Marc's been looking for Dr. Greenberg. We could get in trouble for not following his orders."

"I respect your gut feelings, Vivi, and we're equal partners in this, so I'll go along with what you decide. But you asked for my advice and I'm giving it: turn this over to the FBI and we'll benefit more in the long run. Now, I gotta go. Sammi found a house and we're going to meet the Realtor there."

"Good luck with that."

"And good luck with that." He pointed to the paper. "Do the right thing. That's my motto."

"I thought your motto was 'go with your gut.' Right now the two are at war."

He nodded to someone in the hall. "Here's Nino, eavesdropping like a spy. See what he says."

Nino walked in, not even slightly ashamed to have been caught. "I think you should turn it over to the FBI."

"So I'm outnumbered." She fingered the paper and leaned back in her chair, tipping it onto the back legs, her gaze on the damning words in front of her. "Look at what he wrote, Nino."

" 'Sometimes a few have to die for the needs of the many,' " he quoted. "I've read the letter a few times."

Finn MacCauley was a prick, and so was Sharon Greenberg. And the FBI agent? An unknown element right now.

Nino tapped his watch. "Maybe you can catch that

Lang before he leaves for the day. Then you could take me home to Sudbury. I'll cook dinner for you."

"God, you drive a hard bargain." She let the front legs of her chair slap back to the floor. "Maybe I'm misjudging Lang. You know, if I present this right, maybe he'll let me work with him on the case. That way I could do the right thing and still get a little of the credit."

"He seems like a reasonable enough man," Nino said, waiting as she carefully slid the reconstructed puzzle into a plastic sleeve.

"I don't know about reasonable." Vivi imagined the FBI agent's reaction to her news. "But I have to try. We don't have the resources to follow up on this, but I don't want to be squeezed out completely."

They locked up and headed to the back alley, to the ultimate in prized possessions, a Back Bay parking spot, where they kept the company Expedition. She helped Nino climb into the front seat, tamping down the thought that her eightysomething great-uncle was having a hard time climbing into SUVs. She couldn't stand to think about him getting old.

But his mind was as sharp as hers, and all the way around the common and into the financial district, they talked about the letter and about all the possible words that were missing.

And came up with nothing new. Maybe the FBI, with all their high-tech capabilities, could figure this out. She slowly cruised Cambridge Street, looking for a spot when the brake lights on a blue Scion lit and she slowed to snag the spot.

Just as the car maneuvered out of its spot, which was tiny as hell and going to be a real fight for the big SUV, a man jogged in front of them, headed right toward the blue car.

"Look who it is," Nino said.

Vivi instantly recognized him. "Colton Lang." She watched Lang approach the driver's side of the car, his long, muscular body moving gracefully. Must be all that time on the golf course.

"You gonna ogle him or get this letter into his hands?"

"I'm gonna . . ." Lang jogged around the front of the car to open the passenger door, climbing in. "Follow him."

The Scion took off down Cambridge, weaving into the left lane to pick up speed.

"What are you going to do? Go to his house?"

"I don't know," she admitted. "I can't let this sit all night."

She touched the accelerator and stayed three car lengths behind. Before long, the Scion turned down a side street, picked up Beacon where it headed west, and drove along the side of the Common, then the Public Garden. Lang's driver found a spot and parked. She stayed on the street, inching along as the two men got out of the car.

"That's no FBI agent," she said, checking out the older man who climbed out of the driver's seat. "They have to have an age limit."

"Hey, watch it," Nino said. "Although that guy does look more my age than yours."

"I guess I'll wait until he gets back and grab him when he goes to the car. Interrupting them would just be awkward."

The two men headed toward the gates of the Public Garden, leaving her no option but to slide into a handicapped spot, where she kept the motor on for a quick escape if a cop came while she watched. Deep in conversation, Lang towered over the older man, whose face was tucked under the brim of a Red Sox baseball cap.

"Think it's Lang's dad?" she asked.

Just inside the gates of the park, they sat on a bench, still within sight, the lake behind them. They talked for a few minutes, close to each other. Vivi watched, still intrigued by the meeting—by everything about Lang, she had to admit—while Nino unfolded the letter they'd pieced and taped together.

"You know what I think we should do before we hand this over?" Nino asked. "Call that number."

She'd love to. "But then we really *would* be obstructing justice. Lang'll never give us any business."

"You were ready to bring the guy in on your own."

She sighed. "I know. I'm going to have to beg Lang to work on this case, and I just know that stick-in-the-mud is going to say no."

Nino already had his phone out. "I can star sixty-nine it, then say I have a wrong number."

She was only mildly surprised Nino knew that trick. "What will that get you?" she asked.

"A voice. You can tell Lang if a man or woman answered." He dialed, and Vivi didn't stop him, her curiosity too strong. Once she turned over that letter to Lang, she might be completely out of the loop on this.

The men were getting up, separating from each other. Lang headed deeper into the park, toward the pond where the swan boats were tied up and docked at the side.

"Oh, crap, is he going to walk back to the office? I can't follow him through the park."

The other man shuffled back toward the street, coming through the gated entrance not twenty-five feet from where they were parked.

"Okay, it's ringing," Nino said.

But her gaze was riveted to the older man whose step faltered at the curb, and for a minute, Vivi thought he was going to stumble and fall. Instead, he reached into his pocket and pulled out a cell phone, frowning at the screen.

"Still ringing."

Vivi's whole body went numb.

The man flipped open the phone, put it to his ear, and spoke. She heard the "Hello?" through the speaker in Nino's hand.

"Oh my God," she whispered. "That's Finn MacCauley."

And disappearing into the darkness of the Public Garden was the FBI agent who claimed he wasn't interested in finding him.

CHAPTER 24

There was no satellite service, even when Marc stepped outside to try and call Boston, which wasn't that unusual for these more remote parts of Northern Ireland. Unable to give or get any new information, he waited in the room for Devyn to come out of the bathroom.

Giving him just enough time to hate himself for what he'd just done but accept that he'd do it again.

The ultimate rescue was right in the palm of his hand, literally, and he'd turned it down. Way to go.

He closed his eyes, wanting to picture Devyn naked and wet and wanting him, but all he could see was Laura, spiteful and mocking and hating him. He may have had the power to make her pay for her crimes, but she had the power to make him feel the real pain of loss. How could he ever give that power to another woman?

No matter what she planned to do with it, giving a

baby to Devyn was setting him up for another world of hurt. She'd have to find another man.

Yet, something very elemental in him twisted at the thought. He didn't want her to find another man.

He looked up when the bathroom door opened, surprised to see her dried and dressed...for travel. He'd expected a robe or maybe a T-shirt and shower-wet hair, not jeans, a hooded jacket, and sneakers. She had her purse over her shoulder and a don't-stop-me look on her face.

"You're not going to Belfast," he said softly. "Because I will stop you. With my gun, if necessary."

"Not necessary. I'm going to Boston," she replied. "The inn owner said he'd get me a cab to the closest airport."

He sat up from his lounging position on the pillows, not believing her. "You got phone service in there?"

She gave him a wry smile. "Not the response I expected, but, yes, I did."

"You're not going," he said. "We'll go together, tomorrow."

"Don't worry," she said. "I really *am* going home. I'm not trying to fool you and run into a spy shoot-out at a terrorist cell to save my mother. I've had enough bad ideas for one day."

The words stabbed him. "It wasn't that bad of an idea."

She skewered him with a dark look. "Don't try to make me feel better. I'm embarrassed enough."

Embarrassed? "Why?"

She closed her eyes. "I practically attacked you."

"You did not." He rose from the bed to get closer, but she took a step back, holding her shoulder bag like a shield. "There were two very aroused people and all kinds of consent going on in there."

"Not *all* kinds."

"Devyn." He reached for her cheek, but she ducked his touch. "You surprised me, that's all."

"I know what I did," she said, averting her gaze and shifting her purse to the other arm. "Desperation makes strange bedfellows."

"Don't I know it."

She looked up, confused. "You're not desperate."

"I was, once. Enough," he added quickly, "to understand why you'd make a deal with the devil."

"And you're not a devil."

"It's a figure of speech. I just want to say that it's not you. It's *not*."

"Don't." She held up her hand, fire in her eyes. "Don't give me the speech. I know you think I'm nuts for thinking that what I come from makes me unattractive to a potential...father."

"I do," he said. "I'm not going to lie. But what you wanted me to do, well, at least maybe that means you've come around. Maybe now you believe you're worthy of a child."

"But not *your* child."

"I didn't say that."

"You didn't have to say anything. You showed me what you're made of, and it's impressive. Control I didn't think most men even had." She managed to step by him.

"I'm not most men," he whispered.

Slowly she turned, her lower lip trapped under her teeth as if she could stop the trembling. "That's why I asked." She closed her eyes and let out a soft laugh. "Except I didn't ask, did I? I'm sorry I was so aggressive."

"Don't apologize. I should have stopped it before... before I did."

The words seemed to take the steel out of her spine, and he reached for her again. This time, she let him grasp her shoulders, meeting his gaze. Her eyes were blue pools of pain, locked on him.

"It was a crazy, impulsive idea," she said. "My worst kind. But when you told me about Sharon and the...the terrorist, I just went nuts."

"There's nothing nuts about wanting a baby." He squeezed her shoulders and swallowed. "I want one myself."

"But not—"

"*Not*," he interjected forcefully, "unless I get to be a full-time, one hundred percent father. What you're proposing—"

"I wasn't *proposing*."

"Devyn, listen to me." He swallowed hard, pulling her closer. "I've had..." No, that wouldn't work. "I know the..." No, he didn't really *know*. "This isn't the first time..."

"What are you trying to say?"

"My wife aborted our child without telling me."

She blinked at him, paling. "Oh, God. That's horrible."

"Yes, it was."

"But were you absolutely sure...I mean, you said she had a lover."

"A lover who had had a vasectomy. And, yes, I was sure. And it wasn't an act of choice, but pure revenge after I refused to cover for her. She lorded the pregnancy over me, knowing how much"—he let out a slow, long sigh—"knowing how much I wanted the baby."

She put her hand on her chest, as though she could feel the pain right where he did. "Couldn't you stop her?"

"No. How? It's her body, her baby. The day she was arraigned and set free on bail, she disappeared and I tried to find her. I got my brother JP to use a police cruiser, and we stormed through Boston, searching for her. Searching every clinic..." His throat closed at the memory. "I finally found her. It was too late."

She took his hand in hers, tears of sympathy wetting her eyes. "That was so unfair, Marc. I'm really sorry. I don't quite know how..." She struggled with the words, searching his face. "I would never do something like that, obviously."

"That's why I can't do what you want." He drew her to the bed and pulled her down to sit next to him. "You need to understand that it has nothing to do with you and everything to do with me."

"With *her*," she corrected. "I would never—"

"I know that, but what you would do or not do isn't the point." He looked away, shaking his head.

"Then what is?"

"Love."

She just stared at him.

"I just really believe that a child should come from love. Not desperation, not a deal, not an arrangement. I know it's old school, but—"

"No, it's not." She stood slowly, wrapping her arms around her waist as she walked a few steps away. "It's what we both know is right, and that's why I'm embarrassed."

"Because I don't love you?"

"Because you can't love me."

Who said that?

"I thought we could..." She shook her head. "It was crazy. It was really wrong of me."

"It wasn't crazy." He stood to get in front of her and hold her face to force her to look at him. "The timing is wrong, and that's the only thing that's wrong with your idea."

She tilted her head, rubbing her cheek against his palm, the fight gone from her face, her expression all compassion. "I just want a family."

"I know. But I can't be the one to—"

The rap on the door was hard, loud, and made her jump. "That's my cab."

"I'll cancel it."

"No, Marc, don't. I want to leave. Tonight."

"All right. We'll go together." He walked over to the door. "Can you wait a few minutes?" he called. "We're still packing."

"I don't have a few minutes." The voice was gruff, low, forceful. "Open up."

Marc drew back and glanced at Devyn, taking one step to the left to retrieve his gun from the dresser.

"Get in the bathroom," he ordered.

He peered out the peephole, then snapped the rack of the Glock with a violent yank, jumping to the side of the door, out of firing range. "Jesus Christ, what is it with this guy?"

"Who is it?"

"The person who shows up when we need him most, every time."

"Padraig Fallon?"

He nodded and waited until Devyn was hidden by the bathroom wall. "What do you want, Fallon?"

"Is the lass okay?"

"Yes. What's going on?"

"Let me in and I'll tell you."

"Just tell me from there."

He heard the older man suck in a breath and let it out slowly. "Listen, son, I'm breakin' every fucking rule in the book to help you. The Greenberg woman's in trouble. She needs you."

Devyn was out of the bathroom instantly. "What's the matter?"

God*damn* it. They should have just left when she wanted to.

"She escaped, and she's been shot."

He looked at Devyn, dismay swaying her whole body. "You can't believe him," he mouthed. "It's a setup."

She gave him a pleading look.

"I have a message for her," Fallon said. "For Rose."

Devyn's eyes widened. "Please? Let me hear." She hustled closer to the door, and Marc moved her out of firing range, behind him.

"Then deliver it, Fallon. And go."

"She did her job, and one of our men let her go."

"What job?" Marc demanded, one hand pressing to keep Devyn back. "She works for Baird. She's a terrorist, and we don't give a damn if she's shot or not."

"She *doesn't* work for Baird," Fallon said. "She's undercover for the SIS, as I am. Her cover was blown when she tried to contact Rose to tell her to get out of Belfast."

Was she? Gabe hadn't thought so, and he would know, wouldn't he? Maybe.

"She escaped and was shot, but no one on either side is going after her," Fallon continued.

"Where is she?" Devyn asked.

It didn't matter where she was—they weren't going. "We can't compromise the mission," Marc said.

"The mission's complete," Fallon said. "Baird's got what he wants from her, and we..." He sighed audibly. "God love the MI5, but we are not set up to save martyrs. If you want to find her, my contact told me she's in the cemetery, though that's not much of a pinpoint location considering the size of it."

Marc peered out the peephole again, taking in Fallon's wrinkled face and the hands he held out from his coat to show he was unarmed. "How'd you get this message from her?"

"A young man by the name of Ian O'Rourke, another British agent who's undercover on this operation. He's the person who let Dr. Greenberg escape. He asked me to deliver the message to you. She wants to see you desperately, ma'am."

Desperation again.

"Fallon," he said. "Greenberg is a terrorist working for Liam Baird. This was confirmed by someone in a position to know."

"Unless that someone is the chief of the SIS, lad, then he isn't in a position to know. This operation has been completely dark, and there's misinformation everywhere."

"Yeah, like right outside this door."

"You're wrong, son." His voice was low and quiet. "The doctor was brought in at the topmost levels of the SIS, and she's risked her life on this mission. May have lost it, and she told my son she wants to see her daughter before she dies."

Devyn's eyes went wide and wild. "How can we find her?"

Oh, shit. There would be no fighting this battle.

"Ian said she went over a wall at Crescent Drive.

Across the street from Direct Furniture. That's when she was shot."

"We can be there in a few hours, Marc."

"We're not going."

She stepped away toward the dresser, and he thought she was going to charge the door, but instead she picked something up and held it out to him. The medal that had popped off Fallon in the gunfight.

"Slide this under the door."

He took it and kneeled down, slipping the medal over the concrete while Devyn peered out the peephole. After a minute, she stepped back. "He just walked away and put something in the door."

"This is another wild-goose chase, Devyn. We're not going."

"See what he left."

Marc carefully opened the door, and something fluttered from where it had been lodged in the jamb. He picked up the small square and turned it over.

A picture of a newborn baby. Underneath it, someone had written *Rose Devyn Mulvaney. September 2, 1981. Until we meet...*

"Did you call a cab for an airport run?" A man walked up the path toward the door and Marc backed away, but Devyn had grabbed the picture from his hand.

"Can you take me to—"

"Just a second," Marc said, closing the door in the guy's face.

"I'll be right there," Devyn called, grabbing her purse where she'd left it on the bed. She stuffed the picture in and then pulled out the black and gold scarf he'd bought her in Bangor, wrapping it around her neck twice to hide her face.

"That's not going to protect you," he said.

"But this is." Digging in the purse again, she lifted the hot little Taurus Millennium pistol they'd taken from the agent in the bell tower. "I'll be fine."

Jesus Christ. "We don't need you to wait," he called to cabbie. "We're not going—" Devyn's eyes flashed and she opened her mouth, but he covered it. "To the airport." He lowered his voice to a soft whisper. "We'll take the rental car and be in Milltown in less than two hours."

She breathed a sigh into his palm. "Why did you change your mind?"

"Because it's time you find out what you're made of."

CHAPTER 25

Thank God she kept a spare board in the back of the Expedition. Tossing the keys to Nino, Vivi flipped off her belt and climbed over the console and into the way back to get it.

"What are you doing, Viviana?" Nino demanded. "Going after a fugitive?"

"What the hell would I do with him?" She scooped up the skate board and reached to open the back hatch. "I'm going after the filthy, lying FBI agent instead. Can you drive this thing?"

"Probably. Maybe. No."

"Then stay here with the doors locked." She slammed the board onto the asphalt with a satisfying smack. "I'm not losing Lang."

"You're going to confront him?"

"Hells to the yeah I am." She launched onto the board, kicking away after she slammed the big door down. There was no traffic, so she cruised across the street, jumped the curb, and sidewalk-surfed herself into a fast fly down the path that circled the lake, heading in the same direction as Lang.

That *bastard*. That son of a bitch conniving dirty bastard. Had she, for one insane unmentionable moment, thought the guy was *hot*? Well, that gave new meaning to the phrase "lapse of judgment."

She saw Lang about fifty feet ahead, his phone pressed to his ear, his head down. Anger and betrayal fired every muscle as she kicked her stick mightily, bending low to cut down on wind resistance, zipping like a pro. Just as she neared him, she leaned to the right, shot right by him, then cut him off with a rumble of her neon-pink Spitfire wheels.

She dug her heel into the back, popped the board to flip it into the air, and grabbed it with one hand. "How's it going, Lang?"

He froze, staring at her. "I gotta go." He ended the call, dropping his gaze over her and settling on the board. "I see we've dispensed with titles of any kind. *Angelino.*"

"Who you on the phone with?"

"None of your—"

"A criminal?"

No response, just heat from his gaze. Dark heat. He didn't look so Dudley Do-Rightish tonight. He looked kind of badass and mean. Maybe it was the five-o'clock shadow. Maybe it was the company he kept.

Maybe he *was* badass and mean.

"Who's your friend?" she asked.

"What friend?"

"The old man you hitched a ride with."

His eyes almost gave a tell, just the most subtle reaction. "Just that, a friend. Why?"

"Nobody important?"

"Nobody important." He took a step closer, but she held the board up as a shield. "What's going on, Vivi?"

"You tell me, *Colton*."

"Do you have news? Something happen with Marc and Mrs. Sterling?"

Plenty was happening with Marc and Mrs. Sterling, but she sure as shit wasn't telling *him* what it was. "Why'd you hire us, Lang?"

His brows rose. "You were in the briefing. We don't need to go over it again, do we?"

"Maybe we do." She swung the board, the comfort and familiarity of it in her hand giving her confidence. "Let's see, as I recall, your number-one objective was to get Devyn Sterling the hell out of Belfast."

"Correct."

"But you didn't tell us why."

"Need-to-know basis and you—"

"Need to know why you aren't so hell-bent on shortening that list of FBI's Most Wanted."

He barely flinched. "I explained that to you."

"Not well enough."

His expression hardened. "Where are you going with this?"

"I think you know."

"I think you're in over your head, kid."

The endearment frosted her ass. "I think you're what's known as a dirty cop, *pal*."

"You're wrong."

She took a step forward, looking up at him. "Am I?"

A group of people approached, young professionals heading out of the financial district toward Back Bay, laughing and exchanging barbs. Their presence gave her a sense of security; her certainty gave her a sense of entitlement.

"You owe me the truth."

"I don't owe you anything." At her raised eyebrow, he added, "Except all of Marc's expenses and, should he succeed in the assignment, a flat fee."

"We don't want dirty money."

"Vivi." He came closer, and she held the board higher, ready to whack him with it if he took one more step, FBI agent or not. "You really don't know what you're talking about."

"That was Finn MacCauley, wasn't it?"

He said nothing, just looked at her, his jaw clenched.

"You are connected to Finn Mac—"

He slammed his hand over her mouth, the other one wrapping around her and pulling her into him, the only thing separating them was the board and wheels.

"Shut up."

"I will not—"

He squeezed her, bringing her so close she could smell his musky scent and feel the muscles in his thighs as they met hers. The group of professionals passed around them as if they were stones in a stream. "It's not what you think."

"It's not? Then what is it?"

"I can't say."

She tried to jerk out of his grasp, but it was impossible. "You better say, because I can get to your offices faster than you can on this thing, and I'm sure someone over there will be very interested in your little secret rendezvous."

"You do that, and your cousin's life, and the one he's protecting, will be very much in danger."

She stared at him, letting the threat settle. "The life he's protecting? I thought he was over there trying to corral her out of the country. There was no talk of protection."

"He'll do it anyway. That's the kind of guy he is. That's why I hired him."

She eased away as he loosened his grasp. "Is that so?"

"It was part of the deal."

"What deal?"

He hesitated a few beats, scrutinizing her face, making a decision. "The one we made with Finn. And Dr. Sharon Greenberg."

"*What?* You know about her?"

He nodded slowly. "There are a lot of lives at stake, Vivi. When Devyn got involved, however innocently, we promised Finn—"

"You promised *Finn*?"

He closed his eyes, clearly resigned to telling her more than he wanted to. "Because he's led us, along with the CIA and the SIS, to one of the world's deadliest and most vicious terrorists."

"Finn has." Impossible. Wasn't it?

"Yes, he has. And if we succeed, he'll be pardoned." He let go of her completely, certain he had her full attention. "And if we fail, thousands of people will die. My guess is your cousin will be among them."

Her whole insides went cold. "Why didn't you tell him the truth?" she asked. "Why not send him over there with full information?"

"It's need-to-know on an incalculable scale," he said. "And he didn't need to know. Neither did you."

"Well, I know now."

"Yes, you do." A smile curled his lips, not big enough to show his perfect teeth, but slow enough to make her remember why she'd thought he was attractive.

"Why is that amusing?"

His gaze dropped to her board. "I underestimated you, Vivi Angelino."

"Big mistake."

"One I'll never make again."

Response flitted through her, and she squashed it by dropping her board with a thud. He jerked back, the wheels inches from his feet, but managed to grab hold of her sleeve as she got one foot on.

"Don't say a word to Marc."

She snorted softly. "You've got to be kidding."

"I am not kidding. You could be risking his life. Just let him keep on doing what he's supposed to do—protect Finn's daughter."

"He didn't go over there to be a bodyguard."

"He's too smart to let anything happen to her." He leaned forward, right in her face, nose to nose, mouth to mouth. "Hopefully he's just keeping her warm and safe and satisfied in some hotel room right this minute."

She backed away. "Yeah. I'm sure that's exactly what he's doing."

This was a consolation prize.

Devyn glanced over at Marc, his jaw set in a determined line the way it had been for the entire trip, as he barreled into a dark and deserted section of the Falls Road area, right along the stone walls of Milltown Cemetery.

He hadn't said it, but she could read between the lines.

No baby, but I'll help you find your birth mother. As consolation prizes went, it sucked. But her need to know—and possibly help—her birth mother burned hotter than ever.

"Should I try to get a call through again?" Devyn asked, holding both of their phones, although neither one had been able to hold a signal through the whole trip.

"Actually," he said, "don't. Now it's not safe. If someone traced a call she made to you, we shouldn't use the phones at all. We're getting too close to where Fallon said to go."

"In fact, we're there." She used her phone to point to a small stone marker on the ground. "Crescent Road."

And, sure enough, Direct Furniture on the corner. "We're here."

Across from the furniture store was a thicket of bushes against one of the Milltown Cemetery walls. It was impossible to see in, but not impossible to climb. Not for someone running for her life.

"Let's cruise for a few minutes and check out the parked cars for unfriendly faces, then we'll go in," he said. "But that fence is high. I'm just warning you."

"I've faced worse. Today, in fact."

He glanced over at her, his smile surprising her in a situation that was anything but amusing. "I know you have."

She shrugged off the compliment. "I still don't love heights, but sometimes you just do what you have to."

"So it seems."

At least he'd stopped arguing with her about the mission. Because, she reminded herself, this was her consolation prize.

"There's not a soul anywhere," she said, surveying the streets. "It's eerie."

"It's the middle of the night." And several hours since Sharon had escaped.

He took a quick pass through a few residential streets that backed into the cemetery and slowly drove by the main opening, tightly locked with multiple CCTV cameras visible. After a few minutes, he returned to Crescent Drive and parked the car in the shadows.

"Get your gun out," he instructed. "And stash it in your pants or pocket, somewhere you can get to it fast if you have to. And stay as close to me as possible."

She did exactly as he asked and took one more item out of her bag. Her picture.

Rose Devyn Mulvaney. Until we meet…

Had she ever even seen a baby picture of herself? Her parents—the ones in Boston—had so few pictures of her. Devyn always thought that was because her mother regretted the adoption the minute she'd signed the papers, since the very act itself was an admission of her imperfection and inability to have a child.

And she'd always fantasized that her real mother regretted the adoption as well. The picture, and the inscription, confirmed that fantasy might have been reality.

Finally, they were going to meet. They had to. She stuffed the picture into her jeans pocket and got out of the car.

The streetlights were all out, turned off at midnight to discourage any pedestrians in what was still a hot point of unrest. With a moon lost behind thick cloud cover, there was barely any light at all, easy enough for them to move like thieves across the street, diving into the bushes to flatten themselves against the stone wall.

"First hurdle down," Marc said quietly. "We crossed the street without getting shot."

That was encouraging. "Now to get over the wall."

He looked at her tucking a stray hair under the dark baseball cap they bought at a twenty-four-hour convenience store, his eyes fierce. "Don't do anything impulsive, Devyn."

"Too late for that."

"Okay, more impulsive."

"I promise," she said. "I won't."

"You said that last time."

"And saved your ass," she reminded him.

He leaned down, dipped under the bill of her cap, and kissed her. "I still haven't thanked you for that."

"I think you are right now."

He gave her a boost up to the first brick that jutted out and watched from below as she scaled the wall. It wasn't difficult; with a few high steps, she managed to hoist herself to the top.

And then she couldn't breathe.

He was next to her in a matter of seconds. "You okay?"

"Oh my God, Marc. I had no idea." No map, no pictures, no description she'd ever read could do justice to the size and scale of Milltown Cemetery. She hung on to the stone points at the top of the wall, and even in the darkness, she could get the sense of how vast it was.

She'd read about Milltown. A hundred thousand graves. Miles and miles of graves. Tens of thousands, jammed together so tightly the arms of crucifixes nearly touched. There was no order, no symmetry, no space. Just...death.

How would they ever find a woman who was shot and hiding out here?

Suddenly, this felt like a fool's errand.

But Marc was already scrambling over the top, undaunted by what lay ahead. "I'm going to jump first," he said. "Then you follow."

She looked down warily. "Okay."

He vaulted over the top and hit the grass on the balls of his feet, his knees bending to soften the impact. He turned to look up, holding out his arms, but she stayed rooted in place.

So much for getting over her fear of heights.

"Dev, you're a sitting duck up there. Jump!"

She nodded, biting her lip, and threw her leg over the top. Taking a deep breath, she pushed off, landing right in front of Marc. He broke her fall and held her as they rolled to the ground.

"You okay?" he asked.

"Yeah." She tested her legs—not broken—and stood with him. "I really hope she's on the right side of this situation," she murmured. "Because if we're risking life and limb to save a terrorist, I'll . . ."

"What?"

"Use this freaking gun on her."

He took her hand and stood up. "I'll help you aim. Gimme the penlight."

She handed him the small light they'd brought, and he flashed it to get his bearings.

"Based on that tourist map we had, about a half mile that way is the central area. The most famous IRA martyrs are buried there. But this is the outskirts, and I think she'd go to the most remote possible place to hide."

Around them, the graves were unkempt and thick with bramble.

"The paths are laid out in a grid," she said as they crossed the grass to a narrow stretch of asphalt that cut through a section. "At least they looked that way on the map in the rental car. But, Marc, this place is like a small country."

"Come on," he said, taking her hand. "All we can do is head forward and then we'll come to an intersection, where she would have had to decide to go straight, north, or south. My guess is she's hiding, waiting for light."

Or as dead as all the rest of Milltown's residents.

They walked deeper into the cemetery, briskly, silently, and with each step, she could feel her heart fall like the leaves that floated down from the trees with every light breeze.

"Spooky, huh?" she whispered.

"Fifty thousand graves, two hundred thousand bodies, many of them considered religious martyrs? Yeah, spooky."

A gathering of oaks loomed ahead, surrounding a few graves that appeared somehow extraordinary. Important people, she supposed. They paused at a break in the path, and Marc went in closer, the penlight beaming on name after etched name.

O'Neill. Bidwell. Saunders. McNett.

But no sign of Sharon Greenberg.

An animal cried, and another answered, while a breeze rustled the trees in time with their footsteps.

"My guess is she'd go as deep into the place as she could get," he said. "Knowing that anyone following her would circle the perimeter, not wanting to get lost."

"And you could get lost here," Devyn said, turning a three-sixty as she lifted the bill of her cap.

Something crunched under Marc's foot and he stopped to look at it, freezing at the sight of broken safety goggles.

"Oh my God," Devyn whispered, dropping to her knees. "These are from a lab." She clutched them. "She was here, Marc."

"Maybe," he agreed, using the light to slowly scan the area. But all they could see was grave after grave, crosses and stones, some high, some low, a row of matching flat stones, and a building that looked like a miniature cathedral.

From inside that structure, a soft, pained whimper floated over the air. Not an animal, a *person*.

The thick ground covering almost tripped Devyn, but Marc caught her and made it to the opening first. He held her back with one hand, aiming a gun at the mini-monument.

Devyn's heart walloped against her rib cage, her whole body taut.

The structure was virtually open, a half wall about four feet high that was topped with stone columns to support a roof and a life-sized statue of the Madonna rising above it. The name "McGarry" was carved into the stone trim.

He lifted the light, spearing the darkness with a yellow beam that landed on a body, huddled in the corner.

The figure wore a blood-soaked white jacket and didn't move.

"Is she..." Devyn couldn't finish the question. It hurt too much to say the word. Had she come all this way to find her birth mother *dead*?

Motioning for Devyn to stay back, Marc moved stealthily into the structure.

He kneeled next to the body, reaching toward the woman. Devyn approached slowly and dropped to her knees, speechless.

Marc brushed back the woman's hair, revealing an ashen face. His fingers pressed for a pulse.

"Oh, please don't be dead," Devyn whispered. "Please."

The woman's mouth twitched, her jaw slackened, and very slowly, she opened her eyes, which were eerily silver and very much alive.

"Rose?" she asked.

A tear rolled down Devyn's cheek. "Yes," she rasped. "I'm Rose."

"I knew you'd come." With one more breath, she closed her eyes.

"No!" Devyn cried softly. "No, you can't die!"

"She's not dead." Marc carefully lifted the jacket to inspect her wound. "She's hit in the arm, but it's not fatal. We need a tourniquet."

Devyn grabbed her scarf, sliding the silk from around her neck in one easy move. "Use this."

"Dr. Greenberg." Marc turned her face gently. "Can you hear me? We're going to wrap your arm."

She moaned softly.

Devyn leaned closer, drawn to her mother's face. "Sharon," she whispered. "Please talk to me."

Once again, Sharon's lids fluttered and opened. "They caught me. Baird's men . . . discovered me."

"You work for the SIS?" Devyn asked while Marc gently took off Sharon's jacket and wrapped the wound. "You infiltrated their cell, didn't you?"

She nodded slowly, and Devyn couldn't resist a look at Marc. "We have to get her out of here."

"We will," he said firmly.

Oh, God, her mother was good! Good! The word felt solid and comforting in her heart, infusing her with energy and the will to save this woman and know this woman and, possibly, love this woman.

Of course she was good. How could Devyn have ever doubted it?

"Let's lay her down," Marc said.

"Take me," she muttered as they eased her body straight and covered her in the jacket.

"Shhh." Devyn soothed her, stroking her hair, cradling her head on her lap.

"Royal...Victoria."

They looked at each other. "The hospital," Devyn said. "I saw a sign for it, maybe a mile or two away."

Sharon nodded with great effort. "I can't walk."

"We'll get you there." Devyn reached for Marc's arm. "Please, we have to do this."

"We can't go out the way we came in," he said. "Are you sure you couldn't walk with help?"

"No, no, hurry. They're coming."

"Who?"

"Baird." With superhuman strength, she took a breath and clutched Devyn's arm. "Don't leave me, Rose. Please, don't."

Her heart folded in half. "I won't, I promise."

Sharon managed to shift her attention to Marc. "Do you...have a car?"

"Parked on Crescent," he said.

"Find Curley's."

"The supermarket?" Devyn asked. "We passed it."

"Park there and in the back...three paths...go up

middle one. Will bring you back here. I can make it down that hill." They lost her again.

"Please, Marc, go," Devyn urged.

He nodded, standing. "Stay in here, down behind this wall. Don't make a sound. Give me your gun and I'll rack it for you. If someone comes near you, fire. Don't ask questions, just fire."

She handed him the pistol and he pulled back the slide, then set it right next to her. "Not a sound, not a move. Don't even talk, no matter how much you want to."

"I promise."

And he was gone, silently disappearing into the graveyard.

Very slowly, Sharon's eyes opened and she looked up at Devyn.

"Thank you," she whispered.

Devyn just smiled, finally understanding the meaning of a consolation prize. She was completely . . . *consoled*.

"Shhh," she whispered. "You can tell me later. Rest and conserve your strength."

"Rosie Mulvaney." She said the name like a sigh, a whisper, and for a moment, it sounded just lovely to Devyn's ear. The right name. Her *real* name. "You're just perfect."

"Don't talk, Sharon," she said softly, unable to fight the smile that pulled at her mouth. "We can talk later."

"So much to say."

Oh, God, there was. Tears threatened and her throat closed.

"Rosie Mulvaney," Sharon repeated. "Will . . . take . . . a long time to find you."

It did take a long time, Devyn thought, but didn't

correct the poor woman. Instead she let the name play in her head.

Rose Mulvaney. Should she change her name to that? Because that's who she was, Rose Mulvaney. Daughter of a brave, heroic woman who risked her life to save others.

Devyn leaned back against the cool stone wall and closed her eyes, letting the sensation of warm content-ment roll over her. Marc would be back, they would get Sharon to the hospital, and when this was over, she'd go home with a small, but real, family.

Finally, after a lifetime of—

"*Salam.*"

Devyn jumped at the sound, her eyes popping open to stare into a pair of sharp and silvery ones, right over the barrel of the gun. For a second, nothing processed.

Sharon. Standing. Aiming.

The other hand—with the wounded arm—to her ear with a phone.

What was she doing?

"All right, we can get this done now." Her voice was strong, clear, and directed into the phone. "It's a scrape. I can meet you in ten minutes and deliver the very last thing you need, Malik. An American hostage."

Icy fear and shock washed all Devyn's warmth away. She just blinked in disbelief, sending a tear that had just formed in happiness rolling down her cheek for a com-pletely different reason. "Sharon, what are—"

"I had no intention of dying, Malik. But this person is totally expendable and impossible to trace. Frankly, she's perfect."

Perfect. Devyn's stomach turned.

"By the time they figure out who you have, you'll be

halfway home." Sharon's gaze cut across Devyn, cold, mean, and heartless. "Name's Rose Mulvaney. Oh, and get someone over to Curley's. A guy will be coming into the back parking lot in, oh, about seven or eight minutes. He'll be looking for a path that doesn't exist. Take him down, and make it look political."

Devyn tried to speak, but nothing came out. She felt pain. Searing, black, aching disbelief and pain.

Sharon winced as she stashed the phone into her pocket. "Let's go."

"How can you do this?" The words were barely a whisper. "I'm your daughter."

"You're a mistake I made. Get up."

"Where are we going?"

"I'm completing my suicide mission." The barrel of her gun settled on Devyn's forehead. "Only the suicide is going to be *yours*. Move it, Rose."

CHAPTER 26

Marc squealed into the entrance of the deserted super-market, pushing the little Ford Focus well beyond what the rental car was meant to do. There were two cars in the lot, both dark, a few shopping carts, and no lights anywhere in the store. He zipped to one side, his lights landing on a row of Dumpsters as he careened toward the back.

The grounds of the cemetery ended at a narrow alley behind the store, a nine-foot chain-link fence completely blocking access.

Where the fuck were the three paths?

Maybe there were no paths. Maybe she was delirious. Maybe she was mistaken.

Maybe she was Liam Baird's lying little puppet. That gunshot wound wasn't so serious.

He'd had no choice but to take the chance. Devyn wasn't going to end her tearful reunion with a woman who'd been shot and abandoned, so the only thing he could do was look for a way to get her out of there and to the hospital.

He threw the car into park, racked his pistol, and jumped out, peering into the shadows for a break in the fencing but seeing nothing. Hustling into the darkness, he grabbed the metal and shook it as he ran, peering up the hill behind it. Jesus, there were more graves there, as though they had to use every inch.

An engine rumbled in the front lot, getting closer. He stepped back into a recess of the building, flattening himself against the side.

The car got closer, the lights shining across the lot; then they cut off and the car screeched to a halt. He inched forward to see the car had blocked his exit, and his Ford Focus blocked the other one.

A car door slammed, then another. At least two of them, then. He backed up again, slowly lifting his gun, perfectly still and silent.

But his head was screaming. *Sharon Greenberg sent someone after me.* She had to have—that was the only explanation.

Which meant Devyn wasn't safe at all with her.

Clenching his teeth, he listened to the footsteps, heard a murmur of words. One set of footsteps broke into a run, coming toward him. Marc backed up, ready to shoot the instant his target passed.

He was ten feet away, five, two. He fired the second a shadow passed his hiding place, and the man fell with a thud. Marc jumped out and spun to fire on the next guy, who'd already pivoted and was running back to his car.

Marc vaulted toward him and aimed low, wanting to bring him down, but still get information out of him. He hit his leg, and the man buckled and fell. As Marc neared him, a shot whizzed by his head, fired from his first victim.

Pouncing on the runner, he looked over his shoulder and got off another shot into the shadows, eliciting a grunt of pain from his target.

"What the fuck do you want?" Marc demanded, flipping the guy onto his back and holding him down with a knee and the gun. And a prayer that the one behind him was dead.

Marc ducked as another bullet buzzed by his head. He lifted his hand and slammed his gun against the guy's temple, turning just enough to gauge the position of number one.

He was flat on the ground, pistol in hand, using his last breaths to try and kill Marc. Closing one eye, Marc aimed for a kill and pulled the trigger, the shot echoing through the alley, no doubt about to bring the Irish police.

And Christ only knew who paid *them*.

He turned back to the man pinned under him. "Who sent you?"

The guy narrowed deep blue eyes, sweat glistening on his forehead. "Fuck you. You're in the wrong place," the man said. "We kill fucking Republicans over here for sport."

"I'm not even Irish."

He got a tight smile. "But you'll die like one and those are my . . . orders." On the last word, he got in a sucker punch to Marc's face, the blow just hard enough to give the other man a momentary upper hand. They rolled again, Marc flipping onto his back.

As he did, he got off a shot, which grazed the man's stomach, but the bullet bounced off the bricks of the supermarket. It weakened him, though, and he lost enough power for Marc to crack the pistol over his face again, needing information more than he needed the guy dead.

"Whose orders?" he demanded.

But the guy just groaned as blood oozed out of his wound at the waist, soaking Marc's knees. "Who?" Marc aimed directly at his heart. "Tell me who the hell sent you and how I can find him."

He didn't move, clenching his jaw, fighting pain and the will to live. "At the shipyard. Malik's getting there early."

"And Sharon Greenberg?"

He frowned. "They need a hostage to hold off American fire. She's doing it ... for Malik."

For a second, that made absolutely no sense—unless the Pakistanis knew there'd be a raid. Dr. Greenberg wasn't working for Baird. She wasn't working for the SIS. She was a fucking double agent for the Pakistanis.

And no doubt part of her deal with the Pakis was to either *act as* or *be* a female hostage so they could escape after picking up Liam Baird's delivery of botulism spores.

Unless she could get a stand-in as a hostage.

He glanced at the cemetery behind the fence. No use going back there now. Either Devyn got away or her birth mother was handing her over to a terrorist right now.

Marc pushed himself off the other man and aimed his gun at his face. "Give me your keys."

The man turned his head, writhing in pain. "He has them."

Marc shot his leg and the man jumped and howled, then reached into his pocket and threw a set of keys at Marc.

Hanging on to a hell of a lot of hope, Marc ran to the other car and jumped in, leaving one man near dead and the other unable to go anywhere.

He had to get to the shipyard, before Devyn became a human shield.

Devyn didn't dare stumble, or stall, or even talk.

Her captor, despite her injury, used the gun Marc had left to jab Devyn's back and silently keep her almost at a run. They tore through another unfamiliar section of the cemetery, down a set of stone stairs, around another monument, and through a fence to a side street.

There, they ran to a car, which Sharon made Devyn drive.

Somehow, hands trembling, heart breaking, questions reverberating, she did. When they cruised past the hospital, Devyn started looking hard for a possible escape route.

She slid a glance at the woman, at...her mother. Anything that might have felt like a connection turned to stone.

"Don't even think about it," Sharon said, wincing again and gingerly moving her arm. "I can drive with you dead."

"I've made a mistake, haven't I?" Devyn asked.

"If you mean by trusting me, yes. But you aren't the first." Sharon's pale gray eyes were locked on her, the gun unwavering in its aim toward Devyn's head.

"You can't really be my birth mother."

She snorted softly. "You can pick your friends, but... You know the rest."

Her stomach turned. This was *worse* than her worst nightmare. "You sent that picture of me."

"You? No, sorry, that wasn't you. That was just some baby picture the housekeeper where I was staying had in her wallet."

No. She wanted to scream but kept her voice steady.

"I found a picture of me at your house." That wasn't the housekeeper's picture. That was her.

She let out a put-upon sigh. "Finn MacCauley had pictures of you, not me. I never even knew who adopted you, and I didn't care."

Devyn closed her eyes like she'd been hit. "But Finn did?"

"Evidently. For a man in hiding, he certainly managed to sneak into every public event where you'd be present. Recitals, graduation—good heavens, he even got shots of your wedding."

"He was there?" The words trapped in her throat. Was that possible?

"That's what he says."

She cruised through an intersection, looking for anyone who could help. But Belfast was quiet at this hour. Maybe she could find a CCTV camera and stop in front of one. At least someone, somewhere, would know where she was.

Marc. Another stab to her chest.

"Why did Finn send you pictures if you don't care about me?"

Sharon exhaled again, rubbing the dried blood on her lab coat. "He thought I did. I guess because he did. And he wanted something from me." She smiled, a dry, heartless smile. "I knew he would eventually. It just took a damn long time. Turn at the next street, head toward the cranes, past the airport. We're going to the shipyards."

"What did he want from you?"

"Oh, his second chance." She choked softly. "Finn wants redemption, don't you know?" There was an ugly note of hatred in her voice. "He wants his freedom. So, he came to me to help him buy it."

Devyn frowned. "How?"

"He thought he was so smart arranging this." She waved the gun like all of Belfast encompassed "this." "He worked with the FBI and the CIA and the SIS and God knows who to frame that idiot Liam Baird. He thought if he brought me and my expertise in on it, they really could get Baird. And, of course, through Baird, they could get Malik." She chuckled. "Nobody gets Malik."

Devyn made the turn she indicated, using the excuse to look at Sharon again, the headlights shining just enough to emphasize the wrinkles in her sallow skin, the shadows under her eyes. The wound may be superficial, but the blood loss was taking its toll. She could escape ... eventually.

If she stayed alive.

"So you don't work for Liam Baird or the SIS?"

"No, I don't. They both just think I work for them."

"Who do you work for?"

Sharon laughed. "What makes you think this is work? Screwing Finn MacCauley is my lifelong dream, kid. Ever since the day he used me and left me high and dry, I've been waiting for this."

High and dry? "He left you with me."

Sharon sighed, shaking her head. "I didn't want you."

Oh. Devyn swallowed the lump that strangled her throat, cutting off air, her arms and legs tingling with the heat of adrenaline and agony.

"Sorry," Sharon said with a shrug. "I'm not going to lie. I could have had an abortion, you know. I didn't."

"I know."

"So, don't take it personally. You're not my daughter. You're not part of me. You're a mistake in judgment I made on a particularly bad day when I made several."

Devyn waited for the punch, for some kind of take-your-breath-away blow to her heart as the words settled over her.

But nothing happened.

Except release. The pressure released a little on her chest. The painful truth wasn't so painful at all. It was a relief. This may be the woman who gave birth to her, but she was no more her mother than...than a stranger on the street.

They had no *connection*. So why was Devyn looking for one? Suddenly, she felt free. Light. Liberated from a need that had weighed her down her whole life. There *was* no connection.

But there was the little matter of staying alive. And information was power. "So you're here because Finn asked you to, but you're really here to, what, screw him out of the chance to buy a pardon?"

"Well, there is the money. I'm getting a lot of money."

Devyn shook her head. "Sorry, I've been to your house. Money's not important to you."

"Money is a nice side benefit," she shot back. "Believe me, this was not the first time a terrorist organization approached me. I have a unique and valuable talent, but I always took the high moral ground and said no. But when Finn asked me..." She actually smiled. "Revenge trumps morals, every time."

"Enough that you would let innocent people die?"

"If I can make Finn look bad? Lose his dream of a pardon and a"—she slid a look to the side—"his chance with you."

Devyn gripped the wheel. "That's what he wants?"

The other woman let out a scoffing choke. "He'd say anything to get what he wants, honey. That's what Finn

MacCauley does. And now I'm going to make him look so bad."

"But what about you? You'll look bad, too."

"I'll have the money to not care, but don't worry—I'll finesse this so I look like a good undercover SIS spy. That's where you come in. You know, I'll try to save you. Or make it look like I did. But Finn will be screwed and he will not get his pardon. And I'll be free."

"That's what you want? Freedom from..."

"From hating him. Freedom is a good thing."

Yes, it was. And Devyn had never felt so free in her life.

She had no connection to this woman—none at all.

And that was the "connection" she had never been able to make. She was her own woman, not a product of any man or any woman. They were nothing but bodies who brought her alive.

And right now, she felt more alive than ever.

Except for the gun pointed at her. "Take that right, go around the dock, and pull into that gate. It should be open."

So Finn had tried to convince Sharon to do something good for the government and buy a pardon, and she double-crossed him.

"I'm sorry if this disappoints you," Sharon said, not sounding sorry at all. "I hope you weren't expecting a happy family reunion with me."

"Not at all. You're not my family." *Freedom.*

"Then why are you here, hunting me down?"

Devyn glanced at her, fighting a smile. "I needed to find out what I was made of."

Sharon lifted a dubious brow. "Did you?"

"Yes, I did."

"What are you made of?"

She was about to find out. "Better stuff than you."

"Well, I can say you don't look like Finn or me."

"Because I don't have any part of you in me." No part that mattered anyway. Not her head. Not her heart. Not her soul.

"Through the gate," Sharon ordered.

She drove toward the expanse of the shipyard, which was acres of concrete jutting into wide docks and black water.

"Stop here."

The clang of metal against metal punctuated the order, drawing Devyn's gaze upward to the massive shipbuilding crane standing hundreds of feet in the air. The moonlight and pale yellow lamps along the docks allowed her to make out the giant black H and W on the side of the famous landmark.

She managed a slow, steady breath, and another look at Sharon, who still hadn't lowered the gun. With her injured arm, she somehow pulled out her phone and pressed it to her ear.

"I'm here. How much time do we have until Baird arrives?"

How could this be happening? And *Marc*. What happened to Marc? The question echoed in her head and heart. Had she lost him?

Had she thrown away *that* chance for *this* one?

She should have listened to him when he told her that she wasn't made of the same stuff as her parents, that strings of DNA are meaningless. He was right. Because regardless of the genetic imprint, this beast next to her was nothing to her. Nothing.

In fact, Devyn would kill this woman in a heartbeat. All she had to do was figure out how.

"Okay, I see you now," Sharon said. "Move fast. I'll be on the dock."

Devyn followed Sharon's gaze out to the water, see-ing...nothing. Then something moved, sinister and fast, skimming over the water like a blacked-out shark fin. A dark boat with no lights, no markings, cutting through the waves toward the shipyard docks.

"Get out of the car and don't you dare try to run. You'll be dead before you take your next breath."

Devyn had to buy time. As she climbed out, she eyed the entire space, gauging every option.

There were none.

The entrances were gated off. The docks led to ice-cold water. A long, gray warehouse lined one side of the shipyard, closed tight for the night. The only other place was...She lifted her gaze two hundred feet in the air.

The crane.

Sharon was out and beside her in a matter of seconds, nudging her toward the water. "Let's go."

She pushed Devyn forward. Wasn't there security? Cam-eras? Customs to control ships in and out? She glanced around for one of the many CCTV lenses that she'd seen all around Belfast, but if they were being watched, she couldn't tell.

The boat, visible now despite the black paint, rumbled up to a long concrete dock.

Could she run? Could she scream? Were they expect-ing her, too? Why had Sharon forced her to come? What-ever she needed from Devyn, she wasn't getting it. No matter what.

The boat docked quickly, and a man emerged from the

back, dressed in black from head to toe, his face darkened with grease, barely visible.

With a solid grip on her arm and the pistol in her back, Sharon pushed her forward. "Here she is, Malik."

He barely nodded as another man stepped out behind him, holding a container.

"Jesus Christ." She yanked Devyn back with a gasp. "Baird! What the hell are you doing here?"

"Hello, Dr. Greenberg. Did you really think you could outsmart me?"

Sharon pushed Devyn away like a useless sack, freeing herself to point the gun at Baird. "It wasn't that difficult." She lifted the pistol to shoot, just as he tossed a silver canister in the air. It landed at Sharon's feet. She leaped backward, turning as voices and engines suddenly roared from behind them and a gunshot echoed over the docks.

."They got us!" One of the men yelled. Another shot exploded, and Devyn was forgotten in the chaos. Instantly, she took off, covering her head when a bullet zinged past her, staying low and running as fast as she could in the opposite direction.

Cars charged toward the water. In the air, a rumble and a blinding light from a helicopter. Then to her left, three, four, five large black vehicles appeared from nowhere, lights on, men pouring out, all armed.

She didn't know what was happening, who was good, who was bad, who would kill her, who might save her, so she just ran until she reached the base of the crane. Gunshots exploded, men shouted, and the boat revved to take off. Devyn had no choice.

She'd have to go up the crane, with the hope that it would be the only safe place.

She seized the first rung of rusted metal and hoisted herself up, the bars of the ladder nothing but narrow, slippery bands under her sneakers, her fingers stiff on the freezing steel handles.

Daring a look below, she saw the men in black move like ants around the fingers of cement that formed the channel. They fired at the boat, but it still kept going.

She didn't stop to watch but climbed with every ounce of strength she had.

If the wrong person saw her—Sharon or Baird or whoever the guy on the boat was—they'd shoot her. The wind howled, clanging metal against the giant arm that stuck out another hundred feet over the water.

Finally, her hands hit solid flooring, and she pulled herself up to the arm of the crane. It was a long, narrow pathway made of woven steel, tracks, and twisted cables running along either side. There was a railing, but it was nothing more than two bars designed to hold the harness ropes.

The harness she wasn't wearing. But if she could just wait this out, avoid being caught or spotted, she could get down and get help.

Wind buffeted her, and she automatically dropped to her knees, refusing to look down as her palms scraped the jutting edges of the tracks, her knees screaming in pain from the metal.

Staying flat was the only way to keep from being blown off. Or shot at. She took a ragged breath and laid her face against the diamond-shaped holes in the metal, then closed her eyes, her hair blowing over her face. If she could just stay alive.

If Marc stayed alive.

She *had* to tell him how wrong she'd been. Wrong

about her mother, yes, but even more so, wrong about the genes. That woman—that horrible, heartless, hateful woman—might be her mother, but she had nothing to do with Devyn. Maybe it was coming face-to-face with her, but something inside Devyn had snapped, and she finally let go of those fears.

"Very clever!" The words floated on the wind and fell on Devyn, forcing her to turn around. "You must be my daughter after all."

Sharon's face was bruised and scraped, her hair whipped into wildness. The Indian silk scarf hung useless from her wounded arm, barely hanging on in the wild wind. In one hand, she still held the damn gun. And in the other, a silver canister.

"Looks like I underestimated Mr. Baird. No matter. He'll have no credibility, and the SIS will still believe I'm their agent, as long as I get rid of you."

She took a labored step forward, fighting the wind but managing to hold up the canister in one hand and the gun in the other. "If you can hang on until that chaos down there is over, I'll let you climb down before I kill you. Otherwise, I'll shoot you up here and you'll fall."

Sharon waved toward the ground and the movement freed the scarf, sending it sailing into the air, black and gold, floating like a fallen leaf.

"It's a long way down," Sharon said.

Devyn stole a look at the flying scarf, hope surging. Maybe someone would see it and realize she was up here.

Hope evaporated when the scarf snagged on a hook of the crane, still a good hundred feet in the air. The wind would tear it to shreds before anyone ever looked up and saw it.

Sharon let out a rueful laugh. "Hell, I hate heights, don't you?"

"Yes," Devyn whispered.

"Of course you do," she said softly. "You're just like me."

No, she wasn't. And she'd die trying to prove that.

CHAPTER 27

Marc reached the shipyard at the precise moment that the SIS moved in. In his stolen black Saab, he slipped through the gates with the other cars. When they moved in, he held back, not wanting to draw attention. When the agents finally made it to the edge of the wharf, he parked and followed the shadows, gun drawn, head down.

So far, so good.

"Hey!" A man jumped him from behind, giving his neck a good crack. "Who the blazes are you?"

Shit. They had perimeter guards. He really didn't want to kill an MI5 agent, but he would to save Devyn.

"American," he said. "There's an American hostage."

The man loosened his grip and another jogged over, looking warily at Marc over a Barrett M82 rifle.

"Hey, I know you." His eyes narrowed and his jaw clenched. "From the bell tower."

Marc recognized the MI5 agent instantly. "Nigel Sutton."

The other man shrugged but didn't lower his rifle.

"What the hell are you doing here? Still chasing Dr. Greenberg?"

"She took an American hostage. I think she's on that boat."

The boat was already surrounded, men being thrown on the ground, guns drawn.

"You're wrong," the man said. "She *is* the American hostage. That's part of the operation."

No, it wasn't. And Marc knew that as well as he knew his name. That woman had sent the men to kill him, and she wasn't working for SIS or Baird.

"Listen," the agent said. "I don't know what the fuck you want with that woman, but she's on our side, and unless you want to be collateral damage, this is an official SIS operation and you are not welcome."

"She *isn't* the hostage," he insisted, managing to break one arm free, the one that held his gun. He stuck it right over the Barrett. "And she isn't on your side. She's on that fucking boat with another woman and I'm going to get her."

The other man stared him down.

"Hazmat's here," Marc's first attacker said, inclining his chin toward a team of men in hazardous-material suits surrounding a small container on the dock. Around them, agents were dragging perps away, two in cuffs, one in dark Muslim garb with a gun to his head.

"We got the bastard," the agent said with a grim smile.

Marc eyed the man. "Who is that?"

"Malik Mahmud Khel, the second in command of Pakistan's powerful Shia militant organization, Tehrik-e-Jafria." He grinned at Marc. "Bet the fucking CIA couldn't have done that any better. Though we did have some help from your Dr. Greenberg."

"She's not mine," Marc ground out. "So where the hell is she?" And, Jesus Christ, where was Devyn? His body ached from the need to run toward that boat and get her.

"They'll get her."

A man who looked like he was in charge barked orders, spoke on a phone, and directed the hazmats to place their haul in an armored vehicle. Behind him, three men boarded the boat, all armed with rifles, shouting as they went.

Suddenly, those same men leaped off the boat, shouting. Everyone in the vicinity dropped to the ground.

"Bomb!"

The word settled in Marc's brain the very instant the boat exploded in an orange fireball, flames shooting thirty feet in the air, the noise rocking the docks, cracking the air, rattling the giant cranes above, and throwing all of them back a few feet.

The sound was still reverberating as he scrambled to his feet, starting to run.

Both men grabbed his arms. "Nobody survived that motherfucker," the agent said sternly. "Just consider this a favor and get the hell out of here."

Marc shook the agent off and got five steps away before he had him again.

"Listen to me!" The agent threw him back with the same force as the explosion. "The only reason I'm not putting a hole in your arse is because you didn't put one in mine. Now, go!"

Sirens screamed and more men yelled as his captors took off. Marc stayed rooted watching in disbelief as smoke puffed skyward from the explosion, the hazmat truck already rolling away, their dangerous cargo escaping what was no doubt a suicide bomb planted in case things went wrong.

Was Devyn on that boat?

The only answer was the metal ropes of the crane's empty counterweight clanging on the pulleys overhead, hollow and haunting.

He'd failed. He hadn't protected her. He sure as hell hadn't rescued her. He'd left her with her own mother, and now he followed the trail of smoke into the night sky, his eyes filling, his soul aching.

Did she die thinking she was just like her mother? God, he hoped not. He started to close his eyes, but something caught his attention in the sky, something fluttering from the flatbed that hung from a pulley high in the air.

He couldn't look away from the flash of gold, the shimmer of black, the flapping of . . . *silk*.

He'd just touched that silk, made a tourniquet with it. Breaking into a jog, his gaze locked on the ladder that led up to the base of the crane, he ignored a shout in his direction. He snagged the bottom rung and yanked himself up, launching forward, climbing as fast as his feet would move.

About a hundred feet off the ground, he looked out to the narrow section of trolley line that ran down the arm and hung over the concrete below and saw movement on the track.

Just as his foot hit the next railing, a gunshot blasted through the air, the bullet whizzing by his head. His hand faltered and his foot slipped, his whole body whipping to the side. A blast of wind nearly shook him loose as he fought to swing back into position.

He'd almost regained his footing, using all his strength, when he looked across the crane's arm directly into the barrel of a gun. Behind it, white hair flew in the wind, the same wind that pinned him back so effectively it was impossible to do anything but wait for Sharon's next shot.

Choking on smoke, Devyn's gaze stayed riveted on the fire in the water, her whole being clinging for life as the crane arm swayed from the impact of the explosion.

Another loud noise rocked the metal under her, and Devyn shrieked, turning to see Sharon braced like a gunfighter, the pistol aimed toward the ladder. Was someone coming up?

Devyn fought the wind, determined to see around Sharon, who blocked her view of the ladder. And what she saw stole the breath from her body.

She clamped her mouth closed to stop from crying out as Sharon fired again, the recoil shaking the crane, the bullet missing its target.

Marc gripped the ladder and battled his way up, his face pulled in determination, his life hanging by two narrow metal bars.

With her back to Devyn, Sharon steadied her hands to take another shot. Dragging herself up with superhuman strength, Devyn managed a kneeling position. She gripped the railing and pulled herself to her feet.

As Sharon turned, Devyn kicked out one leg, nailing the other woman in the hip and knocking her off balance. She struggled to get her footing with one hand holding the canister, the other arm flailing with the gun, enough time for Devyn to kick again, her foot aiming for the pistol. She made contact and sent the gun careening into the air.

"Goddamn you!"

"He already did," Devyn said, fury bubbling up. "He made me waste my whole life wondering about you!" She kicked again, but Sharon dodged the blow and lunged toward Devyn, tearing the top off the canister and waving it at Devyn.

"Botulinum in a bottle," she screamed over the howling wind. "More deadly than the gun."

"Then we both die."

Sharon shook her head violently. "I can manufacture the antidote in a matter of minutes. No one knows I work for Malik. The SIS will call me a hero, and you will be...a shame. Good-bye, my child." She reached for the canister.

"I'm not your child!" Devyn spat the words and used the rage in her heart to take one more kick, but it almost toppled her. She frantically reached for the guardrail, missing it the first time, then grabbing hold just as Sharon lunged forward and cracked Devyn's head with the canister.

She let out a shriek and grabbed wildly for the safety rail, but Sharon thrust toward her again. Left hand behind her on the railing, she flailed to fight her off, hitting the cylinder.

As she did, Sharon let go of it, and Devyn's fingers closed around metal still warm from Sharon's touch.

Sharon lurched toward her, folding Devyn through the opening in the railing. She screamed as gravity took her body, grasping the railing with one hand as her hips, then legs, fell through. Only her left hand kept her alive.

Sharon put her hand on Devyn's and started to lift her fingers, one by one.

If she let go of the canister, she had a chance.

The gunshot split through the wind and exploded the side of Sharon's face. Blood splattered, hitting Devyn's fingers, but she managed to cling with all of her power and strength to the bouncing crane as Marc ran to her.

"Devyn!"

Her arm burned in agony, her fingers slipping on Sharon's blood. Marc's powerful hand closed over her wrist, and she looked up to see his beautiful, determined face right above hers.

"I'm falling!" she cried. "I can't—"

"Yes, you can. Hold on."

"I'm going to drop this—"

"No. Give it to me."

But the wind was so powerful she couldn't lift her arm against it. "I have to drop it."

"No, Devyn, you can do this. Fight for it. I'm here. Come on!"

She dug for strength, focusing on him, on the hope and the future and the love he promised. She could do this. She could. She had to.

He was bent halfway over the railing, pulling at her. She finally managed to lift her arm, and he reached for the canister and stashed it in his pocket.

"Now, Devyn!"

She grabbed the railing with her free hand and pulled, kicking her legs, fighting for strength, holding on to Marc. One more relentless gust of wind almost took her, but he clung to her. For one long, agonizing second, she felt the railing slide through her grip and she looked up and held his gaze. This was it. The last time she'd ever see him. The last breath. The last vision.

"I can't..."

"You can. This is what you're made of, Devyn. *This*."

She gripped tighter and fought, through the air, through the railing, into his arms, into his heart, into whatever bliss he offered. When she made it, she let her head fall on his shoulder and shuddered with relief.

"Are you all right?" He brushed wind-whipped hair out of her eyes, searching her face.

She looked down two hundred feet and for the first time didn't feel dizzy or terrified. Just *free*. To live and to love. "I'm perfect."

He took her face in one hand and tilted it toward him. "For me, you are."

CHAPTER 28

I can't do it."

At Devyn's soft admission, Marc moved his hand lower over her abdomen, lingering for a moment on soft skin before inching his way between her legs. She was damp, swollen, as ready as he was for a bout of morning sex.

"Feels like you can," he whispered into her hair, fluttering a kiss against her ear.

"I can't meet him face-to-face." She turned to look at him, her eyes distant, probably off where her head was—anticipating today's debriefing. Her body, on the other hand, was right here in his bed, where she had been every night since they'd returned from Northern Ireland.

Her response to his touch was always positive, easy, and enthusiastic. Her response to the potential meeting with her biological father was exactly the opposite.

"You can't put it off any longer," he said, tempering the words with a gentle caress of her thigh. "We've been back for three weeks. This debriefing of our findings in Northern Ireland is the final official step."

"Why does he have to be there?" She rolled on her side, facing him. "I don't want to meet him. I've met one of my biological parents. That was enough."

"Could you do it for me?" he asked.

"No. Not even for you." She stroked his cheek with one finger, their gazes locked. "But you are welcome to keep touching me like that in a fruitless effort to convince me to say yes."

He traced the inside of her leg again, grazed her sex, then slid his hand around her hip to pull her closer to the erection that he'd fought all night while she sighed in sleeplessness.

"Devyn, I know you're still raw from Belfast."

She just closed her eyes. "I'll get over it."

"Yes," he agreed. "You will. But not completely, not until you face Finn."

Her eyes stayed shut tight, but she slowly wrapped a silky leg over his, closing all space between them. "Let's not talk about it." She kissed him, but he inched away.

"We have to."

"Marc, this is my problem. Not yours. I know you want to help, but—"

"No, actually, it's my problem."

She just looked at him. "How?"

"Until you deal with the demon that you think is Finn—"

"Did you see that indictment list? There isn't a crime the man hasn't committed. I know he tried to make up for it, and getting Malik and Baird was a good thing all around, but why should I give him the satisfaction of meeting me?"

"Because he's in my way," Marc said.

She just frowned, searching his face.

"Until you face him, accept him, and, hell, even forgive him, I don't think you can give me what I want."

She swallowed visibly. "What do you want?"

"For you to love me the way I love you."

The words, spoken for the first time, hit their mark. Her eyes widened, her jaw loosened, her body stiffened.

"Please don't act like this is a big surprise," he said. "I've shown you every way possible. I love you. I'd like to love you for a long, long time. But I won't compete for space in a heart that's still devoted to hating and resenting another man. Even if that man is your father."

She still stared at him, her eyes moist. "You love me."

He let out a soft laugh, enjoying her surprise but a little dismayed by it. "Yes, Devyn, I do."

"When did you know?"

Leaning back on the pillow, he considered the answer. When did he decide that? When she saved herself on the crane? When she fought relentlessly to find her mother, only to learn the worst about the woman? When she dropped from a bell tower to save his life?

"I think when you crossed that rope bridge and trusted me to get you to the other side. I saw your strength and determination and... something else."

"Panic?"

"Guts."

She just laughed. "Buried in the body of a chicken."

"Nope, you have guts. Maybe that's what got stamped on your DNA, and if that's the case, then thank your parents for it. Because your courage is what's going to make you a great mother someday."

She sucked in a little breath, then finally smiled. "I'm not so scared of heights anymore."

"Good. Then have the guts to face one more fear."

The fight raged on her face. She wanted to say yes. She wanted to. He coaxed her with another touch, softer, sexier, enough to make her eyes flutter closed. He kissed her lips, opening his mouth over hers, easing his body on top until their hands and legs and hips and mouths were in place for what had become a comfortable and thrilling connection.

She curled her legs around his thighs and arched her back under his touch. "Guts, huh?"

"You got 'em." He punctuated that with a kiss to her throat, then down to her breast, where he feasted on her sweet, creamy skin.

"Thanks. But I still don't want to do it."

"You want to do this?" He joined their hands so they could guide him inside her body.

"Where's the condom?"

He just smiled. "No guts, no glory."

"Is that what you want?" she asked, her voice quivering with the question.

"Yes," he said simply. "I love you, Dev. And this is what I want."

She closed her eyes in agreement, relaxing enough for him to enter her slowly. Easily. Deeply.

Her flesh closed around him, and he lowered his head to kiss her while they made love. Their heartbeats matched, their breath grew ragged, their moves took on a synchronized rhythm.

"Marc." She gripped his arms, a light sheen of sweat glistening on her cheeks, dampening her hair. "Don't stop. Please, don't stop."

He just nodded, rocking, kissing, connecting, until they both lost control and fell over the other side with long shudders of pleasure.

She slowly wrapped her arms around him and put her lips to his ear.

"You know when I knew for sure?" she asked.

He shook his head.

"Right now."

"Took you long enough."

"And, yes, Marc. I'll meet him."

When Marc slowed their steps in front of a high-end lingerie store on Newbury Street, Devyn had to laugh, despite the pressure that had been building in her heart since they'd left Marblehead to drive into Back Bay.

"Seriously? You want to buy sexy undies now?"

"No, I want to go up there." He pointed to the bay window jutting out from the brick walk-up directly above the store. "The international headquarters of the Guardian Angelinos."

Where Finn MacCauley waited to meet her. "Unusual place for a security firm."

"We're an unusual security firm. You ready?"

She nodded. She had to do this. Had to prove she had the guts worthy of Marc's love and the gift he'd just given her. Inside the vestibule, she took the first step up the narrow stairs, her next breath jammed in her chest.

What would she say to him? What would he say to her?

Already a step ahead of her, Marc turned and gave her hand a tug. "I'm with you all the way, Dev."

Nodding, she continued, counting steps, counting

seconds, counting clamoring heartbeats. At the end of the second-story corridor, a simple, unmarked door opened as they arrived.

"You made it." Vivi Angelino, who Devyn had met a few times at Marc's house in the past few weeks, beamed her infectious smile. She wore the only style Devyn had ever seen her in—baggy pants and a couple layers of tank tops, her hair mussed and gelled, her giant brown eyes unadorned with makeup, giving her a youthful appearance even though Devyn knew she and Vivi were the same age.

The outfit made Devyn feel a little overdressed in silk trousers and a knit tunic, but Vivi hugged and kissed her cousin and gestured them both into the hip and edgy reception room, taking any discomfort away.

"We got the CIA, the FBI, the SIS." Vivi rolled her eyes and laughed. "The conference room looks like alphabet soup."

But what about Finn? Devyn glanced toward the archway that led to the back offices, unable to see anyone but hearing men's voices. "Is everyone here?" she asked.

Next to her, Marc put a protective hand on her shoulder. "She means is Finn here yet?"

Vivi bit her lip, her dark eyes searching Devyn's. "I just found out he's not coming."

Devyn felt a wash of relief pour over her body, weakening her knees. Then they almost folded with an unexpected thud of disappointment. "He's not?"

The other woman shrugged and added a sympathetic hand to Devyn's arm. "I guess he didn't have the guts to face you."

Devyn drew back, then looked at Marc. "That's funny, because I have the guts to face him."

He gave her a nudge toward the back offices. "Let's get this over with, then, Dev. We'll celebrate with a swan boat ride in the Garden."

"Fun!" Vivi said, brightening. "Can I come?"

"No. You have a business to run." The order came from a formidable figure of a man who filled the hall, looking menacing with a black leather eye patch and a decent-sized scar running along his left cheek.

"Zach Angelino," he said, introducing himself by shaking Devyn's hand and adding a slow, genuine smile that instantly erased the darkness of his scars.

She recognized the name instantly.

"A pleasure to meet you, Zach," she replied, taking his hand. "Thank you for all you've done for me, and for investigating Joshua's murder."

"I had help," he said with a modest shrug.

"And now he's marrying that help," Vivi added. "So he should thank you. Come on back, Devyn."

There were familiar faces gathered around a formal conference table, all of them beaming as they stood to great Devyn.

Padraig Fallon held out his arms, and Devyn hesitated only a moment before accepting his embrace.

"I'm so sorry, lass," he whispered in her ear. "She had us all fooled. Even Ian." He stepped back and gestured toward a tall, handsome man whose deep blue eyes glinted under a mop of black hair. "My fellow MI5 agent, Ian O'Rourke."

She reached out and shook his hand. "Good to meet you, ma'am," he said, his Irish thick but understandable. "Thanks for the help on our assignment."

"I don't know if I helped," Devyn said quickly. "I interfered."

"Except that she had us all fooled," Ian said.

"True, and if you hadn't interfered and pursued her, she might have succeeded in her plan," Padraig said.

"Which was?" Devyn prodded.

"She could have made it look like Finn had screwed the CIA and SIS, not her," Padraig continued.

Another man, not quite as tall as Ian but just as imposing, all American and conservative-looking, stepped forward. "She might have even succeeded in pretending to try and save you as a hostage, ensuring that she looked heroic, putting enough blame on Finn that he couldn't possibly negotiate a pardon in time."

In time for what? Before she could ask, the man reached out his hand to gather hers, no smile on a serious but handsome face. "I'm Assistant Special Agent in Charge Colton Lang." His golden green eyes warmed as they shook hands. "Representing the FBI," he added. "The official client of the Angelinos." That warmth deepened when he glanced at Vivi.

"And not our only one," she said. "Since this job has already brought in more business."

Two other men were introduced as representatives from the British Secret Intelligence Service and two men from the CIA.

"We have a lot of questions for you, Ms. Sterling," ASAC Lang said, "but we'd like to start this debriefing by giving you any answers you might need after all you've been through. That seems only fair."

She had many, but only a few this group could answer. The rest were for a man who hadn't had the nerve to show. "Okay, I assume that Finn MacCauley offered to assist you in bringing in a terrorist and stopping this exchange from Northern Ireland to Pakistan so he could qualify for a pardon or lighter sentencing, correct?"

"Precisely," ASAC Lang confirmed. "We closed in on MacCauley the week your husband was killed, and he presented us with this proposal. He knew Liam Baird through his distant relatives in Belfast, and Baird had asked him for help on his project. Finn asked Dr. Greenberg to go undercover."

She managed not to react. "They were in touch?"

"Evidently he maintained contact with her, but only because of you."

Was Sharon telling the truth when she said Finn had tried to get a pardon because he wanted Devyn's forgiveness and a relationship? No, she even said he'd use any tactic to get what he wanted. Otherwise, he'd be here, right?

There she went, dreaming about a connection again. Hadn't she learned her lesson with her mother? Wasn't Finn's no-show enough to confirm that was the case with him as well?

"So, she agreed," Devyn said, pulling her thoughts to the real problems. The ones she'd help to solve, not the ones she imagined. "She told me she'd been approached before but never accepted the job for"—Devyn sighed—"ethical reasons."

"Which was why we agreed to use her," Padraig said. "She checked out as clean."

"What about her run-in with the FBI as a grad student?"

"She told us everything," ASAC Lang said. "We interviewed her thoroughly. Apparently, she was quite the actress, already negotiating with Malik while we were prepping her for the assignment."

She looked at Marc, who'd been quiet but held her hand on his thigh under the table. "Who was trying to make me leave Belfast?"

"Everyone," ASAC Lang said with a smile. "We wanted you out of there for your safety but were concerned you might have already gotten on Baird's radar, which you had. Dr. Greenberg wanted you out until, apparently, she realized you could help her."

"And you?" She looked at Padraig.

The older man smiled. "I was her contact over there, the only call she could make. When you showed up in Bangor, I knew we were dealing with"—his gaze shifted to Marc—"professionals. I decided to let you know just enough to scare you out of there and give you somewhere specific to go."

"Enniskillen."

He nodded. "The SIS own the town, and we knew we could keep an eye on you, keep you busy figuring out how to contact us in the bell tower, then stop you. Didn't expect you to lock our man in the tower," he said with a chuckle.

Vivi leaned forward, her dark gaze on the FBI agent, Lang. "I told you not to underestimate us."

He just smiled at her. "I told you I won't, ever again." Then he turned to Devyn. "Is there anything else you need to know?"

So much, but nothing these men would know. She took a deep breath and asked the only remaining question. "Will Finn MacCauley be pardoned?"

"No," he said quickly. "But he's going to a minimum-security facility to live out . . . what's left of his life."

Oh, so that's what Lang meant by Finn not having time to negotiate his pardon. "Is he sick?"

"He's dying, Mrs. Sterling. He has a brain tumor and I doubt he'll make it to the holidays."

She eased back in her chair as the news hit. He was dying? And he *still* didn't have the nerve to meet her here?

"I see," she said. But she didn't. Not at all.

Under the table, Marc threaded his fingers through hers while the agents asked questions. They answered everything, reliving the few days and nights in Belfast and Enniskillen, putting the last missing pieces of the puzzle together.

But all Devyn heard was *he's dying*.

She managed to swallow the lump in her throat and pay attention to the questions, but they couldn't end soon enough. After they were finished, and all the thank-yous and good-byes were said, and Vivi celebrated being given what evidently was a major check for their services, all Devyn could still hear in her head were those same two words.

He's dying.

She was still sitting in the conference room considering that when Marc came back in from the noisy celebration in the reception area.

"You okay?" he asked, placing a gentle hand on her shoulder.

She looked up at him. "I have one question I didn't have the guts to ask."

"What is it?"

"If he's dying, why go to all this trouble for a pardon? Why not just...die?"

He shook his head, curling his hand under her hair in a comforting stroke. "I don't know, Dev."

"I guess I'll never know." But she'd always wonder.

"Let's go get some air," he suggested. "The swan boats are running."

She didn't feel like a swan boat ride but rose, anyway, saying good-bye to everyone and walking into the cool autumn air of Boston. Arm in arm, they crossed Arlington and entered the Public Garden, the grounds already dotted with the early lunch crowd hungry for the last few days before Boston's relentless winter bared the trees and iced the pond.

They started on the path, and Devyn nestled into Marc, his feel and scent so familiar already, when someone cleared his throat on a bench to their left.

An older man sat alone, in a heavy coat, a navy ball cap pulled over uncombed gray hair. She'd have ignored him, but he was looking directly at her, his face full of... expectation.

And then she knew.

Devyn's knees threatened to buckle, but Marc held her firm and steady. Very slowly, as if each movement was agony, the old man pushed himself up from the bench, then lifted the cap in a silent greeting.

Devyn didn't move.

"You don't have to talk to him," Marc whispered. "But I thought if you wanted to..."

She slid her gaze to him, hoping the gratitude shone in her eyes. "I do."

Finn shuffled closer. "Hello," he said, his eyes watery behind glasses. But she could see their color and knew it well.

So he'd given her at least that one gene. "Hello, Finn."

"I don't want to bother you," he said, his voice gruff. "But I'd like to thank this young man for taking care of you. It was important to me." He reached a weathered hand to Marc, who shook it.

He was so old. The realization stunned her. She never really thought of him as anything but fortysomething, virile, evil, powerful. But this man was pressed to the ground by gravity and the weight of his life, his shoulders sloped, his face sagging.

He turned those familiar blue eyes on Devyn, a soft breeze blowing the white strands that stuck out from under his hat. He just stared at her, drinking in her face, scrutinizing it, memorizing it, savoring it.

"Why don't you ask him your question, Dev?" Marc suggested. "Why don't you talk to him?"

Marc stepped away and she froze for a moment, wanting to reach for him but knowing why he was leaving them alone.

"You're so beautiful," Finn said, his voice gravelly, his eyes smiling. "You've always been beautiful."

Her whole body threatened to crumble.

"Why didn't you come to the meeting?" she asked.

He gave a tight smile, his face like a crinkled map of Ireland. He gestured toward the bench and she went with him, sitting a foot away, unable to take her eyes off him. And he looked at her the same way. Hungry for information, answers...time.

"I didn't want to meet you like that," he said. "So I asked your young man to help me out, and he agreed. In fact, he thought it would be better."

Of course, he was right. "I thought you just...didn't want to meet me."

He laughed softly. "Darling, I've met you a dozen times. Stood next to you, crossed paths with you. I even held the door for you at Symphony Hall once. You were looking so snazzy in a royal blue gown."

Disbelief rocked her. She remembered that night.

"Nothing creepy, I assure you." He made a wave to relax her. "I just... wanted to know."

"To know what?"

"That you were all right." He nodded, studying her face again. "And you surely turned out more than all right."

"And you've been in touch with Sharon? All these years?"

"Before writing to ask her for help, the last time I spoke to her was the day she gave you up for adoption." His blue eyes tapered in disgust. "I'll freely admit I was pissed off. I didn't want you living with strangers."

For some reason, some stupid, insane reason, that thrilled her. "But you couldn't stop her?"

"Not back in those days. Fathers had no rights, and frankly, being what I... what I was, I knew the life you were getting was better. But I never had kids," he said, the words rough with regret. "And I wanted you."

I wanted you.

"Sharon, she didn't want any parts of a child after all. She thought it would keep me, make me leave my wife, but"—he shook his head—"it just worked out like this, better for everyone."

"I landed with a good family," Devyn told him.

"I know. So good I didn't dare do anything about changing your life. I just watched from far away." He gave her another sly smile. "I was in the church when you got married."

She tried to breathe but couldn't.

"I cried," he said.

"I shouldn't have married him," she whispered, her voice cracking.

"I knew that on your wedding day," he said. "That scum already had dealings with some of this city's worst types. Believe me, I knew. But I couldn't hardly walk up to you and stop you, now, could I?"

She shook her head, not sure if she should laugh or cry.

"Anyway, I'm sorry they got him and tried to pin his hit on me." His thick gray brows drew together. "You didn't deserve that kind of deal."

"It's over now," she assured him, her gaze turning to where Marc stood, on the other side of the pond, watching the boats. "I'm okay."

"Found a good young man, did you?"

She smiled, the tears coming despite how much she didn't want them to. "He's very good."

Finn nodded, looking at Marc as well. "Hope he's worthy of a girl like you."

She laughed lightly, and that made her tears fall. "He is."

Finn put a gnarled hand on hers, pulling her attention toward his own overly moist eyes. "I'm not going to be around long enough to see you take that walk down the aisle again," he said.

"Then... why did you do all this?" she asked. "Just for a lighter sentence?" Her heart stopped while she waited for the answer.

"I just wanted to take away some of your shame, child. I tried to convince Sharon to help for the same reason, sent her pictures of you, and told her that maybe she could, you know, have a relationship with you. That happens nowadays, doesn't it?"

"Yes, it does."

He tightened his grip, the purple veins in his hands popping. "As for me? I know the indignity and humiliation of me is an albatross to carry around your neck, and I just wanted to make that load lighter. You know, for the next generation, if you should be so lucky."

A sob rose in her chest and she reached for him, her hands closing around his stiff neck, their heads coming so close her forehead bumped the bill of his cap. "I might be that lucky," she whispered. "And you did lighten the load."

He closed his eyes and tears rolled over the lines in his face. "I doubt I'll see you in heaven, girl," he whispered. "But you've given me something to hold on to no matter where I end up."

She held him for a moment, everything settling into place in her heart and soul, everything feeling right for the first time in her life. She'd been wrong about her mother, and, funny enough, she'd been wrong about her father, too.

Marc's footsteps pulled them apart.

"I have a swan boat for us," he said. "Are you ready, Devyn?"

She drew back completely and looked at Finn. At her father. A dying old man who had made some devastatingly bad choices in life. But in the end, he'd cared about her.

"Would you like to ride with us?" she asked.

His yellowed smile was heartbreaking. "I'd love to, but I don't think that FBI agent over there would like the idea. Go out there, you two, and make your memory."

"I plan on it," Marc said, reaching for Devyn's hand, his smile curling around her heart and filling her with love. "With your permission, Mr. MacCauley, I'm about to ask your daughter to marry me."

"Well, now, that's a pretty word." Finn slapped his hands on his legs and grinned at Devyn.

"Marry?" she asked, her breath caught in her chest.

"No." He stood, chuckling. "Daughter. Mighty pretty word."

EPILOGUE

Chaos. The whole day and dinner had been nothing but a frenzy of food and family. But mostly food. Trays and platters and bowls of so much abundance that Devyn wondered how the entire family stayed so fit.

Luckily the Feast of the Seven Fishes—or as Vivi and Zach said it with the most beautiful, lilting Italian accents, "*la vigilia*"—happened only once a year. But on Christmas Eve, the Rossi house rocked as the homemade wine flowed and Nino, with a lot of help, put out the most amazing dinner Devyn had ever eaten.

She glanced to her side, catching bits of Marc's conversation with his older brother, JP, a big, handsome cop with enough charm to offset his arrogance, and Nicki, Marc's other younger sister, a psychiatrist with a sharp sense of humor and quick laugh.

The youngest of the family, Chessie, kept bringing the conversation back to Gabe, the super-secret government agent brother who Marc had talked to while they were in Belfast.

Listening, Devyn lifted her water glass and took a deep drink, grateful no one, including Marc, had noticed she hadn't touched Nino's wine. He was deep in the conversation, but his hand stayed firmly on Devyn's leg, and he somehow managed to sneak glances her way to remind her that he never forgot her.

"You ready?" he asked suddenly, pushing his chair back.

"We're leaving?" she asked, surprised.

"Like hell you are," Vivi interjected as she scooped some dirty plates from the table. "Not with all that white stuff out there." With her free hand, she pointed two fingers at Marc and JP, like a viper's tongue. "Rossis are going down tonight, baby. We got Samantha on the Angelino side now, and this isn't going to be the blowout it was last year."

"But I have Devyn," Marc said. "And she has a mean arm."

Ah, yes. She remembered the story he'd shared with her in Belfast. The snowball fight, the sled riding, the kids "disappearing" outside while Santa arrives.

In this house, tradition tasted as good as the food.

Marc tugged her up from the table. "Let's find you a nice thick coat, some boots, and gloves. You'll need armor out there. But first, we'll ride."

"I have to sled?" she asked.

Marc guided her to the mudroom closet to pull out a faded down jacket. "You want a present, you get in the snow." He handed her the coat, studying her expression, which she imagined looked pretty uncertain. "You do want a present, don't you, Dev?"

"I already have a present," she replied. A thin blue line in the middle of an inch of white plastic. "You."

He kissed her nose. "Come on, I'll take you on my sled and show you how it's done Rossi style."

"Pffft!" Vivi stuck her head into the mudroom, already in a purple jacket with a blinding orange scarf. "Angelinos do it better."

Devyn was still a little unsure of the sled plan a few minutes later, when they'd lined up five of them at the top of the hill behind the house.

"See?" From behind, Marc wrapped his arms around her puffy coat with a reassuring hug. "Not steep."

"But at least five hundred feet of icy snow," she said.

He turned her around to look at him. "Relax. Enjoy this beautiful night." He pulled her close and whispered, "I love you."

Her body trembled in the down coat, but not from cold. From anticipation and excitement and bone-deep happiness. She covered the shiver by looking around the yard, studying the bare oaks, their empty branches heavy with snow and icicles, the generous full moon bathing it all in nature's spotlight.

Vivi broke the peace by jumping on her sled and flying headfirst into the untouched snow.

"She has to be first," Zach said, laughing as he got on a sled with Sam. "It's like a law or something."

"And she'll throw the first bomb," JP said as he boarded his sled.

"Let's go." Marc urged her onto the board, settling Devyn in first so he could brace her between his legs. "I'll give us a push and guide it. I'll take care of you."

With that, he gave the sled a solid push and they were off, the blades cutting through the powder as they let gravity take them for a ride.

"It's not just me anymore." Her words floated on the air, almost lost in the wind. Marc grabbed the handles, leaned to the left to pick up a little speed, then suddenly jerked to the side, forcing the sled to zip around, sending a rooster tail of powder into the air and bringing them to a swift stop in the middle of the hill.

"*What* did you say?"

Her heart hammered so hard she could barely talk. She looked over her shoulder to meet his gaze. His wondrous, wide, shocked, gobsmacked gaze. "You heard me."

He just stared at her. "Are you . . . can you . . . do you . . ."

She couldn't help laughing. He was speechless and so obviously overcome with joy. Oh, yes, that was joy on his face. And it was all she needed to see.

"Am I what? Sure? Yes, I am." She had the positive test to prove it. "Can I be any happier? No, I don't think it's possible. Do I love you with all my heart?" She blinked at snowflakes and tears. "Yes, I do, Marc. I love you with all of my heart and soul. Hearts and souls. I have two at the moment. We both love you."

"Devyn." His voice cracked and his eyes filled, and it wasn't the frosted air that made them water.

"Hey, you two!" Vivi's voice was distant, drowned out by Devyn's pulse and the look in Marc's eyes.

"What is it?"

"Will you—"

The explosion of snow landed right between them, powder silencing his question and freezing her face.

"I'm gonna have to kill her," Marc said.

"Get in line," Devyn said, already scooping snow.

"Wait, wait," Marc insisted, grabbing her hand. "We're not done here."

"You want to lose the snowball fight?" she challenged. "What kind of example does that set for your son or daughter?" She finished packing the ball and flung it with all her happy might.

It nailed Vivi right in the shoulder, eliciting a shriek.

"You"—Marc spun her around by the shoulders and squeezed—"are going to make a hell of an addition to the family."

"Two additions. Me and Junior." She kissed him fast and bent to get more snow, just missing a missile thrown over her head.

"Just one?" he asked. "I want five."

She buckled with a laugh that came from deep inside. "Five it is." Another snowball slammed her in the shoulder. "If we survive Waterloo."

"Wait a second." He knelt next to her, pulling her close. "You didn't even tell me how you feel yet."

"How I feel? How do you think I feel?"

"I don't know. Sick or tired? Happy or scared? How do you feel about this baby?"

She thought about that for a moment, a tear welling up as the answer came to her. "I feel—"

A soft grenade of snow exploded all over both of them. Even still, she felt completely, totally ... "Warm."

She lives on the edge;

he lives by the rules.

They're on a murderer's trail . . .

and they're feeling the heat.

———————

Please turn this page

for a preview of

FACE OF DANGER

When Vivi Angelino closed her mouth over a wide straw and sucked hard enough to hollow her delicate cheeks, Colton Lang almost got a boner.

Almost.

The state of damn-near-hard was status quo around this woman, so in the few months he'd been sending consulting jobs to her firm, Colt had learned a couple of tricks to ensure that *almost* didn't become *obvious*.

He would focus on her outlandish black hair, made even more so today by the helmet and what appeared to be yesterday's hair gel. Or he'd let his gaze settle on the diamond dot in the side of her nose, concentrating on how much that puncture had to have hurt instead of how it would feel to...run his tongue over the stone.

Or he'd simply remind himself that this skateboard-riding, sneaker-wearing, guitar-playing tomboy happened to have some of the best investigative instincts around, and he wanted to keep the Guardian Angelinos in his back pocket for certain jobs, so acting on a mindless surge of blood to his dick would be unprofessional and foolish.

That was usually enough to quell the erection. Sometimes. Today, finding her in this skate park with a little sheen of perspiration making her pixie-like features glisten and her coffee-bean-brown eyes spark with unexpected interest, the boner might win this battle.

But look at that outfit, Colt. A long-sleeved cotton T-shirt that dangled off her narrow frame and faded green cargo pants frayed at the cuffs. He could never be attracted to a woman who cared so little about herself that she rolled around Boston dressed like she'd shopped at Goodwill.

He preferred a woman who looked like a woman, who wore a little makeup, had hair falling to her shoulders, and maybe strolled – not *rolled* – through a park in a pretty sundress. He'd bet his bottom dollar she didn't own a dress.

"All right, I'll tell you," she said after swallowing the sip she'd taken. "But I swear to God, Lang, don't try to talk me out of it because I want this job."

"What job?"

"You've heard about the Red Carpet Killer, of course."

He held his Coke, frozen mid-way to his mouth. "You don't buy that malarkey, do you?"

She smiled. "Lang, *malarkey* hasn't been sold for forty years. Can you get with this century? And two Oscar-winning actresses in a row are killed in two consecutive years, weeks after winning? You really think that's a coincidence?"

"One was an overdose, one was an accident. But I do

know there's an FBI task force out of LA with an eye on the possibility of a copycat killer."

"Exactly." She pointed at him. "I don't happen to think there's a serial killer, either. But even if the first two deaths are mere coincidence, there are five women in Hollywood who are scared spitless right now. They are ramping up security like you wouldn't believe."

"You think they're going to hire your firm for protection?" He tried not to scoff, he really did. But it was ludicrous. "A brand new firm made up of an extended family of renegade Angelinos and Rossi cousins?"

No surprise, her espresso eyes tapered in disgust. "We are not renegades, for God's sake. I'm a former investigative journalist, in case you forgot, so getting a PI license was a natural move. Zach's thriving in management, which frankly shocks the shit out of me after all those years as an Army Ranger. And, yeah, our core employee base happens to be a few cousins my brother and I were raised with—"

"Don't forget Uncle Nino, providing pasta and daily encouragement."

"Don't knock my Nino," she shot back. "And, for your information, we're interviewing protection and security specialists, including some highly qualified bodyguards. The Guardian Angelinos are experiencing a growth spurt."

He angled his head in acknowledgment. "I know that, Vivi, especially since I keep throwing FBI consulting jobs at you. I just think the actresses who are worried about being victims of a curse or a killer will hire the biggest and best in the protection industry."

"Maybe." She took another drink, her eyes dancing

with some untold secret. "What do you think of Cara Ferrari?"

"I think I wouldn't kick her out of bed for eating crackers."

She looked skyward with a loud tsk. "I meant of her chances to win."

"I don't follow Hollywood too closely, but I did see that remake of *Now, Voyager*. My opinion? She was too melodramatic."

"Fortunately, your opinion doesn't matter. She's got a chance." She gave him a slow smile, revealing that tiny chip on her front tooth. God, he'd thought about licking that, too. "So I think I have a chance, too."

He just shook his head, not following, but maybe because his body was betraying him again.

"Look at me," she demanded, leaning back to prop her hands on her hips and cock her head to one side.

"I'm looking." That was the problem. She was so damn cute he forgot what they were talking about.

"*Look,* Lang."

At what? The way her position pulled the T-shirt just tight enough to outline her breasts? They weren't big but perky and sweet, just as spunky as she was and, well, even on Vivi some things were feminine. Is that what she wanted him to look at? Because, if he eyed them any longer, his hard-on was poised to make a reappearance.

"Don't you see the resemblance?" She turned her face to give him a profile, lifting her chin, closing her eyes, and dropping her head back in a classic movie star pose. His gaze drifted over her throat which was...just another fucking thing he wanted to lick.

Jesus, Colt. Get a grip.

She spun her face around and for one insane second he thought she'd read his mind.

"I look exactly like Cara Ferrari," she insisted.

He let out a soft hoot of laughter. "Are you as stoned as half these other skaters?"

She scowled at him. "Real skaters don't get high, posers do. And look at this face," she demanded, pointing to her cheeks with two index fingers. "Is this not Cara Ferrari's twin sister?"

He chuckled again. "Speaking of posers."

"Lang, *damn* it." Frustration heightened her color, making her even *cuter.* "Everyone says I look like her. I mean, if my hair were longer and I, you know, had some makeup on."

"Like a truckload."

"I get stopped and asked if I'm Cara Ferrari all the time," she insisted.

"And you believe what drunks say to you in bars?"

"Jeez, you're as bad as my cousins. Quit teasing me and take this seriously."

He worked his face into the most humorless expression he had, and he had many. "Cara Ferrari is a movie star, Vivi."

"So?"

How deep was she going to let him dig himself? "I mean, she's a gorgeous icon..."

Deep.

"Not that you're not attractive in your own way...." This was getting worse, but on he went. "It's just that she's all glitz and glamour and gloss and you're..." *Not.*

"I can glam up."

Now that he'd like to see. "All right," he relented, not

wanting to hurt her. He squinted at her, and made a camera viewing box with his fingers. "Yeah, I can see the similarity. You both have dark hair and dark eyes."

She swiped his hands down. "Never mind, Lang. I should know better than to hope you could think outside the box. I should expect you to be all linear, trapped by your rules and the way things are supposed to be done. I shouldn't ever dream that you might approach something creatively. That would just be asking too much from your structured, formulaic, *uninspired* brain."

All right, he deserved that after the insults he'd just heaped on her, but something was really off in this conversation, even for them. "What the hell are you getting at, Vivi? What creative thinking are you looking for?"

"A body double."

This time he just stared at her, a slow realization dawning. "You're not serious."

She thumped her fist on the table. "I knew I shouldn't have told you."

"Told me what?"

"C'mon, Lang, it's the oldest form of security in the world. Put a fake—a *professional* fake—in her shoes until the killer is caught. If there even is a killer, which I don't happen to think there is. But, still, we bait with a decoy and—"

"Stop it," he said, his voice low and harsh, not having to pretend seriousness at all now. "For one thing, all kidding aside, you'd need an extreme makeover to pass as Cara Ferrari."

"Not from a distance."

"Second, if a decoy or bait was used, the job would go to a trained professional, not an outside consultant, ever.

And third, good luck getting to Cara Ferrari. It's easier to get an appointment with the president."

A flicker of arrogance crossed her face. "Maybe I already have."

"What? How?"

She shrugged. "What do they say? Everyone is six degrees of separation from someone."

"You are not six degrees of anything from Cara Ferrari." Was she?

She picked up her drink and then set it down again. "Forget it, Lang. You're right, she sucked in that role. She should stick to the trashy stuff that made her real money."

"Absolutely," he agreed. "Like one of her really early B-movies, the one where she played the undercover cop working as a stripper? I liked that."

"Of course you did. What man doesn't love the raw acting talent it takes for a woman to use her mouth to unzip thigh-high boots during a lap dance?"

"You have to admit that was a memorable scene."

"Yeah, that took mad acting skills."

"And coordination," he agreed. "Just think how many college boys she made happy."

"Were you one of them, Lang?"

"Please. I was in the FBI Academy when that movie came out." Still, he fought a smile. "But it was a pretty sexy lap dance. Although, I guess that's redundant."

She blew out a breath, giving her little Italian hand wave of dismissal. "Yeah, whatever. And can we just forget we had this conversation? It's moot anyway. They say Kimberly Horne has the Oscar in the bag."

He relaxed a little as she accepted the truth. "Vivi, you can't seriously think you could convince Cara Ferrari to let you *be* her for however long it takes to trap a killer, who, by the way, greater minds than yours don't think exists. I think you should forget this idea completely."

She snorted and grabbed her drink. "I don't care what you think."

And that right there was the problem with them. She didn't really care what he thought, what anybody thought. He didn't respond and she sucked the straw again, this time looking up at him with wide eyes as her mouth closed... kind of exactly like she'd look up from a blow job.

Goddamn his dancing dick.

"Just forget it," he said, as much to his disobedient organ as his unintentionally sexy consultant. "It's a cute idea, but—"

"Fuck you, Lang."

"Sorry, I know you hate anything cute."

"You just don't get it, do you?"

Evidently not. "Get what?"

"What I'm trying to do with this business my brother and I started."

"How can you say that?" He pushed his drink aside to get closer. "I believe in your business. Hell, if I'm not careful, my boss is going to start questioning just why you guys have had, what, four or five assignments in as many months? We're supposed to spread the outsourcing wealth, not focus on one firm."

She just shook her head. "This isn't about you and your office. This is about *me* and *my* office."

"Seriously, Vivi. You only started this business last fall. What do you expect?"

"Greatness," she replied without pause. "There are companies doing what mine does and making millions.

They've got multiple offices and hundreds of investigators and bodyguards and security specialists on their payroll."

"And that's what you want?" Somehow, the dream of big business just didn't fit this skater chick. The raw ambition, like so many things about Vivi, surprised him.

"I always want to be the best," she told him. "I don't like to do things half-assed."

"I respect that, but…" He placed both his hands over hers, damning the electrical charge he got every time his skin made contact with hers. "You're not starting with Cara and your body double idea."

She snapped her hands away. "You can't tell me what to do, Lang. No one can."

Obviously. "Consider it professional advice, then."

"Give me one good reason why not, *other* than the fact that I don't look like a movie star, as you've pointed out with great relish and ruthless candor."

"It's dangerous."

"My job is dangerous," she replied. "Your job is dangerous. That's the life we've chosen. If we get the assignment, Zach has three excellent bodyguards who can come stay with me twenty-four seven."

Three guys with her twenty-four seven? Something unfamiliar and ugly rolled through him. Jealousy. "Doesn't matter. With all the nutcases out there, it's too risky."

She pushed back with a disgusted breath. "You are so…*careful*."

"You say that like it's a detriment. I'm an FBI agent, Vivi. Cautious is my middle name. And if you're going to make it in the security consulting business, you'd do well to adopt the same one."

"Well, my middle name is Belladonna," she informed him.

"A poison."

"A beautiful woman in Italian," she corrected him, then raised a palm to stop his response. "Don't. You've dinged me enough for one day. My point is *cautious* doesn't always work in business, Lang."

"It does in the security business." Three bodyguards? Shit, he hated that.

"Nobody gets ahead being safe. It's like that half-pipe over there." She tipped her head to the concrete slopes where skaters flew and flipped. And fell on their asses. "You gotta go big and go wild or go down."

"Yeah, well I've gone big and wild, and went down hard." No, he didn't go down. The one and only woman he'd ever loved had gone down. All the way down. Six feet under down.

"What happened?" she asked.

He shook his head. "Just don't take crazy risks, Vivi."

"Can't help it, dude, that's how I roll." She got up, kicked her board out from under the table and hopped on it. "I gotta head out to my family's house for Sunday dinner. See ya, Assistant Special Agent in Charge Colton Cautious Lang."

"Bye, Private Investigator Viviana Poison Angelino."

She rolled a little, tugging on her helmet, and threw him one last rueful look. "Thanks for the Slurpy and the advice."

She zipped off, giving him a perfect shot of her ass as she kicked into high speed.

There went his cock again.

To make the blood flow north to his brain, he forced

himself to think about her stupid, foolish, crazy idea. Okay, it wasn't entirely stupid, but the last time he took a risk like that, he lost *everything*. Which would also be the last time he let a boner get in the way of his work.

Never again.

The killer she can't escape . . .

The heartbreak she can't forget . . .

The one man who can
stop them both.

———————

Please turn this page
for a preview of

EDGE OF SIGHT

CHAPTER 1

I understand you got into that little law school across the river."

Samantha Fairchild scooped up the cocktails from the service bar, sending a smile to the man who'd been subtly checking her out from behind rimless glasses. "Our trusty bartender's been bragging about me again."

Behind the bar, Wendy waved a martini shaker like a sparkler, her eyes twinkling. "Just a little, Sam. You're our only Harvard-bound server."

Sam nodded to the light-haired gentleman, not really wanting to start a conversation when Paupiette's dining room was wall-to-wall with a Saturday night crowd. Anyway, he wasn't her type. Too pale, too blond, too . . . safe.

"Nothing to be ashamed of, a Harvard law degree," the man said. "I've got one myself."

"Really? What did you do with it?"

The smile widened. "Print money, like you will."

Spoken like a typical Harvard law grad. "I'm not

that interested in the money. I have another plan for the future." One she doubted a guy dripping in Armani and Rolex would appreciate. Unless he was a defense attorney. She eyed him just as two hands landed on her shoulders from behind.

"I seated Joshua Sterling and company in your section." Keegan Kennedy's soft voice had a rumble of warning in it, probably because she was flirting with lawyers in the bar when her tables were full. "I'll expect a kickback."

"That sounds fair." She shrugged out of his grip, balancing the cocktail tray.

"I bet he's a generous tipper, Sam," the lawyer said as he placed two twenties on the bar and flicked his wrist for the bartender to keep the change. "You'll need it for the Con Law texts alone."

She gave him a wistful smile, not too encouraging, but not a complete shutdown, either. "Thanks..."

"Larry," he supplied. "Maybe I'll stop in before you start classes with some first-year pointers."

"Great, Larry." She forced a more encouraging smile. He looked like a nice guy. Dull as dry toast, but then he probably wouldn't kick her in the heart with an...army boot. "You do that."

She turned to peer into the main dining area, catching a glimpse of a party of six being led by the maître d's second-in-command.

Joshua Sterling's signature silver hair, prematurely gray and preternaturally attractive, glistened under the halogen droplights, hung to highlight the haute cuisine but casting a perfect halo over this particular patron.

It wasn't just his tipping that interested Sam. The last time Boston's favorite columnist had dined here, they'd gotten into a lively debate about the Innocence Mission, and he ended up writing a whole article in the *Globe* about the nonprofit. The Boston office where Sam volunteered had received a huge influx of cash because of that story.

"Good work, Keegan." Sam offered a grateful smile to the maître d', who had vacillated between pain in the ass and godsend since he'd started a few months ago. "Count on ten percent."

He laid a wine list on her cocktail tray, threatening the delicate balance of the top-heavy martini glasses. "He tips on wine, so talk him into something from the vault. Make my cut fifteen percent and I promise you we will not run out of the tartare. It's Sterling's favorite."

She grinned. "Deal, you little Irish weasel."

After delivering the cocktails to another table, she headed toward the newly seated party, nodding to a patron who signaled for a check while she paused to top off the Cakebread chardonnay for the lovers in the corner, all the while assessing just who Joshua Sterling was entertaining tonight.

Next to him was his beautiful wife, a stunning young socialite named Devyn with sharp-edged cheekbones and waves of golden hair down to trainer-toned shoulders. Two other couples completed a glossy party of six, one of the women finishing an animated story as they settled into their seats, delivering a punch line with a finger pointed at Joshua and eliciting a hoot of laughter from the rest. Except for Devyn, who leaned back expressionless while a menu was placed in front of her.

Joshua put a light hand on his wife's back, waving casually to someone across the dining room. He whispered to her; then he beamed at Sam as she approached the table.

"Hello, Samantha." Of course he remembered her. That was his gift, his charm. "All ready to tackle *Hahvahd*?" He drew out the word, giving it an exaggerated Boston accent.

"Classes start in two months," she said, handing over the wine list, open to the priciest selection. "So, I'm ready, but nervous."

"From what you told me about that volunteer work of yours, I think you've got more legal background and experience than half that first-year class. You'll kick butt over there." He added a smile to his laser-blue gaze, one that had been getting more and more television airtime as a talking head for liberal issues on the cable news shows.

No one doubted that Joshua Sterling could hit the big time down in New York.

"I hope you're right," she said, stepping aside for the junior maître d' to snap a black napkin on Devyn Sterling's dark trousers. "Otherwise I'm going to give it all up and go back into advertising."

"Don't doubt yourself," Joshua warned with a sharp look. "You've got too much upstairs to push computers and burgers. You need to save innocent victims of the screwed-up system."

She gave him a tight smile of gratitude, wishing she were that certain of her talents. Of course, doling out bullshit was another gift of his. "What's the occasion?" she asked, wanting to get the conversation off her and onto a nice big drink order.

Joshua waved toward the brunette who'd been telling the story. "We're celebrating Meredith's birthday."

"Happy birthday." Sam nodded to her. "We have two bottles of the '94 Tattinger left."

"Nice call for champagne," he said, "but I think this is a wine crowd. You like Bordeaux, right, Meredith?"

The woman leaned forward on one elbow, a slow smile forming as she looked at him. "Something complex and elegant."

Sam waited a beat, as the woman's gaze stayed fixed on her host. Devyn shifted in her seat, and Sam could practically taste the tension crackling in the air.

"Let me get the sommelier," Sam suggested quickly. "I bet he has the perfect Bordeaux."

"I know he does." Joshua handed Sam the wine list back without even looking at it. "Tell Rene we'd like two bottles of the 1982 Chateau Haut-Brion."

"Excellent selection." Was it ever. "While I get that, can we offer you sparkling water or bottled?"

They made their choices, which Sam whispered to a busboy before darting down the narrow passage from the dining area to the kitchen, her shoes bouncing on the rubber floor as she left the gentle conversation and music of the dining room for the clatter and sizzle of the kitchen.

"Where's Rene?" she asked, a smell of buttery garlic and seared meat rolling over her.

"I'm right here." The door to the cellars flipped open as the beefy sommelier hustled toward her, carrying far too many bottles. Two more servers came in right behind him with similar armloads.

"Rene, I need two bottles of '82 Haut-Brion, stat."

"After I help with the upstairs party," he shot back.

"Then give me the key and a general idea where I can find the '82s."

"You're not getting the '82s, sister." The faux French accent he used with customers was absent as he deftly set bottles on the prep deck. "One slip of the hand and you just cost us both a month's pay."

"Come on, Rene. I can get two bottles of wine, for crying out loud."

"You can wait like everyone else, Sam." He started handing bottles to one of the other servers, who gave her a smug look of victory.

The doors from the dining area swung open, and Sam squinted down the hallway, just in time to get a glimpse of Joshua strolling across the room, reaching out to greet a gorgeous former model and her date sitting at the deuce near the bar. So he wasn't in a huge rush for his wine. She glanced at the plates on the stainless steel pass, calculating exactly how much time she had to get this wine poured before her four orders for the old Brahmins on ten came up.

Not much. She wanted the Haut-Brion delivered first or she'd lose her whole rhythm.

One more of the waitstaff came up from the cellar, several bottles in hand. "This is the last of it, Rene. I just have to go back down and lock up."

"I'll lock it," Sam said, snatching the keys.

"No." Rene sliced her with a glare. "I'll get them, Sam. Five minutes is all."

"Come on, Rene."

The door from the dining room flung open and Keegan marched through. "Sterling wants his wine," he announced, his gaze hard on Rene.

"Then you get it," Rene said. "Not Sam."

But Sam was already on her way. "Thanks, Keegan,"

she said quietly as she passed. "You know I'll slather you with payola tonight." As she opened the door, she called back to Rene, "The Bordeaux are in the back nests, the Haut-Brion on the lower half, right?"

"Sam, if you fuck this up—"

"I will dust the bottles! You can watch the video tomorrow," she added with a laugh. As if that prehistoric camera was ever used.

"I will!" Rene shouted. "I just put a new tape in."

She hustled down the poorly lit stairs, brushing by one of the sous-chefs carrying a sack of flour from the dry storage pantry. Farther underground, the temperature dropped, a chill emanating from the stone walls as she reached the heavy door of the wine vault.

A breeze blew the strands of hair that had escaped her ponytail, making her pause and look down the dark hallway. Was the alley exit open again? The busboys were always out there smoking, but they sure as shit better not be taking lung therapy when Paupiette's was this packed.

Tarragon and rosemary wafted from dry storage, but the tangy scents disappeared the moment she cranked the brass handle of the wine vault, the hinges snapping and squeaking as she entered. In this dim and dusty room, it just smelled of earth and musk.

She flipped on the overhead, but the single bare bulb did little to illuminate the long, narrow vault or the racks that jutted out to form a five-foot-high maze. She navigated her way to the back, her rubber soles soundless on the stone floor. Dust tickled her sinuses and the fifty-eight-degree air finished the job. She didn't even fight the urge to sneeze, managing to pull out a tissue in time to catch the noisy release.

Behind the back row, she tucked into the corner where the most expensive wines were kept and started blowing and brushing the bottles, almost instantly finding the distinctive gold and white label of Haut-Brion.

Sliding the bottle out, she dusted it clean, and read the year 2000. In racks stocked chronologically, that made her a good eighteen years from where she wanted to be. She coughed softly, more dust catching in her throat. Crouching lower, she eased out another, 1985.

Getting closer. On her haunches, her fingers closed over a bottle just as the door opened, the sound of the brass knob echoing through the vault. She started to stand but a man's hushed voice stopped her.

"I'm in."

Freezing, she worked to place the voice, but couldn't. It was low, gruff, masculine.

"Now."

There was something urgent in the tone. Something that stilled her.

She waited for a footstep; if he was another server, he'd walk to a stack to find his bottle of wine. If it was Rene, he'd call her name, knowing she was down there, and anyone else . . .

No one else should be down here.

Her pulse kicked up a little as she waited for the next sound, unease prickling up her spine.

Nothing moved. No one breathed.

Praying her knees wouldn't creak and give her away, she rose an inch, wanting to get high enough to see over the stack. As she did, the knob cracked again, and this time the squeak of the hinges dragged out as though the door were being opened very slowly. She rose a little higher to peek over the top rack of bottles.

A man stood flattened against the wall, his hand to his chest, inside a jacket, his head turned to face the door. In the shadows, she could hardly make out his profile, taking in his black shirt, the way his dark hair blended into the wall behind him. Not a server. No one she'd ever seen before.

He stood perfectly still as the door opened wider, and Sam tore her gaze from the stranger to the new arrival. The overhead bulb caught a glimmer of silver hair, instantly recognizable. What the hell was Josh—

The move was so fast, Sam barely saw the man's hand flip from the jacket. She might have gasped at the sight of a freakishly long pistol, but the *whoomf* of sound covered her breath, the blast muffled like a fist into a pillow.

Joshua's face contorted, then froze in shock. He folded to the floor, disappearing from her sight.

The instinct for self-preservation pushed Sam down behind the rack, her head suddenly light, her thoughts so electrified that she couldn't pull a coherent one to the forefront. Only that image of Joshua Sterling getting a bullet in his head.

She closed her eyes but the mental snapshot didn't disappear. It seared her lids, branded her brain.

Something scraped the floor and her whole being tensed. She squeezed the bottle in her right hand, finding balance on the balls of her feet, ready to pounce on whoever came around the corner.

She could blind him with the bottle. Crash it on his head. Buy time and help.

But no one came around the rack. Instead, she heard

the sound of metal on metal, a click, and a low grunt from the front of the vault. What the hell?

Still primed to fight for her life, she stood again, just high enough to see the man up on a crate, deftly removing the video camera.

The security camera that was *aimed directly at the back stacks.*

She ducked again, but it was too late. She heard him working the screws in the wall, trying to memorize his profile. A bump in a patrician nose. A high forehead. Pockmarks in a grouping low on his cheek.

Dust danced under and up her nose, tickling, tormenting, teasing a sneeze. Oh, please, *no.*

She held her breath as the camera cracked off the wall, and the man's feet hit the floor. In one more second, the door squeaked, slammed shut, and he was gone.

Could Joshua still be alive? She had to help him. She waited exactly five strangling heartbeats before sliding around the stacks and running up the middle aisle.

Lifeless blue eyes stared back at her, his face colorless as a stream of deep red blood oozed from a single hole in his temple. The bottle slipped out of her hands, the explosion of glass barely registering as she stared at the dead man.

God, no. God, *no.* Not again.

She dropped to her hands and knees with a whimper of disbelief, fighting the urge to reach out and touch the man who just minutes ago laughed with friends, explained a joke to his wife, ordered rare, expensive Bordeaux.

This couldn't be happening. It *couldn't* be.

The blood pooled by his cheek, mixing with the wine. The smell roiled her stomach, gagging her as bile rose in her throat and broken glass sliced her knees and palms.

For the second time in her life, she'd seen one man take another's life. Only this time, her face was caught on tape.

THE DISH

Where authors give you the inside scoop!

From the desk of Roxanne St. Claire

Dear Reader,

I know it's right out of the *Romancing The Stone* opening credits, but I do usually get a little teary when writing the final scene of a book. Maybe my heart and head are fried from months of storytelling, maybe the looming deadline gets the best of me, or maybe I just adore a good Happily Ever After and can't resist writing one that tugs at my heartstrings.

But when I wrote SHIVER OF FEAR, I admit I shed some *serious* waterworks—and not just because the hero, Marc Rossi, has found true love after never believing he could again...and the heroine, Devyn Sterling, is finally part of a big, happy family after a lifetime of loneliness. I was emotional because I set the scene during *La Vigilia*, also known to Italian families as The Feast of the Seven Fishes. What better place for a happy ending than around the dining room table during a meal that has deep personal meaning for me and for most members of a big Italian clan? No, I'm not Italian by descent, but my husband is "first generation"—the son of an immigrant and, therefore, deeply entrenched in some of the country's best customs. I have no doubt that the fictional blended family that peppers the pages of The Guardian Angelinos series would embrace this time-honored tradition as we do.

No one really knows the origin of the required "seven" fishes that are served on Christmas Eve in Italian families. Some say the number reflects the seven sacraments and others believe the "fishes" represent the seven hills of Rome. It doesn't matter, because most of us go way past seven that night. From the scungilli salad to the baccala amalfi and all of the salmon, swordfish, clams, scallops, shrimp, lobster, and calamari in between…it's a night to celebrate the gifts of the sea and the season. I rarely make it through the evening without looking around at my loved ones, blinking back a tear of gratitude, and going back for seconds on the lobster.

During an earlier scene in SHIVER OF FEAR, I used Marc's description of the evening to highlight Devyn's aching for a family and intensify her belief that she isn't destined to have that kind of love in her life. While he takes the tradition for granted, she is left to imagine the magic of that night and the warmth that comes from celebrating with food and family. Most of the story is set in Northern Ireland, where Devyn and Marc are on a hunt to find her birth mother and discover a hornet's nest of terrorist activity along with an unexpected attraction that soon blooms into love. But when it came time to give the reader the ultimate *dolce* moment—the sweet dessert of a lifetime together—it seemed natural to set that scene on a snowy Christmas Eve with the loud, laughing, loving Angelino and Rossi families gathered to celebrate.

So, I wiped a few tears when I typed "the end" of SHIVER OF FEAR and hoped that whatever traditions my readers honor and celebrate, they can relate to the atmosphere of joy that fills a home during The Feast of the Seven

Fishes. If nothing else, I'll send them all out in search of good seafood!

Best,

Roxanne St. Claire

www.roxannestclaire.com

♥ ♥ ♥ ♥ ♥ ♥ ♥ ♥ ♥ ♥ ♥ ♥ ♥ ♥ ♥

From the desk of Eileen Dreyer

Dear Reader,

Marriage of Convenience. Those three words alone will convince me to buy a book. I can't think of anything I enjoy more than a romance where two people who would never have chosen each other, find themselves having to negotiate a marriage neither one wanted. So when I had the chance to write historical romance, I knew that it wouldn't be long before I wrote a Marriage of Convenience book.

NEVER A GENTLEMAN is that book. Diccan Hilliard is known among Society as *The Perfection*. Suave, smooth, sophisticated, with a taste for only the most beautiful women, he has a keen wit and rapier tongue. The fact that he is also a member of Drake's Rakes, a group of aristocrats caught up in espionage, is a well-guarded secret. That secret, though, leads to marriage vows, when he wakes to find that his enemies have left him naked in bed with Grace

Fairchild, the woman known to his friends as *The Most Notorious Virgin* in Britain.

Poor Grace. As tall as a man, painfully plain with an ungainly limp, Grace has spent her life following her father around the world with the army. She has no female accomplishments, no wish to mingle in a society that has long since shunned her, and even less desire to be shackled to a man who did not choose her, especially since she has long been fascinated by him. But Grace has secrets too. The question is, will those secrets help her gain Diccan's love, or condemn her to loneliness? And will Diccan's secrets cost them not just the chance at a lasting love, but their very lives?

Do you like Marriage of Convenience books as much as I do? What draws you to them? Let me know at my website, www.eileendreyer.com.

Enjoy!

Eileen Dreyer

♥ ♥ ♥ ♥ ♥ ♥ ♥ ♥ ♥ ♥ ♥ ♥ ♥ ♥ ♥ ♥

From the desk of Jill Shalvis

Dear Reader,

Writing a romance called THE SWEETEST THING, which centers around a decidedly *not* sweet heroine, amused me. Tara Daniels is wound a little tightly and likes things her way. She's also a former southern belle who appreciates the fact that she's right. A lot.

The Sweetest Thing? Not exactly.

But her heart's in the right place, always. And, as it turns out, there's a man who melts her like butter on a hot roll. Not only that, but he can soften her in a way that she isn't sure she likes. See, Tara thinks she has it all together, but it turns out she doesn't. She doesn't know a lot about herself. About all she has is the fact that she can cook like nobody's business. Oh, how she loves to cook.

Tara was a challenge for me because—here's where I must admit it—I got a lot of her recipes from my husband. True story. I'm married to a big guy who works with his hands and is the ultimate Alpha Man—and yet he can cook. Don't try to figure him out; it'll hurt your brain, trust me.

Good Morning Sunshine Casserole is all his. Just don't tell him I "borrowed" it and am telling the world that it's my heroine's. It would just go to his head.

Happy reading and cooking!

Jill Shalvis

www.jillshalvis.com

Find out more about Forever Romance!

Visit us at
www.hachettebookgroup.com/publishing_forever.aspx

Find us on Facebook
http://www.facebook.com/ForeverRomance

Follow us on Twitter
http://twitter.com/ForeverRomance

NEW AND UPCOMING TITLES

Each month we feature our new titles
and reader favorites.

CONTESTS AND GIVEAWAYS

We give away galleys, autographed copies,
and all kinds of exclusive items.

AUTHOR INFO

You'll find bios, articles, and links to personal websites
for all your favorite authors—and so much more.

GET SOCIAL

Connect with your favorite authors, editors, and
other Forever fans, and share what's important to you.

THE BUZZ

Sign up for our monthly romance newsletter,
and be the first to read all about it.

VISIT US ONLINE

@ WWW.HACHETTEBOOKGROUP.COM.

AT THE HACHETTE BOOK GROUP WEB SITE YOU'LL FIND:

CHAPTER EXCERPTS FROM SELECTED NEW RELEASES

•

ORIGINAL AUTHOR AND EDITOR ARTICLES

•

AUDIO EXCERPTS

•

BESTSELLER NEWS

•

ELECTRONIC NEWSLETTERS

•

AUTHOR TOUR INFORMATION

•

CONTESTS, QUIZZES, AND POLLS

•

FUN, QUIRKY RECOMMENDATION CENTER

•

PLUS MUCH MORE!

Bookmark Hachette Book Group
@ www.HachetteBookGroup.com.

**If you or someone you know
wants to improve their reading skills,
call the Literacy Help Line.**

WORDS ARE YOUR WHEELS
1-800-228-8813